"What a treasure! Muriel Rukeyser takes us back to those crucial days when Spain became the first international battleground against fascism and hope for democracy, to tell a powerful story of personal, sexual, and political awakening. *Savage Coast* is bound to be an instant classic."

—ROBIN D. G. KELLEY, author of *Thelonious Monk: The Life and Times of an American Original*

"*Savage Coast* now joins the lost brother and sisterhood of Spanish Civil War classics, from Arthur Koestler's *Dialogue with Death*, the desolate modernist novels of the Catalan writer Mercè Rodoreda, Andre Malraux's *Man's Hope*, Josephine Herbst's *The Starched Blue Sky of Spain*, and the reportage of Martha Gellhorn. Rowena Kennedy-Epstein has rescued and edited a great story. Helen and Otto are not Emma and Sasha, nor are they Karl and Rosa, but the American radical poet who tells her story speaks to all of us."

—JANE MARCUS, distinguished professor of English and women's studies, CUNY Graduate Center and the City College of New York

"Muriel Rukeyser spoke of Spain as the place where she began to say what she believed. At the time, Hemingway's and Orwell's male-centered blood and guts novels were greedily devoured, while a woman writing a sexually explicit, gender truthful and politically radical narrative against a background of war was inevitably ignored. Spain changed Rukeyser and her protagonist, Helen. This novel will change the reader. An extraordinary gift!"

—MARGARET RANDALL, author of *To Change the World: My Years in Cuba*

"*Savage Coast* is an astonishing book, too long lost, now a treasure for historians of the Spanish Civil War, equally a pouch of rubies for poets. Rukeyser captures the intensity of the moment—personal, political, and still contemporary."

—PETER N. CARROLL, author of *The Odyssey of the Abraham Lincoln Brigade*

LOST & FOUND / LOST & FOUND ELSEWHERE

LOST & FOUND: The CUNY Poetics Document Initiative publishes primary sources by figures associated with New American Poetry in an annual series of chapbooks under the general editorship of Ammiel Alcalay. Lost & Found's aim is to open the field of inquiry and illuminate the terrain of an essential chapter of twentieth-century letters. The series has published little-known work by Amiri Baraka, Diane di Prima, Robert Duncan, Langston Hughes, Frank O'Hara, Margaret Randall, Muriel Rukeyser, and many others.

Under the auspices of The Center for the Humanities, and with the guidance of an extended scholarly community, Lost & Found chapbooks are researched and prepared by students and guest fellows at the PhD Program in English of the Graduate Center of the City University of New York. Utilizing personal and institutional archives, Lost & Found scholars seek to broaden our literary, cultural, and political history.

LOST & FOUND ELSEWHERE is a unique new series of book-length projects emerging from this research. Working in partnership with select publishers, these books bring to light unpublished or long unavailable materials that have emerged alongside or as part of the Lost & Found project. Available in this series:

Robert Duncan in San Francisco
Michael Rumaker
Expanded edition, with selected correspondence and interview edited by Ammiel Alcalay and Megan Paslawski
CITY LIGHTS PUBLISHERS

A Walker in the City: Elegy for Gloucester
Peter Anastas
With an afterword by Ammiel Alcalay
BACK SHORE PRESS

Savage Coast
Muriel Rukeyser
Edited, with an introduction by Rowena Kennedy-Epstein
THE FEMINIST PRESS

For more information, visit lostandfoundbooks.org

SAVAGE COAST

A NOVEL BY MURIEL RUKEYSER

EDITED, WITH AN INTRODUCTION
BY ROWENA KENNEDY-EPSTEIN

THE FEMINIST PRESS
AT THE CITY UNIVERSITY OF NEW YORK
NEW YORK CITY

Published in 2013 by the Feminist Press
at the City University of New York
The Graduate Center
365 Fifth Avenue, Suite 5406
New York, NY 10016

feministpress.org

First printing May 2013

 This project is supported in part by an
award from the National Endowment
for the Arts.

 This project was made possible in part by
the New York State Council on the Arts
with the support of Governor Andrew
Cuomo and the New York State Legislature.

Cover design by Herb Thornby, herbthornby.com
Cover photograph of Muriel Rukeyser, circa 1936
Text design by Drew Stevens

Library of Congress Cataloging-in-Publication Data
Rukeyser, Muriel, 1913-1980.
  Savage coast / Muriel Rukeyser ; Edited, with an introduction by
Rowena Kennedy-Epstein.
     pages cm
  ISBN 978-1-55861-820-6
  I. Kennedy-Epstein, Rowena. II. Title.
  PS3535.U4S38 2013
  813'.54—dc23
                                    2013004425

CONTENTS

INTRODUCTION

Rowena Kennedy-Epstein

"If this was real," thinks Helen, the protagonist of Muriel Rukeyser's autobiographical novel *Savage Coast*, "it was because it was nearer the sum of everything that had happened before it than anything had ever been." Stranded on a train in a small Catalan town during the first days of the Spanish Civil War (1936–1939), Helen had just had sex with a German socialist who will soon join the first International Brigade, watched Catalonia begin to collectivize, and seen fascist soldiers escape into the hills, a plane flying low above her upturned head, hearing the bombs and rifle fire closer still—it is a perfectly modern moment, at the center of the novel. In addition to its avant-garde and genre-bending tendencies—toward documentary, abstraction, poetry—*Savage Coast* harbors the drama, the psychological exploration and the social critique of the realist novel. It is a bildungsroman of sorts, a "novel of formation," tracing the political development of Helen—her transformation from tourist and witness into activist and radical, from girlhood "liberalism" to mature political engagement, from an "awkward" adolescence of rebellion and anger to a sense of sexual and historical subjectivity found in the collective experience of political action. Helen's transformation is Rukeyser's—she describes Spain as the place "where I was born."[1]

When Muriel Rukeyser sailed to Europe in June 1936 she never meant to go to Spain. Already a successful poet, she had won the Yale Series of Younger Poets prize in 1935 for her first book of poems, *Theory of Flight*, and had already engaged in political activism—she had traveled to report on the Scottsboro trial and was jailed for "fraternizing" with African Americans in 1933, and had completed her trip to West Virginia to document the Hawks Nest Tunnel mining disaster, an experience that would later become her most famous text, the modernist epic "The Book of the Dead" (*U.S. 1*, 1938)—when she was asked to travel to London as an assistant for a couple who were writing a book about cooperatives in England, Scandinavia, and Russia. This was her first trip abroad, and she was put in contact by the poet Horace Gregory with Bryher, Robert Herring and Petrie Townshend, the owners and editors of *Life and Letters To-day*, a prominent literary magazine that would later publish several of her poems.[2] It was through this group that Rukeyser was introduced to the London literary scene, meeting with T.S. Eliot and C. Day Lewis, and spending considerable time with H.D., writing in her diary: "she'll hate all the flaws that show in my poems."[3] She spent a month in London with people "who afterwards would be the Labor Government . . . poets and refugees and the League of Nations correspondent from the Manchester Guardian."[4] When Herring asked Rukeyser to fill in for a colleague and cover the People's Olympiad,[5] meant to be a protest and alternative to Hitler's Berlin Games, and one to which twenty-two countries were sending athletes,[6] Rukeyser gave up her chance to go to Finland and Russia, "for I was driven," she wrote, and set out to Barcelona.

Instead of reporting on the games, however, Rukeyser documented the outbreak of civil war, as the fascist-backed military coup that plunged Spain into violence occurred, not coincidentally, two nights before the People's Olympiad was to begin, disrupting what would have been one of the largest international antifascist events of that period. Only twenty-two at the time, Rukeyser's experience as witness both to the military coup and the revolutionary response in Catalonia proved transformational; she would write about Spain, its war, exiled and dead, for over forty years after, creating a radical and interconnected twentieth-century textual history. Rukeyser was only in Spain five days, from July 19 to 24, just long enough to see "the primitive beginnings of open warfare of this period,"[7] but she subsequently cites the experience as the place where "I began to say what I believed,"[8] and "the end of confusion."[9] In each work on Spain the same narratives, images, and phrases proliferate, re-contextualized inside her contemporary political and literary moment. In poems, reportage, memoir, essays and fiction, and more often in experimental forms that combine these genres, she reiterates, re-imagines, and theorizes her experience as a witness to the first days of the war and to her own moment of political, sexual, and poetic awakening.

Rukeyser's narrative of the first days of the Spanish Civil War appears in four major essays written from 1936 to 1974, all of them uncollected—"Barcelona, 1936" (*Life and Letters To-day*, vol. 15, no. 5, 1936), "Death in Spain: Barcelona on the Barricades" (*New Masses*, September 1936), "Start of Strife in Spain Is Told by Eyewitness" (*New York Times*, July 29, 1936), and "We Came for Games" (*Esquire*, October 1974),[10] which is included in this volume—as well as in the introduction to *The Life of Poetry* (1949), in numerous poems that span her oeuvre—"For O.B." (undated), "Mediterranean" (1936), "Moment of Proof" (1939), "Other-world" (1939), "Correspondences" (1939), "1/26/39" (1939), "One Soldier" (1944), "Long Past Moncada" (1944), "Letter to the Front" (1944), "Elegies" (1949), "Segre Song" (1968), "Word of Mouth" (1968), "Endless" (1968), "Delta Poems" (1968), "Voices" (1972), "Searching/Not Searching" (1972)[11]—and, of course, in the autobiographical novel, *Savage Coast*, which you have here for the first time.

Written immediately upon her return from Spain in the autumn of 1936, *Savage Coast* is the most complete rendering of Rukeyser's experience during the first days of the war, but the novel remained unpublished in her lifetime. It was brutally panned in the anonymous reader report,[12] and rejected by her editor Pascal Covici of Covici-Friede in 1937 for being, among other things, "BAD" and "a waste of time," with a protagonist who is "too abnormal for us to respect." Rukeyser was strongly encouraged to abandon the novel for a "brief impressionistic sketch" of her experience in Spain and to continue working on her poetry. Covici-Friede would publish the long poem "Mediterranean" in her second collection, *U.S. 1* (1938), instead. This is to say, the first critics of *Savage Coast* discouraged Rukeyser from writing the kind of large-scale, developmental, modernist war narrative that she had begun—one that is sexually explicit, symbolically complex, politically radical (much more so than the "communist sympathizing" that the reviewer sneers at) and aesthetically experimental—in favor of the gender-appropriate lyric poetry of her first book and "small" personal narratives. Rukeyser, though, would never return to the more traditional lyricism of her early work, and did not abandon the novel. She continued to edit the manuscript, working on it throughout the war, publishing articles and poems on her experience in Spain in the meantime. It is not clear how much that first rejection letter shaped her editing process, but she did edit the text heavily, over several years. It is unclear when she abandoned the manuscript entirely, and it is unclear if she ever pursued its publication again. It was eventually misfiled in an unmarked and undated folder in the Library of Congress.

Finding this novel now is significant because, as Rukeyser's large body of work on Spain attests, the Spanish Civil War was not only an essential part of her poetic and political development, "part of her inclusive myth, shaping from within her subsequent commitments and writing,"[13] but her work on the subject is likewise essential to the literature of the Spanish Civil War. Rukeyser's lost novel, written before Hemingway, Orwell, or Malraux's major works on the subject, is only one of a handful of novels written by foreign women on the war, and provides us with a more complex understanding of women's political and literary participation in its history, offering a unique view into how women positioned themselves "within historical and social processes."[14] As the discovery of "The Mexican Suitcase" has demonstrated about women's contribution to the documentation of the Spanish Civil War, revealing how many of the most iconic war photographs were in fact taken by Gerda Taro, the discovery of Rukeyser's lost novel reminds us of the important role women played in writing about and recording the political events of this era. Recovering this novel also alerts us (again) to the fact that the recuperation of women writers did not end in the 1970s, and that there is a continued need for archival work that restores feminist and radical texts and puts them in print. As Theresa Strouth Gaul points out, "it remains crucially important to remember that, in the current moment, the availability of women's texts in print still largely determines what is read and taught in classrooms and receives analysis in dissertations, scholarly journals, and monographs."[15]

RUKEYSER HERSELF WAS deeply engaged with challenging the kinds of histories that privileged certain narratives over others, and saw the need to archive, document, and secure in text the stories of those who had been left out of "master narratives"—particularly the exiled, women, and refugees. Like Virginia Woolf and Walter Benjamin, who were writing in the same moment, Rukeyser worked to develop a poetics of history that was particularly attuned to exploring the "latent potentialities"[16] of the past inside the present. She writes, in *The Life of Poetry*, that "there is also in any history, the buried, the wasted, and the lost,"[17] and she recuperates these "lost" histories through an open-ended, proliferating, multitemporal, multivocal, documentary approach, one that "reach[es] backward and forward in history, illuminating all time."[18] *Savage Coast* is essential to understanding this practice, one that she develops throughout her life, as she records and contextualizes the histories of those who traveled to Spain to participate in the antifascist games, many of whom were the first volunteers in the International Brigades, and as she records her own moment of political and sexual awakening alongside the Catalan resistance through an experimental, multigenre form that defies the rigid binaries of the two major literary modes of the 1930s: the "political," didactic social realism and the "a-political," aesthetic high modernism, both of which "were regarded as mutually exclusive of the other."[19] Ironically, of course, Rukeyser's avant-garde and radical project, her "disinclination to conform to the dictates of any aesthetic or political program" or gender role, would prove to marginalize both her and her work for decades.[20]

In this sense the rejection of *Savage Coast* by her editor in 1937 says more about the fraught literary and historical moment in which Rukeyser was working than it does about the novel itself. On the other hand, the Spanish Civil War would become one of the most literary of wars, with "poets exploding like bombs,"[21] and Rukeyser was very much a part of this literary production. At the time of writing the novel, Rukeyser was involved in publicizing, fundraising and advocating for the Loyalist cause in Spain. Her poem "Mediterranean" was printed first as a pamphlet for the Medical Bureau to Aid Spanish Democracy, and she published articles on the subject in *New Masses* and the *New York Times*, among others. Like Rukeyser, many of her generation considered Spain the defining battleground against European fascism, and because of this it immediately became an international war, occupying a transnational imagination, seen as the last hope for the socialist and anarchist ideas that had flourished through the 1920s and 30s.[22] The coup in Spain was also, like the rise of fascism in Germany and Italy, indicative of a more profound backlash against those very social and political changes, a backlash that was eventually absorbed into the Cold War policies of the US. The fascist project to cleanse society of an "impure citizenry"[23]—the urban proletariat, the New Woman, the Jew, the homosexual, the communist, the artist[24]—meant that Spain's "civil war" was also viewed as a European "civil war."[25] Likewise, Franco's military success was made possible only because of the enormous international aid he received from Hitler and Mussolini, and from US corporations like Dupont,[26] who used Spain as testing ground for modern warfare.[27] The non-interventionist stance of Great Britain, France and the US determined not only the trajectory of fascism in Europe, dooming Republican Spain, but as Rukeyser herself noted in many of her essays, it reflected a larger political reality: that Spain was eventually viewed not as the place to stop fascism, but the place to "stop communism."[28] She understood that what was allowed to happen in Spain would be allowed to happen elsewhere, placing the conflict in a much broader cultural and historical context. And she was right: the placation of fascism by the allied nations was not only a suffocation of the Popular Front in Spain, aided by blocking the sale of arms and support to the Loyalist army to defend its government, but it was a way of enervating political dissent and left-wing organizing in their own home countries as well.

As Rukeyser's texts on the subject demonstrate, the Spanish Civil War also marked an important moment in women's visibility in public political life; for both foreign and Spanish women Spain proved to be a site of great potential for the expression of women's political and artistic agency. Women participated in, wrote on, and documented the war in Spain in great numbers, producing a significant body of work: Mercè Rodoreda, Simone De Beauvoir, Simone Weil, María Teresa León, Rose Macaulay, Dorothy Parker, Josephine Herbst, Martha Gellhorn, Genevieve Taggard, Virginia Woolf, Nancy Cunard, Sylvia Townsend Warner, Gerda Taro, and many more. What is striking is how little of their work on the subject is known;[29] and yet women's participation in the war was in many ways the culmination of the decades-long fights for agency in the public sphere, especially considering that Republican Spain had some of the most progressive gender policies for its time, particularly in anarchist Catalonia: women held political office, were allowed to vote, fought on the front for the first time, used and had access to birth control, in some areas were able to obtain legal abortions and request a divorce, and were guaranteed "equal protection" under the law and equal access to employment. They were political leaders like Frederica Montseny, Dolores Ibárruri, and Margarita Nelken, and they were writers and artists who continued to produce work about the war long into exile.[30] Likewise, international women reported and photographed from the front in great numbers, volunteered as nurses and soldiers, and, like Rukeyser, remained dedicated to the Loyalist cause in Spain after the fighting had ended. The Spanish Civil War marked a vital moment in what was an undeniably important series of decades for women's liberation and radical activity, and Rukeyser records and benefits from that history.

The events that unfold in *Savage Coast* reflect the biographical narrative of Rukeyser's trip to Spain. Rukeyser and her fellow travelers, mostly international athletes traveling to the People's Olympiad, were the last to cross the border when their train to Barcelona was stopped in Moncada (Montcada, in Catalan), just as the military coup began and a general strike was called in defense of the Republic. The people she met on the train—a Catalan family, the Hungarian Olympic team, French reactionaries, and American communists, among many others that populate her works—were real, their names appearing in articles she wrote at the same time she was working on the novel. As the novel depicts, Rukeyser witnessed the enactment of a radical Popular Front and the collectivization of the town, the local people burning religious icons, and then the dangerous trip in the back of a pick-up truck into Barcelona, "a workers city," in the first days of the resistance, "jewel-like" and "liberated." Rukeyser continued to correspond with her lover

"Hans," the *Rotfrontkämpfer* Otto Boch, a "Bavarian, with a broad strong face like a man in a Brueghel picture," exiled from Hitler's Germany and traveling to the games as a long-distance runner, after he joined the International Brigades. While the novel ends on the anarchist streets of Barcelona, as Rukeyser is "given her responsibility" by Martín, the organizer of the People's Olympics, who says to those being evacuated, "you will carry to your own countries, some of them still oppressed and under fascism and military terror, to the working people of the world, the story of what you see in Spain,"[31] other renditions of her narrative, like "We Came for Games," describe the evacuation from Barcelona on a boat chartered by the Belgian team (the American consulate provided no assistance). She describes this in the epic poem "Mediterranean" as a voyage of "exile and refugee" to the port town of Sète, where those participating in the local fete-day "raised their clenched fists in a new salute"[32] in support of the Spanish Popular Front, marking the opening of a new era of war and violence. It is on this boat when she is asked the question that frames her life's work, and that begins her most famous book, *The Life of Poetry*: "And in all this—where is there a place for poetry?" She answers, "I know some of it now, but it will take me a lifetime to find out."[33] Many of her poems and nonfiction works provide a nearly seamless epilogue, finishing from where the novel leaves off, fact and fiction overlapping. Sometimes the nonfiction texts specify details, blurred by her fictional narrative, while at other times the poems written across her lifetime extend and eulogize the memory of those who fought and died against fascism in Spain, or to meditate on the body of Otto Boch, who represents all the bodies of the dead in the unending violence of the twentieth century.[34]

Savage Coast, of all her work on Spain, is the most narratively and historically sequential, yet even while Rukeyser insists that this is a fictionalized account, making sure to point this out in a note to the reader, we are also instructed by her to read the text as documentary—from the inclusion of dated newspaper clippings that begin chapters, to the list of the dead that interrupts her own narrative near the end of the book, to the very fact that Helen and Hans are Muriel and Otto, their story and dialogue proliferating and repeated in other essays and poems, the novel itself only one of many iterations. This constant blurring of the boundaries between fact and fiction—the creation of the self inside history, and by extension inside the text—is foundational to Rukeyser's decades long desire to write cross-genre and hybrid poetry and prose where "false barriers go down." It also speaks to the moment in which she was working, when the documentary form was not only de rigueur but was being used particularly by radicals and feminists to challenge and expose patriarchal and hegemonic narratives. The term *documentary*, though, is inherently slippery, for it contains so many possibilities; it implies archiving, recording, witnessing, collaging, photographing, and filming, as well as the hybridization of "high" and "low" art forms; and it can be traced back to the practices of scrap-booking in the women's suffrage movement, left-front politics, social and socialist realism, travel narratives, war correspondences, epic poems, testimony, cinema, and reportage.[35] It is a genre that has, as Paula Rabinowitz notes, "reshaped generic boundaries" as well as gendered boundaries.[36]

Because of its representational mutability, the documentary form held immense potential for Rukeyser, particularly for developing an aesthetics that embodied her political and personal project, one that may be closer to and, appropriately, shaped by the anarchist principles she encountered in Catalonia, where "individuality was dependent on the development of a strong sense of connections with others"[37]—principles that were equally essential to the women's movement and feminist literary praxis. This radical and relational politics is formally manifest in the hybridization of the personal, lyric, and internal, situated alongside and interacting with the historical, documentary and worldly. For example, in the final chapter of *Savage Coast*, during a march through the streets of Barcelona in support of the Republic—made up of Olympic athletes, foreign nationals, Catalan workers, and volunteers about to set out for the front—a message is read to the crowd from the evacuated French Olympic delegation who were the first to flee the war. It is read to the crowd and recorded by Rukeyser, next to and along with her own Sibyl-like lyricism:

THE FRENCH DELEGATION TO THE PEOPLE'S
OLYMPICS, EVACUATED FROM BARCELONA AND
LANDED TODAY AT MARSEILLES . . .

> the tranquil voyage, Mediterranean, the
> tawny cliffs of the coast, cypress,
> oranges, the sea, the smooth ship passing
> all these scenes, promised for years,
> from which they had been forced away
> into familiar country, streets they
> knew, more placid beaches

PLEDGE FRATERNITY AND SOLIDARITY IN
THE UNITED FRONT TO OUR SPANISH
BROTHERS . . .

> the bird flight sailing forced
> upon them, so that no beauty
> found could ever pay for the
> country from which they had
> been sent home and the battle
> which they had barely seen begun

WHO ARE NOW HEROICALLY FIGHTING THE
FIGHT WE SHALL ALL WIN TOGETHER

Here we have the interaction between the documentary text and the lyric poem, imitating Rukeyser's own self-formation inside the collective political experience. The passage contains a double image, a fantasy of the French who have already sailed away and the actual voyage through the Mediterranean that Rukeyser herself will soon take, situated inside the text of a speech unfolding in the present time of the novel. It is the interaction of the lyric imagining of past and future with the factual and documentary text of the present that makes the moment so important, for it renders simultaneously the political implications of the documentary text—the very real possibility that the evacuation of the French Olympic team means that France will abandon Spain to fascism, which they do—and the profoundly individual effect that this experience has on Rukeyser's political and personal liberation, so much so that "no beauty / found could ever pay / for the country from which they had / been sent home."

The autobiographical and documentary nature of *Savage Coast*, though, is not meant to undermine the fact that in this iteration of her story Rukeyser chose fiction for a reason, and out of all her tellings and retellings, *Savage Coast* is the most psychologically internal, most politically radical, most sexually explicit, and, at times, most comical. While not today known as a novelist, it is clear that Rukeyser was not only interested in writing in multiple genres, but was equally desirous of experimenting with the structures and tropes of the novel itself, as she does in every genre, from her use of documentary materials to the way she breaks her prose lines like poetry. The experimental nature of the text is enhanced by the nearly impressionistic, elliptical prose, made up of fragmented images and scenes, pieced together with the documents. It is hard to say, though, if part of this experimentalism is due to the unfinished nature of the novel itself. Because *Savage Coast* was so flatly rejected by her editor, we don't know what Rukeyser would have done with the novel if she herself had in fact prepared it for publication, and if the fragmentary nature of the text would have been smoothed out. I hope it would not have been, because the prose that she writes is always nearer to poetry, and so the text has the feeling of an epic poem inside the realist novel; even the fact that her protagonist is named Helen and is narrating a war speaks to the innovation of a traditionally male genre.

Most avant-garde, perhaps, is the way Rukeyser situates her female protagonist as the mediator, narrator, and embodiment of a changing twentieth-century political landscape, one whose voyage into a war results in sexual awakening, personal liberation, and political radicalism. In writing this narrative through a "Helen"—a name both autobiographical (her middle name) and mythological—Rukeyser also situates herself as a worldly authorial voice, a maker and subject of history, one who has the ability to critique and comment on politics and war. The very fact that at twenty-two Rukeyser positions her text next to and along with the most prominent male literary figures of her time says something about the authorial intent. Not only does Rukeyser buttress her novel with references and quotations from Auden, Spender, Eliot, and Crane, to name only a few—intertwining them with the daily documents, newspapers, and political pamphlets—but her own story ultimately internalizes her male cohorts, so that they become references or footnotes to her history. We might read this as a signal of how she was positioning herself and her work, and it is clear that with this novel she wanted not only to be taken as seriously as the male authors she cites, but to assert herself on equal terms with them.

Consider the fact that Helen spends the entire trip reading D.H. Lawrence's *Aaron's Rod*[38] as she travels through Spain, and Rukeyser quotes it extensively in the text—his narrative structure and heavy prose hang around.[39] Helen is reading Lawrence in the hope that it will provide a "clue" for "a way to reach action," thinking, "perhaps, after trying for it so hard, she could find what she was looking for here. This might carry her deeper in. Lawrence could do that, striking for the heart, penetrating, on a dark journey . . . The book, to produce an equation, To bring an answer." But just like the scene where the message from the French is read aloud, Helen interrupts Lawrence with her own lyric interpretation of the actual events happening around her, and she "clap[s] the book shut." Helen's narrative takes over, she becomes "the clue," the person "that carries her deeper," not Lawrence, not the document alone.[40]

Like *Savage Coast*, *Aaron's Rod* is a quest novel of sorts, but one in which love and women are rendered as inverting forces, and that ends with an anarchist explosion in Italy that destroys the protagonist's livelihood and manhood. Rukeyser both sublimates and refutes Lawrence in the novel: radical politics, particularly anarchist politics, are a force of regeneration for her, as is sexual intimacy and free love; the camaraderie and empowerment found in the collective experience, especially multigenerational relationships between women—the Catalan grandmother, the lady from South America, and Olive—provide the psychological cohesion in the novel; and unlike Lawrence's assertion at the end of *Aaron's Rod* that "deep fathomless submission to the heroic soul in a greater man"[41] will prove to preserve humanity in the face of war (an erie fascist premonition?), Rukeyser predicts that the self, empowered and formed in relation to the development of others, one that keeps moving toward "more freedom," more openness and more connection, will change the future. Nevertheless, there are indeed generic similarities between the two texts. In both, the heroes flee their stifling pasts, represented by the confines and character of the nation state, in search of wholeness and value abroad. The portrayal of the housewife "Peapack" from New Jersey, whose face is always turning to "pudding" when a bomb explodes, embodies this Americanness that Helen is trying to escape. But it is Lawrence's vision, illustrated in *Aaron's Rod*, that "sees human existence as dialectic, a continual process of conflict between elements within the self as well as outside it,"[42] that prefigures some of Rukeyser's early development as a novelist and theorist, an influence that can be seen in the description of the protagonist in *Savage Coast*. Helen narrates her history in the opening scene:

> Her symbol was civil war, she thought—endless, ragged conflict which tore her open, in her relations with her family, her friends, the people she loved. If she knew so much about herself, she was obliged to know more, to make more—but whatever she had touched had fallen into this conflict, she thought, dramatically. The people she had loved best had been either willful and cold or weak In other ways. She was bitterly conscious of her failure, at a couple of years over twenty, to build up a coordinated life for herself.

In this sense Helen is already wounded by "civil war" before the novel has even begun, and so she is herself a symbol for the changing political realities that the Spanish Civil War ushers in. At least in part, then, *Savage Coast* embodies one of the main tropes of the bildungsroman, in which "the [hero]," as described by Bakhtin, "emerges *along with the world* and he reflects the historical emergence of the world itself. He is no longer within an epoch, but on the border between two epochs, at the transition point from one to the other. This transition is accomplished in him and through him."[43]

Helen's quest is to bridge this disunity, and not only to find "a way to reach action" but "to move past fear." Her experience in Spain both exposes her feelings of ineffectuality and dependence and propels her toward independence and agency. Near the end of the novel, Helen thinks, "she had wanted a life for herself, and found she was unequipped; and adjusting her wants, cared to be a person prepared for that life." This articulation marks an important turning point for Helen, in which she is able to assert her need for selfness outside the debilitating confines of the family, social and gender roles in which she was raised, those that leave her unprepared to act and live freely. She describes this coming to maturity in terms of war, as having "the fear of death replaced." As Helen becomes increasingly free on the war-torn streets of Barcelona ("she would always have this street before her for a birthday"), speaking and acting without inhibition, she also becomes more radical; it is thereby that Rukeyser weds gender liberation with sexual agency and political activism. This is why Hans proves such a powerful influence for Helen, both sexually and politically, for he "go[es] toward what [he] most want[s]." Hans is a decisive actor, and Helen describes his life as "single minded." As a literary foil, he is used to model and mirror confidence, freedom and agency for Helen: "all his life, moving so steadily, watercourse! she thought; only let me move, too, keep on pouring free."

Near the end of the rejection letter for *Savage Coast*, the anonymous reviewer states, "This book has been a waste of time—I doubt if at any moment in the writing of it Miss Rukeyser had any confidence in setting down a single paragraph." This sexist interpretation of a perceived textual instability might be read as a manifestation of Rukeyser's and Helen's difficulty in articulating and acting on their beliefs, of making a "coordinated" life, of speaking and acting with purpose and effortlessness, but the text itself embodies Helen's development and reflects the aesthetic and political destabilization that Rukeyser writes toward. Helen's difficulty in speaking, her "stutter," as Susan Howe might call it,[44] her self-made lyric interruption of documentary "facts," is also a way to open up discursive space in the novel: it allows other voices to be heard and to participate in making meaning of history. The cesura opened by this hesitation mediates Helen's own sometimes romantic desire for action, against the actual and often brutal experience of the Catalan people at war. Helen describes her ambivalence as a foreign national unable to interpret the events fully, saying often how she "had never wanted language so much," implying both a desire to better communicate with the Catalans, with Hans, but also a desire for a language to describe and hold the complex meanings of events occurring around her. This ambivalence with language and speaking, though, exposes the actual difficulty in documenting the war as an outsider, thereby subverting any possibility of a singular hegemonic narrative of its history.[45] This is exemplified in the scene where Helen is taken to the roof of the hotel in Barcelona by the Olympic guide:

> "If only I were not outside," she said, looking at him with her peculiar timidity after saying something she felt deeply. But this was a different life. There was nothing, no result of expression, to fear. He was talking. "Not so far outside, because you care so much," he said. "But you still talk like an outsider, if you say brilliant—we have had the waste and the blood and the fighting. We hang on; it will take time for us to see the brilliance, what there is."

The difficulty and fear in saying something "deeply felt" is such a central concern of the text that it appears in almost every layer of the novel—textually, narratively, psychologically, and physically—but more than anything it indicates Rukeyser's attempt to write about and create a form that discloses and explores issues of gender politics, to make a space where women's texts and their speech hold meaning.

From the outset this search for autonomy is described in somatic terms—the very motion of the text itself is made up of the conflict between movement and stasis, between speaking and silence, inertia and speed. The novel opens on a train speeding through France, as Helen describes a feeling of freedom and anticipation, hoping that this experience will "be valuable" and thus give her value. For Helen is filled by a desire for meaning, and to move beyond her gendered body. She suffers from an unspecified leg injury, an oblique disability, "a defect that reminds [her] of a time before this," that prevents her from running, and at times even from moving. The leg symbolizes the barrier to action that Helen must overcome, and Helen describes excruciating physical pain as the bombs explode outside—the internal mimicking the external, the personal and political intertwined. Ultimately, Spain's civil war helps Helen discover a unity and purpose of self that mends her internal "civil war" through political radicalization and sexual awakening. The responsibility she finds at the end of the novel allows her to speak, to move, to act freely, with "choice." Her crippled body is, if not cured, made painless, by the final scenes of the novel, and she has begun to overcome her fears. Speaking to Hans, Helen says, "'I *am* changed . . . I want you to know. You began anew—you set in motion —it is as though I had gone through a whole other life,' she said lamely. But she felt the truth of the words before she spoke them and they became timid and broken . . . 'I was almost born again, free from fear. The ride in, or the morning at the Olympic.'"

It is unclear whether Rukeyser herself had an actual leg injury, though she makes mention of something similar in her diary earlier in the trip, while in England. There is also some biographical evidence to suggest that it could have been the residual effect of the typhoid fever she caught in jail during the Scottsboro trial, or a substitute metaphor for cancer treatment she had recently undergone.[46] Whatever it may have been in reality, it proves a central symbol, not only for thinking through how Rukeyser constructs and writes about issues of gender (Helen is also uncomfortable with her large body, "as a big angry woman"), but as a depiction of the Jewish body: the novel takes place in 1936, as Helen, a Jew, is on her way to document a counter-Olympics against Hitler's Games, in which the perfect German body, as depicted by Leni Riefensthal's film *Olympia* (1938), would be reified. Ultimately, Helen's damaged body is intimately and erotically restored through sex with a German athlete, Hans, who is himself described as near physical perfection:

She walked with long safe strides beside him. He was not at all impeded by the load. The suitcase leaned against his strong thick neck, bending his head with its peasant broadness to one side; he was very tall, in the easy sweater and corduroys, looking high in shadow. The strained muscle in his neck stood out to the weight; it was fine and taut, symptom of his body. His walk was as balanced as before, he was master.

One must assume (or I want to assume) that Rukeyser was intentionally referencing Hitler's "master race" here, subverting and critiquing its ideology, and exposing a decade-long German resistance to the rise of fascism in Europe, since Hans is himself a political exile from Nazi Germany. Hans's "perfect dominance over himself, trained, disciplined, active," will be used to struggle against those forces of annihilation. Like many German political exiles who fled repression and imprisonment in the early 1930s, he viewed the fight against fascism in Spain as "the German chance, in or out of Germany."[47] This Jewish/German love story between Helen and Hans is reflected by the interracial relationship between Peter and Olive, the American communist couple that Rukeyser befriends on the train, connecting the American debate around miscegenation and the color line with the eugenicist ideology of Nazi Germany's Nuremberg Laws. Many of Rukeyser's later poems on Spain weave together the struggle for civil rights in America with the struggle against fascism in Spain. We can see this intertextual history begin in the novel, but, importantly, it is only Olive, who is of mixed race, who comments on the irony of Helen and Hans's relationship: "'Just imagine!' she cried, in a witty voice, 'during a revolution, with a 100 percent Aryan!'"

Rukeyser's brief love affair with Otto Boch (Hans) is one of the most consistent images throughout all her writings on Spain. There are a few letters from Boch to Rukeyser from the front, between July 1936 and 1938, written in German, addressing her desire and unsuccessful attempts to return to Spain, but more than anything speaking of his soldier's life, and his acceptance of their separation, since "everybody has their post in the war against Fascism."[48] Despite the brevity of their time together, their sexual encounter proved transformational. In the novel Helen and Hans meet the second night in Moncada, and with only that youthful kind of physical consent they have sex on the train, as soldier's boots can be heard on the platform, and before they even know each other's names. The quotation that begins the chapter is appropriately taken from Hart Crane's *For the Marriage of Faustus and Helen*. The symbolism of the scene is enormously overwrought—Lawrence's influence may be most notable here—as sex is framed allegorically in terms of unification, of the meeting of countries and continents, of bridging the divided spaces made by wars and borders: "And Europe and America swung, swung, an active sea, marked with convulsive waves, as if supernatural horses stamped through the night; a scarred country, that lies waiting for the armies to meet again." It is a metaphor that will thankfully become more subtle and introspective over the following decades. In the subsequent years, Boch's body, "lying / blazing beside me / . . . / erotic body reaching," turns into the "endless earth," encompassing everything, existing in everything.[49]

After Rukeyser's departure, Boch joined the German Thaelmann Brigade and set off to Saragossa.[50] He would die at the front in 1939 at the end of the war, as Rukeyser records in "We Came For Games": "On the banks of the Segre River, at a machine-gun nest where six hundred out of nine hundred were killed that day. It is in the Franco histories. Their intelligence worked very well. They knew every gun position."[51] Boch acts as a poetic and mythological site, and Rukeyser uses his body and memory to frame the politics of many of her works, calling out to him—the script that runs through her history. In "Long Past Moncada," she writes:

Other loves, other children, other gifts, as you said,
"Of the revolution," arrive—but, darling, where
You entered, life
Entered my hours, whether you lie fallen
Among those sunlight fields, or by miracle somewhere stand,
Your words of war and love, death and another promise
Survive as a lifetime sound.[52]

In 1972, during the Munich Olympics, she published an obituary in numerous German newspapers memorializing him. It read:

In Remembrance of
OTTO BOCH
Bavarian, runner, cabinet-maker,
fighter for a better world.
Any of his family and friends
wishing further information,
please write to ___[53]

At the end of the 1974 *Esquire* article, she connects the Spanish Civil War to the POWs in Vietnam, the 1968 Mexico City Olympics, "where the black athletes made their protest," and the shooting at the Munich Olympics, reminding us of the political nature of the Olympic Games as a site of exclusion and also of resistance. Then she looks back, writing about hearing the news of Boch's death: "Things that endure to our own moment," she writes, "not to let our lives be shredded, sports away from politics, poetry away from anything, anything away from anything."[54] She ends with the image of Boch, the runner, "Going on now. Running, running, today."[55]

It is hard to imagine that the sexually explicit, politically partisan, and avant-garde nature of the novel did not influence Rukeyser's publisher to reject it and encourage her to focus on her poems instead. This says something about the kind of genre that Rukeyser was attempting to take ownership of, and speaks to the increasingly conservative gender, aesthetic and political dictates that were emerging in the late 1930s. The rejection of the novel ushered in the kind of criticism that Rukeyser would receive for the following three decades, from both sides of the political and critical establishment. By the late 1930s, Rukeyser was under constant and continued state surveillance that persisted through the 1970s. Once considered one of the best poets of her generation, by the early 1940s her radical and experimental poetry had been marginalized. As she became increasingly engaged with the interaction between high and low art forms, with the big public works of biography, with a radical avant-garde aesthetic, her work was dismissed. The Cold War containment policies that permeated every aspect of American society found in New Criticism a powerful tool for excising certain kinds of writers from the canon and from history, successfully separating aesthetics from political and popular art forms, denigrating the latter and lauding the former.

Quite famously, and in a vein very similar to the criticism in the rejection of *Savage Coast*, the *Partisan Review*, once a proponent of her early work, attacked her in the early 1940s on political and artistic grounds. In what they themselves later dubbed "The Rukeyser Imbroglio," the editors repudiated her for being both a "bad poet" and for being a "bandwagon" Stalinist, writing that her work "shifted back and forth between the orgiastic diction of D.H. Lawrence at his worst and a style suggesting that of *Time* magazine and a persistent effort to send many telegrams at small cost to oneself."[56] But this political stance was a thinly veiled attack on women's literary and political authority, a sexist position that the *Partisan Review* would continue to exercise in the 1940s and 50s under the guise of New Criticism and anti-communism.[57] Likewise, Louise Bogan at the *New Yorker* spent an enormous amount of time pointing out that Rukeyser's work failed to live up to her notion of female lyricism, writing, "the chief virtue of women's poetry is its power to pin down, with uncanny accuracy, moments of actual experience.

From the beginning of the record, female lyricism has concerned itself with minute particulars, and at its best seems less a work of art than a miracle of nature."[58] Because Rukeyser's work did not shrink itself to fit these very tiny parameters, Bogan described her as having a "deflated Whitmanian rhetoric," meant to imply that Rukeyser wrote merely in a non-procreative approximation of the male voice. Of course, this may be one of her greatest poetic strengths: Rukeyser was working in a form and language dissonant with contemporary readers' notions of women's writing and even American poetry. *Savage Coast,* described as being "too confused, too scattered in its imagery and emotional progression to be real . . . clearly an example of bad writing," is a nascent example of the hybrid textual practice she was working in, a style deemed inconsistent by critics. And it was this "inconsistency" that she was charged with most, as David Bergman has astutely pointed out: personal (often she was described as "promiscuous," both because she had sex with men and women, and particularly because she was an unwed mother), political (she never joined a party), and especially artistic (she was formally experimental and wrote in multiple genres).[59]

Rukeyser, in actuality, appears deeply politically and artistically consistent through the years following the Spanish Civil War: always she resisted totalizing systems that flattened subjectivity and that could inherently lead to totalitarianism; and she worked within "the changing forms" of both her literary genre and her political and historical moment. Against gender norms she asserted political and artistic authority, writing philosophical, historical, and worldly works, with little concern for generic or disciplinary borders. The formal complexity of Rukeyser's work, the "obscurity" she was so often charged with, seems just the opposite; read in the context of her historical moment, her work presents an obvious extension of the difficult ideas, forms, and histories she was attempting to render. The more complex her forms, the more complex her readings of politics and history.[60] Perhaps Sylvia Townsend Warner's "wildly leftist novel" *Summer Will Show,* which Rukeyser quotes inside *Savage Coast* as well, is a logical influence and partner. Published in 1936, the same year Rukeyser was writing her novel and the first year of the Spanish Civil War, Warner's heroine, Sophia, finds subjectivity in political engagement and activism during the 1848 French Revolution, finds liberation in free love, finds herself on the barricades, awakening. But Townsend Warner's work falls short of the radical textual experimentations Rukeyser was making to embody those very politics.

In *Between Past and Future*, Hannah Arendt writes of revolution that "as Malraux once noticed (in *Man's Fate*) . . . it saves those that make it."[61] Rukeyser saw this in Spain, and writes it through Helen, as she watches the small town of Moncada collectivize, as she hears the people of Barcelona speak of transformation in their resistance to the fascist coup, as her lover Hans makes his way to Saragossa, and as she takes in this revolutionary potential as her own, back to her own country. The more Helen participates in the resistance, the more she becomes herself. The denouement of the novel is the miraculous moment when Helen stands alone on a street in Barcelona, surrounded by marchers, workers and soldiers about to leave for the front. She stands without fear, she acknowledges her changed self, describing it as a "life within life, the watery circle, the secret progress of a complete being in five days, childhood, love, and choice," and she listens to Martín's speech, translated in language after language, wave-like, until it finally reaches her, and she is given what she wants: an acknowledgment of her desire for responsibility and value, the freedom to move and act. He says, *"If you have felt inactivity, that is over now. Your work begins. It is your work now to go back, to tell your countries what you have seen in Spain."* Rukeyser finishes Helen's journey, and so we know that the young heroine of *Savage Coast*, standing in the middle of a street, in the middle of war, history, politics, sex—writing from its noisy center—learns to speak deeply, to say what she believes.

NOTES

1. In *Savage Coast*, Helen calls Spain her "birthday," and in the poem "Letter to the Front" Rukeyser calls Barcelona the "city of water and stone where I was born," *The Collected Poems of Muriel Rukeyser*, ed. Janet Kaufman and Anne Herzog (Pittsburgh: University of Pittsburgh Press, 2005).

2. These correspondences can be found in The Muriel Rukeyser Collection, Henry W. and Albert A. Berg Collection of English and American Literature, at the New York Public Library.

3. "Diary" Box I:56, Muriel Rukeyser Papers, Manuscript Division, Library of Congress, Washington, DC.

4. "We Came for Games," *Esquire*, October 1974, 192–95, 368–70.

5. Scheduled to take place July 19–26, 1936.

6. Originally, both Spain and Germany had vied for the 1936 Summer Olympics. The Olympic Committee's choice of Germany proved to legitimize Hitler's regime rather than "open" it, as they had hoped.

7. Introduction to *The Life of Poetry* (Ashfield, MA: Paris Press, 1996), 1.

8. Ibid.

9. "For O.B.," *"Barcelona, 1936" & Selections from the Spanish Civil War Archive*, ed. Rowena Kennedy-Epstein, New York: Lost and Found, The CUNY Poetics Document Initiative, Series II (March 2011).

10. In addition, upon her return she spoke at political meetings and wrote small articles in the *Daily Worker* and student newspapers.

11. *The Collected Poems of Muriel Rukeyser*, ed. Kaufmann and Herzog, (Pittsburgh: University of Pittsburgh Press, 2005).

12. The review was most likely written by her mentor Horace Gregory, as a May 31, 1937 letter from Pascal Covici indicates that he agrees with Gregory's assessment of the novel. This correspondence can be found in The Muriel Rukeyser Collection, Henry W. and Albert A. Berg Collection of English and American Literature, at the New York Public Library.

13. Anne Herzog, "'Anything Away from Anything': Muriel Rukeyser's Relational Poetics," *"How Shall We Tell Each Other of the Poet": The Life and Writing of Muriel Rukeyser*, ed. Anne Herzog and Janet Kaufman (New York: Palgrave, 1999), 33.

14. Rita Felski, *The Gender of Modernity* (Cambridge, MA: Harvard University Press, 1995), 8.

15. Theresa Strouth Gaul, "Recovering Recovery: Early American Women and Legacy's Future." *Legacy*, vol. 26, no. 2 (2009): 262–83.

16. Marina Camboni, "Networking Women: Subjects, Places, Links Europe-America, 1890–1939." *In-Conference, How2 Journal* 2.1 (2003).

17. *The Life of Poetry*, 85.

18. Ibid., 35.

19. Kate Daniels. "Muriel Rukeyser and Her Critics," *Gendered Modernisms: American Women Poets and Their Readers*, eds. Margaret Dickie and Thomas Travisano (Philadelphia: University of Pennsylvania Press, 1996): 247–63.

20. Ibid.

21. W.H. Auden, "Spain," *The Penguin Book of Spanish Civil War Verse*, ed. Valentine Cunningham (New York: Penguin, 1980), 100.

22. See, for example, Beevor, Cunningham, Carroll, Graham, Nelson, Preston, Perez, and Thomas.

23. Helen Graham. *The Spanish Civil War: A Very Short Introduction* (New York: Oxford University Press, 2005), 29. As Graham notes, Franco wanted not just to conquer but to fully supplicate and destroy the enemy.

24. Graham, 29.

25. Ibid., 32.

26. Antony Beevor, *The Battle for Spain* (New York: Penguin, 2006). Beevor notes that many American companies had factories in Spain, including Ford and General Motors. Over the course of the war, along with Studebaker, they supplied twelve thousand trucks to Franco's army. Dupont provided forty thousand bombs, sent via Germany. The Texas Oil Company and Standard Oil supplied more than 3.5 million tons of oil, on credit, to the Fascists.

27. Spain's was the first war in which aerial bombing of civilians was practiced, most famously in the bombing of Guernica by the German Condor Legion.

28. "We Came for Games," 370. Russia and Mexico (though minimally) were the only countries that actively supported the Republican government in defense of itself, and while much has been written about the "communist influence" and the rifts in the Popular Front between revolution and liberal democracy, between anarchism and communism, Helen Graham has noted that the influence, both ideological and military, of Communist Russia was nothing compared to that of Hitler and Mussolini.

29. This is not surprising, considering that "going over" and volunteering in a militia was considered a crucible of masculinity for the bourgeois left, most famously rendered by Orwell, Hemingway, Spender and Auden, in whose works almost no women are represented, other than as sexual partners. Likewise, in literary volumes and poetry collections published in the 30s that addressed Spain, Popular Front politics or proletarian literature, women were almost completely ignored. See Nelson and Wald for a good overview of this publishing history.

30. For more information on women in Spain, see Shirley Mangini, *Memories of Resistance: Women's Voices from the Spanish Civil War* (New Haven: Yale University Press, 1995); and Martha A. Ackelsberg, *Free Women of Spain: Anarchism and the Struggle for the Emancipation of Women* (Oakland, CA: AK Press, 2005).

31. *"Barcelona, 1936" & Selections from the Spanish Civil War Archive*, ed. Rowena Kennedy-Epstein. New York: Lost and Found, The CUNY Poetics Document Initiative, Series II (March 2011).

32. "We Came for Games,"192.

33. Ibid. The question is phrased a bit differently in *The Life of Poetry*, and again in "Mediterranean."

34. Luise Kertesz, *The Poetic Vision of Muriel Rukeyser* (Baton Rouge, LA: Louisiana State University Press, 1980).

35. For a more detailed discussion on the modernist documentary, see Stott, Entin, Kalaidjain, Robinowitz, Wald, and Marcus.

36. Paula Rabinowitz, *Labor and Desire: Women's Revolutionary Fiction in Depression America* (Chapel Hill, NC: The University of North Carolina Press, 1991), 3.

37. Ackelsberg, 21.

39. D.H. Lawrence, *Aaron's Rod* (Cambridge: Cambridge University Press, 1998).

39. Rukeyser writes often in her journal about Lawrence, and his influence on her early work is clear, particularly his explicit renderings of sexuality and his discussion of a dynamics and metaphysics of poetry. Perhaps most important, though, is his *Studies in Classic American Literature*.

40. In *The Book of the Dead*, which Rukeyser wrote in 1937, after the novel, she asserts that "poetry can extend the document."

41. *Aaron's Rod*, 317.

42. Mara Kalnins, Introduction to *Aaron's Rod* (Cambridge: Cambridge University Press, 1998).

43. M.M. Bakhtin, "The Bildungsroman and Its Significance in the History of Realism," *Speech Genres and Other Late Essays*, trans. Vern Mcgee, eds. Carol Emerson and Michael Holquist (Austin, TX: University of Texas Press, 1986).

44. Susan Howe writes that the "stutter," or "what is silenced or not quite silenced," is an essential trope of American literature, *The Birth-Mark: Unsettling the Wilderness in American Literary History* (Middleton, CT: Wesleyan University Press, 1993).

45. This is unique for documentary works of this period, especially for a style that often sensationalizes its subject, and at times fetishizes or fabricates. Orwell has been the subject of such criticism, as well as Auden and Spender. Likewise, the Depression-era documentary projects of James Agee, Walker Evans, and Margaret Bourke-White have been accused of "sensationalism."

46. Thanks to William Rukeyser and Jan Heller Levi for their thoughts on this.

47. "We Came for Games," 370.

48. "Correspondences," Box I:56, Muriel Rukeyser Papers, Manuscript Division, Library of Congress, Washington, DC.

49. Kertesz, 319.

50. A good history of this brigade is in Arnold Krammer's "German's Against Hitler: The Thaelmann Brigade," *Journal of Contemporary History* 4.2 (April 1969): 65–83.

51. "We Came for Games," 370.

52. *The Collected Poems*, 232.

53. Box1:52, Muriel Rukeyser Papers, Manuscript Division, Library of Congress, Washington, DC.

54. "We Came for Games," 370.

55. Ibid.

56. You can read full accounts of the "imbroglio" in Kertesz, Kalaidjian, and Bergman.

57. Michael Kimmage, *The Conservative Turn* (Cambridge, MA: Harvard University Press, 2009).

58. As quoted in Kertesz, 43.

59. Bergman, 570.

60. This is a concept Julie Abraham develops for reading women modernists in *Are Girls Necessary?: Lesbian Writing and Modern Histories* (Minneapolis: University of Minnesota Press, 2008).

61. Hannah Arendt, *Between Past and Future* (New York: Penguin, 1968), 8.

WORKS CITED

Abraham, Julie. *Are Girls Necessary?: Lesbian Writing and Modern Histories*. Minneapolis: University of Minnesota Press, 2008.

Ackelsberg, Martha A. *Free Women of Spain: Anarchism and the Struggle for the Emancipation of Women*. Oakland, CA: AK Press, 2005.

Auden, W.H. "Spain." *The Penguin Book of Spanish Civil War Verse*. Edited by Valentine Cunningham. New York: Penguin, 1980.

Arendt, Hannah. *Between Past and Future*. New York: Penguin, 1968.

Bakhtin. M.M. "The Bildungsroman and Its Significance in the History of Realism." *Speech Genres and Other Late Essays*. Translated by Vern Mcgee. Edited by Carol Emerson and Michael Holquist. Austin, TX: University of Texas Press, 1986.

Beevor, Antony. *The Battle for Spain: The Spanish Civil War 1936–1939*. New York: Penguin Books, 2006.

Bergman, David. "Ajanta and the Rukeyser Imbroglio." *American Literary History* 22, no. 3 (Fall 2010): 553–83.

Camboni, Marina. "Networking Women: Subjects, Places, Links Europe-America, 1890–1939." *In-Conference, How2 Journal* 2, no.1 (2003).

Caroll, Peter N. *The Odyssey of the Abraham Lincoln Brigade: Americans and the Spanish Civil War*. Stanford, CA: Stanford University Press, 1994.

Cunningham, Valentine. *British Writers of The Thirties*. London: Oxford University Press, 1988.

———. *Spanish Front: Writers on the Civil War*. Oxford: Oxford University Press, 1986.

Daniels, Kate. "Muriel Rukeyser and Her Critics." *Gendered Modernisms: American Women Poets and Their Readers*. Eds. Margaret Dickie and Thomas Travisano, 247–63. Philadelphia: University of Pennsylvania Press, 1996.

Entin, Joseph. *Sensational Modernism: Experimental Fiction and Photography in Thirties America*. Chapel Hill, NC: University of North Carolina Press, 2007.

Felski, Rita. *The Gender of Modernity*. Cambridge: Harvard University Press, 1995.

Gaul, Theresa Strouth. "Recovering Recovery: Early American Women and Legacy's Future." *Legacy* 26, no. 2 (2009): 262–83.

Graham, Helen. *The Spanish Civil War: A Very Short Introduction*. New York: Oxford University Press, 2005.

Herzog, Anne. "'Anything Away from Anything': Muriel Rukeyser's Relational Poetics." *"How Shall We Tell Each Other of the Poet?": The Life and Writing of Muriel Rukeyser*. Eds. Anne Herzog and Janet Kaufman. New York: Palgrave, 1999.

Howe, Susan. *The Birth-Mark: Unsettling the Wilderness in American Literary History*. Middleton, CT: Wesleyan University Press, 1993.

Kalnins, Mara. Introduction to *Aaron's Rod*, by D.H. Lawrence. Cambridge: Cambridge University Press, 1998.

Kalaidjian, Walter. "Muriel Rukeyser and the Poetics of Specific Critique: Rereading the 'Book of the Dead.'" *Cultural Critique* 20 (Winter 1991–92): 65–88.

Kertesz, Luise. *The Poetic Vision of Muriel Rukeyser*. Baton Rouge, LA: Louisiana State University Press, 1980.

Kimmage, Michael. *The Conservative Turn*. Cambridge, MA: Harvard University Press, 2009.

Krammer, Arnold. "Germans Against Hitler: The Thaelmann Brigade." *The Journal of Contemporary History* 4, no. 2 (April 1969): 65–83.

Mangini, Shirley. *Memories of Resistance: Women's Voices from the Spanish Civil War*. New Haven, CT: Yale University Press, 1995.

Lawrence. D.H. *Aaron's Rod*. Cambridge: Cambridge University Press, 1998.

Marcus, Jane. Introduction to *Three Guineas*, by Virginia Woolf. Eds. Mark Hussey and Jane Marcus. New York: Harcourt, 2006.

Nelson, Cary. *The Wound and the Dream: Sixty Years of American Poems About the Spanish Civil War*. Urbana, IL: University of Illinois Press, 2002.

———. *Repression and Recovery: Modern American Poetry & the Politics of Cultural Memory*. Madison, WI: University of Wisconsin Press, 1995.

Patterson, Ian. *Guernica or Total War*. Cambridge, MA: Harvard University Press, 2007.

Rabinowitz, Paula "History, Documentary and the Ruins of Memory." *They Must Be Represented: The Politics of Documentary*. New York: Verso, 1994.

———. *Labor and Desire: Women's Revolutionary Fiction in Depression America*. Chapel Hill, NC: The University of North Carolina Press, 1991.

Rukeyser, Muriel. *The Collected Poems of Muriel Rukeyser*. Edited by Janet Kaufman and Anne Herzog. Pittsburgh: University of Pittsburgh Press, 2005.

———. "Barcelona, 1936." *"Barcelona, 1936" & Selections from the Spanish Civil War Archive*. Ed. Rowena Kennedy-Epstein. New York: Lost and Found, The CUNY Poetics Document Initiative, Series II (March 2011).

———. "For O.B." *"Barcelona, 1936" & Selections from the Spanish Civil War Archive*. Ed. Rowena Kennedy-Epstein. New York: Lost and Found, The CUNY Poetics Document Initiative, Series II (March 2011).

———. *The Life of Poetry*. Ashfield: Paris Press, 1996.

———. *Savage Coast*. Ed. Rowena Kennedy-Epstein. New York: The Feminist Press, 2013.

———. "We Came for Games." *Esquire*. October 1974. 192–95, 368–70.

Stott, William. *Documentary Expression and Thirties America*. Chicago: University of Chicago Press, 1986.

Townsend Warner, Sylvia. *Summer Will Show*. New York: New York Review of Books, 2009.

Wald, Alan M. *Exiles from a Future Time: The Forging of the Mid-Twentieth-Century Literary Left*. Chapl Hill, NC: The University of North Carolina Press, 2001.

———. *Trinity of Passion: The Literary Left and the Antifascist Crusade*. Chapel Hill, NC: University of North Carolina Press, 2007.

EDITOR'S NOTE

Muriel Rukeyser wrote and edited *Savage Coast* between 1936 and 1939, but the novel remained unfinished in her lifetime. Because of this, we don't know what she would have done with the text had she prepared it for publication herself. Rukeyser wrote the novel with unusual speed in the fall of 1936, and it was rejected by her publisher in the spring of 1937, but she continued to work on it throughout the war. The opening line, "Everybody knows who won the war," was scrawled in handwriting atop the first page, and was obviously written after the fall of Barcelona in early 1939. The original manuscript has her editorial changes in type, pen, and pencil, indicating the multilayered nature of her editing process, and one chapter was left incomplete, with an outline appended. In this sense the text is still in flux as we encounter it now, especially considering how it interacts and overlaps with other texts she was writing at the time. The open-ended nature of the manuscript seems an appropriate reflection on both the motifs of movement in the novel and the ideas that Rukeyser was writing toward—ones of mutability, interaction, and wavelike discovery. In preparing the novel for publication, I tried as much as possible to follow her editorial directives. Rukeyser was so bothered by the bowdlerizing of editors, their insistence on "cleaning up" her grammar, that she had a stamp made to emboss "PLEASE BELIEVE THE PUNCTUATION" atop her manuscripts. With that in mind, I have tried to leave her words, sentence structures, and punctuation as she wrote them, though I have corrected her Spanish and Catalan spelling where necessary, as well as any misquotations, typos, and grammatical inconsistencies. The paragraph breaks, which are almost like poetry, are hers, and remain. Only in the first chapter was I forced to make a difficult editorial decision.

During editing, Rukeyser crossed out the place names in the opening chapter with pencil, as if to signal that she wanted this beginning scene to be read as a moment in any country, at any historical moment, in any war. The opening sentence of the manuscript looks like this: "The train went flashing down ~~France~~ toward ~~Spain~~, a stroke of glass and fine metal in the night." However, she didn't change the sentence structure to accommodate her editorial decisions, nor did she insert any indication that she wanted to use a kind of ubiquitous proper-noun-replacing Victorian dash, such that it would have looked like this: "The train went flashing down ——— toward ———." If the manuscript were reproduced faithfully, according to her editorial assertions, it would read like this: "The train went flashing down toward a stroke of glass and fine metal in the night." This sounds kind of beautiful at first, but if one continued like this it would be like reading sentences off a cliff: "The train slowed down with a civilized grinding under the shed at." Since Rukeyser did not continue this editorial practice throughout the novel, and abandoned crossing out place names by the second page of the second chapter, I've decided to leave the names in, for sake of clarity and readability, especially since *Savage Coast* is a text that renders, often times quite beautifully, the very specific geography of Spain at the moment of civil war.

—Rowena Kennedy-Epstein

SAVAGE COAST

To George and Elizabeth Dublin Marshall

This tale of foreigners depends least of all on character. None of the persons are imaginary, but none are represented at all photographically; for any scenes or words in the least part identifiable, innumerable liberties and distortions may be traced.

—Muriel Rukeyser

CHAPTER ONE

On Saturday, according to all the latest reports, Barcelona
was calm, and as yet not a shot had been fired.
—Reuters dispatch

Everybody knows how that war ended. What choices led to victory, reckoning of victory in the field with the armed men in their sandals and sashes running blind through the groves; what defeats, with cities bombed, burning, the plane falling through the air, surrounded by guns; what entries, drummed or dumb, at night or with the hungry rank of the invaded watching from the curbs; what changes in the map, colored line falling behind colored line; what threat of further wars hanging over the continents, floating like a city made of planes, a high ominous modern shape in the sky.

EVERYBODY KNOWS WHO won the war.

The train went flashing down France toward Spain, a stroke of glass and fine metal in the night.

Its force of speed held the power of a water-race, and dark, excited, heavy before morning: it was traveling, lapping in the country, in speed.

She got up, bending her head low, twisted the length of the sleeper, and pressed her face against the window. Now she could gather herself firmly in, twist in the sleeper, lie with her eyes washed over by black countryside pouring past, streaming over her as she stared out.

She looked out with an intent look of finality: she expected everything of the day, of the long roll of night-country. In a blaze of excitement, the world changed: to speed, sleep and speed.

The tense, desperate stroke of the train relieved all the passengers: no responsibility, no world, only sleep, sleep and speed in the black, the calm night falling, preserving speed, opening up the shadows, drawing away to morning.

Casual and direct, the tourist train went down, flying like a high whistle across the air.

South of Carcassonne the early morning, and with all the cocks crowing, the landscape was changing now, the neat silvery fields giving way to white hills and cliffs, standing spread, catching the facets of bright windows in the wake of the train.

Helen woke with brightness on her. She lay in the lower sleeper, looking out level at the gray terraces, the gasps of blackness as tunnels enclosed them, the careful white masonry of bridges and underpasses.

High up one of the hills speeding past them, a man stood for an instant, leading a donkey.

The black of another tunnel wiped him out.

The tunnel-roar lasted for minutes, at last exploding into the shriek and light of a train whistling emergence. They were leaning around the shoulder of a mountain now.

"Look!" she said, startled.

The stranger in the upper berth moved her head lazily. The reflection swung in the door-mirror which had opened during the night. She was older and fairer than Helen, not so large, but flabby and lax in the early morning.

"First time you've seen it?" she asked.

"Any of this," the girl answered.

"But there's plenty of cactus in the States," the older woman said, yawning.

The guard put his head in at the door, cutting her yawn short.

"Ten minutes to Cerbère," he stated, and shut the door.

"Better get up, better get up," muttered the woman, clamoring down the trim ladder.

She stood on the floor of the little compartment, very smart in its dull green metal, very compact and comfortable. Lazily, she pulled her underwear to her over the top berth, and started dressing.

Helen lay still, looking out.

The hills dipped into green valleys, climbed steeply up, balanced tiny white houses with tile roofs on their edges, broke again, and rose into mountains. The Pyrenees produced their little churches and donkeys, plaster and stucco houses, enormous sweeps of green forests and bone-white rock. Fiery dark cypresses sprang up along the slopes, urging them up. The spread of the mountains was wing-spread, white and terrible, or tawny, as if blood were beneath.

The woman was out quite soon, looking for coffee down the aisle.

The train slowed down with a civilized grinding under the shed at Cerbère.

Helen swung her shoulders to the other end of the bed, looking out the large window.

Across the double tracks was the bookstall, all the paper-covered books ranged cheerfully.

Two porters, covered with tennis rackets, were helping a party across the station.

The fat man in the beret looked up appealingly, walking alongside the windows until the right one was found, and he might tiptoe and flutter and assist.

On the big walls the poster with its yellow diagonal, "*Pour La Protection des Jeunes Filles*," stared across at her.

Two boys, very daintily muscled, strolled up and down; the one in the maroon silk shirt had his arms across the other's shoulders.

The fine tonic heat rested on the shed.

Helen began to get dressed.

The last station in France. Spain opened up to her, in fifteen minutes!

The twinge of excitement pulled the nerve in her leg. Sun would cure that.

She drew the sweater over her head, and opened the door.

It lay there, just on the other side in a pocket of hill, the old water, the Mediterranean. Gray and trembling with sun, and only a glimpse.

Urgently now, the train began again. Finding its full speed, it whipped around the slopes.

The sea went by, was covered, was laid out full again, cut with sunlight.

Helen found the other woman in the next compartment.

"We might just as well sit here for a few minutes," the woman said. "The frontier's next, and this place is so clean and vacant, just right. Have you changed your money yet? No, don't go, I just want to tell you how glad I've been that you were put in my compartment—not some old Scotchwoman, I always think there's going to be some old Scotchwoman stuck with me. But the minute I saw you—I knew we wouldn't fight about the lower."

Helen laughed.

"And then," she went on, "I was so glad to show *somebody* those photos of my children—I guess I do miss them, no matter what they say—and, in a manner of speaking, we *are* neighbors, aren't we, if you live in New York, and I'm just across the river in Jersey—in Peapack?"

"The river isn't very much, as far as barriers go," agreed Helen.

"And it was nice to talk to you about my friends in Barcelona. He's really very attractive—you'd like each other, I think—you must meet them. Maybe we could all go to a bullfight this afternoon; there are always bullfights, Sunday afternoons, in Spain, aren't there?" said Peapack.

"I don't know. But I have to look up the Olympiad man, as soon as I arrive," said Helen.

"Olympiad? What Olympiad?" asked Peapack. "The Olympic games are in Berlin, aren't they? Why I planned to meet my husband at the end of the week and go on to Germany. He has some letters to some very interesting people there. And then we're going on to Italy, to Milano—we're going to meet some very interesting people there, too."

"These are against the German games," said Helen. "People's Olympiad, against the Nazi games, against Fascism. They are being held in protest against the others. In an entirely different spirit."

"Well," said Peapack, "I like the spirit of sportsmanship. We have some very interesting contacts in Germany. Why should there be games *against* games?"

The newspapers lay unfolded on the floor, carrying the headlines of Europe that spoke of war on every street, knew that the Undergrounds were not safe from air-raids now, put advertisements on its front pages asking for gas-masks recommended for children.

Peapack went on. "I guess there can't be too many games," she said brightly, to make peace.

Helen looked out the window.

Spain began here, hot and confusing.

The white road disappeared behind a church.

A man with a wide black sash waved from a row of peas.

Her mood had changed since yesterday. Then, she had crossed the Channel, gone down to Paris on the fast train, whipped across the city, and come on this one, all in a daze of excitement, carried away with the excitement of it, but still locked into herself, traveling alone. It was all new and must be important, must be valuable, in the same way that she was used to thinking she must grow to be valuable. It was too much to carry, all this self-consciousness, and it was beginning to relax from her in the heat and adventure here. She always drew into herself so painfully, conscious of herself years ago as the white, awkward child, and later as the big angry woman. Being that conscious, she knew enough to train most of it out of her, and had grown into a certain ease, an alliance among components, that resembled peace. But her symbol was civil war, she thought—endless, ragged conflict which tore her open, in her relations with her family, her friends, the people she loved. If she knew so much about herself, she was obliged to know more, to make more—but whatever she had touched had fallen into this conflict, she thought, dramatically. The people she had loved best had been either willful and cold or weak in other ways. She was bitterly conscious of her failure, at a couple of years over twenty, to build up a coordinated life for herself. This trip to Europe was to be a fresh start, in the same way that college had given her a fresh start. And now, nearing the end, with her work done and this week to spend at a People's demonstration, as she chose, the tension was breaking a bit. The nerve in her leg, which had been so disturbing all year, was almost the only reminder. The rest was beginning to turn outward. She could give herself thoroughly to anything that broke down the tension, and this day was beginning to, with the warmth and whiteness, the first-seen cypresses, the inconsequential woman talking away.

Europe, the thought of Europe swelled over the horizon, like a giant dirigible, strung with lights in a dream of suspended power, but filled, in the dream, with a gas about to burst into flame. When the porter had talked to her about war at Victoria Station the day before, premonitions crowded down on her; Paris made it worse, with its posters and notices of gas-masks and the gossip of cellar drills and war ritual.

But all of it was beginning to wear away. France, strongly Popular Front, was a pillar after England's mixed politics and mad conversation. Sun was restoration after London, and Spain, flooded with sun, backing a People's Olympiad, had shaken her free before she reached the frontier.

Let it all pass, American strikes and civil cases, grievance in love, looking for rest, seeing only tensions everywhere, nightmares of coming struggle, the concentration camp, the gas-mask face, night voices, German pain, threat of all forms of war.

Let it pass in bursts like bursts of music, until there is some quiet after, quiet and heat and speed to wave over one, tide that waves over a woman lying on sand under a cliff, a cliff like the one here of white and green and cypress, heat like this heat that one can put the hand into, speed like this speed, a train flying south, quiet like this quiet, now that this train has come to final rest.

Port Bou.

The frontier.

Porters ran screaming up and down the platform, valises fell and jostled through windows, passengers clutched each other, dropping down the perpendicular steps.

The cataract madness of a new language filled the station, she had a porter who was pushing his way across, head down, Peapack had found somebody to take her five rawhide suitcases to the customs office.

There was the young English couple, the fresh girl, the young husband, long soft eyes, long soft mustache, whom she had noticed head up crossing the Channel. His green porkpie hat had a faintly Latin air.

She entered the customs building.

The porter shouted, "First or third, lady?"

Peapack signaled she was going first, as in France.

Helen could see the wooden benches of third from where she stood.

They were filling with Spaniards.

"I'll let you know in a minute," she called back, moving toward third.

Her single suitcase was chalked immediately.

She was at the end of a long line waiting in front of two scribbling officers.

They stopped each passenger before the waiting room.

As she moved up to them and stood before the long table, they looked up with an ironic detective look. They took her name and added it to the list.

"Extraordinary!" said the Englishman.

She passed into the waiting room.

The French express was completely broken up. Its passengers were standing in little knots, waiting for the Spanish train for Barcelona.

She recognized one or two of the other passengers, but many new ones had been added.

There were two groups traveling on collective passports, wearing *Olimpiada* buttons, breaking into little athletic runs every now and then.

Three black-cheeked, well-dressed men, talking tough Americans, stood at the turnstile. One had a copy of *Variety* under his arm, and grinned at her when she stared at the headlines.

Peapack was getting on the train, four cars ahead, as it backed slowly into the station.

It was a smaller train, of eight cars, three third-class, three first-class, one Pullman, and one dining-car.

The teams and Spaniards scrambled up the third-class steps. *Variety* vanished in the direction of the Pullman.

Peapack's head came out of the first-class window, looking vaguely resentful.

Helen was liking the Spaniards.

She went up the third-class steps.

The porter found a single seat on one of the wooden benches, and slung the bag overhead.

With a great grinding, the train started.

CHAPTER TWO

Junction or terminus—here we alight
—C. Day Lewis

The train had not yet reached its speed.
The wooden compartment was a clatter of Cata-
lan, the six dark women filled it, packed it tight with words. They
had been sitting back against the boards when the train started, in
the shadow of the station, pushing back to wait for Helen's fat black
pebbled-leather suitcase to be thrown on the rack, and the blue
coat and large black hat over it; staring. The black and the hot sun
crossed their faces then; drawing out of the station, the train pulled
into the miraculous heat and light; the wheels turned. Drowned
under their talk.

All sound was wiped out.

They were leaning forward, screaming in argument, friendly,
shrill, at the top of the voice, yelling across Helen, filling the room
with fists, round and shaking before each other's faces.

The fashionable one, sitting at the window, would lean back for
a moment in her starched clothes, a quiver of earrings, sighing; and,
renewed, lean shrieking into the center of the compartment.

A large, placid young girl with a long jaw came to stand against
the partition and grin; one of the little boys scrambled over the
woman's knees; two soldiers walked through the crowd in the aisle,
in a blur of olive and black and yellow; the noise continued, whip-
ping around the wooden box, a henhouse madness of argument.

They stopped off a moment to look at Helen. She pulled out the
guidebook, looking for phrases. One of the women smiled across to

her. She smiled back as she looked up. The fashionable one thrust a provocative word into the face, flat and Celtic, of the peasant woman next to Helen; and the "*Buenos días*" was lost.

They descended on the instigator. The earrings shook

Pushing through the tangle of noise, Helen could get words, one or two word-roots came through the Catalan.

The flat-faced older woman threw "*monàrquica, monàrquica*" at the fashionable one, who streamed wrath and contempt now.

All the others flared up, obscuring everything, compartments, windows, hills of shaken silver, dark points of cypress, little rivers. All the others punctuated, "*comunista, república, anarquista*," sometimes, "*socialista*," and often, with hatred, "*Feixista*." It was possible to comb out some coherence; then the shrieking blotted out all but vehemence.

Something quiet was moving down the aisle, bringing quiet. It reached the next compartment. Here it was, a guard taking tickets. Helen pulled out her book of tickets as he punched the women's slips; they stared as he ruffled through the book to find the last page. "Barcelona?" the flat-faced one asked her as the guard passed through.

"*Sí. Olimpiada*," she answered.

They all turned on her, opened, friendly, with O and greeting, questions, appraisals. They thought she was French.

She showed them the letter from London to the committee chairman at Barcelona. The woman on the other side of her took it, nodding at the address, passing it across, all nodding, recognizing, friendly.

"English?" they asked. She told them no; American.

She could catch, in the rush of comment, the words for *Olympic, American, committee, week*. Everything else was lost. The barrier had sprung up immense in a moment; here were friends, and she could not reach over. She thumbed at the list of words.

Lawyer, learn, leave, leave behind.

"Left?" she asked, (straight on, strap, street, string) "strong in Spain?"

They looked, puzzled, quieted. She passed the book. The flat-faced woman pushed it away, and the fashionable one put her hand out for it. She looked at the close columns, and shook her head, smiling, making no sense of it. She said something to the others, and they all smiled at Helen.

"¡Viva Olimpiada!" said the fashionable one. "Visca Olimpíada!"

The train was slowing, noon-hot, hotter than any noon, as its motion's wind died, and it came to a stop.

All the women got up.

Children scrambling, clothes arranged, the pushing hips, the noise, the flourish of good byes.

The compartment emptied in a moment.

Helen moved to the window, and put her head out into the full sun, seeing in one broad view the pale town, lines of washing hung, dark clear hills, the six women walking up a little road, the children at their hands.

She pulled her head in, struck by the blaze.

The compartment was a thin crate of heat, tranced by the sun. The excitement of the Catalan women had kept it alive; now it became stale, filled with dense noon and silent.

The train waited.

Helen crossed again to the window, and went head and shoulders into the sun.

The short blue man stood opposite the car, pointing a rifle at the steps, in readiness, alert bristling, dark.

A gun!

Guns, patrols! she thought.

His rifle moved like a camera, covering the train panoramically.

Soldiers! she thought, the soldiers on the train! Where are they?

The six Catalan women were receding from the station moving down a small hillslope. One of them waved, minutely outlined against a wavering silver tree.

Helen answered the woman. The gun swung round to her, pointed, hesitated, returned. Watching, panicky at a glance, she saw it aimed at two gun-barrels held by the soldiers, guarding the steps.

They were very neat and amazing. Their musical-comedy uniforms, olive cloth, strapped with yellow leather, their reversed patent-leather hats, sideburns, chic.

Their guns.

At the front of the train, the engineer was leaning far out of his cab, gesturing at a group of armed men.

The automobile horn blew ferociously, in a quick triple blast, One-Two-Three, up the road.

From all the third-class windows, heads developed. A dark boy nodded at the man with the gun and smiled. He was pointing to his lapel.

"¡*Olimpiada Popular!*" he shouted.

The man shook his gun high over head in greeting.

The boy's dark head turned, looking up the train toward first class. Most of the heads were pulled in already. It was too hot.

He swung around toward Helen, brilliant, dark and smiling; waving to her to come through, as she answered him, "¡*Olimpiada!*"

He was speaking, waving his arm pointing inside his compartment, describing. She could not understand what he was saying.

The train whistle slit the valley in an atrocious blast.

"¡*Olimpiada!*" repeated the boy, like a signature. He put his hand up, with the gesture of an acrobat who calls his audience to attention for the next turn.

He shouted a word to the man holding the long gun, who replied with a come-on motion.

Leaping down the steps, hurrying up these, he was in the next car, he was hurrying through, he was at the door.

The boy was very gay, dark, his mouth was almost purple in the young, intense face, the smile was a dim archaic smile. Remembered, in Renaissance paintings, the purple curved lips, the youth, this grace intensity. His white shirt and light flannels were ordinary; his coat was marked with the button of the Games.

"Are you Spanish?" he asked, in Spanish.

She told him, repeating what she had told the women, feeling very strongly the oddness of repetition; for a moment, feeling the oddness of recognition in a dream.

He clapped his forehead.

Real, it was entirely real.

"You don't speak Spanish?" She nodded no. "French, perhaps? Oh, well, that's fine then, that's better yet, we'll get on in French." He sat down beside her.

"You in the Olympics?" He was not much taller than she, he could not be much older. She felt self-conscious because she was not athletic, she was not to be in the Games, and it was stupid to be watching, always; the nerve in the leg pulled with a memory of past games, past sidelines, answers.

"Just going to see them," she said.

"American!" the exclamation startled; a scream pointed it, the engine screaming up the track. "You came all this way?" He didn't let her answer. "Is the American team on this train?"

More repetition; she told him her position, her ride from London, the speed, the flight across France, asked him his country. "French?"

"No, I'm Hungarian," he said. "The team's in the next car. Hungarians from Paris—we've all lived there, in the colony there. Antifascist sport club. Vaterpolo."

She could not understand, even when he repeated. Va-ter-po-lo, he was saying, turning his purple mouth around the word. An American sportword.

The train was wrenched suddenly, they fell forward abruptly from the edge of the bench, Helen's black hat settled in place on the rack. They were laughing; she saw; the train began to move. They passed the armed man. He brandished his gun at their car, joyously. The flat pale houses ran by in a moment.

"Oh," she said. "Water-polo."

Outside, the long fields began to take the attention, stripes of blond wheat, purple (thistles, flowers?), walls with long sheaves, long branches laid against them, glimpses of sea that had no color but the light it held, the hot white light, and the little fair brooks that ran blue under the tracks, the pools.

He was talking about swimming, about American athletes, American men who lived with their feet up on desks, high buildings, the Empire State, movies, would many Americans be at the Games, how was the antifascist movement in the United States, the union movement, the students' movement. His father, a jeweler in Budapest, had lived in Brooklyn for seven years while he stayed in Hungary, had taken out citizenship papers, did she know Brooklyn? What games did she like best? Diving, was diving like the American elevators he had heard so much about (his dark mouth curling, laughing over all the words, how do you pronounce *Hollywood*?), did Americans get news more quickly than other people, had she heard the news about Africa that they heard at the border, a revolt of troops in Morocco, something to do with generals, all very vague, but when they had stopped at Port Bou yesterday to go swimming, the Hungarian team had heard stories, the Spaniards seemed to know all about the revolt. But the papers carried small paragraphs about that piece of news, if they mentioned it at all.

Revolt in Morocco!

But all quiet in Barcelona.

All quiet in Spain.

Had she seen the revolutionary slogans on the train? Chalked on the train?

What slogans?

THE TRAIN STOPPED for the first time. Helen got up, crossed a man in a tight, flashy suit who was pushing into the compartment, and went on to the platform.

In big, white-faced scrawl on the red, the words stood: *Viva República España—Viva República Catalunya.*

Guns.

She climbed the next car, dodged through the thick groups in the aisles, crossed over into first as the train got in motion again.

The windows here were larger, the benches were upholstered in pale gray, the white faces turned without interest to the windows were clear and stony against the lace rests. One to a compartment, two here, a group of four, an empty room. She was suddenly completely class-conscious about the fact of the split train, the noise and herding of the wooden cars, the guns. Slogans.

Here, Peapack.

The woman rose as Helen rolled back the door. "Oh, I'm so glad you're here," she was saying, beginning another of her long, trickling speeches. "I was getting so sick of being in here by myself, watching those fields. It makes me miss my husband. I never thought we'd be separated on this trip; but he'll be waiting for me in Berlin, and I'm to wire him as soon as we get into Barcelona. You'd like him; he's good to talk to, and he always knows people, where he is. He gets things done, too. Wouldn't he be sore to be on a train that takes so long! We must be stopping at every little way-station. I thought this was an express!" She opened her pocketbook, and felt about in it for a lace-edged handkerchief. "And it's so hot . . . I get awfully thirsty in this heat. I've just been up to the diner, and it's not open; it closed just as I got there. There are a couple of Americans; they were drinking coffee. And that young couple, with the beautiful Spanish-looking woman. You know, the ones in the second dinner last night. She *is* beautiful, that woman, even if she's such a snob. Wouldn't say a word!"

"Did you speak to her?"

"Oh, just something about the weather. But she wasn't very cordial. Have you met anybody?"

Helen told her about the crowd. And the Hungarian.

"I forgot," said Peapack, "of course, your Games. You probably have to see those people. But I wish you'd move in here. Nobody would mind, and I hate sitting alone when you could be here. Why don't you go back and get your suitcase?"

The suburban encroachments, Helen thought. Two hours more of it! It seemed foolish, surrounded by another race. But she said she would go and see about moving her things up.

"You'd better keep an eye on your suitcase, anyway," Peapack warned her. "How could you leave it like that, even to come up here?"

THE COMPARTMENT WAS full again when she returned, except for her place at the window. The Hungarian boy was talking to the man she had passed on the way out, who was jammed in between the boy and the family with a wicker basket. On the other bench, two young men in white were explaining something to two girls, who shook their heads quietly, silenced by their failure to understand what the men were saying. The four young people had the look of picnics and tennis-parties, and the family across, centered in the old woman, dressed in black, stared openly at their smartness.

The two soldiers were standing in the aisle just outside.

As Helen crossed their knees, the Hungarian boy started to introduce her to his friend. The man's suit creased sharply over his stomach and sides; his legs burst roundly out from the cheap cloth, every muscle detailed and full. He might be a salesman . . .

"This is our manager," the boy was saying. "He's got the whole team on his hands, and what a team, *mon copain*, yes?"

The man cut him short, his hand up in modesty. "Toni's been telling me about you, mademoiselle," he said. "Let's all have dinner together this evening, and see a bit of Barcelona."

"Toni thought we might look for headquarters together when we arrived," Helen told him.

"We won't have to look," the manager interrupted, grinning broadly, and pushing his straw hat back on his head. "They'll be down at the station to welcome us. And tonight is the torchlight procession. They'll be there with banners!" he said, sparkling. He wiped his forehead.

"I wonder about the American team . . ." Helen thought, fine; everything is arranged.

"Oh, they've gone through, they've been there three days. I saw them in Paris early this week, and they were just about to leave," the manager told her.

The train was slowing again.

It was drawing to a full stop.

"We must be coming to a station," the manager said, getting up. He stumbled over the four young people. "I'd better be getting back to the team. No hurry, Toni." He wiped his forehead again.

"He's a wonderful fellow," Toni looked after him. "Goes everywhere. I saw him in Paris last spring, and we mentioned the Games. He agreed to be manager, and left that night for Venice. Three weeks ago, when we all had given up—including his brother, who's a printer by trade; you'll meet him with the team—he turned up at dinner—same café, same suit, same dinner—he'd just come back from Marseilles, and were we in training?" He saw she wasn't listening. The young man in white at the other window was leaning out, looking down the tracks.

They were not stopping at a station. There was only a grade crossing, guarded by a small boy and a dog with a signal-flag in his mouth; but two armed men climbed up beside the engineer before the train started again.

They were reaching a walled city. Pale yellow battlements, the high pale towers of Gerona stood delicately up over the deep hills. And at every crossing an armed peasant held his gun up.

With the familiar grinding, the train stopped at the station platform, and the four young people got off.

The family moved over to the bench opposite, and the two soldiers came in and sat down, facing each other, at the end.

Next to the window, the old woman with the wicker basket, all in careful rusty black, pulled out some almonds and handed them to the young boy. He looked about twelve years old, tall and finely made, his iodine-colored eyes startling behind the clear-oil yellow of his skin, and his fair hair, cropped short and stiff as a blond field. He kept looking for approval to the dark, stout man sitting between them, whose fleshy, deep-grooved face could not have been farther removed from his own. The furrows ran vertically and double between his eyebrows and from his fleshy nostrils around the full, kind mouth. Only the arched nose was a point of resemblance and the smooth curve of his eyebrows, which was identical over the grandmother eyes of the old woman.

"I wonder if they speak French," Toni whispered. "I wish I knew how far we are from the city."

"It would be fine if they did. We could find out if they are olive-trees, and why the slogans are up."

The train was edging along now, never reaching its speed, stopping at every crossing.

"There's a castle!" cried Toni.

GRANOLLERS WAS PAST, and the train hardly moved. The heat hooked on to every board, it seemed, rippling over the window-panes, seizing cloth and flesh.

"I really ought to go back to see the American woman," Helen said, struggling to rise through the torpor, through the weight of air.

"Let her wait, if she's what you say," Toni objected, smiling his purple smile, looking at her sidelong. "And we must be almost there, anyway; we've been riding almost three hours."

The old woman spoke, suddenly with a flash, speaking French.

"We're not more than halfway between the frontier and Barcelona."
Helen and Toni leaned forward together; they could speak, here
was a break made!

"But it's a three-hour ride!" Toni exclaimed.

"Yes?" The old woman's humor was noiseless and gentle, her
wrinkled, lovely face very kind. The Sibylline face, grandmother.
The young boy looked a question at her.

"We've never been here before," Helen said, feeling like a little
child before the old woman.

"We live there," she answered. "I've just been with the grandson
to spend a week on the coast, and my son here just came to take
us home." The boy said something in Catalan to his grandmother.

"Yes," she answered, and turned again to them. "It's a beautiful
coast. Just over those hills—I wish we could see it from the train."

They followed her finger as she pointed. The hills, the fierce
hills, on either side.

"We're going in for the *Olimpiada*," Toni explained.

The man began talking then, in French with a strong Spanish
accent. "Then you won't be like the tourists at the beach about
the rumors," he said. "Perhaps you can tell us something about
Morocco." The soldiers looked over sharply. He sat back. "I suppose it's all rumors," he said.

"Better not to say anything," the old woman spoke slowly, and
laid her hand on his arm. "Some on one side, some on the other."
She turned to Helen. "I know about rumors," she told her, nodding. "First in France, where I come from, and then for forty-eight
years here in Spain. And the rev—" she stopped short.

Helen opened her pocketbook, and took out the cigarette case
which she had filled in London the morning before. She offered
one to the large son, who looked at the gold stamp before he took
it. The soldiers waved their hands, grinning. One was young, with
tender sideburns, and kept glancing at the other, whose green eyes
and creased cheeks reassured him. He wanted a cigarette.

"English cigarettes," the father told them.

"Ah, English," said the soldier in authority, and bent his head with the suggestion of a bow, accepting. The other one took his, and they lit them; after a second they took their guns and left the compartment. They could be heard whistling near the end of the car.

"Better not to talk at all before soldiers," the father echoed the old woman. "But my mother has strong ideas."

"Only about order," she said. "The revolutions here bring a new government in, and we have order for four months, and then we have another revolution."

"Like Mexico," Helen put in.

"In some ways like Mexico," said the grandmother. "The church here!" She threw her head back. "Just let there be a revolution that will hold what it does for a long time and prove itself." The eyes grew brilliant in her face, enlarged in the small skull, whose skin was still soft, like fruit which was wrinkled only in certain places. "The government changed last night," she informed them. "With too much—" she looked at her son.

"Yes," he said. "Too much right wing to it. And I hear another government went in this morning. We'll know when we get to Barcelona," he said. A trail of sweat started down his temple. "In the meantime, it's fine country, isn't it?"

"I wish I knew what cork-trees look like," Helen said illogically, and in English, forgetting language. Toni raised his eyebrows. She started to repeat in French. She had lost the word for cork. "What goes in the neck of the bottle," she described. Toni was still blank. The heavy man nodded.

"I know, certainly," he said. "*Vino.*"

The illustration was easy. "Oh that," the man shook with laughter, "not so important, perhaps. There they are, leaning against the house there, the branches of cork, waiting to be cut." He pointed, but across the line of his finger stood the crossroads figure, the man with the gun.

THE TRAIN WAS stopping now every few minutes, at roads or at arbitrary points, where nothing but a near house broke the fields. They kept their heads out the window, Helen on one side, the young boy at the other, half in his grandmother's lap.

They were reaching a station platform, talking about Madrid, the Scottsboro case, New York skyscrapers, the Berlin Olympics, the tawny cliffs of the coast just beyond their vision, the slow trains traditional to Spain. Their talk slowed as the train slowed. The train stopped.

A whistle-blast shot with finality through the cars.

There was some disturbance in the first-class section. Helen started through again to Peapack. "I'll leave the suitcase," she told Toni.

"You'd better," he said. "We must be almost in. What town is this?" He asked the heavy man.

"It must be Moncada," he said. The old woman nodded.

"Yes, Moncada. A very small town," she told Helen.

"It's a pity we can't see the shore from this train. I was so sorry to leave the sea."

Her son ran his hand over his cheek, brushing the streak of sweat down the dark stubble. The boy watched everything he did very closely, his face flickered at every action. He moved a little closer to the man as the train-whistle yelled again.

"It's too bad they had to come home so soon," the man said, of his mother and son. "They were spending the vacation with so much pleasure. It's very beautiful all along here—" he pointed out at nothing but the line of hills—"*Costa Brava*, it's called: Savage Coast."

"Savage Coast!" Toni repeated.

The noise in first class was growing louder. The old woman sat listening, her lined face turning intent and critical. "Moncada," she whispered to herself.

Helen started up the aisle.

THE ENTRANCE TO first class was crowded shut by tourists. She shouldered past the anxious surprised faces, and came to the center of the group.

A girl in a cotton dress stood at the door of one of the compartments with her back to the aisle and to the two armed boys who followed her, holding their carbines ready. She was talking to three men who sat with their hands in the air. The girl frowned at them, explaining; but they were terrified, and would not listen.

The fever sense of dream, dream unreal, spoke in her head. Dream, she thought, as if she had said it aloud; and, acting as she would in a dream, said "Excuse me" to the first boy, and started to push by his gun. He brought it up chest-high, barring her way, and spoke a word to the girl. She swung around. Her face was broad, active, angry.

"*Fotografies?*" she demanded.

A man behind Helen muttered in rapid French. "*Ils détruisent des photographies*," he said. "*Répondez non.*"

"*Nada*," answered Helen. And, lamely, "*tercera.*"

The girl's face cleared. She turned back to the three tourists. "*Aparat fotogràfic?*" He motioned to one of the boys. As he went forward to open the suitcase, Helen passed. She saw him, with the tail of her eye: he was thumbing through the baggage, while the girl held his gun.

Peapack sat, alone and shaking, in the next compartment, her face gone to pudding. The laxness in her flesh had softened still further with fear; the white skin, which had been groomed and creamy when she got on the train at Paris, was dismal, floury now; her voice shook with an incongruous shiver, menaced and cold in the great heat.

"The bandits!" she said. "They're raiding the train!"

Helen went to her, and put her hand on the woman's soft, cowering arm. Where have I seen a sheep, she wondered, sick and afraid? For herself, she thought; should I be afraid? Examining. There was a sweep of sensation, in the heat, the new country, the peculiar danger, but no fear. Not now.

"Did they bother you?" she asked the woman, touching her arm with an effort, trying to remove the pasty violet-white look from her. "Did they search here?"

The woman moved out of her corner with a soft shuffle of her hips, pulling away from a black box behind her. She drew back her lips in a pale grin of pride. "An Englishman came running through just before them," she said, "the coach was in an uproar. I put my movie camera here, and sat against it. But they went through my suitcase."

"Well, then," said Helen, "put it away. Put it in your suitcase, and change some clothes to the case . . ."

"The Reds!" Peapack was going on. "They must be Reds, violating property that way. I wish to God my husband could be here now, he'd put an end to that sort of thing. Searching innocent people, stealing cameras."

"They didn't take anything, did they?" asked Helen.

"They might have," Peapack retorted, "anything might happen if they're going through the train. Listen to that!"

There was a noise of voices on the platform outside. It was the first time they had realized they were in a station. Helen put her head out of the window, and saw the concrete walk, lined with rows of yellow blossoming trees, the brick station house, the wall around the restrooms marked "Caballeros" and "Señoras." At the end of the coach a few passengers grouped around the searchers. The girl was holding a large camera in her hands, snapping back the hinged flap, and unloading film. She handed the exposed strip to one of the armed boys, clamped the lid into place, and gave the camera back to its owner, a tall German-looking man. He nodded to the girl formally as he took the black case.

"Why in the world should they do a thing like that?" Peapack whined, sinking back on the gray seat. "I'm so upset; are you upset,

Helen?" she started. "I wish you didn't look so calm; I take things so hard. We've got to stick together, that's all; and we've got to find the other Americans on the train. I know there are some, I told you, *you* know, about the diner; but I think they're traveling third—and you've got to move in here with me; I can't stand it if things like this happen. It's only for another hour; when we get to Barcelona, Felipe can take care of us, if there's any trouble."

"Why don't you come to third, then?" Helen was thinking of Toni and his manager; they would certainly be better than any newspaperman who might be Peapack's friend.

"But my suitcase! I've got five suitcases, and who's going to carry them for me? No, you go back, and bring yours here . . . Look," said Peapack, "just look at the pictures of the children once more." Her fingers were trembling at the stiff lock on the rawhide suitcase, at the expensive shirring of the pocket, at the leather case. She was twisting the halftones of the knobby children. She showed Helen the pictures she had brought out last night, rushing through France; the boy in the garden, his infantile knees and stiff hair, the little girl's starched dress standing wide about her legs, making her look narrow and pathetic. "Do go back," said Peapack; "get your things and bring them in; I can't stand these stops."

ALL THE PASSENGERS in third were filling the aisle now, crowding out the open windows, talking to the groups whose heads could be seen, banked thick against the sides of the train, standing on both sides of the station platform. Helen pushed back through the swarming cars, through the holiday knots, laughter, gossip. An arm reached out and seized her wrist. It was the tight-skinned Hungarian, the manager.

"Have you heard the rumors?" he shouted, over the laughter and talk. "All sorts of rumors, already. The English are saying that the Communists have bombed the tracks and that we can't go farther; and I heard the Frenchman say that the engineer has gone on strike, and won't move the train until he gets some kind of extravagant promise." He fanned himself with the straw hat. "But come in and meet our team, anyway." The Hungarians were standing, politeness and warmth ran around their compartment. The fine-faced printer was introduced. "It looks like something real," he said. "But obviously nobody knows what. You probably ought to find the other Americans."

"I know one of them," said Helen. "I wish you'd go down and reassure her. She's on her way to the bullfights, and she turned into jelly when they searched the train."

"They were absolutely correct to search the train," the printer answered. "They destroyed some snapshots we were taking, too. Last spring, they said, the Fascists caught a lot of photographs of armed civilians, and anyone whose face was clear got his. They're not taking any chances."

"But if you've been talking with them—" Helen cried, her face darkening with excitement. "What do they say is happening?"

"They only said that," the printer told her. He was a young student, from his look, his earnest clear glance, but the marks about his mouth and his darkened, blunt fingers showed how long he had spent at work; he looked straightforward at Helen now, obviously telling all he knew. "They were ordered to go through the train; for all they knew, the girl said, it's just an examination, and we'll go right on through to Barcelona."

"Yes, certainly," the manager put in. "They're waiting for us now in Barcelona; at the station!"

"I'll go through and tell Toni," said Helen.

In the compartment, the heavy man was taking down a bundle from the rack. Toni looked up quickly as Helen came in. "What's up?" he asked, flashing, his face concentrating.

"Did they search the car?"

"Oh, they came through," said the grandmother, "but they wouldn't bother us in third; what would we be doing with cameras? We're not tourists, to take pictures of our countrymen, if they're having troubles." She smiled very gently at Helen; "Will you have some sausage with us?" she invited.

"I have a camera in the suitcase," Helen said.

"All right, let it stay there," the grandmother stopped her; "you haven't been making a fool of yourself, you're all right." She was opening the bundle that her son gave her, opening layers and layers of newspaper.

"What's up Helen?" Toni was repeating.

"Your team doesn't know, and they've been speaking to that girl—she's certainly been scaring the people in first."

"It doesn't matter," said the grandmother. "Such people get scared if anyone asks them a question."

"The soldiers left the train the minute we stopped here," her son remarked. "They're not likely to show up again, either."

"What do you mean?" asked Helen. "Have they run away?"

"You can't tell about soldiers," answered the grandmother. "All the generals are the wealthy, here, and all the soldiers belong to the generals. And the generals in Spain are with the church, for the money, for power, for keeping their heel on the land."

"They can do it too," interrupted her son, bitterly. "Seventy-five million pesetas to the church a year from the government, and if I have two chickens, I am taxed; and an army that belongs to the officers, not to the state! And this Civil Guard, a handful, what good is that to the government, even when it is Left?" He had his open hand out, shaking; the young boy was looking at it. The father caught his eye. "What place is that to bring a boy into?" he spoke the words out bitterly, his hand still held out, shaking. His mother looked at him with a narrowed, proud look of knowledge, and held her hand out, too.

"Give me a knife to cut the sausage," she said.

He quieted. They looked at one another.

Toni broke it. "Let's eat in town," he said. "I'll get the team, and we'll find something."

"No, you cannot," said the grandmother. "We have sausage, and almonds, and wine. It is nothing. Stay with us."

Her son was holding the sausage in the crook of his elbow, sawing at it with his knife, saying nothing, sawing angrily at the meat. He looked up. "Yes, stay," he said to them, and smiled. "We have enough for all."

"I'll get a cup for the wine," Toni sprang up, and was going down the train. "Thank you!"

"Let me get something, too," Helen said. "Fruit—would you like fruit?" The young boy's face flickered; he knew a few words of French.

"Oh, we have a great deal," said the grandmother.

"Fruit would be nice," the big man told her. "And they'll very likely come through with bread. And when your husband brings the cup—"

"Oh, no," Helen shook her head quickly. "He's not my husband. He's with the Hungarian team . . ."

"Then you'd better stay with us," said the grandmother, with her kind voice of age and patience. "We may go stay in the town."

"The town!" Helen echoed vaguely. She looked out the window. The platform was covered now with townspeople, walking idly up and down, staring in through the large windows, as if the train were some tremendous sideshow. She could see a blond pregnant woman going slowly through the crowd, little boys in twos and threes, crowding into the yellow trees, dodging under the train-wheels, running up and through the train-doors, whistling; the men, the boys with bicycles, the grave, white-haired man sitting at the station bench, the gray-haired official with a black band in his coat lapel; the whole town, promenading, with a strange intense sound of talk in the air. Not the relaxed gossip of fairgrounds, but breaths of danger, importance, secrecy.

"The town!" said Helen. "But what about the train?"

The grandmother looked like a Sibyl as she sat in her corner, turning her small face up, perfectly certain, matter-of-fact. "This train," she said, raising her hand, palm forward, the wrinkled, small palm waving from side to side, "this train isn't going to move, anymore."

"JUST A MINUTE," said Helen. "I'll bring something back."

She wanted to be in the town. The crowd on the station platform was banked thick, as if it were fair-day. She saw the pregnant blonde walking in the other direction now, with a young man whose head appeared over the rest, rough black. The woman would look sidelong at the train, hardly noticing it, as if it were some public building, and continue with her peculiar sailing gait. The little boys were at the coach-windows again, appealing and beggar-faced, calling "*¡Cigarrillos! ¡Cigarrillos!*"

The grandmother was quiet; she knew these towns. "It's not necessary," she told the girl again. But Helen was already outside, behind the thick line of passengers, whose legs and rears filled the corridors like the hindquarters of domestic animals caged at a feeding-trough. They were hanging from the windows of the train, talking to the people on the near platform. On this side, the crowd was not so heavy, but there were many more guns: armed men stood in groups, smoking. The black sashes, the dark furious hair low over their foreheads, their rope sandals, their controlled silences, contrasting with the train's conversation and acrobatics and the town's promenading, all contributed to one effect. They took on the keepings of a secret romantic soldiery, they seemed to her, struck with the strangeness, to conceal a clue that she must have.

The regular soldiers, in their olive and yellow, had gone. The town and the train faced each other alone.

Once on the platform, in the broad heat, the focus changed: The men with guns were about their business, they were townspeople, they hung around, waiting beneath the row of yellow flowering trees, watching the train. From here, it was the train that was out of place, lying dead in the station. Tourists were leaning from all the windows, even up in first class.

The engine, near the front of the station, was fuming, a gentle ineffectual line of steam ascending.

Hurrying through the crowd, she was very afraid of being left. There were no words. How could she reach any of them without language? She turned to one of the guards, and said, in French, hesitantly, "if the train . . . leaves, will you . . . ?" She saw he did not understand, and pointed, signaling the train, town, herself, the train, the motion that would take it through the station.

The guard laughed, and shook his hand once toward the train, disgusted. "You can go ahead," he told her.

Helen crossed the little concrete square behind the restrooms. The station gate was snapped open, facing a short wide street that led to the main roadway. On one side, diagonally, a row of houses presented their balconies and gardens to the station. On the other, more impressive ornate buildings confronted the platform, separated by grillwork or a strip of grass. At the end of this short street, the little iron tables of the café covered the sidewalk. They were crowded. Colors snapped in the hot air, filling in the street corner. She walked up, entered the bright crowd, hearing the foreign calls after her, the disjunctive music of the radio, the receding station noises. The street ended immediately. This was the Calle Mayor, crowded in both directions.

Sunday noon!

The whole town was out.

There was not a single empty table, you had to thread your way between, escape the tangle of families, the childrens' games. But Helen could see through the low windows; the inside of the café was quite empty. She split the fringe of long beadstrings that curtained the door.

The café was big and shadowy. An old container, painted a shiny synthetic orange, stood on the counter, unused. But deep in the room, the bar itself took shape, ghostly-white. The proprietor was washing glasses; they flashed quickly. He looked up, his high-domed head stood sharply out; dark glasses, long wine bottles filled the shelves behind him.

Helen saw the piled peaches, the flush of fruit color on the bar. The proprietor asked a question in Catalan, the soft burring sounds and the mixture of x's confusing her immediately, throwing her off, by a trick of wrenched concentration fixing her whole attention on the opening words so that she was deafened to the rest. She lost every bit of language. God, she thought! Why should I care about speech this much? The blood pushed up behind her eyes, in her poverty; and then she was over it. She laughed with the man, pointed at the peaches, counted twelve on her fingers.

The proprietor jerked his head back at the train. "*Extranjeros*," he commented.

A hoot, from the shadow, turned them both, shaken. It was the radio: a man, up a ladder at the side doorway, was rigging up an extra loudspeaker. It hooted again. He turned it down until there was nothing but an even, boiling sound, came down the ladder, winding wire in his hand, and crossed the bar.

The proprietor gave Helen her peaches and change in the new-feeling Spanish coin, and gave the man his glass of wine. As she turned the beadstring aside at the door, she saw him bent over the radio behind the bar.

ON THE STREET, they were standing at their tables.

One man lifted his little soft-colored child up to the chair so that he could see.

An open truck stood in the middle of the street. The Ford signature on its hood sprang out, plain as a movie-title.

There were nine boys standing in the truck. None of them could be over nineteen. One had a heavy double-barreled hunting piece, five of them carried unmatched rifles, and the rest held their revolvers ready, self-consciously. No two of the weapons were alike.

Helen stood in the doorway, holding the peaches loose in her arms, still feeling as if her tongue were cut out. No speech, no words to reach any of this. She looked at the truck.

The Hungarians crushed in toward the truck. Toni admired the truck; his fist went up automatically, clenched to greet the boys.

They turned to him, the cry in the throat of the very young one, enraged.

One raked his hand down the air, clawing.

The stocky boy raised his double-barreled gun, pointing it at Toni.

He did not recoil, there were too many at his back; he stared up at their faces.

"Aren't you Communists?" he asked, bewildered.

"Communists!" the youngest cried, and his voice broke.

"We're *not*—"

The stocky one broke in. "We are Anarchists." He was pompous, with a certain defiance.

"We're going to fight in Barcelona"

"To fight!" said Toni. "What for? What do you want, if you're Anarchists?"

"Want?" the little one echoed, again.

The others turned. The driver leaned far out from his cab.

"We want no Fascists," he said.

"No Fascists," they agreed, "no money, no law, no generals."

"All right," said Toni, "no Fascists, that's excellent. But the rest—"

The driver opened his mouth.

"Never mind," he said, against his will, clamping his jaw. "We have a United Front."

Toni's voice came up. The Hungarians were trying to pull him away.

The radio turned on, savage loud, in the café. Shaking the entire street, the music walked through, mastering all motion, Beethoven, the Fifth coming tremendous on the scene.

An old woman rushed frighteningly through the people attached to the back of the truck. From the wide sprung mouth, the cheeks' distortion, it was seen that she was screaming. The music would not permit her shriek.

She laid hold of one of the boys, dragging at his leg, stretching her cheeks again in that blotted-out cry. His face changed; his lips closed twice, mumbling, under the music, as he recognized his mother. No sound came, as if a wind were against them.

The great music continued.

The driver bent quietly over his wheel, reached down, and the truck started to roll, spreading the crowd back on itself.

Dragging, the old woman stumbled a few steps with it, as the boy watched her holding his leg, still astonished, still motionless, unable to be heard.

The truck picked up speed as it shifted gear; she was forced to let go; it moved toward Barcelona, out of the grasp of the crowd.

Only the symphony occupied the air.

Screaming above it, hooting, Helen heard—perhaps! the train whistle! She looked at the mother, to see if it might instead indeed be she; but the cheeks had gone loose, the mouth was shut.

Helen ran back to the train, her arms heavy with the peaches, the strong music overriding everything but her fear that it had gone. There was no train whistle.

The train had not moved.

She climbed into the car.

THE FAMILY WAS still sitting there, eating the sausage. Helen spilled her armful of peaches into the grandmother's lap. "A truck has just gone off;" she was out of breath, and, feeling the childishness of language now, the complete childishness, in an undefined situation, waited for them to speak.

The grandmother was master. "We will finish our meal, and then go into the town," she stated. She wiped a peach off carefully, the bloom rubbing off, leaving the fruit smooth golden against her black skirt, and gave it to her grandson. He took it, nodding to Helen. His skin was only a shade of pink different, more even. Helen was very moved by the graceful turn of his shoulder, his head, refined and delicate, held precisely on the slim clear-oil neck.

"Your son is very fine-looking," she admired.

The man was cutting meat for her. "Is his mother blonde?" she asked. The two heads were dark, of another race. The man nodded.

"Yes, very blonde."

"How old is the boy? Twelve?"

Toni was standing at the compartment, a tin cup in his hand, looking at the boy with his purpled, bitter stare. "Give him seven more years, then, and he'll be old enough to be an Anarchist, and go off and fight."

The father looked up at him. "He could be worse," he answered, the distinction and loyalty coming out in his words.

A boy carrying a large wicker basket of bread came down the train, calling his sales.

"Go after him, go," said the father pushing his son with a little gruff gesture, poking him between the delicate shoulder-blades, sending him after bread. The son turned down the aisle without a word.

"Are they going to war?" asked the old grandmother. She did not look at Toni, but offered almonds from a square of paper outstretched. "I cannot hear any guns," she said. "Is there fighting near here?"

"Oh, I don't know; nobody says anything definite. Come out, Helen, the team sent the printer into town to find out how things were, and he's going to report to all of us."

Bread came, the boy holding the long slender loaf; and they sat eating, passing the wine-cup between the women, passing the bottle of strong bitter wine. It rinsed away the heat and irritation of the train and stop and uncertainty.

They finished. Looked at each other for confirmation.

"Now shall we go?" Helen turned to Toni. "We must find out something."

The father put his hand on hers. "Come back with news," he said. "Maybe the train will continue, after all."

Helen went down the steep steps. The Hungarian team was on the platforms, still waiting for the printer. He could be seen in the distance, running down the street along the platform. As they watched him come, the manager crossed to Helen. "You should find the other Americans," he advised. "There's a lawyer, with glasses, who's looking for you. I told him you were on the train."

The printer was close now. He threw his arm up before him like an exhausted marathon hero. He brought news. Helen thought, what a child I am now! And then, as his hand went up, this is it, this the clue!

The printer could not wait to reach them. He called out, in a hoarse, important voice:

"General Strike!"

CHAPTER THREE

At the frontier getting down, at railhead drinking
hot tea waiting for pack-mules, at the box with
three levers watching the swallows . . . The fatty
smell of drying clothes, smell of cordite in a wood,
and the new moon seen along the barrel of a gun.
                                        —*W.H. Auden*

G ENERAL STRIKE.
        The words at the end of a poem, the slogan
shouted, the headline for gray industrial scenes, waterfront blue-
gray, the black even in the air over mines, the dark sidewalks before
factories, covered with lines of gray parading people. Words printed,
painted out, broadcast in handbills. Not like this.

She looked about the platform.

There, the young pregnant blonde turned, and began her slow
walk toward the head of the train, weighted, undisturbed; the Hungarians began to talk at top speed in their own language, a very
beautiful one with heavy eyebrows, the grasping printer, the manager, Toni staring, and the anonymous rest; the boys called out from
the yellow trees; the pavement was fairground, distinguished and
made serious only by the guards near each door of the train. The
near guard came closer to the team, and nodded yes in answer to
their question.

"*Huelga General,*" he substantiated.

And the scene was intensely foreign, it was a new world indeed,
with these words true.

The train, the frontier.

Now the train was held, as surely as if the tracks before and behind had been blown up, as one rumor said; as surely as if the engineer had refused ever to move again, as Peapack must be thinking; or as if the searching party had found, not photographs, but spy incriminations; more surely.

The anonymous passengers!

"What will you do?" Helen asked Toni.

"The team must decide," he told her. The printer was talking to the manager, repeating the whole story of what the mayor had told him, had told the American who had been outraged, it seemed, at the mention of the words.

What American?

"Not the lawyer," the manager said. "Better find him. He speaks seven languages, too."

"I'll tell the family," Helen suggested to Toni, thinking of the grandmother.

GENERAL STRIKE.

They were already wrapping the rest of the sausage in the newspaper, pulling down the great wicker hamper again, preparing to move. The news had come through.

"Where will you go?" she asked them.

"We'll find places in the town," the father said. "Come with us, it won't be good to sleep on the train." He looked around the compartment, at the stiff wooden benches, the walls, the metal heat of sun on still wood.

She thanked them. "But I'd better find the others," she insisted, "the American woman is alone, too, and they tell me there are other Americans here."

"Yes," said the grandmother. "You'll have to find them. We'll ask at the café about a place to sleep, and, if you want us, the café will know where we went. Here—" she plucked at her son's elbow. He reached for the heavy black suitcase, and set it on the bench.

"Better go up to first," he advised, the slow unshaven smile channeling his cheeks. "There are cushions there, anyway."

They were ready to leave.

The fair-haired boy took the package of food and slung it over his shoulder. He was still eating almonds, and his pointed teeth glittered. As he took his grandmother's hand, he turned suddenly to Helen, with a volunteer look in the startling iodine eyes. "Goodbye," he said rapidly, trying the word in English.

SHE KICKED THE suitcase before her through the connection between the cars, kicking it against the feet of a stranger whose thick glasses seemed over-smooth and blazing on his heavily pitted face.

He dodged to the side, escaping apologies.

"Are you American?"

"No," he answered, still in French. "I am Swiss. There is a Swiss team on the train, but I'm not with it. Are you looking for the Americans who are going to the Olympics in Barcelona?"

She was speaking eagerly, the words falling on each other. If only I were fluent, now, she thought, I need words now!

"They've been looking for you, too," the Swiss told her. "They heard there were two more Americans on the train. You must be the other woman . . ."

"Do you know about the General Strike?"

"Really?" the Swiss exclaimed, his look of surprise sunk deep in the pockmarked forehead. "Is that what it is?"

He picked her suitcase up easily, and turned.

"Come on through," he said, "I'll show you where they are. They'll want to hear."

He led the way through the empty corridor of the first-class car. Voices came from one of the doors, half rolled back on its little groove. He swung it back all the way.

"May I introduce the American lady?" he said, with mock-formality. "And the news: it's General Strike!"

"WE JUST HEARD," the man answered, pronouncing in careful French, his mouth shaded by the brown mustache on the long, sensitive lip. He sat against one window, his head thrown back against the antimacassar, his hand stretched out over the clasped hands of the woman who was next to him. "Hello!" he said, in English, to Helen. "Nice day." And grinned. "We've been looking for you."

"Yes," the dark woman beside him agreed. "They've given us at least five different descriptions of you, and none of them fit. Her cheeks caught shadow, her curly hair turned over her forehead, the broad planes of her face missed being Negroid because of the sharp mouth.

"I was in third," Helen said, looking at the two other women who sat across from the couple.

One was tall, and the red blouse she wore pulled, with its color, at the pointed collarbones, the greenish throat and face; the other shrank, rather sickly, beside her, with her head on one side, listening.

"Wait a minute, I can't hear," interrupted the tall one nearest the window, "the radio's started again."

A tremendous voice, like a voice in an airplane, started to expound. It seemed sourceless, deity; it said a few peremptory phrases, came to a violent close, and the music started again, a soft Spanish dance played from a recording.

They waited until the music started. "There, that's news of the battle," said the man. "The government's sound!"

"God, it has to be," exploded Helen, forgetting tact, forgetting their strangeness. "What is this all anyway, a putsch of some kind?"

"Why, hello!" said the man, realizing her. "Is that how you feel? Well, for Christ sake, come and sit down." The Swiss, not understanding, made a sign; he had to leave. The man went on. "It looks like a Fascist putsch; but the radio says it's failing in Barcelona. It's the government radio, of course; but it's good news, just the same, good news for all of us."

"Are you going to the Games?" Helen asked him.

"Certainly," the woman beside him said, in her low, reedy voice; "and if you want the Party line on the radio, and the frontier, and the armed guards, Peter's the man to give it to you, aren't you?" she mocked. But the seriousness, the intimacy was very evident. When she spoke to him, the women across were shut out, there was actual closeness.

"Communist?" Helen asked.

"Yes," he answered, "and gladder of it right now than about any time. Where are you from?" he asked her, and (through the Spanish music) they knew, New York, a matter of blocks between them, a matter, perhaps, of missing each other by moments in theater lobbies, at lectures, on streets.

"Organization?" asked Peter.

"None," she answered, "but I've been in the American Student Union, and I've done some work for the I.L.D." She looked past them to the platform. She could see the gray-haired man with the mourning band, surrounded by the Hungarian team: he must be the mayor—the armed workers, the town, alert, faces leaning from the row houses. "I wish now, for the first time, that I were really active," she said, slowly.

The two women beside her brightened. "We're in the Teacher's Union," said the sickly one. "We've been reading up."

Peter pointed to a yellow pamphlet in the tall one's hand. "How's that?" He burst into laughter, and the woman beside him laughed, as at an old joke. "She's been reading a French pamphlet on the problems of the Spanish Revolution ever since the train was stopped!" Helen laughed, a full, happy laugh from the lungs. "You should have seen the faces of the girls who searched for photographs!"

Helen was trying to remember. "I didn't see you at Port Bou," she said.

"We saw you, though," said the dark woman.

"Yes, Olive saw you get on," Peter told her.

"We were in the next car—got on first of all, I guess. We'd been swimming in Port Bou—came down from Carcassonne yesterday, so that we could have the night at the border. How's that for perfect timing?"

"Carcassonne!"

"That's how Peter felt," Olive said to Helen. "That poem about never getting to Carcassonne made him go, I swear."

"Such a bad poem, too," Peter was apologizing. "But an amazing city. Preserved, so that the old houses and walls, which should be dead, are full of the living. It was a good prelude to this." He waved at the window.

Helen looked down at her suitcase. The benches were uphol-stered here in the first-class gray. "Next car! Were you in third, too?"

Peter followed her look. "Don't be class conscious when it's irrelevant. We took possession of this compartment. It was quite empty—most of first was empty—and we have to be able to take over, you know."

"All right," said Helen. "I'm beginning to."

"I have even put my feet up, on occasion," Peter went on. His eyes were almost black, seen with the light brown hair.

Olive shook her head, smiling. "*And* took them down again. Hollywood disturbed us," she explained. Hollywood?

"Haven't you met our magnates?" She leaned back. "The three gentleman from Paramount who occupy the Pullman car: item, one executive; item, two newsreel men."

"Arrogant bastards, too," said Peter, sighing.

"They're the prime reason for that search of the train."

"Except it was good common sense," said the tall school teacher.

"Our countrymen!" Olive exclaimed. "And it looks as though we'll be seeing our countrymen, too. It's lucky you turned out all right," she said to Helen, "we were worried."

"You sound like Peapack. She was worried," Helen saw, flash, the green metal compartment of the French express.

"Peapack?" said Peter, sitting up.

"She comes from there, New Jersey," Helen told him. "Five suitcases, didn't know there were going to be Games in Barcelona, means to proceed to Milan and Berlin, asks why antifascist . . ."

"Well, the English can take care of her. *We* won't." Peter was firm. "Have you met the English?"

"No," said Helen. "I've been with some Catalans, and the Hungarian team."

"Well, the English are prepared to do their duty," Peter said. "There seem to be at least three couples, all first, and they're having a meeting now. And there's the chorus; seen them? Six swell platinum blondes, and a self-effacing manager; oh, and some sort of traveling salesman—I can't think of any others. Then there are a few assorted people we ran into: three Frenchman, and I wouldn't be surprised if they were spies, and a German-looking family who've moved up to first, and Olive saw another German get on at Port Bou, didn't you?"

"A fine one," said Olive.

"Well, we met the others while we were trying to get coffee," Peter went on. "They closed the dining car while we were in the middle; locked it up, and put a sign, 'Not Running,' on the door."

"You might go and see whether the water is, Peter," Olive was reminded.

"Oh, no, that's definitely out," he said. "The water gave out on the train a half hour ago. We've been talking to the engineer. He's sitting on the steps of the cab, being bawled out for a dirty slacker by the Hollywood guys. They think he's refused to run the train."

"They act as if he was a mule," said the sickly woman.

"Well, the chocolate's good, anyhow," said the other.

"Yeah, they got a supply in Paris," Peter said. "Lucky we ran into you . . . Imagine, we hadn't seen them in three years, and there they were drinking coffee in the diner on this train . . ."

"Of all places," finished Olive. If we'd got a supply of something like that in Paris—"

"Oh, it was fine," Peter said. He was talking to Helen, in exuberance. "We were there, Bastille Day. A million people on that march, past the Mur des Fédérés, through Père Lachaise through the entire city . . ."

"What's that?" said the sickly woman, sharply, her head on one side.

Peter stopped a moment. He put his lower lip out; he heard nothing. "Don't look now," he cracked, "there's a revolution in the next car."

"No, really," the woman said, "listen!"

"Aren't the children beautiful in this town?" Peter said suddenly. "Remember that boy, Olive? I wish we had a child like that boy." Her face was darkened and sad; some meaning Helen did not understand fell across it.

"Oh, shut up for a moment!" the woman said vehemently.

In the air, the music was changing. From the Spanish dance, the needle of some distant phonograph scratched for a moment, and then, familiarly, the words began:

St. Louis woman
with her diamond rings,
got my man . . .

They laughed nervously, and stopped to listen again.

"There!" said the woman.

Rapid and thin, the high frail sound clapped out between the hills. It could not be the record. That went on:

. . . by her apron strings,
wahn't for diamonds . . .

Crazy and American in this town. Moncada. There, the sound again, high and unmistakable. They had been to too many movies to mistake it.

"Rifles!" cried Peter.

Peter's lip straightened suddenly, vibrated like wire; Olive's face took on an amazing beauty.

"Maybe it's only backfire," said the tall woman weakly.

From up the car, a calling grew. A woman's voice went past as the woman ran loosely down the corridor, shrieking.

"The guns! The guns!"

"CAN YOU TELL where the sounds come from?" Helen asked.

"I don't think John Reed could tell, in these hills," Peter smiled whitely. "We could be in the middle of a thing like that, I'll bet, and not know what was going on."

"Well, he was always at the bottom of a flight of stairs when something was happening at the top, wasn't he?"

"And the story of the waiter—he was asked where he was during the Revolution, and he said, 'It was during the special dinner, sir.'"

The sounds had stopped. Only the radio was still singing blues.

"But this isn't revolution!" the sickly woman said. Her words came trembling. "This is nothing like that!"

"We can't just sit here," Peter was saying sharply. "I want some coffee. Come and find some coffee; I want to find out what this is all about!" He stood up, and the two other women stood with him. "All right," they said, under their breath.

Olive and Helen wanted to stay. Helen could not have moved. To see the gun, the threat, to fear the plane, to feel the radio emerge, meant one thing; but the clap of sound in the hills, the voice shrieking through the corridor!

"Don't go far," Olive said pleading; and, then, looking at his face, "sorry."

His look changed. "No, you're right," he said, and kissed her, bending over her, his hair falling forward as he leaned. "You're right; I'll be right back, I'll just go up to the place where the truck left from."

The women were waiting outside. Then they were gone.

"IT WAS SO tragic, to hear that gun," Olive said slowly. "No matter what it signifies. I don't belong to any party." She stopped a moment, looking out the window. "I wish he hadn't said that about the child."

"He looked as if he wanted a child, very much," Helen answered.

"He does—I don't know why I should be telling you this," she said, shy then, abrupt. "Except that this train makes you feel that you're not in—oh, I don't know—in Europe, in society. Don't let me get whimsical," she mocked herself.

"You get angry at that idea?"

She turned her face away. She knew which idea. "All this war," she said after a minute.

War! In a slow admission, Helen took the word finally. Yes. This is it.

"We've had our heads out of the window," Olive said. "Peter's been talking to some of the men. They talk about having to win, and their look goes bright. Do you feel the fate here? They tell us this is death unless the country is won in this war." She spoke in a rush of feeling, sudden and fatalistic, that made Helen turn in on herself even more, not liking to face the romanticism of the words "fate," and "death" in the bright sun, with Olive's eyes swung on her, firing up steadily.

"It doesn't seem political, even," she said. She was speaking flatly, hating her self-consciousness.

"Marx, in these hills?" Olive laughed.

"No, not like that, this is what I mean." Helen leaned forward, beginning to relax in the effort of explanation. The fact. The story of one or two people. She told about the Catalan family. The story of Toni. She was speaking fast now, wanting to be finished. "It seems more a question of the presence of belief, of feeling."

"That's what gets me angry," Olive said slowly, and her eyes lengthened. They were dark. There was sun.

"The emotion?"

"Not theirs—only that I can't feel it myself. It was that way in France, too. I can't make myself feel it."

Helen's hand came out in a push of denial. "Don't be one of those," she said vehemently. "I hate them most, and I know plenty of them in New York. The spoiled, brutal girls with the disappointed faces, trying for all they're worth to make themselves feel."

Olive looked sharply at her.

"Why should you feel; who are you that you should push anything on yourself?" Helen said, in a loss of control. "Let yourself alone; my God!" Olive was staring at her. Surprise and regret, until the jealousy passed. The look pulled Helen in. She was quiet, and went on evenly.

"Don't feel anything," she said. "That's not so terrible. Only don't try so."

"And what about you, does everything hit you hard?"

Helen sat back against the lace, against the gray upholstery. "Oh, that, it's the last thing that counts, anyway, the way we are. We're to be quiet, and stay in the train. Tourists! To look out the window!"

She repeated the names of the lace border, with pain, and with a certain sarcasm that drew the two women together more quickly than any talk about emotions could. The pattern ran straight over all the lace edges.

"Madrid-Zaragoza-Alicante."

"Madrid-Zaragoza-Alicante."

THE AFTERNOON WAS deepening, and the population of the station platform was growing continually.

From the street behind the station, automobiles could be heard. They must go down the street very slowly—their horns were blowing, a harsh triplicate blowing, One-Two-Three down the road. One of them swung into sight, pulled down the half-street to the station, and stopped. On its side was painted, in white, scrawling letters, "C.N.T.," and the long, new car behind it was lettered "F.A.I."

"What does that mean?" Helen asked.

"I wonder where Peter is," said Olive.

From the car, armed men were hurrying to the train. Two of them stopped at the back of the station house, and the others broke into a half-run, heading up toward the engine.

After a few minutes they ran back to their cars, got in, and with a screeching of tires, the cars pulled off.

The horns went One-Two-Three the length of the village, seemed to turn, and faded.

"I've got to get Peter," Olive repeated, and stood.

Peter was at the door.

"Look," he said gaily, "I lost them. They went back to their compartment,"

"What do you know?" Olive asked.

"Oh, it's complicated," he answered. "So many Anarchists, too. But not like ours—here, they're different, they're in the majority, and it's natural anarchism: they've never seen any party that didn't rob them, the state is always the church and the generals and the other landowners, and it looks as though those are the people who have attacked this government. It's a liberal government, too, voted in OK, nothing particularly left-wing about it—not last night, anyhow," he added with a grin.

"And the cars?" Helen remembered initials.

"That's what gets me," he said, puzzled. "I know some of the letters. C.N.T.—that's Confederación Nacional del Trabajo; F.A.I.— Federación Anarquista Ibérica; and then the other big trade union group (there are more cars in town), U.G.T.: Unión General de Trabajadores. Those are the three great labor unions in Spain . . . Oh, and here's a present," he added, fishing a pack of cigarettes from his pocket. "Bisontes; they must be made by the Lucky people, they're packed like Luckies; one peseta fifty, and the English are stocking up on them. You ought to see their providence and foresight," he waved his hand, "bread, Vichy, candles—they're setting up house on the train. I don't know what they think we're in for; they've bought enough to last a week."

"What about guns?" Olive asked him.

"I think the whole town's armed," he answered. "I didn't see a man without a gun; and civilians are guarding the road up there, stopping every car that goes through. I heard the story about two regiments in Barcelona, and then someone said four—one thing's certain, this is all over Spain. Somebody said the tracks were blown up; somebody else said there was a train stopped in every station all along the line."

"When do you suppose the train will move?"

"Can't say. But they'll let us know. The town's all right," he said violently. "Know what they're doing? Feeding the whole darn Olympic crowd, at their own expense!"

He sat down and opened the pack of Bisontes.

"I met some more people, too," he said. "There's a stunning South American woman with the English, who told me that about the food—that's the mayor's order; and your friend from New Jersey, Helen," he told her, "She's looking for you all over the platform.

"No, leave your bag here," Peter went on, "You'll be staying with us." They looked at her, with their intent grave looks. She had come to rely on them already.

"See you in a few minutes," she said.

PEAPACK WAS HUDDLED in her corner still. "God," she was muttering, "what have I let myself in for?" She sprang up when she saw Helen. "It's war," she cried, "but the Fascists are going to rescue us, I mean the Anarchists—oh, do you know what's happening?"

Helen sat down with her.

"No," she said, "I won't move, Helen, I won't leave this compartment, I can't bear it. Did you hear the Belgian woman rush down the train? She came in here and said that noise was guns. It did sound like backfire, didn't it? Who's that?"

Toni was at the window, calling Helen. She leaned out. He was an old friend, his face was immensely, touchingly familiar, the purple lips darkening in the half-light, his gay dark eyes. He wanted her to come to dinner, she was with the Olympics, the town was standing them all dinner.

"Go ahead, I'll see you later," she promised.

Peapack was behind her, pulling her arm.

She turned to the older woman, the whitened harassed face, sunken with fear.

"Don't leave me, Helen," she demanded, "don't leave me alone. It sounds like war, I can't bear it, we'll never get out of this, don't go, only don't go!"

Evening was coming down. The radio was very loud.

CHAPTER FOUR

*Finally, in times when the class struggle nears the
decisive hour, the progress of dissolution going on
within the ruling class, in fact, within the whole
range of old society, assumes such a violent, glaring
character, that a small section of the ruling class
cuts itself adrift and joins the revolutionary class,
the class that holds the future in its hands.*
                          —The Communist Manifesto

The crowds had drawn away; only a few small boys
were left, concealed and whistling in the yellow
trees. The armed guard stood in front of the station house, speaking
to the mayor, whose band of mourning could scarcely be seen on
his lapel in the increasing dark. A faint gabble of roosters came from
the oblique row of houses.

As soon as the station was deserted, the passengers began to
revive. The Catalans gathered their children, and pulled out the
long loaves of bread. Even the Englishwoman brightened. Poor
Mme. Porcelan, who was so anxious about her husband, stared at
the Swiss across from her in the compartment, and wondered if his
heavy, pitted head, thrown back against the antimacassar, would
ever wake. The Hungarians leapt down from one car suddenly,
laughing and cracking jokes, and disappeared into the town.

It was a signal. The whole train, a string of pale faces pressed
against the windows of first-class, a scramble of shoulders and heads
blocked out in third, assumed vigor. A few Spanish families flocked
on the platform, not speaking, moving into the town.

A radio roared a sentence, shocking the train into full attention; and then digressed into a soft tango, the notes played sliding and loose, the jar and ripple of music reassuring everyone.

Helen sat in Peapack's compartment, tracing the letters in the lace border that repeated *M-Z-A-M-Z-A*. Peapack's face, white and still fearful, stirred.

"All right," she said. "I don't feel so upset any more. I feel hungry now. Could we eat?"

It was a very good idea.

"Oh, but wait," said Peapack in alarm, "supposing the train starts to move, and we're in the town?"

"We'll be called," invented Helen.

Peapack was comforted.

"The café is very close."

The English couple, with their easy walk, was crossing the little square beside the station. The woman with them was shorter than they, who drooped over her slightly. Her dark hair was clawed with gray and fitted to her head, her eyes were deep in shadow. As she spoke, her mouth, russet-colored and startling, moved distinct and separate, drawing attention to itself so that it took a small additional effort to listen to her.

"There is no need," she was explaining, with a strained note in her voice, as though her throat had been struck and was still ringing. "The Spanish gentleman will call us the moment the engineer says yes."

"The engineer?" interrupted Helen, just behind them—"Is there any activity? Is the train going to move?"

The woman turned. Her face did move with her smile, brightened as the small white teeth showed. The radio finished its tango in a shiver of high notes, and a wide final chord.

"Nobody knows, if the General Strike is to last a day or indefinitely. But we have a gentleman—a diplomat, a Spaniard—with us, who has gone to speak with the mayor, and to see whether anything can be done—even a cable would be a lot," she added.

"Weren't you on the London train? Didn't we see each other on the Channel?" The fair English girl dropped back to speak to Helen.

Peapack hurried ahead, she snatched at the girl's husband.

Yes, said the English girl to Helen, they were all going to dinner. They weren't sure yet where they'd go. The five went up the street to the café.

It was the only place open in Moncada. All down the Calle Mayor, there were boarded-shut doorways and shy children in their corners, chain curtains that tingled under the breeze, pale thin dogs running across the street.

The sidewalk was jammed. The five strangers broke into a file and crocodiled between the tables. Every chair was taken, every table was surrounded with chairs.

The big radio announced its Barcelona stations.

The lady from South America stopped, her hand up. Helen and the English looked at her.

"That's why everybody's here," the lady finally commented. "It's the radio. That was an order from the government at Barcelona, advising the people to stand by. As long as the radio goes, the government is in power. The Fascists have attacked the radio station several times today. There must have been terrible fighting in town," she added.

The broadcast had stopped for a moment. There was the click and whine of a victrola being set up in the station, and another dance tune began.

They pushed forward to the marble counter. The lady from South America asked for a table.

"We'll have to wait forever for the sidewalk," she relayed the answer, "but we can go inside, immediately."

The small inner room to the side subdued the radio by putting the wall between them. "This is splendid," said the Englishman. His collar was open; it was a first concession to necessity. His face was very young and clear, and the long mustache only served to soften it further. "What shall we have?" he asked gaily. "Wine? Would you please ask for wine—you'd like wine, dear, wouldn't you?" he swung to his wife, gathering the others in his eagerness.

"And bread."

"And Vichy."

"Oh, come," said the lady, scarcely moving her lips, "we'll have all of that—but something else: spaghetti, or omelettes perhaps?"

They watched the lady as she ordered, as if she were qualifying for some distinguished position. She smiled at them, brilliantly, an actress's smile.

"You're not thinking," she objected, "I've lived in South America and Spain for a good part of my life."

Helen was curious.

"But you're not Spanish, are you?"

"Both of my parents were English," the lady answered. "My mother and son are in Geneva, and I'm going home to my sister's flat in Barcelona—not very rapidly, it's true."

The dark wine and soda water were set before them. The soda water was in a bottle tinged blue, as if ink had escaped faintly into the glass. Helen pressed the little handle, and the water hissed into their glasses. They had not known how thirsty they were.

"Here's to a quick journey," said the Englishman, his long eyes narrowing with a smile, "although blast it all, I did hope we could get to Palma by tomorrow night."

"Are you going to Mallorca?" asked Peapack. "I've heard Mallorca's lovely."

"It's our first trip—it will be, that is, if we ever get there," he said. He went on, turning to Helen, "—You were in Cook's bus in Paris, weren't you? Of course. Well, Cook put us through, too and their man should have known better. He could have told us—why, I asked whether everything would be perfectly safe, and he said certainly it would—"

"I *do* think he should have known, don't you?" asked his wife.

Helen laughed at them. The lady laughed. Peapack looked grave.

"Very well," continued the Englishman, a little weakly. "When we get to Barcelona I'm going to tell the man at Cook's a thing or two."

The omelettes were brought in, the little yellow rolls deliciously streaked with brown, and a long loaf of bread. The waiter set them down, and the lady said something cheerful to him in Spanish. The remark made him look at them all, for the first time. He said to the lady, "There are two gentlemen seated behind you, two brothers, who have walked in from Barcelona."

"Doesn't he look like a brute," whispered the English girl. Helen looked at the table next to theirs. Two men sat facing each other over its small top. The larger of the two had a broad heavy back, turned to them, and when he lifted his head, his furry, close-cut hair took the light. His head came up at every mouthful to face his brother. Smaller, compact, the other man sat eating steadily, never looking up, baring the plate methodically from rim to rim. His hair fell in shreds, dark and jagged on his forehead, and his upper left sleeve was torn. White cloth showed under the rent, and the arm hung loose.

The lady from South America, opposite Helen, put her hand out gently and touched the shoulder of the large man.

The lady's head was thrown back at him so that the jawbone stretched the skin white and brittle, and her cheek made one delicate plane away from it. The attitude was suggestive of ritual, the position of the head was very familiar. For a moment Helen could not remember; and then she saw vividly again the beautiful woman in London, the long cheek marbled with one pale vein, turn her head so against her shoulder, to look back and up at the wooden Buddha in its stance of disclosure, bright with its oily gilting.

The two were talking. In a moment the lady turned back. "Yes," she said, breathless, "there's been a terrible battle in Barcelona today, starting this morning. Over two thousand dead, in the streets of the city, and these men have walked all the way."

She turned back to hear more.

Behind her, the Americans were entering the restaurant—Peter and Olive, and the two school teachers. Helen said *Barcelona* noiselessly, with her lips, looking at the little table.

"But who *is* the man?" the Englishman was asking.

"He says he's a bus-driver in town," answered the lady. "Everything is stopped there, in the General Strike, nothing's running, nothing's open but the chemists' shops, and all doctors are on emergency duty."

"And the battle?" he asked eagerly, half-smiling in excitement.

The man was explaining, friendly, comfortable. He turned so that he could see while she translated, screwing himself around the chair, the creases in his shirt spiraling over his shoulder.

"He says it is impossible to say very accurately, now; but that the government had a smashing victory, starting with the defense of the Telephone Building, and has captured and broken up two rebel troops. They're completely disorganized—they'll be escaping through these hills to the frontier—"

"Through here!" Peapack's face rearranged itself, agitated.

"Of course through here," retorted the lady in a hard voice. "We're on the direct route, aren't we? And they've been fighting in the big plazas" she said quietly, as if recollecting—"they always fight in the four big squares. He says the dead, and the horses and mules, have had to be left where they fell."

The man added something briefly.

The lady from South America told them what he was saying about the United Front. They were strong, everything had been foreseen, all night for two nights men had been meeting, collecting weapons, checking on the African news. The whole of Catalonia, according to the bus-driver, was in the United Front: only the church, the generals and the wealthy had rebelled. "And," added the lady, "he says everyone is with the Anarchists this time—the Front is really strong."

The radio yowled suddenly as a record was skidded off. An announcement followed. The lady from South America looked up from her omelette. Her face was taut in fatigue and nausea. The whole restaurant was straining for the sound. The bus-driver's head pulled up; his brother glanced at him and went on eating.

"What is it? Tell me!" said Peapack frantically.

"Sh—General Goded—captured, going to speak," the lady answered under her breath.

There was a blank of silence, and then a harsh, broken voice came through.

"*La suerte me ha sido adversa y yo he quedado prisionero. Por lo tanto, si queréis evitar el derramamiento de sangre, los soldados que me acompañábais quedáis libre de todo compromiso.*"

A burst of noise poured from the other room, cheering, laughter. The American table was very excited. Peter rushed over.

The lady drew her eyebrows tight. "How *can* he?" she said, contemptuously. "He says that he has fallen prisoner, and advises his soldiers to stop fighting, actually. He says to stop the flow of blood, he releases them from their duty. They must have held him to the microphone. A general!" she exclaimed.

Peter said, "My father spoke in that desperate voice all through 1930 . . . "

The voice had changed.

"*Ciudadanos: Sólo unas palabras porque estos momentos lo son de hechos y no de palabras . . .*"

"Acts, not words—that's Companys!" said the waiter, arriving. He stopped at the table, listening.

". . . Acabáis de oír al general Goded que dirigía la insurrección y que pide se evite el derramamiento de sangre.

"La rebelión ha sido sofocada. La insurrección está dominada. Precisa que todos continuéis a las órdenes del Gobierno de las Generalidad, ateniéndos a las consignas.

"No quiero acabar sin hacer un fervoroso elogio de las fuerzas que con bravura y heroísmo han luchado por la legalidad republicana, apoyando a la autoridad civil. ¡Viva Cataluña! ¡Viva la República!"

They came to their feet in the burst of cheering. "*Visca Companys!*" they shouted.

"He said, 'The Rebellion has been suffocated.' He praises the forces who fought so heroically for the republican regime," relayed the lady.

The short man looked into his brother's eyes during the blare of cheering. His nostrils stiffened and pointed.

The radio put on another record. The stammer of machinery done, the words issued, crooning, native, absurd:

Alone, alone with a sky of romance above.
Alone, alone with a heart that was made for love,
There must be someone waiting
Who feels the way I do.
Whoever you are,
 are you
  are you, alone?

They left the café.

THE WOMAN STUCK her head out of the train window. All the little boys had climbed out of the yellow trees. They had gone off to bed; from the row of houses slanting to the station, their voices still came, moving from window to window. The houses were full of running children. The radio was shouting down at the Worker's café. But the children stopped, one by one; the radio was turned off. The deep quiet rose from the ground. The train was deadly still.

They all sat in the compartment—Peter, Olive, Helen, the two school teachers who were uneasy, the pockmarked Swiss.

Rising from the ground, following the quiet, a deep roar came, a zoo noise of some sick enormous animal.

They looked at each other in despair and ignorance, the long fearful look of the haunted.

Olive said in extreme disbelief: "Storm, in the mountains . . ." She lit her cigarette with heavy sighing puffs.

It came again, eager and deep. They all knew what it was.

The Belgian woman pulled the compartment door open, slamming it back fiercely in its groove so that it slipped half-shut as she cried out: "The cannons are coming! Don't you hear them coming nearer?" Her hair was pulled in disorder, her fat soft shoulders rocked.

Helen trembled. The woman stood above her, agitated and moist, pushing at her forehead as if she had gone mad.

The great sound boomed again.

"Oh, God," said the Belgian woman, pushing at her hair, "somebody come back with me to my compartment. I can't stand it when they come nearer." She was appealing to the two school teachers. They did not move. She threw her hand out.

"You babies!" she shouted. "What do you know about guns!"

That pulled them to their feet. The sickly school teacher took the Belgian woman's shoulder and steered her through the door; the one with the long teeth went out after them.

The sounds came up like giant plants around them, a forest of noise.

Peter lit cigarettes for Helen and himself.

"She has to think it's coming nearer," he said.

"She's Belgian." He grinned in sick humor, the grin of pain that sick babies show.

"We have to have something to do," Helen said suddenly. "From the minute they said General Strike, I've been wanting to push through until we could do something."

"If there were only something close to us, beside the noise," said Olive. "Why should it be so remote?"

The Swiss in the corner looked sharply at her. He had not said a word. He did not understand at all.

"Well," said Peter, "if this were a meeting—"

Olive laughed, "It's manifesto time," she said,

"OK, Olive."

"She's right it is," said Helen abruptly.

"Yes," Peter answered, on two slow notes. "From the train to the town—a manifesto. A letter."

The Swiss began to understand. His slow, kind face churned. "And a collection," he announced.

The two women were back in the doorway. "Collection?" asked the sickly one. "The Belgian woman went in with the English."

"Come on in," said Helen. "Come help us. We'll take a letter through the train, to tell the town we're with them."

"It isn't true," Peter contradicted. "The train's not."

"We have to do this well," said Olive. She found a sheet of paper. The Swiss leaned forward.

"We'll compose," he said. "Write: 'The passengers of the train standing in the Moncada—'"

Olive looked out of the window for the spelling. The station sign was directly outside their window, half buried in leaves, lit by a raw white light.

"'—wish to thank the citizens of the town for the courteous treatment they have received—'"

"No. 'Treatment received during their stay at the station.' You can't tell how long we'll be here."

Helen and Olive looked at each other, startled.

"'—and to express our sympathy—'"

"We can't," said the Swiss.

"We're foreign nationals," explained Peter. "It was like that in Paris on July fourteenth. The government asked all foreigners who wanted to march to mingle with the demonstration, and not to go as foreign nationals. Can't, in a revolutionary situation . . . Incorrect."

"To express our understanding of the hardships of the people's cause, and to present this, this—"

"—small sum collected on the train, for the care of the wounded and mutilated in today's battle—"

"Oh, no," said Helen. "If we can't sympathize, we can at least give them money for their own uses."

"OK," said Peter. "Collected on the train for the town to use as it sees fit."

"Yes," said the school teachers. "That's it, if anyone will sign it."

"No signatures," the Swiss declared, waving his hand before his marked face.

"OK. What'll we do, go right through?"

"Well, it should wait until morning, we ought to give it as we pull out," said the school teacher.

Helen said, "We can give it then, if you want, but we ought to see how the train feels about it now."

"Yes," said Olive. "You go with Peter, Helen." The school teacher agreed.

"We'll report to the rest of this committee on the way back," said Helen. Peter interrupted. "We'll start the collection here."

The Swiss drew out his wallet, thumbed through it, and laid a fifty-peseta note in Peter's beret.

They were startled. "Oh, no," said Peter, flustered.

"Never mind." The Swiss's face did not move.

"THE SWISS IS good," said Helen, "He gets more and more like the lion for the Swiss Guards."

"He does!" said Peter. "But those two bitches are beginning to get me.

"I don't know," said Helen. "The picture of the green one reading *Problems of the Spanish Revolution* was worth a lot of annoyance. How do you want to do this?" She was very glad of the activity.

"Let's split them for language, and then you take men and I'll take women. I'm all right at meetings; I'm not sure about trains." He laughed.

There were three men in the next compartment, busy reading *Gringoire.** Helen tried in French. They talked among themselves a minute, and Peter shook his beret. One of them slapped down two *duros*.

"That's as close to fascism as we can afford to get," said Peter, outside.

"Oh, no," said Helen. "You've been talking to leftists. They'll go on reading *Gringoire*, but they're human."

"You've been in England," Peter retorted.

"Let's ask the English," she said suddenly. "They are decent, and they've got the League of Nations man with them."

The Belgian woman was just leaving the English compartment.

"I'm better now," she answered Helen. "I'll be all right, I think. It's only the big guns." She hurried down the train, blowing her nose softly.

Peter opened the door and leaned against it. The Spaniard's long face looked up mildly. "Good evening?" His graying sideburns added meekness and courtesy to his expression.

"We have a letter to the town, from the train—" Peter began.

"Yes, we hope'd you'd translate it for us, if you approve. We're going through the train with it."

"*Through the train!*" repeated Drew.

The lady from South America smiled at Helen. "Perfectly

*A right-wing weekly in France.

— 66 —

groomed," Peter had said. Her mouth moved. "Oh, yes," she said. "But give it to them tonight; at least they'll know we're not against them. I'll sleep better. She held her wrist against her temple, and the light caught her bracelet.

"Do give it to them tonight, by all means," the Spaniard advised gently. "It is a very polite gesture; it will be our . . . guarantee for the night." He waved at the open window. "We are perfectly exposed here, you realize."

Helen spoke aside to young Mrs. Drew. "Is he really from the League of Nations?"

The Spaniard looked up before she could answer.

"What an idea!" he said. "No! League of Nations! I am a professor at the University of Madrid."

"If I were from the League, I might be able to put a call through," he remarked wistfully. "As it is, my family is waiting for me to come for them . . . But this," he said, tapping the sheet of paper, "this is a very politic gesture. It will at least insure us a quiet night."

"We'll have guards—" Drew looked at the professor for confirmation.

"Indeed yes," the professor granted. "The mayor has promised."

"They'll be armed peasants, of course, who've never handled a gun before," Drew said. "But they're probably the best persons to have on the platform. It's really decent of them to be so considerate—the letter's right—whether the consideration means anything or not." He was very hopeless looking. His silk mustache was stuck on to the face of a young, worried boy.

The professor was translating rapidly, writing in pencil under the English letter.

"There!" he said, finishing, with approval, as if it were an examination paper. He pulled coins out of his pocket. "Let us know what happens, won't you."

Drew nodded. "Good luck," he said. "D'you think sleeping will be all right? We've got our candles."

His wife had swimming blue eyes; she was nervous. She laughed. "We'll hope to wake up in Barcelona."

They went on to the chorus' two compartments. One of the girls saw Peter reflected in the window-mirror. She paused, holding her eyebrow pencil an inch away from her face. "Maybe he knows!" she said eagerly.

The three perfectly-tinted silvery heads came up. "Have you seen our phonograph?"

"Did you see any of those men in sandals carrying a case away?"

Peter said no, showed them the letter, explained about the diplomacy of the move. They drew eyebrows, agreed, contributed.

They went through the first class, speaking to the rest of the chorus, a little dark Spaniard, a Spanish family which sat apart, the mother stony and tragic, the father with his arm about a weeping daughter. The daughter wept; the father motioned them away.

They turned, going down toward third. Many were asleep already, the timid light from the bulbs strung in the corridor did not disturb them, even when it lay on their faces. The Catalans slept on the wooden benches.

Peter and Helen passed the open compartments where there were sleeping children. A group who were still awake, collected money among themselves, nodding and asking about the battle. They had been eating on the train when General Goded's broadcast came through, and were delighted to hear of the victory.

Others groups gave and approved the message; their intense colorless eyes watched Peter and Helen read it, they scraped together *céntimos* and *reals*, they asked for news. At the end of the second car the Swiss and Hungarian teams occupied several compartments; the Swiss were singing softly, led by a tall, academically handsome athlete whose tightly curled hair caught the weak light.

As they reached the teams, Toni stood in the corridor. His dark mouth smiled, the lips appearing almost black, his female dark eyes softened by the shadow. "We looked for you," he said gently, reproachfully, to Helen. "I tried to find you. Did you eat?"

"I went off with the English."

"The mayor gave us dinner," Toni said proudly. "Big dinners in a *restaurante*, for both teams. But there will be more fighting tonight. Did you hear the cannon a few minutes ago? And the mayor has sent *camiones* into the hills tonight to capture rebels. Now that the fascists are in retreat, these hills are important."

"Did he say how the United Front was?"

"Everybody is either Anarchist or very proud of the Anarchists," he answered, "and this may mean a free Catalonia."

"Are you all Hungarians?" asked Peter.

Toni came along with them into the next car. He was very impressed by Peter's Hungarian.

They continued up the next car. It was in complete darkness. The first compartment belonged to an Italian, taking care of his old father. "Such a day!" he breathed. "And God only knows what is happening at Barcelona and all over Spain tonight."

"Haven't you any light?" Helen asked. He picked at the switch. It clicked blank.

"There hasn't been any light all evening," he said. "The cars must be connected on separate batteries," Peter said to him. "The English have candles. Would you like one?"

"Oh, thank you, no," the Italian protested. "I would like it if my father would get a little rest: the dark is *benigna*—gentle."

More than half of the darkened compartments here held sleeping figures, the drawn-up legs and cramped restless shoulders half-seen through the glass, or guessed-at behind the blinds. One woman stood out in the corridor, leaning on a bar, her head stiffened and listening.

The radio was going again, full blast, opposite the locomotive.

"Do you speak English?" she asked. "If I only knew what they are shouting."

"They were celebrating a victory a little while ago," Helen said. She had not seen the woman before. She supposed they had overlooked others on the train, anonymous fellow-travelers. She wished she had the Spanish family to talk to, for a minute she missed them keenly, the old generous grandmother, the heavy man's warmth, the fine beauty of the boy.

The speech stopped abruptly. The woman sighed as she contributed, "That's some sort of workingmen's restaurant," she said, "they have an excellent radio. I wish I knew what it was saying." She lowered her head as a sheep might.

In the next compartment, a man with a gray beard lay on his bench, already asleep, looking comfortable; but his companion, a sallow Frenchman, jumped up and came into the corridor to praise the letter and pay his French money. The beret hung down in a heavy point. It was almost full of French, Italian, and Spanish coins. Toni admired the fifty-peseta note.

Peter said, "The note helped a lot."

The English couple in the last compartment wondered about it. "It's real," Peter said, controlling his voice, edging toward mockery.

"I'm afraid I can't match it," said the Englishman. He turned with a long uxorious drink of a look to his tall wife. She acknowledged him with a lip-motion, repressed and formal. "And I do think it's a little steep for tonight's lodging."

"No. It isn't like that," said Helen.

"They've all given only if they wanted to and what they could," Peter was saying incoherently.

"I suppose English money's acceptable?" the man asked, eyeing the mixed pile and sticking two fingers in his vestpocket, cutting the conversation off.

"Don't put anything in until you've heard the letter." Helen read it to him quickly. She could feel him stiffen at the phrasing.

His tall wife turned her square modern face to the window in a deadly gesture of exhaustion. The man fished out a half-crown.

He spoke directly to Helen, avoiding Peter. "It should hire a quiet night, but it does go a little against the grain," he began.

"Oh, but don't give anything if you don't think—" she said.

"Sorry—I didn't mean it that way." He put it in the beret, and hunched his shoulder in an awkward self-conscious spasm. His whole body apologized. His wife watched him now, aroused.

The entrance to the Pullman was locked.

"Never mind," said Peter, "we'll go around. We won't pass these birds up. The Hollywood trio must be in here."

"Hollywood?" asked Helen. The flash of *Variety* headlines she had caught at Port Bou station recurred under her eyelids.

"Our magnates; I looked for you with them, before we found each other."

"How do you say that word?" Toni asked. "*Hollywood.* I had an argument over that in Paris."

They went outside. The radio was on again. A wind sprang up in the Pyrenees, washing down over the valley.

Toni made a face. "The refuse is heaped under the train. Bad smell," he said. "In the sun, it would be very very bad."

The outside door of the Pullman was locked.

Peter rapped against the metal side of the car directly under a lit window.

The man had blue-shaven cheeks and a candy-colored shirt.

"Do you speak English?" Peter asked, following the formula they had used throughout the train.

The man shook his head.

"You don't speak English?" Peter asked, confounded.

"*Non,*" said the man. The other two appeared at the window.

"*Kesker say?*" the first man demanded, with a strong New York thickness in his words.

Peter was disgusted. He explained very shortly. Helen took up recital. They read the letter in French, feeling fools. The men grinned, and gave them French money.

The dining-car carried its NOT RUNNING sign, and the waiters and the engineer were asleep in the baggage room.

They could see the Workers' Café. There was a full sidewalk in front, where thirty men were listening to the radio.

THEY SHOWED OLIVE the beret. It held about 140 pesetas and some foreign money.

"But the Swiss has to take back his," Peter said. "There's no proportion, this way. And ask him to come with us to the mayor."

He came, lowering his bulk gently down the laddersteps. He became the leader of the group as soon as he saw a knot of boys standing in the street behind the station.

They crossed the cement-paved court.

The Swiss walked ahead; his broad shadow increased on the ground. He spoke to the boys in Catalan.

"Wouldn't the mayor be at the radio?" A burst of shouting expanded, issuing from the Workers' Café.

"They say we can find him at the *farmacia*." The Swiss was authoritative.

The boys swirled around them, curious and polite. They all turned down the Calle Mayor. The night, a new element, entered the street. Houses were distorted by it, their clearness discolored, their angles thrown out of joint, each block and tile focused. The darkness changed shapes like wind, like an organism deranged by fearful wind the town changed shape.

The *farmacia* still had lights on. One burned raw behind the gold plait over the window: *Centro de Específicos*, another lit the rows of surgical scissors and labeled jars and bottles.

Peter stepped forward. "We are from the train—" he said.

The Swiss put up a great conclusive hand. "We have a document from the train for the mayor," he declared, in Catalan. "And a small collection for the town."

The chemist was profuse; his sideburns were agitated by his apologies. He was glad to inform them that the mayor was certainly at his home now, he had left the shop not more than ten minutes since; he, the chemist, was afflicted that he had detained them with his disquisition; he would be honored to accompany them, but he had sworn to keep the *farmacia* open all night and to remain on these premises. In case of emergency, they comprehended; they foresaw emergencies during the *madrugada.*

He took them to the door, and thanked them for their good wishes.

They beheld the silent street.

Crisis at night, or at dawn!

The Swiss had metal plates reinforcing the heels of his shoes. They rang on the pavement, a high, wild sound, recurring like a sweet stammering flute, bells, ritual music. The wind blew down, the cooled air falling from the mountains.

Beside these, there were no sounds.

The mayor's house was past the restaurant, across from it. The Swiss dropped the knocker. A young girl opened the door a crack, showing her pale forehead and two wings of gleaming hair. She said she would call her father, and twisted her fine throat, calling on two notes. The mayor appeared at the crack, and threw the door open. His coat with the mourning band on the lapel was off, and he looked younger and more tired. The Swiss started to explain the train-message.

Helen watched the mayor's face lighten with sympathy as the Swiss spoke.

"Good night, *vuestra merced,*" the Swiss said, finally.

"¡*Compañeros!*" acknowledged the mayor. The shift of level hit them hard. An excitement passed through the group. The faces changed slightly; the light fell as the door shut.

"What did the mayor say?" she asked Peter.

His face had lost its look of knowledge. He was very startled. "The mayor thought it was too important for him to accept. He sent us to the secretary."

"What secretary?" she asked.

"I don't know."

It was a low modern building, banded broadly with chalk-green and white stripes. It was the only building whose door was lit.

The Swiss led them past the guards and up the high steps. At the head of the stairs was a balcony, with offices branching from it. An armed workman stopped them.

"The mayor sent us," said the Swiss, in Catalan.

The workman opened a door.

It was a high, hot room, lit with naked bulbs whose white unbearable dazzle made them narrow their eyes. The walls were ranged with straight wooden chairs. At the far side, behind a square dark desk, the secretary got to his feet.

"You are from the train, they tell me?"

The Swiss explained that they brought a message from the passengers; as he spoke, the secretary signaled with a nod to four of the men in the anteroom. They came in and closed the door behind them softly.

The secretary motioned for them all to sit down. He spoke a few words to the Catalans, and came back to the Swiss. "Tell them what you have told me," he said.

The Swiss repeated their mission. The four men sat there, not answering with any motion. The Swiss handed the letter to the secretary, and Peter emptied the beret carefully on the glossy desk.

THE SECRETARY READ the document. Even sitting, bent over paper, his body had dignity, and his long face, the cheeks crossed and braided by lines, dominated the room. He leaned over the desk, stretching the paper towards the nearest committee-member.

The two lines of people faced each other—the four dark Catalans sat opposite the Swiss, Peter, Helen, and Toni. The secretary turned his engine-eyes on them. The first man passed the paper on to the second. With a long hooked gesture, the secretary pulled a light steel table to him, spooled a sheet out of the typewriter, settled a new page, and began to type lightly and rapidly.

No one said a word. Helen leaned over to Peter with a full, rich gesture, bending forward from the breast to ask him a question. She was looking at a large photograph framed on the wall over the secretary's desk. The Catalan who had just finished the letter followed her eyes.

"Who is he?"

Peter shrugged slightly, and asked the Swiss, they had dropped into whispers. Peter put his mouth near her ear.

"Lluís Companys, President of Catalonia."

The committee-man nodded.

The secretary finished the lines he was typing. His lips tightened, the deep sharp groove down his lone upper lip became lighter, and his lined forehead cleared. He reached over his desk and inked a seal. The room was quiet, now that his machine had stopped. The stamps of rubber seal on paper had a final, military note.

The secretary stood up, and began to read in a flat voice.

"The Workers' Committee of Catalonia hereby thanks the passengers of the train of the Madrid-Zaragoza-Alicante line, now detained in the Moncada station, for the expression of their recognition of the position in which Catalonia and all of Spain has been placed. The committee wishes to assure the passengers that every effort will be made to continue to provide for their comfort and complete safety. *Por el Comité Trabajador de Cataluña.*"

The secretary sat down and drew a telephone toward him. Peter and Helen stared, fevered with the sign. The secretary was speaking softly. Then the lines were up, the people held the communications. The brightness of the room, the heat, the promise that the telephone meant!

The secretary turned his typed sheet over to the Swiss.

"Say that some of us have our sympathies in theirs," whispered Helen. "We can tell him, at least!"

"Yes," Peter said the Swiss. "Tell him!"

The Swiss had a settled face, pitted and firm. It shifted, entrenching further in solidity. "No," he answered. "We have no place in their politics."

"Foreign nationals."

It seemed impossible to continue without any indication, without making any sign or giving a partisan clue.

The secretary folded his hands. "Is that all?"

They stood. Everybody stood. The door opened.

The Swiss moved forward to shake the secretary's hand. He turned then to the committee.

Each of them did the same. The two files met, grasped hands, and passed. They shook hands with a smiling curious intensity, trying to find language in that touch. It was, again, a humiliation to Helen not to be able to speak. But there was no constraint: they shook each others' hands: they could count on the transmission: they were sure.

Foreign nationals.

"It was like that on Bastille Day," Peter whispered. Heavily, they moved down the sharp steps.

A man with a long gun hurried down with them, at Helen's back. She could feel the gun pointed at her, feel a passage bored through her back, a tube leaving a cold fear through.

They walked, a little apart, down the street. The man with the gun was running in the other direction, and then he was gone.

Secret, furious, the night grew. The street rested, but the black air was alert, waiting for its game to start, its sun to approach, its act of will to resolve this war.

Peter and Helen walked slowly. "The night," she said.

"Vivid and black."

"Those people are, somehow, historic facts."

"Realer than any, more strong than any, more the clue?"

"No," she said. "We romanticize."

A cold flaw ran over their faces. They reached the station. They said good night to Toni and the Swiss. They all were bound to each other insolubly, it was a grief to part, the good night protracted.

Peter and Helen walked down the platform. The yellow trees swung on the low wind, yellow, perfume of lilac. The small lit blossoms were clear; perfect and blond in the night.

"Mimosa?" she asked. They stood under the bright tree, the yellow light fell over their faces. He peered with a scientist's squint into the tree; she turned white and quiet. Her dark hair was tinted with light.

"I never knew," he said "Maybe. The words came again."

"They came up once today, stronger than ever before, creating what they said."

"General Strike?" he asked

PEAPACK WANTED TO go to sleep. She asked Olive to come in with her and Helen. They were better off than on the wooden benches of third. The gray cushions were heavy, but upholstered. Helen's leg jumped; sleep, she thought.

Peter came to the door. "Good night," he said, and kissed Olive.

"Where will you be?" she asked.

"The Hungarians have captured three compartments," Peter answered triumphantly. "I'll be in there. I'll come by early—first thing, dear," he said, and shut the door.

The three women lay down.

Helen snapped the light off. As she shut her eyes, knowing the train lay dead in a dead station, she felt a powerful muscular motion around her: the train, the secret hills, the country, the whole world of war rushing down the tracks, headfirst in conflict like a sea, unshakable, the momentum adding until the need burst through all other barriers: to reach the center, to will continuance.

SHE DREAMED THE sea: a green streaked sea, with black tremendous currents. And headlong, plunging through the stream, a force rushing, which carried her along; until she ceded her will to it in a huge gesture. In that moment she revived, she drew will from the enormous source, and thought, even in the dream: O Parable.

And passed, during the voyage, faces.

Of all these, two came clear; husband and wife, the poets, their looks like light, their beautiful heads. She saw them changed, the fine familiar bones tapering down, planted tight in seabottom; and the currents swept over their faces, but could not change their steady look. She felt a hammering of love, faith in them, in the force which carried her memory upon the looks she loved so much and trusted, she called to them loudly: You are my legs; and swept by in the immense currents. In blackness.

OFTEN, THAT NIGHT, she woke to the motionless train and the laughing cry of cocks.

CHAPTER FIVE

'Where can we get a good meal?' . . . .
'I am not sure if it can be managed,
I expect everything is shut' . . . .
'But why should everything be shut?'
'The Revolution—'
She had overlooked the Revolution again—
an affair of foreign politics.
                              —Sylvia Townsend Warner

It was the bomb that stopped the roosters. The soft, tremendous explosion shook the town, their cages, the
train. Immediately a ghost of smoke rose from the village, a dark
escape in the morning air.

All the eastern sky was mottled brilliant.

Helen pulled herself stiffly off the suitcase and cushions, slid the
door open behind its green shade, and left the compartment. There
was no water. It was not until she gave up the idea of washing and
stepped down to the platform that she remembered what woke her,
why she had hurried from the train.

If they were bombing the village!

Smoke evaded the arms of the woman who bent over the dirt.
Helen watched, leaning against one of the little yellow trees. The
peasant woman had set her baby down, against the next tree, away
from the blowing smoke, and was feeding sticks into a small fire.
The covered red pot was set on the stones piled as a fireplace.

The green branches went slowly, and their smoke smelled like
brine, vivid and stinging.

But the baby was on the safe side; its eyes, holes burned in the expressionless face, were turned to the flame. It was colorless in the early morning; transparent, it showed the grass behind the fire.

The woman looked up and nodded.

"Café?" Helen asked.

"No. *Sopa.*"

Peter came up behind her. "Soup," he said.

They stood and watched the fire.

"Was it a bomb?" she asked.

"They bombed the church," the woman said.

They heard the soft waking noises from the cars, the beginning of fretful voices, the sighing return to consciousness of the train.

THE ENGLISH WERE coming down from the next car. Drew's sweater was limp; and young Mrs. Drew was quite crumpled. Only the lady from South America looked polished and beautiful. The Belgian woman could be seen in the background, following them up the platform, her scarf flying behind her, all gem-clean like some fatal figure in contemporary painting.

The lady from South America patted her silvery head. "I despise letting myself go this way," she said to Helen, "but I couldn't sleep at all, and there's nothing one can do . . ." She drifted to a whisper. The mouth, still russet-colored, hardly moved.

"*Did* you hear the explosion?" screamed young Mrs. Drew. "They've bombed the church and arrested the priest, the Spanish gentleman says. We're not to go up to that part of town today."

They were walking up toward the café.

Peapack caught up with them. "Don't leave me, don't leave me!" The English looked at her coldly. "Was that a cannon?" She sat down next to the Belgian woman, who began to illustrate the sound of guns. The proprietor of the café was arranging the wine bottles behind the counter, listing the levels on a long sheet of paper.

He said something to the lady from South America. Her face

changed in passionate horror. Her hand lifted in a sharp, beautiful gesture, denying everything, the words he had spoken to her, the world. The proprietor came to the tables for orders.

"What is it, what's happened?" Helen leaned over Drew toward the lady. She turned the helmeted head.

"He's just told me they caught five Fascist officers this morning—early, before four o'clock—and shot them and cut their throats."

The proprietor, bent over Helen, added something.

"*Leche*," she answered.

"Milk? Don't you want coffee?" asked the lady from South America, automatically. "He says they're on view in a cellar in the next block—we should go see them."

"God!" breathed Drew. "Does he say the train will move?"

The proprietor looked at Drew as the lady translated, he grinned. "*Huelga General*," he responded. He told the lady more of the story. She seemed to become more frail and fashionable as he piled on horror.

Peter and Olive came in, pulled up a third table, and listened.

The lady relayed: "He says the men who went out of town last night stopped the Fascists' car in the hills. It surrendered immediately, and the captain who led the men said: 'Do whatever you want with me. I've killed two or three hundred of your men, and it doesn't matter what becomes of me.'"

"So what did they do?" asked Peapack.

Peter laughed her down.

But another Englishman had crossed over to them, a shortish, pale little man, with a hanging nose and chin. He smiled pleasantly and asked in a Jewish Cockney accent: "But what did they do?"

"Shot them," answered Peter.

"And slit their throats," said Drew, drawing a line with his finger.

"They're in a cellar down the street," repeated the lady from South America. She turned back to Helen. Her head moved again with the precision of that London Lady. "I don't know whether it's going to be worse here than in Barcelona," she said, contemplative. "The only chance to consider is that they might have a telegraph line open in Barcelona. If I could get word through to my son and mother . . ."

Helen asked about her flat in the city.

"But that is nothing. My sister's family will try to take care of it for me. They're in the suburbs—" her face changed, "but they're not just fighting in the square this time. If I could get word to Geneva, my son—" She broke off again, with an exquisite final note in her voice. Hopeless and beautiful, deposed.

"Perhaps the train—" cut in Drew.

She overlooked him. "He's a striking boy," she continued, looking at Helen, making her words personal and significant, as if here was a secret clue; "he's twenty-two." She spoke the words with a subtlety beyond anything she said, an exquisite inflection, tender and naked. "My dear," she said directly to Helen, "I might be your mother."

THE WORDS CAME, shaking the blood inordinately, filled with a compassion that was unlooked-for, indeed undesirable, filled with every softness, an echo of the need of the other world which had just ended; and they were strong enough to strike through the conversation of the little Cockney, deep in Coffee-and-Tea, prices and stocks, with Peter, through the pudding solicitude of Peapack, the vanishing vitality of Olive, the handsome Drews. The softness reached her, the unhappy older woman reaching with a phrase, taking her hands, stroking her with the words, recalling all old unhappy softness. And through the windows of the café, the break came.

Through the windows they saw cars pass, splattered U.G.T., C.N.T., carrying the men with the effort set in their faces, carrying loudly through the village heavy guns.

They could see the boys who drove them.

They could see the mark, the bullet hole, the streak along the hood. And the vicious machine gun.

"U.G.T.—Unión General de Trabajadores. C.N.T.—Confederación Nacional del Trabajo," said Peter.

"Oh my God," said Olive. "The guns."

"*Les mitrailleuses!*" screamed the Belgian woman. She stood up, puddling the coffee, pale with milk, before her.

"Let's go back," said Drew.

Helen picked up a newspaper as they went back to the train. "Morning routine," she smiled at Drew. He spoke gently: "It would be nice to wash. I'll see what I can do."

From high up in the hills, slapping across hill to hill, came the first wild sound.

"Rifle fire!" exclaimed Drew.

Helen hurried ahead to the lady from South America. She had not answered the lady's phrase; she hoped she had shown how closely it had touched, how it had canceled the wish for softness. She spoke hurriedly and impersonally.

"Look," she said, "you have a family in Barcelona, and I have a letter to the head of the publicity committee of the Games. It won't do me any good to get in a bit sooner"—she stumbled over words, the lady said nothing—"the letter doesn't identify me except by name, it's good with the government, they're People's Front games, it'll get you past the officials. Take it, you take the letter, you should be there."

In that moment, before the lady said anything, Helen wondered at the step of the possible sacrifice she was making. Because of the fragmentary half-caught resemblance to a woman in London who had been kind to her? The broken half-suggestion of a banal phrase? War between worlds?

The lady moved the beautiful russet mouth. "You are extravagantly kind," she was saying.

A shot came like terror out of the hills.

"But I mean it, I mean it," Helen pressed. "You can pass for me, it's only my name. I want you to be there. They say a bus may come. There's a rumor."

"I'll speak to the doctor about it," the lady was answering. "There's a doctor on the train who got on at Gerona. I've been talking to him. The authorities here are quite severe, stricter than your Americans. I've been speaking to this little doctor"—her voice descended melodiously, became confidential—"you know, I've been suffering so, I haven't been, for two days—I can't bear going to the W.C.s here. They're not clean. I'll talk to the doctor again. Have you found a clean bathroom?"

Helen said no, but about the letter—

"You're a dear to suggest it. If you really wish." The lady consented, gracefully, with her neck. "But I must speak to the doctor."

They had reached the station platform.

It took Helen a moment to accommodate the change. From the exquisite, caught-in-a-revolutionary bottleneck, to descend to these physical intimacies—! She saw how ridiculous she was being. It was true that the sun was high over the fetid train, that the small refuse-heaps at either end of each car were apparent now to everyone; the flies were atrocious.

The lady's delicate hand went out. Her chic red bracelet flashed. "There he is, now—and the professor, the gentleman from Madrid!"

THEY ALL SAT on the bench in the waning shadow of the station, laughing at the professor.

". . . nobody was arrogant, everybody's trying to help," he was saying. "I went to the *restaurante*, as you suggested," he nodded to the Englishwoman whose compartment was opposite the Workers' Café, "and engaged a waitress in conversation. We thought we could get meals wholesale for the train," he added parenthetically, in a charming, modulated, classroom voice. "I went in and asked her for a menu, 'Oh, we don't have anything like that,' she said, very much put out. 'Well, what have you to eat?' I asked her, and she laughed. 'Anything you like, sir, anything at all, we have your favorite dishes,' she said. 'But *what?*' I'm afraid I was very insistent. 'Ask for something,' she told me. 'Veal?' I said, very tentatively, you know; they should have some sort of veal. 'No, no veal today.' I could see she was on the verge of tears. She did want to please. 'Well, you tell me,' I said. 'We have a lovely omelette,' she suggested. I asked her how much it was. 'It all depends—how much omelette do you want?' 'I don't know,' I told her—it was getting very complicated. 'How hungry are you?' she finally asked; and I told her I wasn't at all hungry."

Drew howled with laughter.

"It's such an old joke, too," said the professor, "if only it hadn't happened!"

"What are we going to do, though?" The English woman's long face took on vertical marks of hopelessness.

"I'd like to wash," said the lady from South America.

"All right," said Drew, "that's the easiest yet. I rigged up something for my wife this morning. Wait a second."

He came out of his compartment with a shallow tin basin. "Water down the street!" he shouted, diminishing toward the café.

"The town's given us its other pump," the professor said. "Erratic, but water. Seriously, though," he looked around. Peter and Olive had come up. "You're the reliable people on this train," he said to the group. "We've got to do something to keep the morale up. What with the Belgian, and the woman from Peapack, and those Hollywood people . . ."

Peter grinned. "Deck games, or lectures," he proposed. "You lecture, sir, on Spanish history. It would do us all a lot of good."

"I doubt if it would quiet anybody," the professor answered. "What I was thinking of," he twinkled over his tall, placid face, "was the chorus. What about a rehearsal?"

"God, that would be wonderful," said Peter. "Except they have the town already. I don't suppose this place has ever seen anything so blonde."

"They're to open at the Tivoli," the professor continued. "That is, they should have opened last night. They must be all right."

"Or the teams could play exhibition soccer," Mrs. Drew added. "Everybody ought to do something." The talk about the chorus was getting her visibly nervous. She looked over her shoulder for Drew; he was coming down the platform with a pan of water. The lady from South America wrung off her bracelet and ring, and accepted the towel and the tiny lump of English soap. The professor watched her as she began to wash at the next bench.

"Yes," he said ruminatively, "that's right, we all should. We ought to talk a bit about pooling our money, too. The bit of Spanish money most people changed at the border isn't going to hold out forever."

"What do you mean, forever?" The voice came from behind them, and they all turned. It was American, and sandy. It was the Hollywood executive. "Who said anything about staying in this dump?"

"We only thought we should make the best—"

"Yah, thinking!" the man exploded. "That's not going to make this trolley move. What we need is a little action, instead of taking what they hand us, and by God I'm going to see that's what we get! I want to get out of here as quick as wheels can go, and I'd a damn sight rather be at the frontier than go to Barcelona."

The lady from South America scrubbed her face dry, and looked up at Hollywood. "What do you propose to do about it?" she inquired. All the contempt of the truly cosmopolitan was in her voice, and her oblique look; hatred of cowardice, of coarseness, and swagger; and besides she had just washed.

He faced her directly. "I'll do what I can," he answered, with stubbornness. "I've got money to get out. I'll hire a car. No," he said, "I'll commandeer a car, if that's going to be the style. I'm going to the mayor now. Give me ten minutes, time enough to find out the mayor's price, and I'll have that car."

He strode off down the street; they watched him go. Drew started down after him with the empty pan, to get water for Helen. The professor said, sadly and wearily, "Shall we place bets on Hollywood?"

THE LITTLE SHOP was crowded with townspeople, lined close, three-deep at the meat counter, keeping the butcher chopping lengths of sausage, steadily, as roll after roll of meat gave out, snatched from the meathooks, lifted hungrily from the wooden slab of the cutting-block.

What was left of the vegetables was going very fast; cheese after cheese was handed out; and a tall stack of cans was vanishing away, its top sinking lower by the second.

Hardly a word of conversation was heard, but the shop was full of noise: the prices of food, the rattle of heavy paper as the meat was wrapped carelessly by the butcher, the arbitrary clockwork of the chopper, descending like a judge's gavel, significant, irregular.

The foreigners stood at the fringe, almost against the far wall, next to the two sacks of almonds and dried fruits. They looked at each other in confusion: the need for rapid action, coming on them suddenly, made it impossible for them to speak. They saw the piles of food disappearing, as by some slapstick trick of a camera; and, casting about for help, they realized that the lady from South America was the only one who spoke Spanish.

She stood a little apart from the group, watching the butcher, paralyzed by attraction; she was counting the blows of the meat-chopper, her lips moved visibly. Drew took her by the arm.

"We'll get the other things," he said. "We can just hold them out and say *cuanto vale*; you go and get the meat, won't you?" He stretched out his long fingers, pushing her gently, enough to start her one step toward the butcher. It was the same gesture the Catalan father had used on his fragile son, sending him affectionally into the third-class aisle after the basket of bread.

The lady said nothing, but her eyebrows drew together; she was still concentrating on the chopper. She moved a few steps up, but a woman shoved her back as she ran before her to the other counter.

Helen turned away.

They must hurry.

The cheese was gone already. There was hardly any meat left.

She walked over to the low shelves beside the grocery counter, and picked up a large bottle of mineral water in each hand. A stream of people crowded her away from the counter, trying to pay for their food, trying to order from the inaccessible shelves. It is at moments when action is called for that we fail, she thought; get deeper in this, no trembling here! She stood there still, the long silvery bottles hanging like clubs, her money in her pocket, as the women crowded up to their marketing.

Mrs. Drew came up to her. "The lady is ill, I think," she said, in a low voice. "But she'll be all right the minute she pulls herself together. Can't you pay for these?" she asked, taking one of the bottles from Helen. "Get three," she said, "three between us, and I'll take the lady next door to get some fruit."

Drew came up behind her. "There!" he took out his handkerchief and rubbed it between his hands, "she's paying for the meat now. I just steered her through all the people, and she asked for sausage as though she were sleepwalking. Makes you feel funny, though, even buying food—there doesn't seem to be terribly much in the stores."

"I wish you'd pay for water," said Helen, "and get some bread. I can't get through, either." She smiled at him weakly, handing him her purse. He opened it, and whistled at the note.

"Going to be hard to change this!" he said, "I haven't seen any paper money yet."

"I changed all I had at the border," Helen said.

Mrs. Drew and the lady were leaving the store. It was filling all the time; nobody seemed to be leaving. As Drew gave the note to the grocer, the family with two little boys in playsuits came in. They were speaking German, counting over their money; they said hello to the train-people. "Hard to get anything, isn't it?" the tall German said sociably to Helen. "The fruit store has a few rotten bananas left, and they're going like gold. The sausage seems to be all that's left." He looked around the shop. "Nuts, too dry; dried fruit, thirsty stuff; hate to eat from cans." He marched over to the meat-counter.

"Have to wait for change a minute," called Drew, deep in the crowd, waving a loaf to get Helen's attention.

She stood back against the shelves, holding the three bottles.

The sound of the shop was rising; since they had come in, it had lifted from the chattering monotone of a great many women buying food, going chromatically up to screaming sharpness that was broken only by the gavel, the chopper fallen on bone, as if order were being constantly and futilely demanded.

One of the men said something about civil war. Helen looked at him without understanding, hearing only the military words. He began to repeat, but nothing could be heard. The orders, the crowd shifting in haste, payment, hunger, were too loud. And now another sound became evident: the shop divided.

HELEN STOOD UP, disengaging her foot. "I want to go down the train a way," she mumbled. Peapack was winking as she tried to think of the Spanish for "Excuse me," and came stumbling out through a vapor of cucumber-cream, over the knees of Catalan boys. Helen went blind with fury; all she wanted was to lie down, on grass, and look at the Lawrence book, and let the last day arrange itself somehow in her brain.

The three Frenchman stood aside in the corridor, holding the Saturday *Gringoire* flat against their chests, in clown's positions, reading an old paper about another world. She went down the platform. The Belgian woman put her head out. "I think the sound of a cannon is coming closer," she said mechanically, like a signature.

Peter was talking to the engineer. He walked toward the schoolhouse with her. "He's keeping up fuel," Peter remarked.

"Does he recommend anything?" asked Helen, more quietly.

"He suggested a look at the five Fascists. I thanked him . . . Oh, God!" he said. Peapack was in obvious retreat down the platform, the Catalan boys bewildered but following.

"She winks when she can't pronounce her verbs. It throws them off the track," said Helen, with a tired amused smile.

"Are you going to the schoolhouse?" Peapack shrieked. "I do want to see the school. Tell me," she said, intensely, to Peter, speaking as she would to a ticket agent, "is it safe to leave any valises in the train and sleep in the schoolhouse, or should I stay in the compartment?"

"Oh," he said, not answering, "you could have them taken to the schoolhouse, and sleep there, among them, on them, under them . . ."

"Oh, *would* you?" she sang out, "that would be lovely! Is this it?"

They had cut across the tracks to a clay lot with grass growth knotted flat in the middle, patches of weed, and an incline of gravel sloping toward the school. The square, two-story building was the newest in Moncada. It stood at one corner of the town, and the asphalt road ended before it. Its cream walls were cut by immense rectangles of glass, its halls smelled of plaster, the front steps could not be schoolhouse steps, foursquare as they were, with not a sign of erosion in the center.

Peapack ran in, squealing, and Peter started to follow. He looked back at Helen, standing dark and quiet in the glare. "Go on," she said, "I'm going to find a tree."

"Wait a moment," he said, "wait for me."

It was the first minute she had been alone. No, she remembered, the compartment was empty when the train stopped for the first time and the women got out; but that had been before. Everything that had ever happened had happened since then, in blistering sun, like this sun on the gravel bank. She looked at the triangle of streets whose peak she faced. There was no shade on all those hot squares of houses; up the bare cliff behind her marched the power-lines, and before her the soft hill, half-grown in olive-trees, receded in a scum of sun-haze. She walked over the grass embankment at the tracks. The long sharp leaves were coated with dust, and hot to touch. She was standing there when Peter came out, hurrying.

"All right," he said, "let's find a tree—Peapack's inspecting the shower."

They walked to the entrance of one street. The road went as far as the telegraph office, and turned to baked dirt.

"The Hollywood people were all for breaking the door down this morning," Peter jerked his head at the barred, padlocked office, "they want to send an SOS themselves, or buy the telegraph company, or something."

"Did they see the doctor start off to Barcelona?"

"No," said Peter glumly.

A rout of chickens were scratching among the wheel-ruts. At one of the doorways, a thin tall woman was emptying a pan of water, and the chute flashed and fell, staining the rich brown. Peter asked her where there were trees. She was sure there were none in Moncada. Up in the hills, plenty. But in this town, no.

"Ask her about the canal!" prompted Helen.

Canal—there was none, really; there was a little stream that the boys went swimming in—her boy could show them, it was up the road a little way, if—

Peter said it would be all right, they could find it.

—if he were here; but he had gone off to Barcelona, to the battle. Yes, said the woman, he was a good boy, it would be as it came.

Had they seen the five Fascists? Well, they ought to; and they would find the stream, up a little farther.

"I suppose we'll be talking about this for the rest of our lives," Peter said, on the road. "I keep thinking: we mustn't dramatize it." But as he spoke, the village rose up about him, the chalk-bright houses, the black sashes of the men, the guns, the challenge of trucks pounding the blank road. He looked at the girls, and laughed.

Answering his mood, Helen said, "But they dramatize it, don't they? It dramatizes itself. They know, sooner than we, that it is the historic moment."

"When I can think about it, at times like this," he said, pulling at the long grass of the lane, "I resent the train. It's such a damned device."

"I hate, too, the way we classify everyone by country. Even the tags everyone's acquired, all place-tags: the lady from South America, the lost Frenchman, Peapack, the Swiss—it's very insidious."

"I don't know," she answered. "The line hasn't fallen that way. When there's any barrier, it's come between the ones who are for the town and the ones who feel this is spoiling their trip."

"Don't you feel at home?" she asked.

"That's not witty," he scolded. "And I don't. I don't ever. What are we here? Wasted—"

His hand pushed air.

CHAPTER SIX

Look on the world, my comrades! It's aflame!
fire-tongues in the sky, new sword-blades at its core,
cutting the dry dead harvest that it bore
a generation gone, in all the lands of earth.
                                    —Edwin Rolfe

There must be a way to reach action.

Helen turned back to the Lawrence book. Perhaps, after trying for it so hard, she could find what she was looking for here. This might carry her deeper in. Lawrence could do that, striking for the heart, penetrating, on a dark journey.

The flies came in as she read, settling on everything, cucumber cream, remnants of food, the gray cushions.

The book, to produce an equation,
To bring an answer.

"But won't they act?" cried Josephine.

"Act?" said Aaron. "How, act?"

"Why, defy the government, and take things in their own hands,"
said Josephine.

"They might, some time," said Aaron, rather indifferent.

"I wish they would!" cried Josephine. "My, wouldn't I love it if
they'd make a bloody revolution."

They were all looking now at her. Her black brows were twitching, in her black and silver dress she looked like a symbol of young
disaster."*

*From *Aaron's Rod* (1922) by D. H. Lawrence.

But on the window little yellow trees
and the hand claps of rifle bullets and
behind the book scenes her head produced
scenes of faces ranged to mock at all of
this and the mouths that mocked were those
that cried most loudly War: streets of
stone, streets of stone, dark rooms, no
rest, no sleep, mockery

She looked farther down the page.

"But, Josephine," said Robert, "don't you think we've had enough of that sort of thing in the war? Don't you think it all works out rather stupid and unsatisfying?"

"Ah, but a civil war would be different. I've no interest in fighting Germans. But a civil war would be different."

"That's a fact, it would," said Jim.

"Only rather worse," said Robert.

"No, I don't agree," cried Josephine. "You'd feel you were doing something, in a civil war."

"Pulling the house down," said Lilly.

"Yes," she cried. "Don't you hate it, the house we live in—London—England—America! Don't you hate them?"

"I don't like them. But I can't get much fire in my hatred. They pall on me rather," said Lilly.

"Ay!" said Aaron, suddenly stirring in his chair.

Lilly and he glanced at one another with a look of recognition.

*"Still," said Tanny, "There's got to be a clearance some day or other."**

A wagon marked LLET going down a
small pale street followed by a
machine gun mounted in a produce truck,
a shot spat against a stucco wall,

*From *Aaron's Rod* (1922) by D. H. Lawrence.

— 94 —

a handful of almonds whose shells
are rubbed off between the fingers
five slit throats and a red-bound wound
a red-bound book on a stopped train
with the track All Clear Ahead

She clapped the book shut.

The Hungarian printer appeared at the door.

"*Olimpiada* credentials?"

Helen nodded.

"Get ready. The truck is coming for us. How many pieces have you?"

"One," said Helen.

"Good," answered the Hungarian. "Then you're ready now."

He looked around the compartment. "I'll be back for you in five minutes, when the team is together."

Helen took down her hat and coat.

A few compartments down, she could hear the chorus. "O lord here's the gramophone under the bags." Laughter came through.

Peapack was standing on the threshold.

"What's up?" she was asking. "What's all the excitement?"

"The truck is coming for the Olympiad people," Helen said.

"And you—you're getting out of here!" Peapack cried. "Oh, Helen, get me out—you've got to get me out!" She was weeping. Her face was swollen dark.

She hauled down the first of the rawhide bags. There was nothing to do.

Helen raised all the questions: the lack of credentials, the necessity of sticking to a story—of saying they were traveling together—the movie camera, the fourteen hats. Peapack wept.

At the height of the confusion, when the compartment was fully littered with hats and the five valises, Toni appeared, smiling beautifully.

TONI LABORED BESIDE her with the suitcase. As they passed the last first-class car, the lady from South America descended, and walked along with Helen. Toni pushed ahead, bent over the thick black bag.

It was impossible that the lady's helmet of gray-black hair should lie so smoothly.

"That was a curious thing you did this morning," she said, with the peculiar provocative motion of her lips.

Helen was puzzled.

"About the letter, I mean," the lady continued.

"Oh, you should have said yes," Helen answered. "You might, still, you know." They both looked at Toni, halfway to the school-house with the bag.

"It's very curious," said the lady, in her accented, violin way. "Things you never dream people will do . . . If only there were a bathroom in town . . ."

"The school's not as bad as the station," said Helen. "—And I don't believe there's going to be a lorry for the team," said the lady. "But if there is, and you reach Barcelona, will you take a message?"

Helen produced a postcard. The lady from South America scribed across it—"This is brought by a companion in misery who has proved very kind. Try to get word through to Geneva that everything is all right. Will be in Barcelona as soon as possible." She addressed it to herself. "You'll find the place," she said. "It's in the residential section—anyone can tell you. There—that's my name: Mme. de Trébilhan—Mrs. Trevelyan, I suppose, in English," she added, smiling. The black eyes dilated, the rims were very dark.

Helen made her way through the crowd in front of the school-house door. The whole train was standing there, looking at the two teams who were ready to go. Slicked down as shiny as possible, the athletes were revived and optimistic. The others were getting tired, breaking a bit. Some looked in envy at the naive Hungarians, who were repeating their detailed instructions. Toni stood over her suitcase, with Peter. She went over to thank him.

"Hello!" said Peter. "Going out?"

She was embarrassed. "They said to come," she explained, diffidently. "It's the letter I have to Tudor, the Olympiad man."

"Stop confessing," said Peter. "Is Peapack going?"

"She says she's coming. *And* the five valises."

"To Barcelona! But how? Did she dump herself on you?"

"She's to be traveling with me, she says."

There was Peapack and the Catalan, heavy-laden. The rawhide had an expensive look.

"If you said something friendly but critical—" Helen suggested to Peter.

He grinned, and crossed the lot to Peapack.

Toni turned around. His lips were almost purple. "Dirty-face!" he said, mockingly.

"Where?" she asked, humbled, like a child, but gratified to be commanded to do anything simple, like washing.

He showed her the smudged place, and she started upstairs. My pleasures! she thought. There was running water.

Reaching the door as she came down, she heard one of the sickly bitches explaining to the Englishman with the tall wife: "—But only four million are organized in America, out of twenty-four million workingmen eligible for such organization, and, no matter how conservative English trade unions are, they've covered more ground than . . ."

Peter and Peapack were standing together. She was being convinced. Helen jerked her head back at the school teacher, "Those are the figures I should know."

"Trade union figures?" asked Peter.

Peapack put up her muddled face. It shifted, like stirred pudding. "I've been thinking," she announced. "It's an awful responsibility, and the roads are probably not as safe, even, as the train. And, then, I'd have to lie."

"Whatever you say," retorted Helen, and walked away. She was sick of the whole thing. The hills were losing light gradually, standing out in detail as the sun left them. The jagged hill at the back showed ruddy. The roads were empty, shaved clean against the woods.

"Am I a little cleaner now?" Helen asked Toni. Her cheeks were shining from the cold water.

"Oh, you're insulted," he said, miserable. "You're insulted!"

She laughed. It had been lovely to be ordered to wash. The water had been very clean and cold, almost as cold as the well-water. Toni saw that she wasn't insulted. And smiled.

The lady from South America watched the starved dog cross the lot. "Any news of the lorry?" She made it a statement; it was evident that she was convinced there never would be news. "Oh," she said quickly, bitterly, "nobody knows who holds the roads, or if they're torn up, or if the army's on them. How can anyone promise a lorry?"

IN THE MIDDLE of the lot, Olive was calling Helen. She went over slowly, swinging the large hat. "Anyone who can wear sneakers and a big black hat—" Olive smiled fancifully.

"I like the hat. I like the shoes. It's very simple," Helen laughed. "Any simple pleasures we find, just now—" she broke off.

"I know one," said Olive. "Come and see the church. The Hungarians say there's a rope which makes a ghetto of the Fascist section, and they're fed by the town across the rope."

"Just a second." Three young boys were standing at the edge of the lot, their heavy guns in their hands. They were comparing bullets. Their sleeves hung in rags, one had a rag about his head. When the two women came close, they looked up, grinned.

"Big," said one of them, holding out a bullet. Helen put out her hand, involuntarily. "*Por favor*," she said.

He placed the silvery end of the bullet on her palm. It rolled over into the deepest place and lay heavy. She looked down at it as if it had a word written on it. "That's the business end," said Olive.

The boys caught the remark, and nudged the spokesman. He held out the shell. "There!" he said. The shorter boy raised his finger, "one moment," and shook something into his hand. It was a little mound of iron-black, square bits, like children's mosaic, or beauty patches.

"That's gunpowder!" exclaimed Olive. "Powder," she repeated to the boys.

"Sí, pow-der," they answered, delighted. The short one went through the motions—he poured the powder into an imaginary gun, took aim, clicked his tongue. "Pam-pam!" he said.

"Yes," said Helen.

A quick double shot came down from the wooded hill nearest the school, like a pain in the head. The boys gripped their guns and set off, running up the dirt road. Two men caught up with them from their doorways, the guns jolting with their arms. The five hurried to the foot, stopped to talk a moment, and then spread in a fan up the hill, disappearing into the grove one by one.

Olive and Helen recrossed the lot. The hand with the bullet tightened, setting to the weight and the consciousness. Another shot flew from the wood. They hurried. Peter came to meet them. "There's a story that officers are in the wood," he said, a little breathless.

The whole train was standing in front of the schoolhouse, looking up the hill, perfectly quiet. One of the Rodman Truesdale Young Ladies pulled the professor's elbow. "Perhaps we ought to go into the school," she said in a flat little voice. He did not answer. Nobody said anything. Nobody went inside. There was no choice but to stand there. To look at the hill. The rounded, small trees went up it in rows to a line near the top, where they ended abruptly, and the soft hill rose from there. There was nothing to be seen. A few women came to their doors, drying their hands, staring up the hill. Slowly the sunset began to wash color above it, a russet finish, like sunset-glaze on a wide river, leaking over the sky.

Peapack stumbled noisily down the stairs, babbling. She was very nervous. She giggled. "There's a Rodman Truesdale upstairs, sitting on her suitcase in the backroom," she shook with little screams of laughter. "And you know what she said to me?" Peapack continued, failing, stumbling, the words falling over each other, trying an Oxford drawl, "in her English accent, she says, moaning, 'I'm only eighteen'—she was almost crying," and Peapack shrieked, 'I'm only eighteen, and I don't suppose I'll ever live to see my nineteenth birthday.'" Peapack saw that everyone was watching the hill, and grew quiet, suppressing little gusty shrieks of laughter.

The Englishman with the tall wife came over to Helen.

"If you get in," he asked, smiling with his eyes in his blocked-out, austere face, "will you send a cable for me? To my wife's mother," he said. He put his hand in his pocket for a pencil, took the postcard she offered and wrote a few words on it. His pencil moved slowly over the card, and jumped once at the end, as if his hand had been struck. A loud shot banged down, echoing, slapping among the hills. The Englishman turned with the rest. His forehead wrinkled as he stared against the bright sky.

Near the top of the hill, at the line of demarcation where the trees ended, a little man was running, lightly, with little darting motions, shuttling behind the last row of trees. He was short and dark, and wore a wide black sash around his waist. A shadow, shadow of cloud, moved over the hill, covered him for a minute, and then he was visible again, running, scampering between two lanes of trees. The hill stood clear, in maplike clarity, very impersonal. Everything was quiet still. There was no way of telling who the man was.

A hundred people stood watching.

Then slowly, he could be seen moving out, holding his gun ready, looking down the slope, looking around with a reconnoitering look. He glanced once at the summit, and suddenly turned and hurried over the open shoulder of the hill. It was not until he was well over that the firing started again.

Nobody had spoken.

One of the Swiss cleared his throat. "They're hunting down Fascists," he said hoarsely.

The Englishman, still holding the postcard, turned to Helen. His face had changed, his eyes were full of excitement. His controlled, assertive face flickered with the excitement. "I think he was a Fascist," he said, with joy. "I think he was—and I hope to God he got away. I hope he's legging it over those hills for all he's worth this minute." He was speaking rapidly, in a transport. He stopped for breath, and noticed her face. "Oh, no need to look like that," affecting lightness, "I'm on the right side, I know the working class is on its way into its own. But the *bravery*, the sheer bravery of these men—cornered, broken up, fighting it out in these hills. And do you know they cut them down without a trial—they give common criminals a trial, but these fellows, they stop them in the roads and shoot them down without a word. That *brave* man, this morning, without a chance—that captain, do you know what he said? He said 'You can do what you like with me,' and they shot him down and slit his throat and exposed him to the village with his four men, I saw them in the cellar. He may have been a vicious fool, that captain"—Helen saw Peter turn as the Englishman's voice rose— "but he was *brave*. And I hope they run like hell."

"The Fascist captain? The son of a bitch," said Peter, bitting the words.

The Englishman sneered through his nostrils. He was carried away. His face flickered. He stared at Peter.

"You'd get a trial if you committed a crime!"

From behind the hill where the man had disappeared, a sound spread, filling the sky, drowning out the quarrel for a moment. The crowd had already broken up, but people straggling across the lot stopped and looked back. For a moment they thought it was a new, protracted bombardment, the sound streaked along like a line of sonorous bombs. It was not until the plane appeared over the ridge that the fear changed and took shape. The high sweet sound of the engine ran through them. They might have been ready to be executed, strapped in the chair, the current might be shooting through them, the constraint of terror stabbed them so. Helen looked curiously up at the plane's clean progress over the even sky. Her mind seized on it like an abstract idea, in its successful motion. It approached; it was almost directly over them. And she thought, how calm I am, she could feel the trickle at the corner of her mouth. She licked her lips to cover the fear. When she moved her tongue, the fear did go; and it seemed to have left all of them in that instant. They all went on talking, the Englishman and Peter caught up in their quarrel, the teams discussing possibilities of a truck. They hardly looked up as the anonymous plane passed harmless overhead, marking the ground swiftly with its shadow, and turned away down the sky.

HELEN SWUNG AROUND. Olive was sitting on the low stone wall, looking at her and at Peter quarreling. She was saying, "Come now, and look at the church." Helen moved over to where she was.

"I can't stand just waiting here." She pulled at her lower lip with her teeth. "What's Peter fighting about?" she asked.

"The Englishman's sporting instinct," answered Helen. She grinned. "He thinks the captain should have had trial by jury."

"These English and their 'being sporting,'" said Olive, with her hand flung out. "At home they're being sporting to Hitler, in the Mediterranean with Mussolini, and here they want to play games with the generals. Look at them run and line up with the Fascists. That's what I'm afraid of." They walked on a bit. As they came to the railroad tracks, they saw that the train had been moved up the track about a hundred feet. The mayor must have let the town move it. There would be a better smell that night.

"It's a fine town," said Helen.

Olive did not answer. She was watching four people, loaded with bags, who were coming down the street to the tracks. They were the professor, Peapack, and the Drews. They hallooed. "Gunny-sacks!" called Drew across the street. "Very cheap! Admirably clean! Almost soft!" He took a breath. "So cheap! Six pesetas! And if a peseta equals sixpence—" he ran out of breath again. "To sleep on!" he yelled, as they crossed the tracks.

"Drew is lovely," said Helen. "So cheap, so clean—he's almost sold me one." She laughed.

"I suppose that really *was* a government plane," said Olive softly. There was somebody calling them from behind. Olive turned. "Oh, God," she said, "one of the bitches!"

"Wait for me," called the one in the red blouse, running prominently up the street, her breasts shaking. "Are you going to see the church?—I've been wanting to see the church all day."

"I didn't like to go alone," she gasped, as she drew up to them.

They turned into the main street, where shadows were beginning to fill the doorways. The loud radio could be heard, turned on full blast in the café. A car, loaded with guns, initialed C.N.T., F.A.I., came down the street, its horn shouting, three times, pause, three times. The air was darkening.

The shell of the church stood, new yellow-brick walls darkened by smoke. A wooden beam, fallen just inside the portal, was not yet completely burned. A strand of smoke turned in the air, rising, issuing up, pointing at the inscription, cut in stone, "The house of

God is the gate of heaven." Rags of red and gold cloth littered the steps. Within the arch of the portal was the arch of the stained-glass window over the shattered altar. The glass had been blown out by the explosion, and the blue sky was, through it, grotesque and untouched.

"I don't suppose there are many whole churches in Spain tonight," said the bitch fatuously.

"See the rope!" Olive's hand was tight. Helen turned. There it lay, broken across the street, looking more like a guard against a fire area than like a boundary. Did they feed Fascists across a taut rope?

The sullen air touched them. The dusk became feverish and volcanic. A few houses down, some boys with guns were hammering against a door.

"Let's get going," proposed the bitch.

They started down the main street. As they passed the door hurriedly, they could see the scars of the gun-butts that were ramming against it. It was a heavy brown door, carved. The building might be a parochial school, or the storehouse of an absentee landlord.

The bitch was looking the boys up and down. "They stare at you in such a funny way," she observed, lasciviously.

Olive lost her temper, made a sound of dismissal, and walked faster. "Well," said the bitch, "maybe you haven't found it to be true; but—"

Two boys stood over a large doll. One of them looked at it angrily. The street was quiet except for the hammering of the gun-butts on the door. The boy took the doll by the legs and threw it savagely on the sidewalk. Its head cracked open with a loud report. One of the legs tore loose. The other boy picked it up, laughed, and raised it over his head, whirling it. Behind them, the hammering was faster, and a sound of splintering.

They broke into a half-run, and stopped at the turning. Helen felt foolish. "Don't . . . let's," she said, "if we go fast, that's enough." They hurried down to the tracks. Two soldiers were at the crossing. The uniforms were back, the attractive olive strapped with yellow. But the army! The soldier smiled as they approached. "*Guardia Civil*," one called in reassurance. He was fair, and his teeth were lightning-white against his skin.

"Handsome," muttered the bitch.

A shot was fired.

A young girl, walking along the ties, crossed herself.

Evening was closing down perilously fast, now.

It was only the second night. As if she had watched the passage of seasons, with the deepening, Helen thought, I know what is going to come now. I know a little of what is going to come.

The color deepened, melodiously, melodiously.

. . . SHALL BE THE HUMAN RACE.*

A thin tan dog ran across the tracks.

There, the wagon marked LLET was pouring, while women stood with pails.

Helen began then to be very thirsty. "I want some of that milk," she said.

"You have nothing to put it in," said the bitch.

Do I need something? thought Helen.

"It's not pasteurized," Olive observed.

"Wait, we'll have dinner."

"Here comes Peter."

Peter walked over, through the dim light, bringing the other bitch with him. It was growing dark.

"One minute," said Olive, "I've asked the German to come along with us." She stood and waved, isolated.

How thirsty I am! thought Helen.

He was walking across the lot, his brown head carried a little forward, his hips perfectly timed, perfectly at ease in a controlled walk. It was almost night.

*A phrase from the "Internationale."

— 105 —

"Who is he?" asked the bitch.

"He's a German," said Olive. "I like him. Isn't he nice, Helen?"

"He walks well," answered Helen. It was quite dark. They all started up the street again, walking three by three, the German going ahead with the two bitches.

OLIVE SAID TO Peter, "The town's cracking. It's very jumpy now, like this," teetering her hand from the wrist. "They're breaking into some places on the main street."

"Hemingway doesn't know beans about Spain," said Peter.

"Oh, Hemingway was all right," answered Olive. "Who won, you or England?"

The German stopped, waiting to look at the three of them. He had deep brown eyes, or black. It was night now. He had a dark face, darker than his hair. As he passed under a light, it was plain. Sunburned dark. It had a carved rigor, the snub nose and wide peasant mouth, with keen lines on either side. Like carved wood, Helen thought, a Brueghel face, with active living, philosophic eyes.

"Rule, Britannia," Peter was mocking. "Britannia keeps the rules."

Olive and Peter went over the question of English sportsmanship, their mechanical answers echoing in the dark.

Helen felt that, at any other time, the quarrel would have been real, the issues plain. But that set of habits fell behind. Here there were only the weird scenes: the church, the man on the hill, the plane, following so swiftly and inconsequently that there was no way to stop and set them in place, no way for the speeding mind to arrange them.

Nightfall. That was real. Black and physical upon her, the only thing known.

Not that it was a matter of *real* scenes, *real* feelings, as it was with Olive, who felt most strongly and looked most moved during fear. It was all absorbed, immediately, too soon, in the way that the danger from the unknown plane had been accepted by the time the plane had reached its position, able to let fall its bombs. The gun-cars could pass now: one had passed behind them as they criticized the fruit that morning, it had passed tooting, and they had not turned to face the guns. It was perhaps that there was no imaginable future. They had by common consent stopped saying, "*If* we reach . . ." and everyone said, "When we reach Barcelona," but without conviction, without belief in their own imagining.

The street was dark and furiously real, Helen thought: the night was, all unidentified objects were real: the pregnant woman on the platform, the boy in the *camión*, nameless emotions, Peter's wish for a child, her own turning toward the lady, the anonymous German walking so powerfully before her. And the fear with which they were already familiar, the conventions which they had already adopted, so that they were unbearably aroused by mention of the captain's bravery. Criminal bravery, Peter was saying, and Helen thought how weak she was to let everyone talk on so, and to enjoy hearing them, to think always that if she had the poetic genius that produced the clue, she could find them, hear the real sound that could be spoken only at a moment like this, during such a night.

There were hidden causes.

The armies covered the world.

Let them win, let them only win, and we can bother about this later, she thought, helplessly.

All the moments flew, colored and clear. Now is my life, she thought. It comes to this night.

Only wait.

THEY WERE IN back of the main street, on an easy incline. The bitches had stopped, uncertainly. Peter called out to them, "There's a little tunnel, to the left," and hurried ahead. The black street grew tense and alert. When they entered the tunnel, there was a shiver behind them in the roadway and the women seized their children's shoulders, snatching them into the houses. There was a tremor of heavy wheels approaching.

The restaurant faced the little tunnel. They opened the thick door; a burst of heat met them like a host, and drew them inside.

"Shut the door, and come in!" said the woman, not waiting, pushing the door too. "The machine guns are coming."

"Oh, Peter," said Olive, "let's not stay. Let's go back to the train." The room was almost empty. Under the radio, a man leaned back, his mouth half-shut, pouring water into it from an earthen pitcher held at arm's length. The bar was shiny with empty glasses, lemonade bottles, spilled wine. In the next room, at a large table, sat the German family with two of the Spaniards from the train. The father, with his head down, concentrated on a loaf of bread crooked in his elbow, distributing slices, sawing and pulling. At a smaller table, three soldiers balanced on their chairs, sitting back on two legs. Their braided collars stood open, and the strong veins of their necks were distended purple as they drank and laughed. Their guns were in a thin pyramid beside the table.

"You don't want to go," Peter answered in a hard voice. "You don't want to be out on the street for the next few minutes."

The woman said she was crowded, she could not serve them for a few minutes, would they care to rest inside or in the back room?

"I'm very thirsty," said Helen, in a lost voice, ordering lemonade. The German looked narrowly at her.

SHE AND OLIVE stood at the bar and drank, while the others went to say hello to the train people. Olive spoke to the waitress. Yes, the machine guns would probably come down the street. Fascists were hiding in that street. No, there was no danger here, they would keep the restaurant open, there were three soldiers in the front room, there might be a little shooting, but how could there be any danger?

"There's a garden in back," said Olive suddenly. "I'd like to be in the garden." She looked at Helen. Her face, with its wide dark cheeks and immense eyes, was at its most beautiful in such a smoky light.

"I like you," said Helen. She finished the warm pale soda. "I like your attitude toward machine guns."

"Yes," answered Olive, moving away with her, "It's a nice attitude, isn't it?"

One of the soldiers leaned forward listening.

"I won't have this danger. It subjects us so to fear, when we are not allowed to have a part in it. I care, it makes all the difference to me. Peter would give his life for it, I think; and we're foreign nationals, and we were that in France." Olive spoke in an extremity of grief. "Here we are, and the machine guns are coming, and we have nothing to do with it, nothing at all."

Europe, cracking wide apart, the split going down to the families, the trains, and to be engulfed, not cast up, not assimilated in the struggle!

Only wait.

Only we cannot be lost in the waitings, while the guns bear down! While Europe is the dark Leviathan, raging!

THE LITTLE GARDEN, where the others sat, was walled and leafy, under leaves like shallow water. A cicada made a tiny shrill sound. There was an arbor in the center of the garden, and cards were scattered on an iron table. The German came over to Helen, as she picked them up one by one. The exotic yellow stamping was a curiosity. He recited their names.

"Here, the three of gold, and the five of gold, and the queen of cups, and the prince of gold, that's for good luck . . ."

A line from *The Waste Land* flashed across her.

"No, I'm not sure," he was saying. "And the games are different, also, bezique . . . Do you know any of the games?"

Helen fumbled in German. Oh no, she thought, trying, the others can speak to him. They changed to French; both were confined, but it would do.

One of the women jumped up. "I thought it was a soldier," she said as she started. It was the man with the square gray beard, who with the sallow friend was looking at two blue birds in a cage. He greeted them in his polite French; he believed that the woman was prepared to serve them instantly. They filed into the back room, looking through the doors vacantly for seats. There was no room in the front. Peter and Olive sat at one end of the long, white-covered table, and the others crowded near them at the corner, close. The German looked at Helen.

"Isn't there any way we can shut the door?" asked one of the bitches in open nervousness. The garden door was nothing but a square cut in the house-wall.

Peter looked down the long, half-empty table, receding in white perspective. "It's a table for the Last Supper."

Helen turned to the vacant place beside her, stretching her arm along the cloth. "Where is Jesus?"

There was a splatter of gunfire in the street that wiped out the words.

"Is it a woodpecker?" Olive began, facetiously.

"Did you hear that?" Peter was still listening, sitting attentive. Wine and vegetables were on the table, and soup. "I heard a shot, and a child crying."

Nobody answered.

"I heard a shot, and a child crying!"

Everyone went on eating. There were vegetables.

"It's all right for you," said one of the bitches, viciously. "You're at the end of the table, not right in front of the open door, where I'm sitting!"

They looked at her with a morbid spectator's stare, as if they were an audience who had watched a tight-rope artist's fall to the stage before their eyes and could not stop staring at the accident.

CHAPTER SEVEN

Accept a lone eye riveted to your plane,
Bent axle of devotion along companion ways
That beat, continuous, to hourless days—
One inconspicuous, glowing orb of praise.
                                        —Hart Crane

The German was pouring wine with a flat elastic gesture of the wrist that was fascinating them all; he was master of the group, and poured the wine into all the glasses, now pulled close together before them, huddled at one end of the long white table. None of the Americans dared speak much after the catastrophe. The bitch refused to recognize her fall; but they saw that she was shaken with fright and the humiliation which she was choking back.

The shooting had somehow stopped; and the radio was playing Spanish dance-music that, with the strong dark wine, swayed slowly along their veins.

And, now that the room was warmer than ever, the sensual night walked through the open doors, from the garden, the room with the radio, the wine, the deliberate talk of the German.

He was describing Barcelona, its waterfront, its green wide promenades, workers' centers, a gay and tortured history of brilliance and wars for freedom. He outlined the city for them with the impersonal accurate strokes of a stranger who has listened to stories and studied maps, who has wished all during his youth to visit a place, and summed up accurately, in a passionate memory, the details of a city to which he has never been, a life he has never known.

He spoke almost directly to Helen, refilling her glass.

She wished she could answer him. She watched the rhythmic muscles as he poured, and glanced at Peter's face, where a soft twitch near the mouth betrayed his anxiety and effort. The German was controlled, he went on speaking, centering the attention of the entire group, making them see the immense city on its coast, although his head too was stiffened up and fixed to listen for any street-sound.

They were rubbing the paper-thin almond skins, laughing at his story of the Catalan sailor, when the radio snapped off the music. He pushed his chair back. They could hear the chairs inside all pushed back. "Come and hear the announcement," he said to Helen.

She was suddenly satisfied. It was enough that she understood what he said, could respond to the smallest inflection of his voice. With a roll of relief, she was freed from her need to speak, which had weighed on her since she crossed the frontier.

THE RADIO WAS speaking of the frontier, and of towns between it and Barcelona. All the restaurant listened. With the breakdown of the Fascist forces, the huge voice warned, the roads, the railway line, the hills, would be dangerous; isolated rebels, attempting to escape to France, would swarm along the short way to the border. A workers' militia had been organized at Barcelona; but, in the outlying towns, citizens were needed now to guard the roads, to watch among the hills. A government plane was searching for groups of Fascists. Many had been intercepted. But the remainder were fighting as individuals, desperate, defeated, single . . . In an hour another bulletin would be issued. The voice stopped abruptly, and the phonograph resumed, distant and receding in the heat . . .

Two of the men who had been eating were leaving with the

three soldiers, walking noiselessly, their sandals passing with animal silence.

The bitches looked after them. The green-faced woman exclaimed: "And they're the ones who guard us!"

"What chance have we?" the sickly bitch put in. "Directly on the railway line—"

Peter cut them short. "Come on back to the train," he said roughly.

Helen remembered, with a shock of terror. "I've left my suitcase at the school!"

"You're not going to sleep there, are you?" Olive asked her.

"No," she said. "The station—"

"Come along then," the German said, at her side. "We'll get it and take it to the train."

He looked after the Catalans, at the heavy door.

THE STREET WAS not hot, as she had imagined from the heat of the restaurant, but frozen with wind running down the mountain spur, and with the million lights of white gigantic stars.

They separated after going silently through the tunnel. The street remained empty, the four Americans turned off toward the station, and the German and Helen went on down to the crossing. The cold night shivered against her, rousing the senses, storm and exhilaration after the soaking heat.

The German took her arm. He was speaking of the men who had left the restaurant immediately and with their blazing look of belief, when the radio-call came. "The whole legend is on their faces," he was saying, "our whole belief, freedom, this war . . ."

A bulb turned down over the schoolhouse door lit the heavy body of the pock-marked Swiss, sitting straight on a stool. He stared out across the lot, into the blackness from which they emerged.

He nodded to Helen, and moved his hand on the air. "Fine night. Streams down, like water."

"Has the truck come?" she asked.

Nothing had come. But the Hungarians were waiting inside. They thought they would wait a little longer. Everyone else was going to sleep, envying the gunnysacks of the English.

The German went indoors to look for her suitcase. They had all been taken in to be lined up in the hall or used as beds.

The guard looked up at Helen from his low stool.

"Will you stay here all night?" she asked tenderly.

"It's the least—" he shrugged. "During this bravery, the magnificence around here—" he could not finish. The wind swept across his thick lonely body, passed the door, the bulb wavering, and gave way, returning the night to its sensual pleasure, its warmth, the blackness, the rocking secret valley.

And now the German was coming out in the bright, half circle, holding the heavy suitcase. He swung it easily and high, to his shoulder, setting his head on one side as prop.

"*Compañero*," he said naturally to the Swiss, and took Helen's arm again.

"Good night," she added over her shoulder. "Good watch."

She walked with long safe strides beside him. He was not at all impeded by the load. The suitcase leaned against his strong thick neck, bending his head with its peasant broadness to one side; he was very tall, in the easy sweater and corduroys, looking high in shadow. The strained muscle in his neck stood out to the weight; it was fine and taut, symptom of his body. His walk was as balanced as before, he was master. The identification struck her. He was an athlete; a member of the Games! She did not have to ask. They hardly spoke on the way to the train.

Up the street a cock crowed, a syllabled call. The night was changed by it, split like a black unearthly melon, opened, revealed, and utterly dark.

SHE BEGAN TO know what was to happen. The knowledge turned her thought, irrationally, to her country. America, she thought, far, far, vivid, asleep. This Europe, boundaried, immense in meaning now, throwing its signals brilliantly ahead.

She was pulled back by the sight of his face, brown and intent, Asiatic because of the set, half-smiling mouth. He took over leadership, his strength was open in his body and his walk; the curious wide peasant's face with the philosophic eyes pulled all attention to itself and to his meaning.

They climbed up the steps of the nearest car. His following face caught the filtered trainlight on its austere planes, the rough leather of the suitcase bulked on his shoulder. They started down the train, silent and moving slowly, stopping at each door, in search of a compartment.

The train was asleep. Through cracks at the drawn shades they could see the long bodies of sleepers, on all benches, at length tonight because now there was more room. Half of the train was at the schoolhouse; but the first-class compartments were all filled.

They reached Peter and Olive, who were almost asleep, and yawned luxuriously. "Come in—sleep here," invited Peter.

Helen spoke levelly, as if she had known she would say this. "I'm going to look for a compartment, you should have the room—But will you keep the suitcase for me?

The German slung the bag up the shelf.

Helen went on. "When I find a place, I'll call for it."

"I'll come," said the German.

They said their good nights, and were in the corridor, in the night simplicity. The German looked quietly at Helen.

"Good," he remarked.

The compartment next to Peter's was empty. From the lamp over the town's name, blocked on the platform-sign, a ray fell over the upholstery.

A wind carrying perfume and cold ran down the Pyrenees.

His face was cut wood. He stood aside to let her go into the compartment, and came after, sliding the door to.

She had walked across to the window, and half turned as he shut the door. Her hand came up toward the light-switch.

He met it, raised in air, and his other hand covered her breast. He swung her to him in a quick decisive motion, pivoting her through the small, black room to reach his mouth.

THE TORRENT, MOUNTAINS demand, steaming night, marvel-black, daring to sweep away, daring to answer, to announce, to find. A radio promulgation, night-manifesto. And the fierce country, blazed across the brain: urgent and cypressed, the granitic cliff, the shock of parent sea. The mouth, strong summer on the mouth.

Gap. The door of the compartment, opening.

Frenchman. Polite. Interruption. Pardons.

They sat for a moment, looking out the window, at the blank distinct brick wall. The station, and the militant tread down the platform. Soldiers. The attack!

The radio spoke one loud tremendous sentence from the Workers' Café. The heavy iron-soled tread climbed the car. Slid doors back, steel on steel. Reached them.

The jaundice light oiled the shine on patent leather hat, olive shoulders, bright yellow straps.

"*Guardia Civil*. Good night. All quiet."

And night restored, black and imperative night.

THE RADIO SPOKE again, rising through seas of night.

But he was delicate wood, brown wood, white wood, struck by the pale night-light, behind shades, from the station, not speaking, only subtle, delicate, only strong.

She looked up as the radio stopped, turned her head up and

backward, seeing at the end of the arc the blond small blossoms on the flowering trees. And coming back, his clear power, the imminent grace, discoverer, victor.

Under her cheek, she knew his heartbeat, the grave pulse and delicate after-tremble. She meant to lift her head to speak to him; but, a little ruefully, thought how clumsy her French must be, how she could not bear to tell him in an over-simplified jargon that he was more reassurance to her than anything had ever been. She lay relaxed, remembering city, hypnotic conversations, the strained and wordy love. Beneath her face, beneath her flung arm, was his fine peace, soft and vivid.

Very gradually, she became conscious of place. There was a thin light in the compartment, raising in the night the lace design of the antimacassars, and the firm muscles of his ribs and belly. She lifted her face to the brilliance pouring through the sky; a thread of cloud reached under the heavy moon. His forehead caught the light on its surface, and his cheeks and wide lips, like a new country. She hung over his face, learning it; and the thought of the plane flew over her, hanging on the hills in the turning afternoon. All the fierceness and implication of mastery in the thought of the plane had passed out; she shifted on the narrow seat, returning down, seeking to find her former position. Then she saw that his eyes were open.

He lay there still, breathing in the same rhythm. His hand went gently and luxuriously across her long back. "Ah," he said softly, as his breath went out, "you are so much life!" He smiled, but his eyes held, gripped on her face. The smile quieted; she could feel his recurring motion; he put his head far back, the long neck-muscles stretched.

"The pure life!" he said, and all his energy lay concentrated behind the words.

With a simple liquid motion, he turned his whole body, like a white rush of waterfall.

AND EUROPE AND America swung, swung, an active sea, marked with convulsive waves, as if supernatural horses stamped through the night; a scarred country, that lies waiting for the armies to meet again. The upraised fists, the broadcasting station, shake in the air, complaining, bragging, threatening, raised from the surface like final signs of those who drown and, instead of the grasping frantic gesture, raise their fists in the last assertion.

Here is your sea, sailor! Floundering with life, prophetic with rising land, peopled.

We are all swallowed in it.

Only, when we are cast up, it must be on firm land, we must not have lost ourselves. Because then we are going to be asked to rise and walk away.

HE PUT HIS hand out and it closed on her arm. After a little while she lifted his hand and kissed it. A long ripple went over him. "What is your name, my love?" he said.

"Helen," she answered.

"Hel-len," he pronounced, slowly. "Helena, Helena."

She lay in the darkness, across the narrow space. Her name sounded foreign, classical as he spoke it.

"Mine is Hans, Hans Sachs," he offered quickly, not wishing her to have to ask him.

She said nothing, letting herself go quite drunk at the sound of the two names, their soft aspirate rush going through her nerves.

Then her curiosity roused. "Where do you live?" she asked him.

There was no answer.

"Where do you live, Hans?" she repeated, her head dropping sideways toward him.

He spoke in a blurred, swollen voice. "My mother is still in Bavaria," he answered. She thought it was no answer, but she did not press him.

"I live in New York," she said. "I have been staying in London."

"Yes," he said.

From far off, the radio shouted a few sentences, and then ceased.

"What will you do in the Games?" she wanted to know, she was most anxious to know now what he did.

"I am in the races—the hundred-meter—on Thursday," he said softly.

A runner! she thought, exulting, and put her free hand on her hip. It was quiet now, the pain was all down.

"You will be there," he was saying, so softly she could only guess at the words, to himself.

She was half-asleep, with the faint breeze over her skin. Then he stood over her, tremendous in height.

"My love—my love—*me dar-ling*—" he said, attempting English.

Words from a poem chased through her head, coming into place:

Über allen . . . in allen . . .
Warte nur, balde
Ruhest du auch.

As his face enlarged close, the words rang loudly and evenly, in triumph.

She shut her eyes. She did not care that she heard a heavy boot on the train-step. Secure, she recognized the tread of the *Guardia Civil*.

CHAPTER EIGHT

The knocks were beginning again. This blind, stubborn patience could only be that of a prisoner; and such care, such concentration on the manner of knocking could not be those of a lunatic . . . And meanwhile every noise in the prison was becoming like a distant knock . . .

—André Malraux

The light struck past the shade in a steady pale vibration, milky still, early. Helen woke with Hans's hand on her: his face was whitened and clear. The outlines would never be soft, all the planes were hard, the muscles were held, the jaw had clamped tight for years; but the day, and its light in the small compartment quieted all hardness, in the same way that sleep had rested the strain.

"Morning and so soon," he said, and looked down at her mouth before he smiled. The lines drawn down were thin and distinctly Chinese over his cheeks.

She was waking slowly, in the blur of daylight and his words. She reached her arm over his heavy shoulders, around the ring of brown, edging in white where his sweater ended.

And even as he kissed her, repeating the ritual tenderness, light visibly grew, working through the still air.

"I think the truck went during the night," he told her.

"Oh no! You should have been—"

"It's better here," he said. "My love."

His hands were brightened now, she saw them in daylight for the first time, square, tan and fine-grained. He reached up to the rack for his sweater. He pulled it over his head with a white, fluent motion. He was in perfect dominance over himself, trained, disciplined, active. Day: so soon!

"I'll go over to the schoolhouse," he was saying, "I'll see about the trucks. I thought I heard only one; perhaps it was a scouting party from the town."

"I'll come after you."

HE STOOD IN the doorway as she yawned and stretched. "Stay, and sleep," he said gently. "I won't be gone long." The door unlocked with a snap.

"Red Front!" he said, smiling, and was gone.

Shutting her eyes again, she lay quiet on the gray bench. But could not sleep.

In a few minutes she got up and dressed in the sweater and dark skirt. She went down the brightening corridor, out onto the platform.

Somnambulist daybreak. The clock said 4:45 a.m., as on that other morning, when the bomb broke. But now there was no noise, the platform was empty, all the sleepers need not be shocked awake today. The train, moved up the track, did not lie along the station: the engine was almost at the crossing now, and the cars faced the row of heavy square houses on the near side. Light touched the molding and the carved birds which bracketed one, the grillwork on another. There were no shadows, light fell evenly.

Up the walk, alongside the locomotive, Peter was standing, talking to the engineer. He saw Helen come down the car steps, and waved. He walked up a way to meet her.

"This is what I meant," he said. "A morning like this. This is when I want a child."

They walked up to the engineer together. He was eating a sandwich, and a tin of coffee sat beside him at the big door of the cab. He said good morning as they passed, nodding at Helen.

Peter suggested they go to the school immediately. "The engineer says that a truck went off," he said, as they went down the white walk, touched with a faint color. "Early, in the dark. He wants to get in, too—they can stop *that* rumor—he's got a wife and four children in Barcelona, and they live near a big square." He stopped to point out the Swiss, who was sitting before the schoolhouse.

"He must have been there all night, in that position," said Helen. "He looks like the lion on the monument."

Peter told that to the Swiss as he came up to the door. The kind pockmarked face relaxed, he smiled his gentle reassurance. It was true, then; the truck had gone.

"During the night!" exclaimed Peter. "Or while we were at dinner! And what about you, Helen? We thought you'd come back."

"I found a place," said Helen.

Hans was in the hall of the school, shiny with scrubbing, a small towel over his arm. He nodded to Helen. "They did leave," he said. "But they know that there are more to go in. There's wonderful cold water upstairs." He was gay, Helen understood, it infected Peter. She ran up the long stairs in one long run. She could feel the stilled, breathing morning completely about her, a marvel of light, a morning belonging to Hans, ending one kind of reality in this renewal. He called from behind her, at the foot, looking up, the towel raised to her.

Hans flung the towel; it spread and flew up the staircase into her hand, like a dream-object in its obedience. She laughed delightedly; she was completely stilled and released. As she heard herself laugh, she remembered a winter afternoon when she had watched a golden little boy dance in the middle of the floor, spreading his arms, spinning erratically as the towel spun, and how she had sat with a desperate smile and envied him for spreading his arms. She stretched her hand to Hans, half for love, half for the proof that she could move in ease; and he laughed back at her from the stairpit.

When she came out, Hans had gone, and Peter stood where he had been, looking up at her with almost the same smile. The dreamworld continued in this washed, still morning, moving and braiding the currents, changing love for love, truth for truth. She descended to him.

"How you smile this morning!" he said to her in wonder. "They spoke about your triumphant bearing on the train at once; but you gleam, you smile beyond that, even."

She watched his sensitive shaded mouth. She was proved in happiness, hearing him, it confirmed her, it bound her to him also.

He wanted to walk, and they went out. The sun was raised now, the pink sheen on the hills was dissolving before it, and the cocks stopped crowing. Only, faintly, one sang out from a long distance, its softened cries issuing like four words of a slogan, reaching them small and distinct; and a quadruple blare of response followed from the village before quiet returned.

Nothing moved as they crossed the lot. The Swiss had gone away. Only colors moved, the high stain spread the sky, the olive hill took green and gayer silver as the mist wavered up in a fantasy.

The street they entered began with a nougat-green house. The windowsills being lake blue and polished, the vivid tiles collected light as the light grew.

Peter spoke quietly. "I like, too, the way you put your hand out to the tiles," he said. "I thought, for a moment, they would extend to meet you."

"The color is so clear," she answered. "All these pure, warm lights—it is all perfect—the marvelous brightness, in daytime, and the dark fleshy night. I've been wanting a country like this for a long time; I thought perhaps there was none."

They seemed not to move down the street. The early coolness had not dissipated, although warmth was beginning. A knocker was dark iron against a pale-green door, holding a round fruit in the curved fingers, dropped from the frilled wrist to fall against the door. They stopped to look: it was the only decoration beside the tile and flowers.

But, as the street receded around them, they were again looking at the knocker: the charming hand, falling with its fruit against the door.

"The same one!" Peter exclaimed, looking back. The knockers were identical.

They looked down the street, filled with milky light, translucent and lovely upon the housefronts, the colored walls in the impossible morning.

On all the doors fell hands. Reproduced in a dream of sameness, a row of soft iron hands, holding fruit.

THREE WOMEN WERE at the street corner, at the end of the doors. Two sat on the wide step before the corner house, and the other leaned against the door. As she spoke to them, Helen recognized her. She was the girl who had searched the train for cameras.

"How is the train?" she was saying. "We heard about the money and letter you gave the town. Nobody knew you people felt like that."

"You certainly frightened a lot of the tourists," Peter told her. They all laughed together, the girl first in astonishment and disbelief, and then in a kind of pleasure. She had a soft full face, very strong.

"Did you hear that?" she said, laughing, to the other women. "I frightened"—she said, laughing—"all those dressed-up—" laughing, "tourists." She looked solemnly at Peter and Helen. "They should have known how I felt," she said, and ducked her head forward with a little giggle.

"How's the fighting?" asked Helen.

"Oh, it's coming," the girl answered, "the hills are getting cleaner every hour. But the town! It's got to stop soon, or we'll need help with food, and we can't ask: all the towns will be having that."

"And you let us buy provisions," Helen said slowly.

"We're not like you," the girl said, kindly, "we've got our houses. How is that train to sleep in, *hein?*"

"Oh, it's all right," Peter put in quickly. They all laughed. The other two women said something gaily to the girl. She bobbed her head in the direction of the train.

"What a smell to sleep with!" she said. "These two were saying the same thing; and the first thing this town will do after the war is have one big laundering. We haven't had anything washed since the fighting started." She pulled out her handkerchief, and made a face. "Full of egg!" she said. "There was a little business of egg-throwing in the beginning."

Helen got out her handkerchief and offered it, but it wasn't much better. The girl refused. "We'll have a washing soon," she said. "This will be over very soon in Catalonia. The people know how soon."

"Many dead?" Peter asked.

"Very many," she said. "About twenty from the town yesterday. There has never been anything like this."

It was full morning now.

"Well, good luck on the train," they said.

"Good luck in the town."

"Long live the Catalonian Republic," they said.

The women moved off together down the street, into the beginning blaze. Peter and Helen stood looking after them, their swinging loose hips, their easy shoulders, the gentle back that had frightened the tourists. They turned down the corner, stopping to stare up the brightened olive-hill that was now perfectly quiet, looking over the garden walls, pointing out cactus, unfamiliar trees, clambering plants, a hutch of fat-skinned white rabbits with sensitive spinster lips and dark reflective eyes.

"Their eyes should be ruby, shouldn't they?" Helen asked.

"Not necessarily. Why?"

"I thought—" she laughed at herself. "Someone once told me, and it hurt me, too, that I acted in the country as if I were in a museum."

"No," said Peter. "You are very much at home, here. And the train is so definitely home, now. In the tired moment I imagine flying high over the Atlantic; so high that all of America and Spain could be seen in the same coasting view. Nothing could be more familiar now than the train and the people on it."

"I have that, too." She was still very rested, covered with the languid flushed dawn, but set square and alert at the same time, ready. Now it was easy, she dared think; even if she were shot, she let herself think, it was all happy for a moment; she was beginning to have a place here.

They walked down. Little trees hung over the low walls, and from one, clusters of rosettes leaned at the wall's edge. Peter reached across and broke one off. The intricate pink buds were as hard as fruit. He held it by the black stem, thrusting it through the loose weave of Helen's sweater, at the breast. She looked down at the close group of curious roses against the limp wool that had been lived in, and at Peter's hand that set it there, fine and white behind the sumptuous rose color.

Shadow washed on them as they reached the underpass, having swung back to the tracks. Over them, they saw through ties the rods and wheels of the last car, a barred Venetian blind of light.

A triple horn. Blowing.

It started them wide awake; as the full car roared down the street, full of men, equipped, thorny with guns. The car blared up the underpass, slowed, stopped opposite them in the faint shadow. A gun pointed directly at the cluster of roses. Helen could feel the channel of flesh behind it, running through her body, shrinking from the gun-bore. Through the open car she was suddenly conscious of a green-and-purple poster glued against the far wall of the underpass: a lurid advertising portrait—Jimmy Cagney, grinning in green-and-purple, both hands full, the pistols pointed at the car, pointing at her. And the men's hands on the rifles.

Peter stiffened his neck. The tunnel shut them all in together. "*Extranjeros*," he described. They nodded abruptly, and started off.

"Let's be getting back to the train," said Peter. There was only one way to go. Up the little street to the Calle Mayor, and around the station. The church was cleaned out now, everything was cleanly destroyed, the streets looked neater, the meat-shop was already open and preparing for the day.

"At six o'clock!" Helen exclaimed.

"Sure; the same thing, everywhere. Haven't you ever seen the east side butchers opening at five in the morning?"

The man was hanging sausages and waved at them.

"Does it mean the strike is over?"

"Maybe, although food wouldn't prove that. Look, I'll go and wake Olive." They could see the English, trooping up to the café for breakfast. "She may take a bit of waking, if yesterday's a sign. We'll meet you at breakfast."

"I'll find Hans," Helen said. She went past Peter's compartment, looking for the one they had found. The view from the corridor window was the landmark. She swung back the door. It had been the compartment next to Peter and Olive; her hat and coat were on the rack, flies were circulating at the mouths of someone's beer bottles, old newspapers were crushed in a corner of the gray bench. Hans was not there. It was the first time Helen saw the room plainly.

Young Mrs. Drew walked along the platform, looking up at the windows. "Hello there!" she called. "Come on to breakfast. The rest of the car is just waking."

THEY SAT DOWN in their usual places at the café, and as the late passengers came in, they took their seats confidently, like guests under a formal régime. All the women were lined on one side of the chain of tables. More subdued than before, they drank their coffee without speaking. Hans sat at the far end of the men's side; as Helen came in with Mrs. Drew, he swung his shoulders toward her seat. She was beside the lady from South America again, who for the first time was looking tired and afraid. She did not think that the train would leave.

"They say that the train may start this morning, or that a lorry will surely come by noon," she was telling the table.

"But the Hungarians have gone already," said Hans.

"Gone!" cried the lady, and the Belgian woman echoed her.

"What's that?" the man in Coffee-and-Tea asked, coming in. One of the young ladies was with him. "What's that?" he repeated officiously. He was looking very well set up, and stared at the platinum hair continually with a patronizing look of ownership.

"Something will follow it," said Hans, repeating the news for his benefit.

"*That's* what we heard during the night," said the lady.

"Were you well off in the school?" Helen asked.

"On the benches, with those gunnysacks?" the lady laughed. "The bench tied itself into wooden knots under me all night—it's a wonder I missed the lorry, I can't say I slept though!"

Peapack came in with the professor, and the rest of the chorus. They had left out any attempt at makeup, and looked oddly fresh and English. The morning around them still kept its clear, water-quiet quality, although bright light penetrated every crack, and the heat was rising.

The manager was putting the pale coffee and glasses of milk on the table. Coffee-and-Tea was asking for rolls.

"Do you notice," he said to the rest of the table, "that they're not bleeding us? I should've thought there'd be a rise in food prices immediately. After all, we're foreigners."

"And they're afraid of a shortage," said Helen. She thought of the goats and rabbits she had seen. "Even though it's not immediate."

Coffee-and-Tea went on. The young lady admired. "I mean,

there's no profiteering," he explained. "The prices are just where they always were. And they could have asked any price from us. In our predicament! Why, do you know, we're better off here—why, we're living here for *nothing* and in a hotel, I wager they'd—"

Hans cut in. "It's a criminal offense," he said, in German. "I was speaking to the mayor. No prices are allowed to move a centime during the state of war."

"What's that?" the lady translated.

Peapack looked up from her roll. "But nobody would know what they did, way out here in the country," she mumbled, and went back to her food.

"That's what I mean," said the Belgian woman in a cracked voice. "Anything can happen to us here, and nobody would know!"

The table was silent.

Peter and Olive came in, found places at the far end, ordered, and were already eating before there was anything else said. Then, all together, Hans was explaining to the Belgian woman how wrong she was, Helen and Olive speculated about the truck, the professor was outlining a plan for pooling all the money on the train that evening. The chorus had no cash left, and everyone was begging to borrow from the few who had changed their money at the border.

"Of course, let's pool!" said Peter. "On the same principle that the young ladies should stage a rehearsal, if only on that!"

"Definitely," said the man with the tall wife. "Although we'll surely move by tonight. There's a story I heard that the General Strike is over, and the Giral is now president of the Cortes."

"How does it touch the fighting?" Peter asked.

"Oh well, if that's how things stand, I've got to learn Spanish," Coffee-and-Tea said abruptly, pulling out a little handbook. He opened it, breaking its binding. "Here!" he said to the lady. "You'll help me, won't you? Handy little glossary. Here—you be a shoe-store, and I'll ask you in Spanish for three pairs of shoes: one brown, one black, and one patent-leather—"

Terrible clamor broke into the transaction; harsh, foreign, and beautiful, a bell rang, the telephone bell behind the counter, the first bell they had heard in all that time. It struck down their conversation, turned them all toward it, coffee-glasses lifted, roll halfway to the mouth. Telephone! Then the lines, the communications—?

Helen's look flickered, startled, across to Hans's look.

Peter leaned back in his wire chair. He prepared his remark. "If that's for me, I'm not in," he cracked, and waited for laughter.

There was none. The man with the tall wife forced an unlucky, stiff expression into his eyes. His glare blazed then explosively over Peter's face. "So the lines are up!" he shouted.

"Certainly," said Peter to the air. "The secretary telephoned to his committee when we took the train letter to him."

"Even if they are," commented the lady from South America, in a ravaged voice, "there will be nothing for us. Nobody will help us."

Drew burst in. He was at the door, sweater out, hair uncombed.

"Oh, come down to the station!" he said. "A couple of men are in from Barcelona, and they're letting the stationmaster out."

All their chairs went back. Mrs. Drew ran over to her husband, and started down the street ahead of them all.

"What stationmaster?" asked Helen, in confusion. She was watching the Drews. In this moment of sight, she saw the ridge that Mrs. Drew's heel was going to catch, and in a slowmotion catastrophe, saw her go down. The morning was changing: the hysteria here was evident. Hans was firm; the walk with Peter, even, was away from this. But here everything shook and fell in fear and increasing conflict.

Mrs. Drew was helped to her feet. The square bruise on her knee was out and ugly, beginning to bleed. Drew stared in fear at her, and then, in a moment, was charming again, bandaging it with a handkerchief.

Hans was next to Helen. "They're losing their heads," he said.

"I'll be in the compartment," Helen said rapidly to him. She went on to the Drews. "Better wash it," she said.

"Yes," answered Mrs. Drew. "With what?"

"I don't trust the water in the schoolhouse."

"I know," said Drew. "We'll use the Vichy. It won't sting as much as iodine."

"I've got some extra handkerchiefs," Helen offered, and remembered the girl who had searched the train.

"Fine! I'll be down for them in a moment."

Helen hurried ahead.

The two men from Barcelona were sitting in the center of a little knot on the platform, talking to a train official. The stationmaster! Helen called over, "Is the General Strike over?"

"No," they called. "Not yet."

She turned back to Hans, waving to him to talk to the men, and hurried into the train. The suitcase was in Peter's room. It was lying where Hans had left it. She took it into their compartment, and pulled open the heavy strap. A shadow fell. Drew was in the doorway.

"Never mind," he was out of breath. "Thanks. The professor has gauze.

"How is her knee?"

"Oh, I don't know," he said. "It's getting stiff."

"Better keep it clean."

"It's so hard to keep it clean, or anything else for that matter. Such a ghastly thing to go through, this trip! We're supposed to be in Mallorca now," he said bitterly, "and if we ever do arrive there, I'm going to ask for three more weeks' vacation to get over this."

"That should be easy enough," Helen said. He looked as if sleep were the only thing he had ever wanted.

"That man at Cook's!" he said. "Thanks awfully. The knee is probably nothing at all." He went down the corridor.

Helen sat in the corner of the compartment. The newspapers were piled on the bench across from her. Outside, the sound of the crowd around the two men was growing louder and louder. Flies accumulated in the hot train. The smell of the refuse and stale provisions was heavy. She saw, as the nerve in her leg began to throb again, the boxed paragraph on the open page of the French paper:

> On Saturday, according to all the latest reports, Barcelona was calm, and as yet not a shot had been fired.

THE NERVE PULLED and pulled, regularly, with the accent of the sentence, with her memory of the early Pyrenees frontier when first she had seen the newspaper, of the audacity of that landscape, which never could flourish in a more temperate zone. The nerve pulled with the beat of footsteps in the corridor. She felt she should recognize them; listened, and failed. As they stopped, she looked up from her corner. Hans was in the doorway for a moment before he was on the seat beside her, kissing her question still, twisting against her as he turned on his back with his head heavy in her lap.

"The men say the General Strike is still on," he said, answering in his monotone as if he were making love to her with words, "except for four industries: gas, water, electricity, food."

She hoped he would not speak of it now, if he had heard that the train was to move.

He looked up at her, pressing his face against her, deep in her light wool sweater. "I do not think this train will go." The words mumbled; she felt them as if they had been spoken in her body cavity. He threw his arm out, hanging his hand over the floor, swinging it in to her arm on his chest. She was looking out, memorizing the building opposite: the train would stay—that would make it impossible, and soon all the oddness would fall on them, their burden on the town, their equivocal tourist status, their condition as foreigners, having to act differently.

"What a life we could have together!"

She came back to his words with violent suspicion. These were the phrases that the eyes recalled, treacherous complicated fools promised their lives away and then withdrew. She knew about this.

But his eyes were single minded, his eyebrows locked against a vertical line of thought. He continued.

"First we must find our work. And that may be quite short; look how the government is winning here! If it is only a question of Spain, we may see a free republic, everything will be ahead of us." He closed his eyes, and the line was erased. "You will not know how long it has been since I could see the future."

Always, return. For in the hills, again, the crackle of rifle-fire.

His eyes broke light with each sound. The bullets might have ploughed through his eyes each time.

"They do not contradict us," he said, to convince them both. "I am used to them; this time, they do not need to cancel what we have."

Passengers began to come back from breakfast. Hans tightened on her arm, lay important and like sleep for a moment against her; and brilliantly sprang up. "Shall we look at the newspapers?" he invited politely as the German family and the two children passed the door. He picked up the sheets in the corner, assorting them, and laughed at the masthead. "Do you know where we are?" he asked. "The compartment of the French reactionaries!" He watched her. "We might walk," he suggested.

She said no, the heat.

"Your leg! They told me you had pain."

She said no, there was nothing wrong, a little humiliated because he was an athlete, thinking what histories she had come through from her logical past, when she would have taught her body its place, and neither over-valued nor been embarrassed at such a point. No good, this does not tally, this is better, she thought, not allowing herself to think What Next? this immediate response, this taking fear and responsibility and love in one's full grip. A defect that reminds me of a time before this is nothing, she knew, as ghostly as a habit that one falls into again after years of disuse, like her young-girl habit of wringing her hands, that would not be recognized as hers by any of these friends, or any of the friends she had left, but only by people who had made her miserable in her early youth and whom she now despised. For Hans, I am well, and soon I will be well.

"Then we will read newspapers and be a family sitting for a moment after breakfast," Hans was saying. "Do you prefer the first section—no, here are two papers," he laughed. "Very nice, very bourgeois; five minutes of this will be quite enough. Who will win the Davis Cup?"

"These are old papers," she said. "They've played it off by this time."

"In Australia! And I am very impatient because our sports-column is out-of-date. Did you see Perry play in England?"

He turned the page. "Look!" There was a large photograph of a port flashing with boats. "A bombing! One of those yachts that sit so gracefully in the bay off St. Maxime. Shelled! Do you know the coast?"

"I don't know any of the country,"—her voice sounded remote, as voices in a fast falling elevator—"from London."

"We must see that soon," he said. "St. Maxime and St. Tropez and that worldly little bay, where now they are bombing yachts."

The taboo on any talk of the future kept her quiet, she picked up the other paper and ruffled through it. A line of portraits and a page-long story stopped her. They were all portraits of one man, his success, his passionate floodlight genius, his asylum: Nijinsky. Snuffed out, the article cried, in a rant of sentiment.

Peter and Olive came in, and dropped on the bench. "If you want to go, there's a Red funeral at the end of town—mass funeral. The Swiss team's up there now. The English are collapsing," said Peter. "Mrs. Drew's knee. And the constipation of the lady from South America, which makes her more and more hopeless. But the professor says that the mayor is confident the train will move."

"The professor is a very polite gentleman," said Olive. "Under the circumstances, I would tell the train just that. Everyone's at the edge already: just tired enough, just hungry enough, jumpier than the town. Nothing to *do*."

"But in good company," Peter bowed formally.

Hans was looking at Helen. Olive noticed: "Just imagine!" she cried, in a witty voice, "during a revolution, with a 100 percent Aryan!"

"What is that?" Hans wanted a definition.

"You. *Du bist*," answered Olive, "*echt deutsch*."

He was irritated, and humored her.

The heat and the flies made it noon already. "Let's play anagrams again," said Peter.

"Fine," said Olive. "Until I fall asleep."

"Come on, Helen." She saw Hans's impatience. "In German, please," he asked, stiffly.

"Oh, God," said Peter. "I don't know. Anagrams, word-games, *Wortspielen*—is that right?"

"Word-games!" said Hans. "You'll excuse me. I'll be back Helena." He swung out the door.

They started to play anagrams.

The pale miraculous morning, the rows of hands lying upon the doors, the harsh bell, worldly bay, Nijinsky, anagrams.

Olive was asleep on Peter's lap. As the sharp gun sounds came down out of the hills. As the little group of young men came around the corner.

They were followed by two old men who trailed them curiously.

There was a noise in the corridor. The tall bitch stood at the door, gasping the words out. "They've just taken over the mansion on the corner—that's the Socialists," she forced the words, "and the U.G.T. have that big place on the Calle Mayor. We saw it rammed in yesterday."

She went down the corridor. They could hear her, stopping at every door, repeating her breathlessness, fainter, until the group advancing down the street drowned her sound out. They were discussing loudly. One of the boys had a gun. It was obvious that they had reached an agreement. They turned to the old men for confirmation. Several very little children, the eldest about six years old, came up around them as they stood.

"There's the way to hold a meeting," said Peter. "Look at the row of houses, all solid and decorated. Objective right before them—two minutes, they face it; three minutes, they determine on procedure; four minutes, all approved. That's a meeting for you!"

Olive sat up, slow with sleep. "What's that about meetings, forever?"

Peter put his head back against the lace, looked at his wife, chanted softly.

"I love Leon Trotsky. Leon Trotsky is my sweetheart."

Olive laughed. "He always calls me names when he can't depend on the answers," and she looked at him with her soft look of familiarity that Helen so envied.

"No, really. The sharpness of this: you can't discount the bravery, all the sacrifices, the directness of method here. Even if they lose their heads, the white-hot conviction carries them through."

The sound was coming down the street. The little group reached the first of the houses. Its ornate door met them; it looked as if it would withstand centuries.

They reached the door and pounded on it, with their hands and with gun-butts when it scarcely shook. The leader called down the street, and two more boys with guns came running up, and the three rammed at the lock. It broke at last; they pushed the door in. Olive held up the window shade, her mouth open in anger.

"I don't like that!" There were steps in the corridor. Peapack was running down the corridor, and Coffee-and-Tea, and the bitches. They stopped at the door.

"Opening houses!" Coffee-and-Tea said. "We're all getting our baggage ready. Pile up the suitcases, there's no way of telling where they'll stop. We've got to get into the baggage-car!" He ran past with Peapack. The bitches came into the compartment.

"What do you suppose that means?" the tall one asked.

The others were looking out the window. Two of the unarmed boys were coming out of the house, their arms piled high with sheets of papers and boards. As they spilled the sheets at the feet of the leader, it was easy to see from the train what they carried. Paintings, engravings, drawings; they held the largest framed painting up for the leader to see. It was a daub of the Last Supper. He nodded, and then one of them put his foot through the canvas, upended the square, and began very methodically to break the frame. Another boy came out of the house, carrying four crucifixes in his hands. He threw them on top of the pile. One of the drawings spun around as he kicked the heap together, and Helen could see that it was an Ascension.

"Religious subjects!" she exclaimed. They were all shocked; the forcing of the door destroyed something for them.

The group passed on to the next house. The door was barred with wrought iron, and would not splinter. They drew away from it, into deliberation on the street. The little children were looking at the pictures on the pile, holding up the gaudiest, showing each other the halos.

"I don't like it about the children," said Olive. Peter turned away from the window to look at her eagerly. His face softened. "I think this will be all right," he said to her.

A boy was being sent over the garden wall, boosted up by two others. He disappeared around the side of the house, and a moment later the fracture of glass could be heard, and the dashing of fragments. The door shook, and the boy unbolted it to let the others through. Small children crowded at the door; and, in through shadows, the somber, carved hallway could be seen by the passengers, over the heads.

The lady from South America was coming through the car, calling for the professor.

But the boy appeared at the door, carrying more paintings, crucifixes, iron candelabras, plaster statues. He threw them down on the spreading heap. A plaster saint rolled down from the top, turning eccentrically, its blue plaster robe collecting dust. It rolled away from the pile.

The leader had a long cloth case in his hand, and pushed it back, taking out the shiny, expensive-looking gun. All the others crowded about.

"They can use that," Peter said.

The leader handed it to one of the younger men. As they stood close to him, one of the little children, a tiny dark boy, ran into the house. The boys were pointing the gun into the crowd, finger on the trigger.

"Oh, God!" Olive said, with a twinge of panic on her face, and drew her shoulders together, head down. The leader knocked a hand off the trigger, knocked the barrel up until the gun pointed at the ceiling of the hallway. The boy pulled, and the little click of the unloaded gun surprised them all.

The minute the boy had his orders, he ran down the street, carrying the gun in its case very carefully.

At that moment the little child dodged out of the doorway, and started running the other way with his baby's short run. He had something under his arm. He put his black head down, running hard, and charged directly into the skirts of a woman standing in the roadway. He was lofted a few steps back, and looked up, recognizing his mother. The woman pulled the bundle from his arm, separated the three white towels, and caught the boy's shoulder.

"Look!" said the sickly bitch. "She's spanking the kid!"

He stood wailing, his fists up to his eyes, and the woman marched up the street to the leader, who was watching before the heap. She shook the towels under his face, scolding, blaming, pointing at the child, and finally slapped them down into his hand. He nodded. He gave the three towels to one of the other children to put back, and the woman marched back to take away her child.

"There's your looting," said Peter. "There's your Spanish violence! I hope Drew saw that—I hope the whole goddamn train saw that." He put his head far out the window. "Couple of people next to the station house, still talking to the stationmaster," he observed. "They're watching . . . and the Englishwoman with the deaf husband, about to break into tears."

One of the Spaniards reached their door. "Horrified?" he inquired. He smiled showing his mottled teeth, and sat down. "The train is prostrated: Señora Drew with the wounded knee, and the Peapack, and the three questionable Frenchmen, whom I believe to be spies . . ." he looked around.

"We've just seen some looting," said Helen. "Little boy with towels. His mother was magnificent." The bitches left.

"Oh, the peasants," answered the Spaniard. "All honest, all courageous, here. I hope the gentlemen from Hollywood report *this* incident accurately. Where will you go from Barcelona?"

Outside, the group had moved on to the next house, and were repeating the process, mechanically, in a business-like way. Helen looked out. The doors were standing back, rich furnishings, tapestries, heavy tables could be seen. Nothing was brought out but the images, the paintings, the heavy crucifixes.

"Well," began Peter, "we thought Mallorca now, and we want Helen to come with us." She said nothing; knowing it was impossible. Where was Hans?

"That's fine," said the Spaniard, "you can get a boat from Barcelona. Every day. Or a plane—it's wonderful to land on an island by plane, and it costs less than—oh, but planes, I don't think that's practicable now." He smiled.

"If the boats run every day—" suggested Olive.

"And when you get there, don't let them steer you to Chopin's

Villa just because you're American," he went on. "Take a trolley all about the town, an open one, with a little awning. You can see the whole town best that way, and it goes high up over Palma, up the mountain—take the trolley." He was talking too rapidly, nervously; he looked out the window continually. He was very nervous. They were breaking into the fourth house.

Somebody cried out up the train. Coffee-and-Tea could be heard, reassuring his girl from the chorus. The Englishwoman's head appeared below the window; her mouth hung open lengthening her face, she was staring at the pile. The tallest boy took out matches and struck fire to it. The unframed drawing caught and began to blacken.

The Spaniard looked out, and bit his mustache. "You'll love Mallorca," he said, with a still smile, "*Mucha ilusión . . .*" He trailed off.

"Glamour," supplied Olive.

"Excuse me," he said. "I'll be back. I have a circular of the Balearics . . ."

The boys went down the row of houses, closing the doors firmly and quietly. A maid came to the garden wall of the corner house, watching the burning pile. All the doors were closed tight, softly.

"I like that," Helen said. "They're closing the doors so gently. They've taken the proper things. There's nothing worth saving in that heap. And, God, that gun will be good to have! None of their guns match."

"Nice shutting of doors," said Olive heavily. "Do you feel tired?"

They were suffering the lapse. They felt the fear, and the sense of time after fear.

Peter looked at his watch. And up at Helen. "It's like the poem—the Gregory poem you said. What was it?

Come, come, Minerva, close the door softly as I no longer wait,
Felling the earth downplunging in darkness, sink in deeper earth,
I say quietly: 'It is very late;
It is later than you think.'

"I'm glad now I belong to the party. Much later."

"When I saw them shut the door, I wanted to join," said Helen. She laughed. "Do you carry application cards?"

"No," Peter answered. He rubbed the watch-stem, winding it. "See you in New York."

An old woman came up to the burning pile, and looked at the white clear flames in the light. She stared at the heap of paintings, and made a face as the wind stirred, blowing the smell her way. As she turned, her turning foot kicked at something, and she bent. The old woman straightened, holding the little plaster saint in the blue robe, she smashed it down on the hot ground saying a word. But only the face broke; the body would not break. She bent down painfully, and picked it up again, looking at it long, with a look almost of superstition, it seemed, a curious blank stare, holding it up in her hand oddly, as if she felt strongly about it in love or hatred or curiosity. She might be about to take it, or lay it gently down. But it was not love, or curious superstitious hate. She examined the statue closely and finally; and at last, with a substantial, business-like gesture, her hand closed tight on it, that had held loosely, like the iron hand on the knockers. It hardened, it might have been a fist raised to smash in a door, and brought the statue down, smashing it on the stone. The old woman turned on her heel and walked down the station platform, past the Englishwoman, exhausted with horrors.

Peter and Olive got up and left.

Down the corridor Helen could hear the voices of two chorus-girls and Coffee-and-Tea, calling for a fourth for bridge. And beyond them, the complaining, rising screams of the Belgian woman and Mrs. Drew, and the Polish of Mme. Porcelan, trying to quiet this hysteria.

CHAPTER NINE

Official Welcome to Assembled Sportsmen
Boxing
Wrestling
Gymnastics
Addresses
Theatrical Performances
                    —Program, People's Olympiad

Helen stayed in the train after the others had gone. She did not believe any of the talk about Mallorca, and the trolley-line that would take one all through Palma. It was grotesque to plan; there was no Mallorca.

She saw from the window the row of houses and the heavy carved doors softly shut; the palm swung in the private garden; there was a breeze now; it turned up the edge of one of the burnt *óleos*, shoved it a step or two along the dirt, and swung it around, facing the train. It was the gaudy drawing of the Ascension. The Englishwoman was hammered into the ground—she still stood there, her two long feet pointing at it, her long upper teeth hanging bare. One of the Spaniards, talking to the stationmaster, looked at her as her limp hand rose. She made a little catching motion when the wind swung the picture away from her, and then blew her nose and walked away. The Spaniard said something very funny to the stationmaster.

Helen picked up the old *Gringoire* again, and turned to the story about Nijinsky. His pictures goggled at her from the page—one worse than the other, a Hollywood version of a wealthy jeweler aging fast. She turned down the paper and got up. The train was assured, the town was real; that was all. She might never have lived a day before, she thought; and immediately realized how insane she was being. Everything contributed to this—if this was real, it was because it was nearer the sum of everything that had happened before it than anything had ever been.

Hans knew that, perfectly; he was complete, he moved surely, he was the only person here who was not swamped by strangeness. He knew, she was sure, that they were not engulfed, even though for the moment they might believe they were, but that nothing foreign had swallowed them; this was the logical stream.

She wanted to find Hans.

THE MOMENT SHE stepped down to the platform, she was part of a new crowd that had formed around the professor and the French delegate.

"No," the professor said, definitively. He had never spoken so sharply before. "The mayor is doing all he can. He can't get us in, and there's no word from the Hungarians. A man came out this morning saying they hadn't reached Barcelona."

"Hadn't reached!" said Drew indignantly. His hair fell loosely; his sweater was not tucked into his trousers; his morale had collapsed.

"But nothing is certain," went on the professor, unperturbed. "A truck has been asked for to take the Swiss team in, as vehicle, messenger, sacrifice—what you will—and we hope to have a report after that."

"And in the meantime? What about us?" The Englishman with the tall wife came stamping up. "We *must* stand together," he declared, speaking to the crowd, but facing Drew. "We *must* look out for ourselves, since obviously no one else has the wish or the power. And poor Drew's wife, with the hurt knee," he continued.

"And no communications—yes, I left my cable form on the table in there with the rest to be sent," he said, full of mockery, "when things begin to move again."

"How can we stand here?" The Englishwoman finally burst out. "How can we see this vandalism and call ourselves civilized? The churches—the houses—the holy images—"

"Someone must get through to Barcelona."

"I'll go," said Drew. One of the Germans patted his shoulder.

"I suppose you'll rent a bicycle," Peter put in savagely.

"I'll walk," Drew answered, carried away. The thing burst over them. They were all volunteering, they would all walk.

"Ah, but gently, *messieurs*," the French delegate said. His bright blue eyes snapped light, and went sad. They drowned him out.

"We'll set you a committee," said Drew, officially. "We'll set up an international committee."

"Splendid!" applauded the Englishman with the tall wife.

"Someone from each country represented here will walk to Barcelona. There will be enough of us to ensure complete protection. Perhaps the mayor will even give us flags—certainly we will be given identification. We'll be there in no time, and in touch with the proper authorities." He enlarged on the idea.

"With whom?" asked Helen.

"I don't know—somebody will be there to help us—Cook's, or the consul—"

"You're mad!" Olive shouted, from the edge of the crowd. The Belgian woman turned and faced her, shrieking, pulled about as though by rage.

"He's right. Somebody has to be there! Somebody! Some ambassador or consul!"

"We'll walk," the man with the tall wife dictated firmly, his lips pressing together, his shoulders squared, triumphant that at last somebody (and that somebody, he) could promise action, to save them all in one brilliant exertion.

"Let's go find lunch," Olive was saying, tugging at Peter. "Helen, let's get out of this."

The crowd around the professor was growing noisier, offering advice, talking faster. A few more compartments emptied, and the ether-buzz of voices, the shiny hysterical eyes, pressed closer.

"Come out of this, fast," said Olive. The last words hissed as she caught her breath. "You don't have to join any walking trips. Let the English commit suicide." She was pulling Helen and Peter as she spoke, edging between the people on the margin of the crowd. She hurried them across the little station's square into the hot still street. On the wall, the palm branch shriveled, smooth and vanilla-colored against the rough stucco. The voices could be heard halfway down the street.

"Oh, God," Olive was going on, "it cracked up, it cracked up. Helen, did you see the Belgian woman? Everybody went crazy all at once."

The café was perfectly empty. A little child standing behind the chain curtain looked at the orangeade container, and shifted from one foot to the other. The manager polished glasses, looking at them critically against the streaky light.

"You're not walking in, Peter, are you? You're not walking anywhere. How do they know how the roads are?"

"They don't," said Helen. "They're no good to anybody now. There's no sense sticking to the train any more. They might as well be fighting us . . ."

Two girls called over—did they intend to walk to Barcelona? Olive gave them some powdered chocolate to drink in their milk. The tragic sense persisted. The train had cracked, nobody could be trusted on it, the town was engrossed in war, the roads impassable.

From the high shadow over the doorway, the radio repeated its announcement.

"*Aquí emisora EAJ-15 de la Radio Catalana. Barcelona!*"

The click and fizzle followed, and the distant victrola bellowed jazz:

You, you're driving me cra-zy
What did I do?
What did I do?

and it was five maybe six years ago
to the three of them in a speak
a dancehall a moviehouse a street
in a college town in the cold flawed
December which followed the crash
and Manhattans and the soaked
cherries the icy olives the inevitable
kiss came back riding on a hot
gust through the air and the flies
circulated over the lemonade

my tears for you, make everything ha-zy
where are those skies
        of
            blue

and the sharp faces the raccoon
coats, the lion lip of the dark girl
the one who died the pale square
beautiful face of the blonde most
persistent most invading the
dim-toned bricks of a college tower
ivy and furs and a dash more gin
please because the bankrupt sky

One of the girls sitting at the door shrieked like a locomotive, and rushed into the street, leaving a puddle of chocolate milk. Olive was up and at the entrance.

"It's moving! It's gone! Look!" the French girl yelled, "There's nothing in the station!"

The two girls ran down, stood under the tacked-up palm branch, staring. Peter and Helen had jerked up from their chairs. She sat down again, very dizzy.

He faced her. "Did we tell you about Carcassonne?" he asked gently. He was playing for time. "We've just come from Carcassonne. Legendary. The old town is still there, inhabited, the old stones, preserved. Museum life."

"Are the towers crenellated?" she asked dully. She had no wit.

"No one shoots from them," he answered, and his voice snapped. "Do you suppose the train has gone off?—and all I could think of among those rocks—" He broke off. He ate several olives very quickly, popping them into his mouth and chewing on the tiny stones. "I'll go and see—"

He went down the street.

The radio was playing:

—you could hurt me,
when I needed you—oh you—
You're driving me cra-zy—

They all came slowly down the middle of the street. A dog yapped at Peter's fingers. They were talking cheerfully to each other.

Olive and Peter came in and ordered more salad. "Catch the train?" asked Helen, keeping it up.

"At the next station," said Olive, and her face relaxed. "They shunted it over to the other track. Sanitary measure. The mayor came over to look at the station, and didn't like the conditions under the cars."

"And the train's not moving?"

"It's done its work for the day."

The French girl was explaining sadly to her friend, with delicate little gestures. The café sank back, as the radio let out one final saxophone-wrench, and the record was heard scratching in Barcelona. Somebody lifted the needle, and it stopped.

"Tell Helen stories," said Olive. "Tell anything. Tell the story about the French cop."

"Go ahead." He selected a leaf of endive.

"No, you," said Olive. "It's his story, Helen—after the thousandth time, it's his."

"It has to do with a gendarme who was walking down a street behind a gentleman who was for one or two reasons attracting attention. So the gendarme walks up to him and says, '*Il ne faut pas uriner ici.*' The gentleman apologizes and assures the gendarme that he won't. But the gendarme having nothing better to do, walks on behind him and soon notices him again. '*Mais, monseiur,*' he says, angry this time, '*Il Ne Faut Pas Uriner Ici.*' 'All right,' says the gentleman, outraged, 'nobody intends to.' 'Oh, excuse me, sir,' says the gendarme, with great relief, and he throws his fist up in salute, '*Vive le Sport!*'"

"Provocateur's story," said Helen.

"Well, not for the committee-meeting." Olive was enlarging on political humor. A car came speeding down the street, blowing its horn in staccato puffs, bursting the street-air with sound. It carried the big mounted machine gun.

This time Helen got up. "It's no good," she said. "We can't change the train. The train's done for. Let's do something." They looked at her. "Let's go for a walk."

"It won't help," Peter said thickly. "Let's get tight."

"All right," said Helen. "Let's get tight. Let's go for a little walk and then get tight."

They were speaking with difficulty, as if they had been drinking for a long time. As they paid for the food, little coins rolled and fell, and they slapped their hands on the money drunkenly to keep it still. They were surprised at the shifting darkness in the dim room, the immense rolling distance from the table to the door, the faces (like weird fish shining deep-seas down) of the girls.

In the street, the elastic waves of sunlight arrived in a flood, shocking them, beating at the temples, insistent.

They looked up toward the church. Butcher's, closed; fruit store, closed; grocer's closed; a block away, though, a crowd had gathered, filling the street corner.

"Probably opening houses," said Olive.

Helen wanted to go up. She remembered their retreat from the church the night before. All these houses must be opened now, she thought. "They must have started this section, last night," she reminded Olive. "The boys were ramming in the door."

They passed the door on their way up. It was broken, half-open, lettered C.N.T., F.A.I. Through one smashed shutter they could see the overturned tables, ransacked shelves, broken crucifixes of the parochial school.

The crowd was standing still. It was not carrying guns. Only two men at the corner, and one who stood in the middle of the crossing, had rifles in their hands.

Across the street, a long robin's-egg-blue bus stood surrounded by people who put their hands on the bullet-scratches, traced the long roads cut in the enamel with their fingers. Two boys with a can of white paint were daubing large letters on the snub hood and on the rear of the bus.

GOBIERNO.

"That must be the government bus for the Swiss," said Helen. There was a spick round hole in the windshield. The heavy glass caught sunlight in the hole-rim; bright stripes of light ran outward in a sunburst.

Peter followed her startle, calculating. "That couldn't have missed the driver," he remarked.

The boys went soberly ahead with their lettering, and the crowd, pressing about the truck, commented, told stories about the road, crossed and re-crossed, shouting to women leaning from windows.

Helen looked at her hand. On it was printed, in a violent after-image, the bullet hole and glassy light.

But the crowd was backing up to clear the street. A car cruised down and guns stood out from every window.

The man in the road raised his clenched fist.

He wore a red band around his arm.

The driver's fist was already held out of the window, his elbow resting on the windowframe. And all the other men, in the car and on the streetcorner, raised clenched fists.

In a wonder, as if the car had come to save them, as if this were her dream that she was dreaming now, Helen raised her arm and shut her fist.

"The first we've seen!" said Olive. The tears rose to Helen's eyes, sprung; and stopped.

"Long live Soviet Spain," Peter answered, completing her thought, all his wish clear in the words.

Order, like a steady finger, covered the street. The crowd looped back, remaining on the sidewalk. The second car came, lettered P.C.—*Partit Comunista*—and the shouts and fists up as it passed. The long black car was full of men, and the driver and a woman sat in front, smiling and holding their tight hands to the people.

Helen turned to Peter. "How beautiful it is now!" she said. She looked as if she had just slept. She found the same safety in his face.

"Now it's all right," he answered, and took her arm and Olive's. They walked to the edge of the crowd, and cars kept passing like shouts, with lifted fists. Another man stood on the curb, stopping the cars for passwords. The last one started in second, clashing its gear, hurrying down the road. He stepped back and smiled at the Americans. His eyes were the absolute of black, night tunnels of distance. They smiled.

Peter stopped. "*Comunistas hoy?*" he asked.

The man's eyes slid smiling. "*Sí, compañero,*" his proud singing voice rose. "Today and Tomorrow."

"It's later than we think," Peter quoted.

Helen's face flared. "I want to go back," she insisted. "I want to tell Hans."

"Yes," said Peter. "This is all right."

"Now I'd like to get to Barcelona," Helen pushed out. "This is what it meant. I'd like to see a city like that."

"It's not like France, is it, Peter? You know," said Olive, abruptly, "It's the first time this has seemed at all real to me. It's the only thing I've felt, really—except for that moment when they shut the door this morning."

The hurrah of gunfire started in the hills, and ran for a minute.

One of the bitches, the sickly one, ran up the station street wagging her hand in the other direction.

"Down there," she panted, wagging. "The Swiss are leaving—"

They started to run down the street. Peter was alongside the bitch, he could see the sad, bruised eyes were swollen, the wrinkles were almost erased.

"Upset?" Peter ran alongside.

"Well," she said, and the fret and suffering obscured her voice, "it's the Swiss—they're getting out of this hellhole."

Helen slowed down with them. The words fell icy on her, she had moved so far from that state. Now, with a shock, she saw the sick, pathetic woman plain, and behind her a whole intelligible world she melted into, like a weak animal protectively colored. And with a counter-shock, Helen remembered her own impatience, a tourist spasm, when the train had for the first time stood interminably long in the way stations. The words had wiped that frantic itch for comfort away. But she was, in mood at least, prepared for General Strike, and it could change her effectively at once. The bad leg was all that stood of the past now. There was no time for it. It was later than that. Nothing but the knot of Swiss, waiting on the corner, their battered suitcases and knapsacks heaped ready.

The bitch was being scolded.

Townswomen came to the corner, drawn down from the other end of the street, where the guard blocked the road. They stood near the Swiss, marveling at the little Alpine hats, the stiff tiny feather that dissolved in tufts, the crisped handsome leader.

The sallow secretary and Mme. Porcelan walked up from the tracks. Hans was with them.

As Helen crossed to meet him, she could hear *hysteria, political, unnecessary.*

He put his hand out to Helen. "You were right not to go back to the train." The large, tight hands moved impatiently. "They've all gone wild, down there. I came up as they got their committee together, and I guess I've been looking for you since then."

She told him about the road.

"Yes," he said, "in a flash, the level's changed. But it was like that. In the morning, while they opened the houses. While you were playing word-games," he added. She felt the blood move at her eyes. "I went into the street. A committee did that. They have truly a Workers' War Committee."

He moved his arm, and stood with her in it. The Swiss were afraid that the bus would not come through. The young runner came over. He patted his pocket.

"I've got your card. If we get through, he'll get it." He cocked his head, his gay voice shifting. "—and if anything comes through to take us in, we're going in stat."

He was tapped on the shoulder. "I'm afraid we have our obligations to the town," he said, formally, and wheeled around.

Windows opened, children ran out, the sun-filled cars stopped to look at the circle. Six of them stood in a ring, their heads together over it, and just outside the leader waited. He shook his head, and all the little waves glittered like water.

The deep music started, a bass beating the pulse—and then the yodeler, standing apart, threw back his admired head, the tune rang loudly, cracking into treble, and the icy outland sound climbed and changed and broke back into tenor, rising high, fine again against the rub-a-dub bass, splitting, outclimbing birds, and with a final slide, a clean ski-track, closing.

Bursts of applause. Sensation.

The black-and-coffee women flashed in the sun, the hot ice-cream colored houses opened blinds and sprouted children, the town turned out big eyed as if a glacier had slid halfway through their street.

The horns went One-Two-Three in rapture, the notes went blinding high, a white delirium caught the town, the children hugged themselves, the gods were quieted.

Nobody seemed to turn in time to see the French delegate run unsteadily toward the corner, crying, "Come! But fast! The autos!"

Then, a moment after, the street was still, emptying fast. The Swiss ran in an erratic line, shouting good byes, and disappeared around a corner.

"Shall we see them go?" Hans asked Helen.

"I've see them leave once today," she smiled. She stopped, caught by a woman's necklace. "What a contradiction!" she started to say. "Look, she's wearing her religious medallion—"

But the delegate was still at the foot of the street, and his arms thrashed. He was still shouting.

"Come! All!"

They broke into a stampede, the cry smashing through. Helen's leg buckled under her. She stopped again in the wild fear of physical impediment—she could not run, she knew in that moment that the one thing she was there for, the one thing she had ever been alive for, was to push through this to its center, to the place where she would be named—as an individual, and an anonymous member, as a job assigned. That was all there was in the world: the great struggle around her whose outlines were springing clearly out against a fantastic voyage, her need to push to a conclusion, the leg's refusal, the clenched fists. Hans.

He was watching her eyes.

"Don't, love!" he said. "Walk, I'll get your valise—" He was running, incredibly fast, down the platform.

She followed.

The train was full of people staring from compartments, hanging out of windows. Moved to the far track, it was exposed and solitary.

The lady from South America met her at the steps. "It's not true, my dear! There's only a car for the chorus, nothing for us, there's not a thing for us!" she said melodiously.

Peter was down the steps already. Olive handed him a knapsack.

"She says no, Peter—" repeated Helen.

"We'll look. We'll be ready—"

Helen climbed up. Hans had her bag and coat, and the big hat. She took the clothes he gave her, and followed.

The truck was ready, full of Swiss, backed to the station, engine running. The automobiles were lined up. The chorus filled one and left room in the other for the French delegate and his secretary. Another open truck stood empty.

A tall yellow-faced man stood beside it. "This is for anyone connected with the Olympics, and then for anyone who cares to try the drive with us," he said, in French and English. His long face was like intellectual metal, yellow and refined sharp; and further lengthened by the high V of baldness which ate into the fair hair, baring the skull ridges.

"Who is coming?" he asked. The truck began to fill. Olive was on its floor as the suitcases were thrown in. "Is there much danger?"

The tall man looked up. "There is steady fighting; but we have a guard." A thin boy with a white handkerchief around his head climbed in. He smiled with all his teeth, he patted his rifle. Olive made room for him, and he took his place at the front of the truck, leaning on the roof over the driver.

"Then it can't be like this," she said, and called to Peter and Hans to stop loading.

Helen climbed in. She pulled the suitcases over from the center of the floor.

Olive was busy. She was sure now. She up-ended all the bags.

"Stack them around the outside," said Olive, setting them straight and close. "We've got to have some walls. We've got to have some order." Her face was clear and active at last.

They built a wall of baggage for the truck on both sides. In front, valises and the driver's box reached breast high. Olive was in charge, she moved everywhere, quickly, with Helen.

"All right," she said. The tall man nodded, and helped the others in. The bitches came running. Mme. Porcelan, attended by the pock-marked Swiss, brought baggage. They climbed in.

"Ready?" asked the tall man in a father's voice.

The driver was ready. Another guard climbed into the seat, holding his gun out the window. From the truck, the muzzle could be seen, and the oily gleam of the barrel.

"Slowly, through the town," the tall man said.

Hans and Helen were beside the guard. He reached out behind the guard and took her hand for a moment.

The boy smiled and looked at his gun. "Everyone is safe," he said. He was very handsome.

Peter and Olive were crushed against them. Helen was glad to feel their weight. They are very good friends to have, she thought. The space left between the walls of suitcases was narrow.

The truck started, blowing its horn. And it turned down the main street, Helen could see the women who had listened to the yodeling, standing in the same place. Hans's fist was up, saluting the town. She clenched her fist, and the women in the street replied. There was a flash of *vivas*, and the little tunnel blacked out the street.

Their truck led the way to the top of the hill. Halfway up, at a sharp curve, the town petered out in a ravel of old houses and meat-stores. The truck made a half-turn, backed, and stopped.

"God!" said Peter fiercely, "what's the matter?"

"He's just turning," Olive suggested.

"He could make the turn—" said Helen.

The street was barred by children; they leaned against the walls, dodged across the road, sat on the curb. Their streaked faces were full of curiosity, and all their heads turned together like newsreel heads of tennis-match spectators, as horns began to blow. The two cars and the other truck pulled up the hill.

"We probably all have to start together," said Peter.

The yellow man got out and called the drivers together.

His face was the most disciplined face Helen had ever seen, one end of civilization. Down one temple the skin was thin, as if an old burn had left it fragile, and the blood showed dark beneath. He was speaking to the drivers in an extreme of conviction.

Peter pulled her elbow. His face had knotted with the delay, and he was contagiously wound tight. The three of them felt undercut and excited by the same shock of drunkenness they had felt in the café.

"Look at the baby," he said, as if he were telling a joke.

She followed his finger. The little boy was no more than two years old, and was sitting on the curb. He was staring at the trucks and masturbating absentmindedly.

"Infantile—Infantile—"

"Auto-eroticism," Helen supplied.

"Not at all," he said gravely. "*Vive le sport!*"

Olive howled and the athletes turned in surprise. The yellow man looked up as he finished speaking to the drivers; he crossed to the space in front of the trucks, and held up his hand. The thin lavender mark was streaked, distinct on his temple.

"We are starting now," he said in a direct, high voice. "We know we can rely on you to work with us, so that everything will go well. From our reports, the road should be well-guarded and quiet now; but you must remember to watch constantly for snipers, and to duck if the truck is fired at.

"Above all, we count on you to maintain with us discipline and proletarian order. If there is too much trouble, we will stop on the way; but, whatever happens, the strictest order must be kept. The guards are not to fire until it is necessary; until they see" — he pointed to his own—"the whites of their eyes." He looked at the passengers, and raised his fist.

"To Barcelona!" He was in his car, leading the way down the cryptic road.

Their fists came up. Peter danced from one foot to the other in an anguish of excitement. He laughed and exclaimed, pompously and dramatically, in the voice of Groucho Marx: "Of course they know this means War!" Olive and Helen laughed with him in one long shriek. The other truck was starting.

Everyone stopped laughing and looked down the road. The red hill stood above them, the pylons marched over it; it was a different view of the cliff, and the profile of the red sand-cut was clear for the first time. The hill looked entirely new. This was unknown country. The truck got underway, shifting into high gear immediately, racing full-speed and roaring into the open road.

CHAPTER TEN

*The sum of force attracts; . . . man is attracted; he suffers
education or growth; he is the sum of the forces that attract
him; his body and his thought are alike their product; the
movement of the forces controls the progress of his mind,
since he can know nothing but the motions which impinge
on his senses, whose sum makes education.*

—Henry Adams

Far down the hill the tracks extended, minute and
vulnerable. The train stood grotesque, stiff, the only
motion being the thin black fume above the waiting engine. The
fume rose straight and sacrificial in the still air.

But up here, faces were whipped by wind, beaten with the speed
of flying. The open truck ran out into wide country. The high significant hills stood: the farms waited: only the truck raced checkless
on the roads.

To those faces, upon those eyes, it was the land racing, the
world, high, visionary, unknown.

They were tense, held high, the eyes seemed wider set, like the
abstract wide eyes of dancers. All the faces looked up the road.

On either side, the long grass, the wide farm-swathes, the walls
of farmhouses.

The truck stopped where a car was headed across the road. The
driver showed his pass-slip to the guard, a woman in overalls and
rope sandals. A band about his forehead meant a suffering wound
or a badge or a means to keep the hair back, it matched the band
that was around the head of the young guard standing in the truck.

Then they knew they had not reached their full speed. That barrier marked the town limits; now they were entering contested country.

The guard sitting with the driver leaned out and shouted up a word of encouragement. Then they let the motor out. The illusion of great speed was partly the product of a fierce dream, standing on the leaping floor, holding to each other and the walls, receiving the iced wind on skin used to the stagnant heat of the trains.

But the truck itself was moving fast.

At the right, the blue-and-white Ford sign was a grotesque. And here, along the farmwalls, bales of hay, stacked solid for protection.

The overturned wagon at the door, its front near wheel still spinning.

The black bush on the hill.

Barricades.

And all these rushing past, the speed of fear, the hands in the doorway, the fists on the hill all raised, clenched, saluting.

Put on coats, they thought, the cold will strike you dead! Watch the road, the black eyes are wild concern, the fingers loose the trigger to point to the wild eyes, crying with that pointed gesture: watch for guns!

On exposed rides, passing the pale houses, the tiled roofs, red now, now darker, shadowdark against the low sun, fear passes, the faces clear and become fresh and happy, filled with this youth that speed gives, the windy excitement of fear, the exploration opening new worlds with a lifted arm.

A quarter of a mile down the road, they saw the men waiting for them.

And all the sky drawn colored toward the sun.

The men grew larger.

Racing down the stretch, the fields slanted away from them, precious and quickly lost, the pastures gleamed under rich lights like grass-green jewels, the house stood lovely and forbidden.

The floor of Europe leaped shaking beneath their feet.
The men stood before them, signaling. Guards.

"Slowly, now. Watch closely."

Air relented on the cheeks. Everything was displayed clearly and minutely, even during speed, standing so high; and now, the dust on the roadgrass, the purple-flowered fields, farmhouses, mules, were rotated past methodically. The railway tracks slanted across their view again, and the ominous culvert reared above them, broad and solid stone.

The guard raised his gun to his shoulder. He pushed the handkerchief tight around his head.

Darkness ran over the truck safely. They were on the other side, where the road was fenced with steep sandslides.

The flaring trees at the top. The deathly bushes, yard-fences, a man sliding down, his legs braced stiff, come down to take the pass.

And another clear run, the road straight, the country-side changing, farm giving way to smaller gardens, large estates replaced by factories, closed and empty, but well-kept and waiting, as on holidays.

So many windows.

Watched the walls as they had watched the bushes. Each thought: guns! There is no way to watch, raking a wall of windows, for a narrow bore. Instinct, the pure ruler quality, wipes away remembrance, the countryside of the mind replaced from a moving car. In a shock of speed.

They watched; waited for city.

A nightmare gun-bore stood black and round in the brain.

They had expected city.

They saw nothing but street: a passage, impossibly long, bending from country road, where the barriers were far placed and long dashes could be made, to an avenue through glimpsed suburbs, and now this, which must be city, if the mind were free to look, but which seemed only street, broken by barricades at which the truck stopped, and the fringes could not be noticed, the faces, the piled chairs, corpses of horses. Then a spurt of speed, wind, and tight hands; and immediately, a gap in the road, blind; after that second, recognized.

At such moments, the sides of the road may be discerned.

The sidewalks, the rows of houses, blocks of low-lying buildings. And ahead? A wall.

The passengers drew in their breath as the men before it turned, the levers held in their hands, and the man with the gun came forward. For the levers chopped the street. The street was lifted to make this wall. The cobblestones were built high.

On the barricade, the red flag.

Again, as the guard stopped them with his fist, their fists came up.

From then on, the fists remained high.

The streets were those of an outlying district. Every man on them raised his fist, timed to come up as the truck passed.

The guard kept his gun up.

Now, from the windows, white patches flew, hanging truce flags of white, lining this street which was taller as they raced deeper into the city.

The barricades were up.

The barricades, recurring every hundred yards. Here, a young soldier, helmeted, behind a machine gun, trained on the highway.

Speed, two minutes, blindness, the road.

Another stop; another wall, a glimpse of street corners.

And the children who played, the families who passed walking, all their fists lifted. The movie house on one side; the sudden heat blown from the church burning on a square. The piles of firewood heightened in flame: vestments, statues, gaudy cloth, images to be carried head-high.

The truck swung down a wide avenue, and far to one side, the quadruple black-and-white spires of the Sagrada Familia rose intact.

Stores, promenades, evening.

And everywhere, the million white, the flags pendant from the windowsills, the walker in the street who lifts his hand.

The hands lifted from the truck, held tight and unfamiliar in perpetual sign.

They lost themselves, travelers exposed in this way, totally unforeseen, strange. This was a city they had read on pages in libraries and quiet rooms, leaving the books to find a hard street, bitter faces, closed silent lips at home.

But there the boy stood, his face raised in recognition, his hand, like all theirs raised.

The car swung ahead.

The bullet cracked.

From the confusion as they all bent, head and shoulders low in a reflex of dread, Helen looked up to Hans's unmoved head, either risen immediately or never changed.

The truck wheeled sharp, on two wheels, to the left, and they caught at arms and hands in confusion, straightening now, recovered.

Avenues opened wider and wider, the plane-trees, the oranges, the palms. Cars passed them now, and each time they blew, One-Two-Three, stopping to race the cars loaded with guns, spiked with guns. Each car carried the white letters of its organization: U.G.T., C.N.T., F.A.I.

The chopping of paving stones was loud at the street corners.

And now, down the long Rambla, past riddled barracks, shell-torn carnivals, bomb-pocked hotels. The dead cafés, their chairs piled on the sidewalk, before the drawn steel curtains.

Wind, fast wind increasing; the long view of a brick-orange fortress, impregnable and high. The high column, the long blue strip of sea.

And the truck turning.

Avenues opened into a great circle, a public square, mastered by two tall pillars, holding subway stations, statues, overturned wrecks of cars, candy-colored posters, full-rounded walls, cafés, the guarded front of an immense building out of which streamed warmth and talk, files of young people streaming.

The truck circled, slowing.

It stopped at the building's entrance.

The travelers jumped one by one.

Hans dropped cat-quick down, and swung his arms up for Helen. She placed her hands on his cabled wrists, and jumped. It was then that the four pains in the right palm were noticeable, and, looking down, the four blood-dark crescents were seen, the mark of the clenched fist, clutched during the voyage.

A guard in a blue uniform, rifle slung at his back, was standing with them.

He smiled at the hand.

They answered.

She asked, "and this?"

The building was large. It streamed warmth.

He looked at the travelers.

"Hotel Olimpiada."

CHAPTER ELEVEN

Olimpíada Popular
Comitè d'Honor
President: Lluís Companys
Ventura Gassol, Joan Lluhí, Josep M. Espanya,
Pere Mestres, Martí Barrera, Joan Casanovas,
C. Pi Sunyer, J. Serra Húnter, Comandant Pérez Farràs,
Josep A. Trabal, Pere Aznar, Joan Fronjosà, Miquel Valdés

Manifesto
In recent years, and especially since the World War, sport
has developed into one of the most important social and
cultural factors in the life of nations. The industrialization
which, in most countries of the world, took complete
mechanization of the methods of work which has not yet
ceased, along with the notoriously low living standard
of the working masses in the majority of countries, have
exercised their pernicious influences over the daily life of the
working peoples.

The working masses intend to counteract the harmful
effect of their hard toil by sporting activities and now with
the exception of a few countries the world recognizes the
vital importance of sport to the health and cultures of the
broad masses.

It is shameful that in the present-day society there
are elements who abuse sport, exploiting it for their
militaristic and warlike ends. Taking advantage of the
eagerness and enthusiasm for sport, they lead the youth
along the road to war. Under the pretense of strengthening

their bodies and adding happiness to their lives, they systematically subject the youth to a strict military discipline and a thorough technical and ideological preparation for future wars.

It is especially in the Fascist countries such as Germany and Italy, and also in various other countries where fascist tendencies exist that sport is being abused for militarist purposes and where, almost openly, recruits are being trained for the fascist gangs and fascisized armies.

Fascism changes the true spirit and meaning of sport, turning a progressive movement for peace and brotherhood between peoples into a cog in the machinery of war.

The Olympiad, founded thousands of years ago and reborn in our own times, has heretofore maintained its character as a symbol of fraternity between men and races, but now it is losing this significance. The Olympic Games now being organized in Berlin are unquestionably a disgraceful sham, a mockery of the Olympic ideal. In a country where millions of sportsmen are forbidden to continue their social activities, where thousands of the best sportsmen are suffering in prisons and concentration camps, where the greater part of the working masses are persecuted for their opinions or for their religion, where a whole race has been outlawed, it is impossible to find the real spirit of the Olympic Games.

The People's Olympiad of Barcelona revives the original spirit of the games and accomplishes this great task under the banner of the brotherhood of men and races. The People's Olympiad not only brings together in friendly competition the leading amateur sportsmen of Spain, Catalonia, and Biscay with those of other countries, but also promotes the general development of popular sport; at the same time giving an opportunity for enthusiasts in

the more modest categories to try their strength against
sportsmen from other districts and countries.

The People's Olympiad of Barcelona must show the
sports-loving masses that it is neither chauvinistic nor
commercialized, with the production of sensational
publicity for stars as its objective, but rather a popular
movement, which springs from the activity of the toiling
masses and which gives impetus to progress and culture.

Catalonia and its capital Barcelona must be the country
and the city chosen for the celebration of this magnificent
demonstration. The working people of Catalonia have
struggled heroically for centuries against social and national
oppression. This people, which has known and still knows
how to fight for its liberty, will fraternally welcome the
representatives of the toilers of other countries and unite
with them in a solemn undertaking to always maintain
the true Olympic spirit, fighting for the brotherhood of men
and of peoples, for progress, freedom, and peace.
—From the Spanish-English-German program
of the People's Olympiad

The big entrance was filled with athletes. Streaming past the information desk at the far end, crossing to the stairs, breaking up to watch the truckloads arriving. Tall boys in sweatshirts ran out to the trucks to help carry the baggage into the waiting room. A tall man with heavy yellow eyebrows watched the athletes arrive and a stocky fair Spaniard with an official badge, *Serveis Generals*, stood at the door, acting as a guide, ushering the strangers to the right.

In the waiting room, they lined up before the brilliant-faced guard, to have their passports and credentials examined. From the center of the line, Helen saw the French delegate and his secretary present their letters. A service man showed them out, and the guard went on with the examination. He was separating them according to one classification: those who were accredited participants in the People's Olympiad, or in any way connected with the Games, were sent through; the rest remained in the waiting room.

Helen took out the letter to Tudor and presented it with her passport. The guard recognized it.

"*Comitè Organitzador*," he said and smiled electrically. "There's a problem."

"If I could reach Tudor—" she attempted.

"Nobody can reach Tudor," his brilliant smile apologized for the publicity director. "He is out on the streets, fighting." He put his head around the door, calling. The official who had been acting as a guide came through.

"Assign mademoiselle to a place with the representatives of organizations. Here is her letter to Tudor," he said.

The guide looked down at the letter. "He is going to be a hard one to find. He has been on the barricades, since Sunday morning." He had a strongly cleft face, tanned and Teutonic, and was slightly shorter than Helen, compact. He crossed the room for her suitcase. The latest arrivals were sitting on their baggage. Helen turned frantically, searching for Hans. "Tell Hans I'm looking for him, and show all your credentials," she said as she passed Peter and Olive. The guide was already at the door.

She followed him through the wide glass doors behind the desk. When he shut them, the sudden quiet was too quick; it was a violence done to the nerves, releasing her abruptly. He put down her suitcase, and spoke to the French delegate and his secretary, in the middle of a bare room whose walls, covered with circus-colored posters of the Games, had the clean naive look of a kindergarten. The guide bowed to the delegate.

"Have they done anything about hotel reservations?"

The Frenchman turned to Helen, his eyes pointed with humor.

"What a revolutionary order they have established here!" he exclaimed, rising slightly on his toes. "They ask about our accommodations!" He clapped the guide on the shoulder. "René," he said gently to the sallow secretary, "go find out about hotel rooms for all of us." He waved an inclusive hand.

Peter and Olive appeared through the glass doors.

"Greetings!" said the delegate, "we shall have a veritable train reunion. Another room, René!"

"Yes, Mr. Corniche," answered the secretary, sliding behind Peter.

"But are you official?" asked M. Corniche. "Are we all official, we Madrid-Zaragoza-Alicante tourists, *hein*?" He chuckled, delighted, he caressed his beard.

Peter explained, shuffling the papers in his hand. "We thought we should be representing our organization at such a time."

"It is a historic fact, this week," said the delegate. He looked up at the posters. "Whatever becomes of it—" The bright pictures advertised a week of Folk Lore, a week of Sports, there were the high colors of tilted skirts, gypsy colors swirling out over the arena, the foreshortened perfect legs of a poster pole-vaulter, the block printing of dates and days and games . . .

THE SECRETARY WAS standing helplessly near the desk, shouldered aside by athletes asking the way to their rooms. Helen saw a familiar head. "Toni."

He spun on his heel. He was laughing, gay, one could hardly notice the bruise-color circles at his eyes.

"We heard you were lost!"

"As good as lost," he agreed. "We were fired on, and we spent the night in a cinema palace. Imagine!"

"Or in a train!"

"Or here!" he finished. "Have you your mattress?"

She echoed him, stupidly.

"There are two thousand athletes here, sleeping on mattresses or on the floor," he mourned. "And we're in training! You'll eat bread along with us—or beans, but probably bread."

"You should have taken the mayor along to feed you," Helen laughed.

"God, why didn't I think of that?" he agreed. He looked past her. "Oh, the Swiss are in, with you! Who else?" he asked. "The seven-language lawyer? The bitches? The lady from South America?"

"Not the lady," she said. She started to tell him about the crack-up of the train.

A line of soldiers, walking four abreast, informally, broke between them. The night shift was going on guard duty. It was quite black outside. They were all as young as the athletes, and carried blue-and-white Olimpiada pennants in their hands or tied to their bayonets. "*V'la les drapeaux!*" one of the Swiss called to Helen.

"*Una banderola para usted,*" the guard said with a flourish of courtesy, handing her the little stick. He was with a girl dressed in the blue shirt and trousers of the guard, a dark, exquisite girl whose long bayonet reached high over her back.

Toni was carried back to her on another wave of athletes. The torrent of foreigners filled the hall.

THEY MOVED INTO the little space before the waiting room. Olive was sitting there, on a mattress in the corner. Her mulatto face was distorted and darkened with fatigue. Mme. Porcelan leaned against the wall, her head thrown back and passive. "She's waiting for her husband," Olive commented. "Sit down. Hello, Toni."

"Peter?" Helen asked.

"Seeing about rooms," she answered.

Their sentences had become as economical as possible; it was with a stiff effort that they moved their lips at all. They both looked with wonder and unbelief at the hall. It was filling with an international warmth; the conversation ran so easily. Toni was at home in the immense building; Helen watched, but could not relax; Olive was paralyzed in the remoteness which was thrown over her, a sheet of distance under which she slept, her dark face withdrawn and still.

The sickly bitch thrust her head around the waiting room door. "There you are!" she said in an ugly voice. "You got there, and we're still stuck in here. We'll probably have to sleep here," bitterly.

"Credentials," said Helen.

"Yes, letters," added Olive.

"We have letters, too," said the bitch.

"Show them with your passport," Helen explained.

"Nobody told us to show anything." The bitch was close to tears. Someone called to her from within the room.

"Nor us," said Helen.

Guards were running to the door. The broad sidewalk before the Olympic was full of guards. Quite close, the dulled fall was heard. Helen's face came up.

"A bomb," she said.

"When?" Olive asked.

Toni leaned out the window.

"Just then. And there!" Helen's white face took on the signs of relief, in tired recognition.

"You can tell now," Olive admired.

"I know the difference between a bomb and a cannon," Helen said.

"Confusing." Olive leaned her head against the wall. Mme. Porcelan cried softly in the corner. She did not want to be comforted; it was better to leave her alone. Two guards and the guide who had met them came over.

"Still coming," the guard said. "All day long. Let the foreigners see our revolutionary order, *viva los extranjeros, viva la república.*"

The guide smiled. "You won't be frightened by the bombs, will you?" he asked the women gently.

"You were right," said Olive to Helen.

"They were close," whispered Mme. Porcelan.

"They were our bombs," said the guide. "We're laying a line of them—to frighten the Fascists."

"Yes," said Olive. She got up. "I want Peter," she said vaguely, and wandered off. The guards watched Mme. Porcelan.

"Perhaps you could help me," she ventured, and began to describe her husband. A great crowd of athletes hesitated at the door. They all held yellow booklets.

The guide followed Helen's eyes. "Food tickets," he explained, and ran away, returning with one. He pressed it into her hand.

"The passport man," he smiled, "told me you were from New York, that this is your first visit to Spain."

She nodded.

"This is a first impression that must be very difficult to swallow," he said, looking down at her with his northern, analytic look. He had changed character; how different he is in authority! she thought. He seemed taller alone.

"Impossible to swallow," she answered. "More brilliant than anything in the world. I've heard people talk theory a little. To see it suddenly sets it all in a drowning flash." She was waking now, coming back. The ride in the truck was really over.

"If only I were not outside," she said, looking at him with her peculiar timidity after saying something she felt deeply.

But this was a different life. There was nothing, no result of expression, to fear. He was talking.

"Not so far outside, because you care so much," he said. "But you still talk like an outsider, if you say brilliant—we have had the waste and the blood and the fighting. We hang on; it will take time for us to see the brilliance, what there is."

He looked around the hall. The crowds were thinning, they were going to dinner. A team of Norwegians stood inside the door, examining the rifles of the guard. But there was not the whirlpool of languages there had been; things were easing down.

I can get away for a few minutes," he said to her, with a certain excitement in his speech. "You speak of brilliance. Come up on the roof, and I'll show you—you've never seen Barcelona by night."

SHE WAS MOVED by the love in his voice.

They went to the big staircase and up the empty stairs. The flight rang with their steps. Turning at each landing, she could see the mattresses thrown on the floors, the signs tacked up, the many passageways. On the third floor, regular footbeats frightened her until the guard appeared to salute them.

"*Compañeros.* There is a guard posted at every outlet."

"Good," said her guide. He explained to her, "There is a degree of danger. We are in one of the most partisan of buildings. The Fascists have been infuriated at the thought that this city is to be used for a People's Olympiad."

"This is a good time to be partisan," Helen answered, surprised by the finality of the phrase, coming from her. My God, college! the level liberal days. How far have I come? She thought, going up flight after flight of stairs, a tower of stairs. Never mind, she followed. I know where I am.

He opened a door, and the cool purple air flew against their faces across the square roof. She was facing a machine gun, set opposite the door, pointing like a telescope to the harbor.

They walked to the railing. They might have driven over a mountain. About the building lay Barcelona, clear in the shining dark night, half-lit as every other streetlight burned.

"It has always been like standing in a jewel," the man said lovingly. As she watched, growing accustomed to cool and the night color, the air burned purple, she saw, dilating like a flame. Across the water, the wide harbor flamed white, the water burning itself white under a high piercing moon. A black spike struck up across the shine.

"The statue of Colón," he said. "The Fascists set up a machine gun beneath the feet." He stared. "Let the man turn," he said vehemently, "let them discover us. This is a new city. It belongs to a new people."

The wide avenues, the Ramblas, branched away from them, and directly across the plaza the two towers of the exposition marked a great black swathe. "The park," he said. It made a monster blackness. He led her over to the second side.

The circle before them had painted its shadow, elliptical and fantastic, on the ground, and there was no clue to this lunar landscape. A crescent of moon-colored ground filled out the shadow, but the pieces would not conform. She could not understand. The wide ring rose around its distortion of shadow and the pale segment, swinging around as her sight swam, turning grotesque cartwheel circles in the irrational lighting.

"Bullring," he said; and it fell into its shape, built up in violent lighting and shadow. "And beyond," he said, pointing up the length of another Rambla, "the Plaza de Cataluña, scene of heroic battles, the largest in Spain. He turned her half about, until she faced the cliff and the range. "Did you see the fortress as you rode in?" he asked. She nodded. "Up there is the Tibidabo; you see where the lights run straight, in parallels. That's the new city, all modern buildings, supplementing the old city."

"And there" he continued, softly, "the harbor and the red-light district, the 'Chinese Quarter,' where the entertainers are men who effeminize themselves and wear breasts, the great hotels that are fired on now, the cathedrals that burn over the city—see! there, and there," he showed four flaws of smoke that rose coiling through the cool air, "and there, the Sagrada Familia, our church, people's property, which will not be touched."

He leaned on the wall. "New city!" he said, his night-pale face turned down. "Here is the new city. There are our monuments: do you see the car overturned there, that has been burned? Five fascists tried to fire on our guards from it this afternoon. And over there, the subway station, where citizens were killed as they came up to the ground—and in the streets where they burn the dead horses, and there, that broken statue, under whose arm died ten civilians, two of them women; and in the burial office, where tonight they are filling out the records."

They turned back, facing the roof, noticing the mattresses thrown down even here.

"And this building!" he said. "We have a city that has been alive since Sunday; and we know its landmarks already, they are scars on our bodies so soon!"

WHEN THEY REACHED the bottom, the hall was empty. The man at the desk said that the last group had already gone to dinner. Peter and Olive with them. But the guide, saying he would look for the French delegate, was disappearing into the office. Helen turned sharply at the sound of English spoken at the door. A fair, tall boy had just come in, saying good night to the guard.

"American?" she asked.

"No," he said. "I'm with the English team—tennis. Derek's my name. Are you American? Oh, your friends were looking for you, I think."

"Yes," she answered. "I'm looking for them."

"They've gone."

"Yes," she said. "What do you make of it all?"

"Of course," he stood, considering, "I'm tennis, and prejudiced, I expect, but there's not a court that's properly marked, and I don't suppose we'd have had balls if we hadn't brought our own. The *queerest* trip for tennis!"

The French delegate and his secretary were coming out, with the tall man who had greeted them, and the other.

"Ah!" said M. Corniche. "And now, dinner!"

They went out into the Plaza de España. It was a soft night, even in the square, and warmer than the roof had been. A black heavy car was waiting before the Olympic. The driver held the front door open for the man with the gun, who got in, brushed the glass splinters away, and primed his gun, pointing it out the window and ahead. It was not until Helen came quite close to the car that she could see the gashes in the paint, and the windows, spangled with bullet-holes. It was not until she was inside that she saw the long dark blood-stain on the upholstered back, and the two bullet-holes clean through the rear glass, behind her neck.

"The car has seen service," observed one of the Frenchmen.

"Sorry, *M. le délégat*," said the tall man, who wore an official Service Committee badge, deferentially. "I couldn't get one with whole windows."

He screwed up the pane as he spoke. "Put on all the lights," he said. M. Corniche, sitting beside Helen on the back seat, leaned over his secretary and snapped on the center light above him.

"Not that one, the rear ones," the man ordered. M. Corniche turned the center one out, and lit the two corner lights. All five heads stood out clearly, built up by the pale frosty rays, reflected against the night outside.

"Better that they should see us," the official added.

Helen could not speak, but cringed away from the stain behind her, the flesh pulling and wrenching in a passion of dread. "Lean back," said M. Corniche to her kindly. "It is better that the outline of your head be distinct." She leaned back, with a strong conscious set of the muscles.

"All right, driver," said the official. "To the stadium."

The car started smoothly around the great monument in the center of the plaza. Helen could see a swarm of young people advancing across the open space, moving irregularly, vast contortions of light changing up the mass-fringe before it entered the shadowy square. As they circled, her heart clenched with terror, the light caught the lettered sweatshirts of the front line. It was the first group returning from the stadium.

The car passed between the pillars at the entrance of the park. It was possible to piece together the shapes of trees, the tall hedges, the blur of shadows that meant colored patches of flowers.

It was a good hiding place.

"They've picked off quite a few in here," the official said.

"It is a beautiful garden," answered M. Corniche with great politeness. "It is very celebrated. I have heard it described with praise many times."

"Yes," said the official. "There are many rare botanical specimens—many sub-tropical plants—in these gardens."

Helen could not speak. Her shoulder-blades crawled against that stain. The official and M. Corniche were discussing the war.

"It is a very educative experience, for the French," M. Corniche was saying. "We are learning a lot from you in Spain."

"There is not enough organization," said the official with abrupt bitterness.

"It is out of these times that organization comes, comrade," answered M. Corniche gently. "These times do not derive from organization." He paused. "We have seen some very fine things in the last few days."

"Such things do not happen in France," exclaimed the sallow secretary, half-turning in his seat.

"Sit still," said the guide. The car took the turn rapidly, skidding a bit.

"NO," CONTINUED M. Corniche. "In France, nothing has changed very much. But we had there, you understand, something in the nature of a coup. Not a life was lost—not a life; with one exception," and he laughed, "there was one hot-head who ran amok and killed his employer. But that was all. That does not make a revolution."

"Slowly here," the official raised his voice to the driver. He spoke in his natural tone to the passengers. "We are coming to a bad place."

He looked very tired.

The car came abreast of the screen of poplars, seemed to hang on the curve, and, with a swing that pushed the grove and the road, pivoted around it. They could see the Stadium, at the end of a formal wide approach.

As M. Corniche got out of the car, a young French boy came laughing down the steps, his hand out to the older man, who stopped, speaking to him affectionately. More of the French team ran down the broad flight. The steps were crowded with the French, running down to the base in a motion like the entrance of a ballet, standing around to listen to the delegate.

The official handed Helen out of the car. She still did not trust herself to speak.

"I hope you won't have any more rides like that one," he laughed, looking down at her with his slanting look.

"No," she said—"it is you—you Spaniards—who go through—" she did not finish.

They entered the stadium. Entering the immense wing, they could hear the soft sound of many people eating in a large place. The hall had been transformed into a giant refectory. Cooks in wide aprons stood in the arches, watching the last groups finish. Boys ran between the long tables with pitchers; dark steaming platters were carried up the aisles. The whispers and assents rose in a strong uneven noise.

They sat down at the table. At the end of the hall, the early tables were beginning to clear. Little groups stood at the wall, waiting to collect fifty, so that it would be safer to walk.

One of the platters was brought up to them, and brown fuming beans were heaped on their plates. The boy ran around, and poured water for all.

"Could we not have, for example, a little wine?" asked M. Corniche, sadly.

The boy shrugged his shoulder. "Sorry, *compañero*," he said, apologizing, "No wine."

M. Corniche looked at him. "I will be glad to buy some wine," he suggested, a little hope in his voice.

The boy stood there. "No wine," he repeated.

The secretary looked at the official.

"I think he's in earnest," said the official.

"Fortunes of war," said M. Corniche, twinkling. "*Vin du pays.* Your health," he pledged, raising his glass of water to Helen. "What do you intend to do?" he asked her.

His secretary was looking at the water as though it had insulted him. M. Corniche nudged him. "Drink it," he advised. "Good for you."

The secretary looked up, his sallow face darkening. "My doctor told me to *be careful*," he complained, with a wry smile, "—four days ago, let me see, yes, four days, would you believe it, I was in bed, confined with a grave temperature, and my doctor would not have permitted me this trip to Spain if he had not made out for me a list of the food I should eat during the journey—"

"Fine list of recommended food you've been eating, *hein*, René?" M. Corniche cut him short.

Helen raised her glass over M. Corniche's shoulder. Hans was sitting at the next table, with the bitches and the Hungarians. "Have you seen the others?" she shaped these words with her lips. They've just gone back, the answer came.

M. Corniche was speaking to her. "What are your plans?" he asked, and did not wait for the answer. "I am going back with the French tomorrow—" he did not stop at her gesture of shock—"and it would be good, I think, if you were to accompany us to Paris. We should be pleased."

"I thought I'd stay while there's a chance of Games," Helen said, lamely. "I thought I'd look for the Americans—"

"A brave girl," M. Corniche said to the official. He raised his glass of water solemnly.

Helen was humbled, after the automobile ride. "Are the French really going back?" she asked swiftly. "What about the Games?"

"Oh, the Games—we all want them," said the official. "But nobody knows. The teams were shot at this afternoon. Have you seen any actual shooting, M. Corniche?" he inquired.

The delegate put his fork down. Veal chops were being served. He looked hard at his chop, in accusation. "This afternoon," he said, "on the way in to Barcelona. You remember the shot, just before we changed route?" he asked Helen.

She nodded.

"We saw that," he said. "There was a young man walking down the street, with a friend. When the shot came, from nowhere, it penetrated his chest, piercing it completely, and passed out on the other side. We saw him spin and fall, and our driver determined on the other route."

The group at the next table, with Hans, was leaving. Helen watched him rise with the even controlled motion she loved. He looked at her.

The official said curiously to M. Corniche, "Tell me, before you came, did you expect to see such things in Spain?"

M. Corniche laughed. "I sat in my garden," he said gaily, "I did not expect. But Spain—one may not be surprised if the sky falls." He looked around. "Is there really nothing but water?" he asked, like a child.

"Nothing but water," retorted the guide, lifting his face up from his chop. He had been occupied, eating.

"Ah, well, then," breathed M. Corniche. "Fill up the glasses." He nudged his secretary. "*Bon digestif*!" he said, patting his vest.

They were the last out of the hall. The car was waiting outside. "Have you eaten, *compañero?*" the official asked the driver.

"*Sí, compañero,*" he replied. "But we have a new guard." This one carried a hand machine gun, with a short, vicious muzzle.

They took the fast, dark drive home without a word.

IN THE HALL of the Olympic, M. Corniche asked Helen about her accommodations for the night. He would try to arrange for her hotel room, he said. The bitch in the red blouse was standing in the deserted entrance. Helen, slack with fatigue, ran over and over one thought—she would find Peter and Olive. She tried the bitch. All the bad teeth showed—"Aw, go ahead," said the bitch irritably. "They've forgotten about you." Helen thought she would wait for a minute. She was changing shape, needing sleep, she felt— her mouth, her eyes and ears, all loosening, as if the sense-organs were at the tips of rapidly lengthening antennae. M. Corniche was shrugging, saying he would see what he could do, and vanishing among the doors to offices.

Peter and Olive were coming down the stairs.

"Where were you, where were you?" cried out Olive, hurrying over.

It was cleared up in a moment. The bitch was gone. The hall was empty.

"And a room?" asked Peter. His eyelids were thickened.

"I thought you—" began Helen.

"The Hungarians said something," Peter said weakly. "I have to wait to hear from them." He took up his position against the door-post.

Hoops of fatigue fell over them, holding them in place, increasing distances. At the entrance, the guard said good night, and walked off with the exquisite girl toward the faint sound of shooting.

"Come on, we'll find Corniche," said Helen.

He was in the inner office, with his secretary and five officials. They were all dragging pallets into position against the wall.

"My hotel accommodation," he flourished, loosening his collar with the other hand. "And you?"

"Have none," answered Helen and Olive in one voice.

"But that is unthinkable," he said, letting go of his tie. "Go in then, immediately, and say that you require mattresses."

They said good night and knocked at the last door. Two boys were in the room, feet up, smoking Bisontes.

"Have one," the thin boy offered. "Just like your Lucky Strikes!"

"Oh, no," said Helen, "only mattress . . ."

Olive wanted a cigarette. Helen could not stand still. She walked out, and sobbed once at the door. Olive came in a minute.

Helen held herself still. "And the mattress?"

"There aren't any more." They stood there. "Peter will get something," she said trustfully. "Look, he's talking to the Hungarian . . ."

The beautiful Hungarian was speaking to him. He motioned to the women.

"How would you like two rooms and three mattresses!" he shouted in a frenzy of exhaustion.

They dragged the suitcase and the two knapsacks from under the desk, and upstairs.

If only we did not act as if we were all sunstruck! thought Helen. "Where is Hans?" she asked suddenly. They stood in the washroom, sluicing water over themselves. She leaned on her knuckle in the white basin. The water was ice-cold.

"He went with the Swiss," answered Olive. "They had an extra mattress." She shook the water from her hand at arm's length, in the posture of an academic pianist preparing for finger exercises. "He's a good man, I think." She splashed more water up her long arms. "Cold water—cold water," she repeated voluptuously.

The room was between the Hungarians' and Peter's. Toni, the

beautiful Hungarian, and the printer came in, carrying pallets, laughing. The Hungarians were having a meeting with the French, and things were going well. Hundreds of people wanted to stay, everybody loved Spain, certainly there would be Games, they said.

They slapped the mattresses down and went for more canvas sheets. "We'll arrange them," said Peter. His voice was very dull.

The room was tall and white-washed, empty except for a Venetian blind and a naked bulb in the ceiling. Her suitcase lay open on the floor beside her. Behind the second door, the Hungarians were laughing and humming songs.

Olive came in with another length of canvas. "Not very elegant," she said thickly.

"*Very* elegant."

Helen snapped off the light. She rested with her hands crossed over her breast, in the position of the dead. From where she lay, the ceiling receded like a dark sheet of flame, eluding tissues and tissues of shadow. The tall Venetian blind threw slats of street-light on her wall. They would be waked, at seven, two thousand foreigners. The room wavered, tall and dangerous. She fell asleep immediately.

CHAPTER TWELVE

10:00 a.m. Conference in the Palacio de Proyecciones:
Objectives of Popular Sport and methods of developing it.
—program, People's Olympiad

Helen went immediately to the window, hauled up the Venetian blind, and stood in the broad panel of sunlight that struck across the room. The gunfire continued. Facing her, a curved wall of arches surprised her, thrown block-long and receding; it took her a second to recognize the tiers and galleries of the arena, the slim pillars which were so perfect for snipers. Her eye ran over the shaded colonnade with animal speed: she had become vigilant, it gave her a tremendous sense of health and freshness to wake without fear and speculate on concealed rifles.

The angle of the Olympic cut down across her view to the right, and she could see nothing but a boarded up café, a filling station, and the radiator and front wheels of the overturned car. But to the left lay the new city, ruled square, block after block of new apartment houses patched white with flags of truce. Behind them stood the high fortress on its strip of cliff, cutting the mountain range abruptly to an end.

Olive and Peter were lying awake in bed.

"That was the seven o'clock bell, wasn't it?"

"That was the beginning of the shooting," laughed Olive. Correct response, thought Helen. She came over to the window in Helen's room. "They said something about leaving the blinds drawn."

"I don't know," Helen said slowly. "I don't mind an open window on a street, so much, today."

"I think I'm finished with all that, too. Peter and I were walking to dinner when we missed you; Peter had just said something about the truck-ride and fear when a car came up. The driver asked us to get in, and we didn't think anything of it. There was a guard with a submachine gun; everything seemed proper until they started driving and took us for miles through the country, or park—darkness, anyway. They didn't say a word to us. Then we began to remember things—we hadn't noticed the initials on the car, fascists can drive cars too, we didn't speak Catalan, the car had only one door—all of those things."

"It's a big park," Helen said.

"A goddamned big park. But it may have cured me."

They hung out the window. At the filling-station, cars were already lined up, C.N.T. and U.G.T. cars for the most part, and the proprietor and two assistants were supplying them, lifting the dripping nozzle out of one tank and dropping it into the next without bothering to check the stream of gas.

"They're going to run short of cars," Helen remarked under the grinding of gears as they rushed down the street.

"The State's requisitioning cars from dealers," said Peter, from bed.

"There was a Ford sign on the road."

Helen knew she would always have this first morning of complete confidence. Peter and Olive had it too, she saw, reading their faces. One more lie to hold against the books! she reflected; the foolish irrelevant stories of people's characters changing like wind which shifts.

She had wanted a life for herself, and found she was unequipped; and adjusting her wants, cared to be a person prepared for that life. I want greatness, she thought, the rich faces of the living. All the tenseness stood in the way, and see how it removes! One morning, and the fear of death is replaced.

She would always have this street before her for a birthday; she was proud in herself for a moment: this is how I come of age! she thought. The long street was half-filled with sun, a brilliant dark man strode up in his blue smock and beret, at the far crossing two boys led a flock of blathering sheep that pushed their faces up in the air. The filling station was kept at high-pressure speed.

"There's Mme. Porcelan!" said Olive.

The Polish woman stood at the corner smiling up at them, her arm about a man who stood above her. The white face was the color of light.

They waved. "She's found him, anyway." Olive turned to Peter. He was dressing.

"American consul," he said, and pulled on his sock.

Helen came out in a moment. "All in white!" said Olive.

"I'm celebrating," said Helen.

Peter started downstairs with her. "Used to the shooting?" he asked.

"I can tell the difference between a bomb and a cannon, but not between a motorcycle and a machine gun."

"We must all feel the same thing this morning," he said. "Incipit. It can't all be due to a good night's sleep."

"What comes to replace the fear?" Helen asked him. She was following her own question.

"I don't know. I think a kind of resourcefulness must come. Power over it, mastery—I think continually about the Germans in concentration camps, the immense power they must be developing, the victory after fear."

"They are in jail," she answered.

The hall was almost empty. Behind the desk, the Service Committee man was trying to help the little Englishman from the train who was in Coffee-and-Tea.

"By George," he was saying, "I simply must get to the British consulate—" ending in a string of explanation.

"Please repeat," asked the official.

"By . . . George," he repeated in a slow loud monotone, "I . . . simply . . . must . . . get . . . to . . ." Peter touched his shoulder.

"Hello, old man!" the Englishman shouted, "I didn't know you were here. Could you help me make this fellow understand that my office is probably going wild at home, that I've got to get to our representative or the consulate and find what dispatches are going out?"

Peter translated for him, and gave him a slip of paper with the address written out. The little man shook his head, thanked everyone mournfully, and left.

"What happened to the chorus?" Peter called after him, but he had gone.

Olive came down while Peter was being directed to the American consulate.

"It's straight up the Rambla," Peter said. "Let's see what the consul has to say to us. He might be able to tell us when we can leave for Palma."

The milk-wagon was making its rounds and swung into the plaza, avoiding two towing cars which were removing the burned and shattered chassis near the café and subway station.

The Rambla was quiet, and the promenade up the center empty. The lettered cars passed at intervals, blowing a triple signal, but they were growing used to that sound, and were scarcely conscious of their passing. It was still cool, the sun was not high, and the broad street was fresh and shady. At the second corner there was a café whose steel curtains were all down except one, rolled six feet up, and they went in.

M. Corniche, his secretary, and the guide were drinking wine in a corner. They nodded and sat down at a table beside the French.

"Will you sail when the French do?" M. Corniche asked Helen. "I imagine we will depart this afternoon." His smile contradicted the meaning.

Peter cut her answer off. "We'll see what the American consulate says," he told the delegate. "They've asked us at the Olympic to make other arrangements, if we can, because they expect more athletes in today."

"Better not go to your consul if you don't want to be put on a boat immediately," the guide said.

"We'll just give him the names of the Americans we've been with, here and on the train."

Three girls came in, and M. Corniche beamed. It was part of the chorus.

"All friends," he said, and stroked his beard. "How are you? Where is your hotel?"

"We had mattresses in the Olympic," answered the platinum blonde. "How do you say breakfast in Spanish?"

"*Vino*," said M. Corniche.

The chorus and the Americans drank *piña* and Vichy. M. Corniche waved a piece of sausage at them.

"*A votre santé*," he said, courteously.

The chorus thought they would look for the British consul, but their manager was against getting in touch with anybody but the manager of the theater where they were booked. If a boat took them into France, they would be stranded without working papers. England would be awful and would mean that they'd be looking for a job again—he was all for staying.

"We'll ask the head of the English delegation to get in touch with you through the consul," said Helen.

"Let's find him now," said Peter.

On the Rambla again, he wondered if it was the intelligent thing to do. "I've never had anything to do with a consul," he said dubiously.

A Red Cross car passed, full of nurses, and swung down a street marked with a tremendous hospital flag. The armed worker stood in the promenade, staring after the car. Peter stopped and saluted him. He had a brother in that Hospital. He knew, of course, where the American consulate was—he was going in that direction and would walk along with them. He introduced himself: member of the citizens' militia established by a decree, published and broadcast yesterday by Lluís Companys; his brother, Coronel Tomás Temporal, had deserted to join the *Guardia Civil.*

They stopped at a kiosk to buy a newspaper. The *Día Gráfico* carried pictures—*Notas Gráficas de la Sublevación Fascista*—with the strained shoulders of soldiers in uniform bent over machine guns in the defense of the *Telefonica*; street-fighting, the gunwagons rolling through, the man in overalls standing, gun up, his legs spread solid against a wide and monumental public square.

The soldier pointed at the picture. "That's the Plaza de Cataluña," he said. "It's straight ahead of us. That's where your consul is. I turn off here. And the papers . . ." he said, slapping his with the back of his hand, "they only tell half. Now we're making order. The Fascists are beaten; we are cleaning the city, little groups are wiping out the Fascists who are left. Now we build revolutionary Catalonia."

The Plaza de Cataluña opened before them. The great stone square, broken by formal lawns, walled-in short arcs of marble, punctuated by lavish heroic statuary, was covered with pigeons that, as they watched, rose in a volley of wings, wheeled, and settled again. The plaza was filling with morning crowds, men without coats, handsome and fineboned, dark, glowing women. They saw the American flag hung over a bank building.

"There it is," said Olive. "Official, protective; will they believe that the Communists rescued us!"

The heavy glass plate behind the wrought iron door held a bullet hole like a jewel. The stone here and all around the plaza was pitted with war.

"Sorry, can't come in," said the attendant. "Bank closed."

"*Consulado Americano,*" Peter answered curtly.

On the second floor, the door held the big eagled seal. They went in. Helen's leg was beginning to hurt. The first room held two tables of American magazines and a few straight chairs. In the second, three young men stood behind a long blotter at the L-shaped desk. One of them, a man of about thirty, with an adolescent face and a crew haircut, was trying to placate three dark Americans. Their backs looked familiar.

"Christ!" said Peter, "the Pullman!"

"You've got to get us out," the largest man was demanding, "and we must get in touch with Hollywood. You can't conceive how important it is for us to get out of the country. The studio will arrange for everything, we can pay for whatever services we get. We'll get a car"—The adolescent shook his head, sorrowfully—"we'll charter a bus, we'll *buy* a bus, only we must get to the border."

The adolescent sucked his teeth and drew a circle on his blotter.

The Hollywood man went on. His assistants nodded as he finished each sentence. "It's incredible, monstrous," he said, "that this should be allowed to happen in a civilized country. You can't conceive—it's unbelievable, the guns that have been distributed to just anybody on the streets. Sixty thousand guns given away, to the scum of the earth, with orders to shoot fascists, and no questions asked. And a fascist is anybody who hasn't got dirty fingernails."

The adolescent looked up sympathetically. "The consulate is aware—" he began.

"I don't like this," said Peter.

"Wait a minute," Helen said. She had been listening to a white-haired, florid man, with intricate purple veins in his cheeks, who was talking to someone with a Panama suit, a clipped mustache, a businessman's gestures. "I want to talk to that man."

"We'll just file our names," said Olive.

Another clerk, a towheaded young man with white eyelashes, asked what he could do for them. He wanted first to tell them that Lluís Companys, the president of Catalonia, had advised the American consul that he would not be in a position to guarantee the lives of any foreigners. The consul was asking all Americans to leave as soon as possible, and would give them safe conduct to the border. Boats? No, no boats were sailing. No, he could not supply transportation to the border. And the safe conduct? Why, no, of course it meant something, it was a sort of—well, a sort of pledge—

"Oh, for Christ's sake," said Olive, "let's go find the team, Peter."

Their names? Well, of course, if they'd like to leave their names, the consulate could take them. And the consul was making arrangements with the British consulate and one of the banks to have the bank open for an hour later in the day to change foreign money and traveler's checks.

Peter listed the Americans who had come in: Olive, Helen, the bitches, himself, and the one left on the train—Peapack. The Hollywood people had proclaimed themselves.

In the other corner, the businesslike man was saying to the flabby one: "And you can tell your paper that I was in the Hotel Colón when it happened, early Sunday morning." He looked over at Helen and Olive and said, vaguely, "that's where it all started, you know." He went on, "I got up and they were shooting from the street, and their fire was returned from directly beneath me. I got dressed right away, and all the hotel guests were put in the dining room at the back of the hotel. But the bombing began—you could see the lamps shake—and they sent us all down into the American bar. That was probably as safe as an air-raid cellar, dug deep in, you know. You can imagine, though, how I felt when I got upstairs and found my bureau all shot to hell and my mattress up in front of the window. Fortification!—my mattress!"

He was working himself up to it. The florid flabby man had his notebook out now and scribbled fast.

"That's not the worst of it," he said, his voice rising steeply. "The vandalism is what we must protest. They've destroyed works of art that whole civilizations cannot replace—on Sunday, they burned the Chapel of Santa Lucía, which dates from almost 1300—and some decoration in other churches went back to the seventeenth century. All destroyed! And God only knows what's happening in Seville and Toledo. What haven't they razed to the ground? What's happened to the Escorial?" He was drawn up, his hands out, his shaking voice pitched high. "What is there in this city that isn't burned?"

Peter turned sharply to him. "The Cathedral of the Holy Family hasn't been touched." The brick-red flush swept up his jaw and cheek. "And there's a guarantee that it won't be: it's people's property, and hasn't been standing on their necks since the seventh century, or the year 1300."

The flabby man put up his hand pacifically. It was bloodless and blown up. The businessman was enraged. "The people!" he spat the sound. "A lot of trigger-loose savages riding wild through the streets, so you don't know whether you'll be killed by cars or bullets!"

"They returned the fire from the Hotel Colón, didn't they?" asked Peter. "Who held your mattress as a shield?"

Helen suddenly turned and left the room.

"Come on out," Olive insisted, and put her hand on Peter's shoulder. "Helen has misery. She ought to do something about it." They looked down at her. She sat next to the litter of magazines.

"I'm all right. I'm all right. I'm healthy," she said. "It's those people. All the art of Europe—we care, too. Priests hid Fascists in the churches—they told me in Moncada. There's no sense arguing with them, Peter."

"You let them go on and on," he accused angrily. "I don't feel that way. I don't want to hear what they say." He picked up a copy of the *Boston Chamber of Commerce Journal* and riffled the pages.

"It's what the papers will say—it's what all the New York headlines must be saying today."

"And Mr. Rockefeller—"

"Yes," said Olive. "Mr. Rockefeller will feel better about Rivera because a man in a Panama suit in a consulate in Barcelona thinks the people here should let themselves be fired on from the churches without shooting back."

They sat there for a minute. Helen wanted to lie down, and they asked for a couch. An attendant took them into an inner office full of files marked TO BE DESTROYED. "Nice secret agent situation," Olive whispered. The office irritated them all very much; they went back to the waiting room. The florid man came through, smiling.

"You mustn't mind him," he said. "He's just had a great disappointment."

"Your friend, the businessman?"

"He's neither—he's an art professor here to do some work on Spanish architecture, and he's heartbroken. Most of his thesis has been shot away from in front of him, and I don't think he's got the nerve to go out and see whether the rest is still standing. What he cares about now is getting a news story out, and maybe a little publicity at home." He winked.

"What paper are you?" asked Helen.

"Oh—sorry. I'm Spanner—Barcelona correspondent for the *Paris Herald-Trib*," he said, "and this has been keeping me pretty lively. Where did you come from—been here long?"

"Just since last night," answered Peter. "The Communists brought us in from Moncada—our train stopped there."

"Hm. Well," said Spanner. "The Communists! Is it true that the tracks have been ripped up between stations? How did they treat you?"

"They were fine to us," said Helen. "There was a guard on the train, and the Olympic teams were fed by the town. We didn't see the tracks."

"Are you with the Olympics?" Spanner asked. He looked at them narrowly.

"Came to see them." Peter wondered where the man stood.

"Oh, well, then," he said heavily, in his uncle's voice, "you're all right. You just stick with the American team—have you looked them up yet? It's very funny," he said, troubled. "They seem to have drag with the government; they say they're sent by something called the International Ladies' Garment Workers of the World. You just stick to them."

Olive nudged Peter. Helen was still talking to him. "How do things strike you?"

"Oh," he said, "it'll be all right, if they don't kill each other off. I've lived here for nine years and I've seen a lot leading up to it. As for me, I'm all right—everybody here knows me, they know I'm a newspaperman, they know I don't give a damn one way or the other, who wins." He laughed and looked down at himself like a little child. "These days, I walk around without a coat, and they think I'm a worker. And when the cars come by I give them the fist with the rest of the boys."

They all laughed with him. He told them how to find the American team, all the hotels are together down there, they're with the English, he said. Was there anything he could do for them?

"Yes," said Helen, "one thing. When you go out, and when we pass barricades, they point at their eyes and say 'Watch for guns.' How can you, *in* a street?"

"Well, it's like this," said Spanner. "You can't. But there is a pretty sure sign. When everything's noisy and going on as usual, you're likely to be safe—but when the street quiets down quicklike, and you look around and everybody's gone, and the cars are out in front maneuvering for position, then you pick yourself a good deep doorway and stay there until the shooting's over."

She thanked him.

"No," he refused, "even that's not *practical*, and it can't be. No advice can be given. You'll move instinctively, and so will the people fighting. No rules of war—civilian warfare isn't like that. Your nerves go and your house may be shelled, and nobody can shoot any better than you could if you were given a gun. It isn't like going to war as part of an army, into trenches—not at all. Come and have a drink with me."

They got out of it. They had to find the American team. Spanner left them at the bullet-pocked door, and hurried off down the Rambla, round, white, cheerfully waving as he disappeared in the crowd.

"There's your fourth estate," Olive looked after him. "He'll never get shot, because both sides know he doesn't give a damn."

Peter laughed uncontrollably. People turned to stare. A car full of boys, spiked with guns, stopped as he laughed. "International Ladies' Garment Workers of the World!" he gasped, bursting.

THE PASSEIG DE GRÀCIA, leading away from the square, and the great Plaza de Cataluña itself, were full of people, swarming coatless, many with guns, lifting their fists each time an auto went screaming One-Two-Three by. Whole families spread across the promenade; children played, calling and dodging through the crowds to find their parents; the kiosks were open, half shattered by bullets. The wide *passeig* flew banners, wore gala, was celebrating General Strike. Flags of the trade unions flew, and the white squares of neutrality; and at intervals, the red-and-yellow stripes of Catalonia, the red-yellow-and-violet of Spain, and the Anarchist flag, halved in black, were flown.

They walked once around the plaza, seeing the fractured lampposts, the heaped bodies of horses, overturned cars, and the exploded walls of the Hotel Colón, before they entered the *passeig*. The plaza was so immense that they could not feel the crowds; once in the avenue, they received the impact.

The streets were fuller than on any holiday, fuller and more alive—for the crowds were exhilarated with a kind of laughter that ran over their heads for blocks, a triumph and rest in the middle of battle. Quick as water, they responded to every impulse; and in the same way that the expressions of the guards at the Olympic the night before, in their stress and waiting, became romantic and ardent, these faces, in triumph and preparation, were seeming of happiness and rest. On cruder, stonier faces, the rigor might remain apparent. But these faces, so many of them fully alive and beautiful, softened the look of shock. And these were, as yet, not the army. There were the working people in a storm and celebration of loyalty; they had not as yet been called to fight.

"Should they all be out, before the streets are safe?" Olive watched the armed cars keenly. They slowed into a traffic snarl.

"It's the thing to do—everybody out during General Strike," said Peter. "You know: out on the streets May first."

"I'd like to see a May Day that looked like this."

"This is May Day," Peter answered. "This is what we rehearse."

They saw, cutting the lines of other flags that shook and glittered over the street, the red flags. The crowd cried "¡Viva!" as it passed, gaily and thankfully. The first story of the wide stone building was boarded up and marked with bullet holes, but over the second floor flew the huge flag, gold printed:

WORKERS OF THE WORLD, UNITE!

The windows were thrown open, red velvet chairs bordered with gold were pulled to the narrow balcony. In these immense soft thrones, their tired faces refined with effort, the crowd recognized the party men who sat, fists raised, saluting the street of people. And, standing beside a chair, his fist up and unmoved, his yellow intellectual face turned to them, they recognized the leader who had brought them from Moncada.

Beside the men stood their rifles, flying the little red pennants.

"Look, it's the man!" said Olive, saluting.

Their fists were up. They felt the same warmth of safety that had reached them in the moment he spoke to the armed trucks in Moncada, magnified infinitely, until from that balcony, those flags, it filled the street, touching their faces with the same rest and laughter that had puzzled them on the faces of the Spaniards.

As they continued down the street, consulting the corner signs for their address, they saw that, every two blocks the paving stones were being pried up. People with picks and levers were working over them, tearing up the streets, rearranging, building new barricades.

THEY WONDERED IF they had been given the right address. The street was no wider than a hallway; it carried the NO HORSES PERMITTED TO ENTER sign. It was jammed tight with signs that dovetailed and were hidden, receding in one shadow and blinding metallic on the other side: PELUQUERÍA, BISUTERÍA, HOTEL CONDAL, HOTEL EUROPA, HOTEL INGLATERRA, FARMACIA, HOTEL MADRID.

"The Europa sounds right," said Peter, "wait a minute and I'll see." He came back with a dark, grinning boy in a blue sweatshirt with OLYMPIAD sewn in white letters on it.

"Johnny!" cried Olive.

"Hello!" he sang out. "Red Front!"

"When did you get here, Johnny?" asked Olive. "This is Helen, a fine woman to be on a train with for three days anytime; this is Peter, whom I married; and I suppose you're in charge of the American team and not clerking at a law office anymore?"

"Not for a whole month now," he answered. "We got here last Wednesday, so we got to know the town pretty well before anything happened."

"You were here for the beginning?"

"Damn right. There were all kinds of meetings Saturday—everybody knew it was coming—and Sunday morning early, the whole city cracked open. The boys thought it was backfire."

"How did they like it?"

"They like it fine—the town, the girls, the way they handle things, the unions. And the town likes us. You should have seen the demonstration we put on for them yesterday! Bagpipes—the

Scotch played all the way to the stadium—they got the biggest hand of anybody except us. Funny, too, when our team was the smallest," he said, reflectively.

"You're not very developed politically," said Olive with contempt.

"Never mind that," Johnny answered. "We got a big hand anyway. But they wouldn't let us march home, because the demonstration was fired on—some went by car, and the rest of us dodged around doorways. Some of the practice was fired on, too. We were glad to get it, though—we're all out of training."

"Have you been eating beans?"

"Not here," he said. "Why don't you stay in this street?" he went on, when Peter said they wanted rooms. "This one's full, but the English are in a bigger hotel, and the section's full of them. Come on over and see the English anyway—they're having a meeting about Games."

"When will there be Games?" Helen asked. He sounded very confident.

"Oh, tomorrow or Friday at the latest. They'll have to catch up with themselves, too—the whole U.S. team wants to start today. All the teams are meeting at noon to talk this over."

They went into the dim corridor of the Condal, across the street. It was lined with wicker chairs. In the far corner, facing the door, sat a brisk, tanned, obviously English man, about forty years old, who got up as they came in.

Johnny spoke to him. He answered in an annoyed voice, "They're all out, except the ones who have been meeting upstairs. I told them not to leave the hotel. I've been sitting here all the time." He turned to Helen. "One of the French team has been shot, you know."

"Shot!" she echoed, stupidly.

"Badly," the Englishman said, "He was told not to go walking at six o'clock last night. It's all very well to say it was a stray bullet," he said irreverently, as if he were trying to answer himself, "but the demonstration was fired on—and I wouldn't like to tell anybody's family that their son was shot, he'd been warned not to go on the street."

"Now you do sound like a manager," said Johnny.

There were no rooms in the Condal, either, but they knew of a Hindu down the block who was trying to change all his money. He was afraid of the government's not being able to keep money stable, they said, and was guarding against a drop in the peseta. But the government was perfectly reliable, had issued rulings fixing the value of money, regulating prices, threatening prosecution of any war profiteers, and the street of foreigners was using the Hindu only until the banks opened. Johnny and Peter went down to find him. As they left, the tall tennis-player, Derek, came in the door.

"Hello, captain! Hello!" he said to Helen. "Left the Olympic?"

"They want anyone to go who can possibly," she told him. "Fresh batch of athletes expected from the country."

"Well, they'll be disappointed, too." He was making a statement to the press, saying a few words for Paramount, jumping over the net to congratulate the loser while all the cameras turned. "Whatever this trip is," he said, repeating himself from the evening before, "it's a washout for tennis. The courts aren't marked, and there isn't a tennis ball in all Spain."

Olive stared at him. She looked as close to puritan as she could ever look. "They're busy," she said.

The Englishman was laughing. "You ran into some other balls though, didn't you, Derek?"

The tall boy ran his hand through his blond soft hair. "I never had to do such a thing in my life," he said hopelessly.

"They shot at our people while they were practicing yesterday," the Englishman tried to control himself—"and our Derek here was forced to lie flat on the courts while they fired over his head!"

Derek turned a hot color and protested. "I don't see why we have to be subjugated to anything like it," he said.

"For the Games—" said the captain. A stout Spaniard came in

and sat down beside them. "Olympiad," he repeated. The Spaniard nodded gravely. "*Viva l'Olimpíada*," the Spaniard said.

"Above all, the Games," he continued, "will mean everything to the city and the army that we carry on with our plans. After all, we are the only ones capable of making an international United Front gesture at this time. They are so anxious about the rest of Europe."

"And if the Fascist press got hold of that, if we *didn't* play," said Derek thoughtfully.

"The only thing is," said the captain, "if the government itself doesn't think Games are in order just now——"

"Two thousand foreigners, in a city at war! The French are conscious of that," Helen said, remembering M. Corniche.

"Yes, and a city afraid of epidemic and food shortage," agreed the captain.

"God, I'd hate to leave," said Helen.

"But in case, mind you, in case!"

The dedication, she thought. Give me something to do for this.

"Oh, in an extremity," Derek was saying, "if the consul wanted, we could get a couple of boats sent up from Gib."

"You must have something extra in the Mediterranean now," said Helen.

"I don't know," the captain considered. "They were supposed to have been recalled."

"Oh, there must be something down there, you're right," went on Derek. "They could pop us around by way of Gib and the Bay of Biscay, and we'd be home in no time."

The captain looked up. "Collins!" he said sharply. "Where the hell have you been? Out all night, and off the first thing in the morning, while I sit here like an old lady."

The Spaniard smiled smoothly back and forth at the captain and the Irishman standing in the doorway, grinning wildly, showing the gaps where his teeth were gone.

"I've been doing the town with a couple of Catalonian lads," he said in his broad speech. "And if you don't mind, I'll sit here beside you." Helen liked his shiny cheekbones and length of arm. "They're a fine race, the Spaniards; they remind me of the Irish."

He waited for the laugh and the questions to stop. "It's their attitude toward the church that I refer to especially," he went on. "It makes me a happy man, to know I can feel at home in a strange country. And I'm a happy man these days; it brings back to me certain days in Ireland."

"He's been out until two in the morning, collecting dead priests," said the captain.

"Oh no, not just that. I've been looking up some places in town, and I've stood a good many drinks," he said. "I used to be a sailor, and I know Barcelona. And the people are princes. They have a fine feeling about the church."

"Is it true that priests fired from the cathedrals?" Helen asked him.

"Fired?" he cried. "It was all they could do to get them off the rafters. I saw one priest's body—he'd been firing from the highest place he could reach, firing right onto the street, and he didn't stop when they burned the church. He was burned all up one side"—he ran his hand down his hip—"and all one leg before he fell, burning and shooting."

There was a silence. "He collects priests," repeated the captain. He said something he had wanted to say for a long while: "I was in the war—three years service." They all looked up at him. He was the oldest of them. "That fighting was nothing like this. Only the nerve was the same. And here, the government has to win. All of Europe is taking sides on this."

"I hope France is sending guns in a mile a minute," Olive exclaimed.

The talk split. The Irishman was telling Helen a story about nuns who had also fired on the people and had been driven naked from the convent. She was skeptical. The Convento de las Carmelitas had surrendered, and many stories might have circulated, he said, but it still was a good idea. Across the floor, the captain was being cornered in a debate on the victims of war, pushed further and further away from his logical argument on the destruction of poverty, until he was cornered into the athlete's *reductio ad absurdum*: destruction of the unfit, the diseased. Peter came back, and interrupted.

"You're playing into the Nazi's hands," he said. "What about Diogenes, Steinmetz, Pope? They were all cripples." He began to tear the captain's fallacy apart.

"The legal mind," said Olive, and winked. "He was pushed into that statement, Peter, and he's an athlete."

A tall, Semitic-looking girl, all thin arms and legs, came in and sat down on the other side of Helen. "Oh, my goodness," she said, letting her head fall back and trying to sum Helen up, "Are you Jewish?"

"Yes," said Helen.

"Well then, my goodness, what are you doing for food? I haven't had anything to eat for three days, and I'll never be able to play tennis on that."

"Three days!"

"Yes," she said miserably. "I went to the stadium, and even the beans had Christian meat in them."

"But, God," said Helen, "you're in a different world now. You'd better eat!"

"Well, I've had some bread," the girl said, "but I can't help it. I can't eat anything else. My goodness," she went on, "are you from New York? Will you take a card to New York for me? I've got relatives."

Helen suddenly remembered the lady from South America, her large beseeching eyes, and the postcard. The girl was still talking.

"I've got other relatives, too," she said. She was a very dumb girl. Peter looked up from his unfit-discussion and grinned, returning to the incapacitated.

"Perhaps you know them," she said, dangling her long leg from her other knee. "They live in a large city."

She sat there in the dark lobby trying to place them, Helen and Olive (the others left one by one) reeling off, caught deep in Spain, American place-names: Chicago, Yonkers, Beverly Hills, Wounded Knee, Cleveland, Sandusky, New Bedford, Minneapolis, Tuscaloosa, laughing (and Peter joined, his scores all settled) Kennebunkport, Taos, Gary, Chapel Hill—no, like Nashville, she insisted, laughing as the names got trickier, more unfamiliar, rolling like praises from them as they forgot in maudlin listing all the wars, Far Rockaway, Topeka, Moberly. Oh no, my goodness, she said (Collins brought in a larger hero-faced woman in a polo coat, introducing her as the *London Daily Worker* correspondent, veteran of thirty years of revolutions), they were pretty rich, they had retired from the bakery business.

"Cincinnati!" said Peter.

THEY WENT TO the next hotel. Its black doors carried Negro hands with African black fruit in them, exotic knockers magnified from the chaste delicate fingers of Moncada. Great hammer blows fell in the halls when they let fall the hands; and finally, a little exasperated Frenchman in a white coat let them in. "Understaffed, understaffed!" he muttered as he led them up the pitch-black double staircase. "Hall porter at the wars, crazy antifascist," he croaked on the threshold to the vestibule, the bottom of a white shaft, sunk through the building, lit by skylight, decorated with palms, a closed-up brilliant patio of a reception room. "You'll want lunch," he said, leading them across a black-and-white checkered floor; "there'll be rooms ready when you bring your bags, the beds'll be made," (bed, bed, thought Helen) and he sent a waiter along.

"A table, in a hotel, with dinner on it," said Olive, ordering.

Peter and Helen came up from the soup in the same moment with lavender things in their spoons resembling Spanner's hands.

"Journalist—inkfish—octopus," said Peter.

The two Americans at the next table, one very dark, scholarly anemic, one dead blond and healthy, turned, friendly. They were the leaders of the team. They wanted Games, speaking about them the way the English had, in anxiety and distress. Helen saw in their words her own impatience with the days: nightmare of action, streaming passionately fast, flashing by, a stroke of brilliance, which cannot bring the deep resolve, the moment when this stagger dance of danger and war changes into responsibility, moment of proof. She pushed herself back with an effort; looked at Peter for confirmation of this wish, and found none now; he was talking about the street.

"Take rooms here," the muscular blond said, "it's a safe street; fifty Fascists were killed here between Sunday and Monday."

"Outside?"

"Fighting, and in their homes; there are small squads going through the city now, looking for known Fascists; the problem is as much cleaning-up, establishing the order, as of driving the enemy back to the west. The city is under control, unless troops push the battle into the town again."

"And the team?"

"The team will stay, all of us want to: only if the government asks us to go—in the meantime, we can see the city. Moscow may have looked like this in October."

The brightness, the hot color, the flicker of joy! The windows of red chairs rimmed and carved in gold; the black sashes, yellow leather straps, the romantic silver hills, fading down to the rows of young faces, held in pure effort, the boy in the *camión*, the party men's salute. That was the common seal.

There was no instant to collect this. The athletes moved and talked; up the black steps arrived the two bitches—"they told us at the Olympic you'd be with the teams—" the waiter ran with more piled plates—the athletes spoke for a minute, then said goodbye.

"If we're not wearing jewelry, it's because we're taking advice. A fat white newspaperman said, 'No coats, no jewelry on the streets. Let them think you're workers.'"

"Spanner!"

But Spanner himself came running up the steps, purpling breathless. "Go to the consul," gasping, insistent.

"You're not backed—by an athletic association—are you?" he wrenched out.

"No. A union," said the dark one.

"Well, better go round," Spanner said. They left, and he sat down with Helen, Peter, and Olive. The bitches went to arrange for rooms.

Spanner watched everyone leave. Olive filled his wineglass.

"There," he said. "Thanks." His cheeks were swamped with little veins, but his egg-blue eyes were schoolboy's, innocent. "Consuls are not notoriously of dispositions such as would make them particularly friendly to a People's Olympiad team—or to a situation like this, for that matter. Do you know the make-up of the town, at all? Well, the three biggest plants—and this is the only industrial city other than Madrid—are Ford, General Motors, and Armstrong Cork; and Ford is talking about moving his plant out of the city proper into the seaport areas so that he can avoid Spanish taxes on cars shipped to Mediterranean markets. And then there are the British firms. But, no matter what foreign companies there are, the labor is Catalonian; with a strong precedent of labor war, nationalist fighting—always fighting for freedom, and they always will. Unless they all kill each other off first.

"But right now the consulate's watching out for business interests first. After all, he's looking out for his own. And hell, there's something else—with the dealers turning in brand-new cars, and those kids racing around in them, and the Fascists doing likewise," he laughed, and his neck shook over the open shirt collar, "between racing the brand-new cars and shooting them up, there's not much time for checking and repairs. Everybody's eyes are on the automobile plants—"

"Are they socializing industry already?" asked Helen.

"Well, of course the strike's still on. But they look to have the *tranvías* and *soterráneos* going by tomorrow or the next day—a lot of people were killed at those subway entrances; you saw the one at the Plaza España. The telephone service is on again between here and Madrid, but nobody knows for how long. And a plane is leaving tonight—this is inside stuff—for Zaragoza, Saragossa—that's the front the fighting will be on after this."

"Can you get your stories through?"

"They go up to the border by mail or courier, and then by plane to Paris. I guess, after this, I can get them out by wire, but you won't be able to get reports out by commercial wire or cable, I don't think." He glanced at them with a notebook look. "Do you imagine your Games will come off? Well?"

"We want them to, very much," Peter said eagerly. "Everyone wants them. What do you hear about the chances? They mean so much—and now!"

"The city's at war, of course," said Spanner, deliberately. "The temper of the people isn't so good for games. And it might be foolish for them to expose themselves in a stadium; also, I'm sorry, but is there time?"

"The Fascist press will make a big thing of it if they don't come off," Peter remarked. He looked at Helen. "I wish we could do something."

Spanner laughed paternally. "This is headlines for the Fascist press, no matter what develops—for any press." He was grave again. "I've heard it compared to 1914," he went on. "Well, it's too close to get any perspective, but it's the cue for the next war, certainly. And after Ethiopia! You wouldn't remember," he said, looking at them for signs of age, "but everyone thought Ireland would blow up—Ireland was going to be it in 1914, until Sarajevo threw the whole thing over to a corner of Europe—a feudal corner that nobody took seriously—like Spain."

"You can see the crack-up from here," said Peter. "The train split on the war, the teams think about their countries now; if they'd only stay the hell out!"

"They're in now," answered Spanner. "You heard the Italian consulate was burned—what the papers outside of Spain won't print is that the reason they burned it was that the consulate set up a machine gun when the fighting began, and sprayed the street with bullets before they set fire to the building."

Outside of the door was the sound of horror.

"And Italian guns and money are pouring in . . ."

A long thin athlete took the stairs four at a time. He had been standing in the street before the Condal as they came out.

"Well," said Spanner, finishing off his wine.

"The French!" the athlete cried in a raw Welsh accent. "Your team said to tell you—the French are leaving."

CHAPTER THIRTEEN

Il n'y a pas de Pyrenees
—Vendredi *headline, July 24*

Above a charred ring, reddish and high over the city, the fortress stood in profile, the angle of its walls narrow as the bow of a ship, pointing to the full sea.

Emerging from the city, they saw it constantly; and now, past the jostled houses, the fumes of burning carcasses, the closed streets, over the marked walls scored by bullets and the flimsy bullet-swayed carnival, the statue of Columbus, shot spout-high above the harbor on its black pillar, a jet of monument leading up to his explorer's eyes.

Beyond that, the cement breakwaters and docks, the idle ships with their shadows that float and circulate, the little sharp Mediterranean craft.

The waterfront was crowded now, and they were walking into the crowd's density, passing young couples, boys going in rows down to the docks, families with little children running in snatches about them, their brief shadows flying on the ground. The even sound of a great crowd talking and laughing was broken, each few steps, as the noise of voices grew louder and the laughter was wound a pitch higher. The water was broken everywhere by sun. Sun sprang in bursts along the sides of ships hanging over the gay water, outlined each cobblestone with its band of narrow shadow, ran in a glassy flash over all faces as a porthole window swung to catch it and throw the light over the harbor.

Peter looked across the fire-bright reach. In a glimpse, superimposed on it, he saw the gray, choppy water off beaches he knew. "It's so brilliant here, in spite of the war," he said, and pulled back his shoulders until the blades met.

"It's altogether different from our strikes," answered the Welshman, going with his jagged walk beside Peter and Olive and Helen. "We have the miners, surprised to be in daylight, and all the black . . ."

"Where are you from?" Olive asked him.

"South Wales," he said, "the grimmest country: its life is nothing like this—" with a reaping gesture of his great length of arm.

Helen saw over the harbor to the curve, where the black circle had stamped the ground around it with scorches. "What was burned there?" Helen asked.

They looked over. "It must have been the yacht club," said the Welshman. "There were tons of ammunition discovered there; it exploded as they set fire, the soldier told me."

The boats that were warped in were very quiet. One sailboat stood idle at the edge. Peter glanced at Olive and Helen. The man on the boat was swinging an end of rope, whistling. Under his foot as he leaned on the rail, were the words JEFE-PALMA.

"Come on," said Peter, "there's our man."

He crossed the stream of people passing in the other direction. The three others stood to watch. The Welshman with his long head on one side, his throat crooked and long, grinned against the sun, talking gaily. Olive and Helen smiling, the contagion completely caught.

Peter stood with his foot up on the edge. The boatman kept his position, moving only his head, so that his forehead wrinkled like a monkey's as he looked up.

"*Buenos días, compañero,*" said Peter in a little rush, and slowed to equip himself with the words. "Is the boat sailing for Mallorca?" He turned to the others. "We'll get to Palma, yet," he prophesied cheerfully.

The man grinned back, dangling his rope.

"*Nada, compañero*," he said. "*No hoy.*"

Peter's voice went weak. "You're right," he said to Olive. "The boats won't move today." He took his foot down, and stepped back, and then, remembering something, he went on hopefully: "*¿Mañana?*" he asked the man.

"*No mañana.*" The man spoke as though he had been repeating the answer all day. "*Huelga General*," he said, lifting his fist. The rope was released farther by his hand's motion. It struck the water, breaking it in circles.

"*Viva*," said Peter. "Where are the French boats?" The man pointed and explained.

They thanked him; and went on. They were almost there. The port buildings, Inspection, Health Inspection, Police, were between the docks. "No Palma, no streetcar, no glamour," said Olive.

"I wonder what happened to the Drews," Peter said sharply. "They'll never get to Mallorca, they won't be able to cable for more vacation—"

"They're probably walking in from Moncada," said Olive. "The Drews and the other couple, the men on the outside, helping the ladies over the barricades, carrying their country with them."

They reached the second dock at an intersection like a public square, jammed with lines of people hurrying on the docks, crossing, returning. The cars with their triple horns were covered with baggage. A big car painted CONSULADO FRANCÉS, its hood covered with bunting, was cutting a road with its horn. Children crowded out of its way. The three Gypsies dancing on the dock, in red and flame-pink crossed the track of the car, lifted their clenched fists in greeting, and went back to their dance.

"Gypsies!" said Helen, with a little gay laugh. "The Gypsy Soviet!"

"That's something to work on," said Peter gravely. The sun caught all the Gypsy's jewels as she danced in a rain of pesetas. The

French were digging in their pockets for their last Spanish money, dropping it, throwing it; it whirled, ringing on the dock.

The French were lined three-deep at all the rails of the first white boat. Athletes ran over the upper decks, sat on spars like rows of strange animals, identical and high, their feet dangling, shouting and waving to the crowds on the dock, staring into the sun at them. The *Djeube* was the first of the two, and it was full already. The only passengers still going aboard were the officials and the men carrying extra baggage, going in loaded with suitcases and returning to the heap of trunks and suitcases on the dock. The main stream, however, was passing the first boat, continuing to the second, which was already half-full.

They stopped at the gangplank of the *Djeube*. The noise had changed; there was little conversation now. It had been replaced by quiet against a background of dock movements, the shouts and ticking of pulleys, the strain of the gangplank as each man at the top of the line stopped to show his passport. But there was no sound of talking, none of the thorough tone of the enlivened waterfront.

Helen became quiet as they turned onto the dock; and Olive and Peter looked at her suspiciously, as they looked with suspicion at the French, moving wordlessly up the gangplank. Suddenly she started; a man with a gray beard was waving directly at her from the main deck.

Peter followed her eyes. "That's the French delegate!" he said, excited. "He's waving!"

She had seem him clearly. "No," she said. "It's the beard, it's a twin beard."

Olive, tentatively: "You could have been on that boat, Helen."

"Could you have!" exclaimed the Welshman.

"But the Games!" Helen protested.

"I take it back," said Peter in a little boy's voice.

Helen felt a beat of sickness at the scene: the tangle of errands on the pier, the refugees sitting on their baggage waiting their turn, the men behind the slat of the public urinal, who turned as each car shouted One-Two-Three behind them, the false, suspicious excitement of the foreigners who were to stay. All along the pier, among their baggage, the familiar faces struck her sight with a quick bullet-slap: the French boy who had run laughing like a ballet dancer down the steps of the stadium; the tired, weak smile of Mme. Porcelan, standing delicate beside the tall husband she had at last been able to find; the sturdy, irritable German family with their two children. One of the little boys moved obliquely behind the other, his fingers outstretched, preparing to pinch the soft flesh behind his brother's armpit. The Swiss team stood, looking provincial among the French, who were so entirely at ease boarding their own boats— the close mechanical crisp in the yodeler's hair was very fashionable, very out of place in the confusion.

Olive wanted to say goodbye to the Swiss.

As they moved down the pier, they could see, behind the two white boats, the great flat destroyer.

The Welshman threw his arm up to shade his eyes.

"It's the Union Jack!" he was shouting in amazement. "They must have called a destroyer up from Gib. By God, will they be shoving us on a boat after the French?"

"That's bad," Peter said in a low voice, "all the foreign boats are coming in."

One of the Swiss heard that, and turned. "There are a German boat and two Italians outside the harbor now," he said. "The sailors don't like the look of things—it's what they said all along," he added after a moment. "Everything's all right, all through Catalonia, the government's strong; the only thing now is to hope the rest of Europe won't step in."

The yodeler turned, too. "—The rest of Europe!" he repeated contemptuously. "Do you think Mussolini will let the government win? If there are Italian boats out there, or German either, I'll wager they've got guns on board, and money too, for any of the rebels they can reach."

"Or they're hoping for stray bullets—anything they can make an incident out of," said Peter.

"But there's a British boat!" the Welshman was saying. "Why should there be a British boat?" He pulled Helen's elbow. "Let's get to the end of the pier, where we can see it better!"

"Why shouldn't there be!" answered the yodeler, with his trick of repeating phrases. "Do you think England's going to sit back, with Italy and Germany in on this?"

The Welshman came back a step to face him. "You aren't lining *England* up with the Fascists, are you?" The words were a threat. "Because you're making a frightful error if you are," he went on. "England's got rotten faults, but she's liberal—God, the country *cares* about freedom and democracy. It couldn't stand for—" he made a stiff hurling gesture at the open sea.

Behind his spread fingers lay the destroyer. Officers barked on the low deck, their uniforms pasted white against the fierce sky. Some drill or inspection had lined up a row of white sailors, who broke ranks as they watched, scattering over the boat.

The Swiss were being called to the gangplank. As the last one said goodbye to Helen, he put his hand into an inner pocket, smiling. He pulled out the postcard she had written at the Moncada station.

"This was never delivered," he said. "Did you find the man? I couldn't reach him—he's been out on the streets, fighting."

"He's been fighting every time I've asked, too," she answered. The dark Swiss smiled, as at a delicious and complicated joke.

"Good trip!" she called after him.

He put up his clenched fist.

The Welshman was halfway to the end of the dock, thrusting

his knees out, staring still as if he could not bring himself to believe the destroyer.

There were a few other Englishmen at the end of the pier, leaning against the bulkheads and arguing. Four boys swam naked off the end. The strip of water between the dock and the boys was rotten with oil; the corrupt beautiful colors lay as though they would never float away.

One of the Englishmen, a stranger, rushed up to where the Welshman stood, and started to speak rapidly, pointing at the boat, pronouncing his words with a strong Cockney accent so that the Welshman craned his neck sidelong and down, amused.

"See that? She sailed in there three hours ago, without a by-your-leave, and the navvies have been kept polishing brass ever since, all the time, except for the drill just now, and do you know what the blasted lieutenant had the cheek to say, over and over again? He's drilling the men in full view of this victorious city, on that flat lizard of a gunboat, and he has the cheek to keep on yapping out at them: 'Left; Left; Left;'"

Peter roared. "What's the destroyer here for?"

"She may very well have come for the *express* purpose of polishing the brass," went on the little Englishman. "But if the balance of power . . ."

He was cut short by an immense blast, as the *Djeube*'s siren cut loose, the great painful sound speeding in circles that shook around them. The French were leaving.

"I didn't think they'd really go," said Helen. She was trembling. "Let's go back. I want to see them."

The four boys had turned, heading for the pier. They swam close, striking the oil, distorting all the color, reaching the shadow of the bulwark, treading water to watch. The Welshman was lost in discussion with the English.

"Come on then," said Peter in a low sad voice.

He and Olive and Helen started down the pier.

Behind them, the dock had changed. All the confusion had been resolved, the refugees cleared, passengers and baggage heaped on the boats, the crowd thinned out, leaving nobody but the rows of spectators on the dock. They all turned toward the boat, with all the faces up at one angle.

From the high bow, the French sailors waved their caps, the long ribbons swinging against their lifted arms. The decks were crowded, the boat was filled to triple its capacity, and the relieved faces crammed at the rails on the shore side, like an overcrowded travel poster advertising a luxury cruise.

The three Americans stood in the light, looking up with blank indeterminate faces. Olive held up her arm to wave, but pulled it down and waited helplessly. She spoke without any object, "It is true that they are safe now." Peter glanced at her, and did not answer. There was no answer, no proof available; only some earthquake occurrence could prove to these crowds what they were. The dock was waiting for that. The French, leaving before the Games had been celebrated, remained undefined, their Popular Front, the mountains between the two countries, became equivocal, unknown values, stranger signatures.

The dock looked up, their faces set at one tilt.

The boat pulled slowly out, forcing itself under weight. The churned water boiled up, livid over the white side. Engines strained in the starting-effort. It was like the attempt of a heavy bird to take off from the ground, with awkward runs and a pitiful flapping.

At Helen's side a little girl cried, while her family comforted her, and on deck her aunt waved and blew kisses. The water widened slightly between the dock and the boat. Families shouted warnings and messages. But, as the strip of water settled to wider and wider blue, over the boat the handwaving stopped. The single messages were sung out into a deep quiet. Helen looked through the crowd on the dock, looking around at the faces near her to discover a reason for the change, at the tremor that moved gently over the dock, the beginning of some act, the will in the air; and, as she turned from the silent tilted faces, the motion spread from their few clenched fists and became general. With a tremendous crisis, those thousand arms went up, as if the boat itself were taking flight. The rows of raised fists ran solid and white before the rows of faces, like cries issued from the mouth, and the sound of that cry came at last, in a victory, from the French boat:

POPULAR FRONT

And, in one motion, to meet the words, the crowds left on the dock pressed forward, the loiterers advancing from the walls, those in the middle following with the same steps to the water's edge, their clenched fists all up; and along the boat, along the quieting water, hurried the sound of music, choking the watchers with its meaning, caught with new impact after the days of war, as the boat ran out to sea. The words came through, the dock taking them up, until both sides were singing the "Internationale" together, the harbor was shaken by the music, and a second longer cry came from the French, repeated and narrowing on the wide water:

SOVIETS EVERYWHERE

THE THREE TURNED away. They could not have seen the second boat go out. Very quickly, they walked down the waterfront. The sun was low in the sky, knots of soldiers were gathering before the government buildings, getting their orders for the night, a few armed cars passed, blowing their horns, and the dead quiet followed. Gunfire was beginning again, in the old city; they heard the sound.

They would have to go back to the Olympic and take the baggage to their hotel. Dispiritedly, the crisis passed and their condition upon them for the moment, they walked up past the shattered carnival. The gay swings had fallen, the carousel was torn and twisted as if a transmontane wind had whirled the booths about.

Beside the carousel was an empty lot, full of old bricks. They would be useful; at the street corner, armed men were building another barricade.

There was a shout from across the street, and Helen turned swiftly. It was Hans. He crossed the street, and took her arm.

"We've been seeing the French sail," she said, in explanation.

"Did they really go?" he asked.

"Two thousand of them," Peter answered.

"It's just as well," said Hans. "The Frenchman died this afternoon."

"Oh, no!" exclaimed Helen.

"He was really shot, then!" Peter said to Olive. She looked at him, smiling, with an inclination of her head.

"It's correct that they go," Hans went on. "The United Front is more important, and there will be 'incidents' enough, without the French athletes having to be involved."

He would go with them if they were going to the Olympic, he said.

"Don't be unhappy when you see the hotel," he warned them. "It's changed since last night. There will be no Games."

They stared at him.

"Officially?" asked Peter.

"I think it was decided when the Frenchman died," said Hans. "Although the committee probably had voted this morning."

When the news came, it was only confirmation, after all. Helen looked at him, fearfully. His wide tan jaw, the stretched mouth gave an Oriental cast to his lower face. She thought she knew what was coming next. Peter was asking what the other teams would do.

"They've given us the Palacio—next to the Olympic—to live in, and asked the consul to make arrangements."

"And you—what will you do?" asked Helen painfully.

"I will stay in Spain."

She was filled, it was the same exultation and certainty that had possessed her in the dark compartment when she had asked him what he would do in the Games, and he had answered to tempt her bad hip, "I am a runner." He had his place, he chose with his full will!

"But what will you do here?" Peter was pressing in schoolboy excitement. Olive turned to him also for a direct answer, but he did not give them one, rather steering the conversation to the day's news. He knew that Madrid was strongly held by the government and was sending out troops. He and Peter dropped into German. Peter was telling him what Spanner had said about the city, laughing over the picture of Spanner, coatless, playing worker, dodging into doorways, conscious that he was not wearing jewelry.

They were walking up the Rambla. At every other street corner, barricades were being repaired or going up. The trucks full of machine guns went past, and armed cars with boys lying along the fender, holding their rifles ready. The street was warm in the sunset, and populous; many had turned the café tables right side up again and were sitting around them, although the café's iron curtains were all down and nothing was being served.

CHAPTER FOURTEEN

Forgetting the song and singing the refrain:
Everything that happens, happens in the street.
(song lyrics)

Plaza de España. Sunset, the long lights struck the avenues into heroic distortion, rounding out bravely the great circle, with its inner and outer lanes of traffic, the massive statues, the corner booths where already the evening edition of the few newspapers still in print were selling out, the beautiful faces of the group of boys at the bullring corner. The face of Hans acquired the philosophic planes Helen had noticed in the Moncada evening; day left him active, reduced his forehead and cheeks to live-wood vigor, but evening, night, touched his mouth and eyes, making the thought apparent.

Plaza de España, the bullring corner, with its new sign up, MOBILIZATION CENTER

They saw that first, as they came down the Rambla: the two boys standing with their arms locked, head down, talking quietly a moment before they went into the entrance. The guards stationed there stopped them with questions, then motioned them in with their carbines.

Hans was reading a note in the late paper. "Saragossa's threatened," he said to Helen. "That's close. That's likely to be a new front . . ."

Peter cried out. "No banner!"

They all followed his stare. "Wrong building," Hans pointed at the Hotel Olympic. "The banner's still up."

The banner, *OLIMPIADA POPULAR*, still hung, but the entrance had changed. It was deserted. One guard at the door, and the guide talking to a single soldier inside, where last night streams of athletes had given the building a meaning of warmth and safety.

"You're the last," the guide told them. "They've all gone to the Palacio to wait for their boats, and I guess the *Djeube* took two-thirds of the foreign athletes, and the French colony, too." He kicked at the pile of posters on the floor. "We'll change the date," he said, "we'll have the Games in October, when the war is won."

"See you then!" Olive was trying to be brisk. "We'll all go to the October Games together."

The hall was empty; there were no knapsacks. In the corner stood two suitcases, with Mehring's *Karl Marx* lying open across them. Olive turned the cover, and looked at the name in the book. "I knew it! The bitches, they've left their baggage, too; we'll never be able to carry it all."

Hans walked over to the table where Helen was sitting. It was the one before which they had filed to show their passports. The guide was suggesting that they get a car, he thought he could manage one of the cars marked *Extranjeros*; he left for the Palacio to get an official pass. Peter and Olive started for the fourth floor; they nodded to Helen, they would bring her suitcase.

"Bad leg?" asked Hans.

She nodded. "But not so much that; I hate to hear them talk about coming back. It seems impossible to leave now."

"You feel that, too?"

"I love your *knowledge*," she said. "You know so clearly. It was so rare on the train, and the train was very small; here, with all of us disturbed and undecided, you are the strong one still."

"My choice is very limited, I go toward what I most want. You. This war, which is my World War. The French athlete died, and a Spanish athlete, too; and they can prove already that guns from Italy and Germany were behind all of it. So soon! The guns were in the country before the war. That means too much. But you see what it does for me, it gives me a country."

"It becomes my fight, quickly. You know," she said, in a voice of wonder, remembering long distances, histories, "I came in as a tourist, with tourist eyes and wishes."

"You were started. Think of Peapack." He laughed shortly. "And how we kept them going in the restaurant with wine and sailors' stories about this city. You have been moving all along."

"There must be some way to stay."

"They are thinking, there must be some way to get out."

"I know," she said. "Every time they speak of it, I see you. They talked to a man about sailing to Mallorca, at the docks. It's the only times I'm not their friend."

"We can't be children," he said, and kissed her. "What about your leg?"

"I'll be all right," she said, mechanically, in the tone she had used at the consulate. She saw sharply again the shiny photos in the trade journal she had held. "I'll be fine."

"You know," he told her, going back to the thought in both their minds, the growth that was surprising her constantly, as his coming had surprised her, breaking in on her life with unforeseen conditions, the sum of what she had wished for in people, action and grace and security of thought, "I had no political party; so many of these people have been set for a long time. In Bavaria, I was a *Rotfrontkämpfer* before Hitler and during the early period, before the exiles; and then I went to Italy, did some professional running, some furniture designing, other designing to make my living, among all the organizing. And, after that, I was in France a while, arrested there for activity, lost my passport . . ."

"You can't go to France?" All the ways were being cut off, slowly and scientifically.

"It doesn't matter," he said. "There is always now only one thing to do."

The guide was coming back. "Stay inside, stay inside!" he shouted. "Are the others still here?"

"What is it?" Hans asked. "We're all here."

"Fighting in the plaza . . . There! Hear it? Automobile fighting, again, just outside the door. There's still a lot of that going on; evenings," he said, trying to catch his breath. "I wish we had enough cars."

"But you've got the plants here," said Helen.

"We'll probably take control tomorrow," he answered. "All these cars requisitioned from dealers. But if the fighting gets worse tonight, we'll need more, and we'll take over Ford and General Motors. The same thing will happen there that's been going on in other factories: owners closed them down, and the workers have been forced to open themselves, and take over. The strike should be over by tomorrow or the next day."

Olive and Peter were coming down the stairs. The guide ran up to take the black suitcase from Peter, and Olive slung the knapsacks down. "We'll stay in a few minutes more," the guide said, "listen; the sounds are pretty far away now. Our car will be along as soon as it gets back."

They stood at the doorway, looking out into the blue plaza, at the few cars turning around the circle. The city was intense blue now; and, as they watched, the street-lights bloomed, every other one lit, but hardly penetrating the color in the air.

"Come to the hotel, Hans."

"Helena!" he said. "I can't. The other Germans are all going to the Palacio; a few more came in today, and there's to be a meeting."

"At any rate," said Olive, "you'll be coming along to the party the English are giving at the Condal."

He looked at Helen. "I'll see you there," she said.

A car was parking at the inner drive. Its horn blew three times, and the driver waved.

"All right!" said the guide. "I'll come with you, I have the pass."

"Let's take the bitches' baggage, Helen," said Olive. She laughed. "*And* the literature!"

They piled the suitcases into the compartment and on the floor of the car. "It won't fit," Peter was pushing the last suitcase into position. It could not stand on the floor; the driver's rear view would be cut off. "Come on," said the guide. "It's getting dark. It's better to make the two trips and keep moving than to stay still on the street for any length of time."

Peter waved them on. "Go ahead," he told the guide. "I'll wait here for you to come back. It's not more than a ten-minute drive."

"Oh no," Olive was pushing at the last large suitcase, "there must be some way . . ."

"There isn't," said the guide imperatively. "We must go now, and we'll be right back. Be sure to wait." He nodded to the driver. He bent to release the break, and the car started.

OLIVE TURNED ONCE to Peter, who stood vaguely at the edge of the inner curb, looking after the full automobile.

Helen was pinned by the bitches' large suitcase. She could not move. She looked into the little mirror over the driver, trying to find Hans in the road behind them. He had disappeared in the evening, blueness after obscurity of blue cutting him off as he hurried toward the Palacio.

The car passed into the traffic in the circle of the plaza. The driver snapped his headlights on. They made watery marks of brightness on the ground before the car. It was not yet dark enough; he turned them off.

As they came to the outlet of the circle, an armed worker doing police duty jumped on the running board and asked for their pass. The guide saluted as he showed it; hardly slowing down, the car was let by and entered the avenue. The driver nodded; cars were coming up in the opposite direction; the two men thrust their fists out, holding their arms braced on the car doors. "All of us," the guide advised, and the women followed.

He did not turn his head to talk to them. "Almost all the fighting is cut down to this suicidal automobile warfare," he was saying. "And the sniping. Although there are rumors of planes. Seville and Madrid have been radioing about bombardments, and Saragossa is threatened. The plane and the radio will fight this war with the soldier, in the cities, at any rate. The sniping should be over in a day or two. Nobody should be allowed on the streets at night," he said in a low planning voice.

"I'm glad they're going back for Peter," Olive said in English to Helen. "Hans should be all right; he only had to walk one block." She looked narrowly at Helen, caught in her vise behind the suitcase.

"Don't worry about him; he'll be fine," she said.

They were the only car on the avenue now. The quiet was unnatural; they slid forward in silence. On the sidewalks, people seemed pressed back against the houses, near doorways and arches; and the blank facing of steel curtains closed the wall of the street.

At the next corner, five men stood waiting for them, guns up, signaling with a white flag. They leveled their guns at the car while the pass was taken, and the man with the flag spoke a rapid sentence to the guide before he allowed the car through. Helen looked at Olive. They waited for the guide to speak, but he sat there, his neck tense, controlling his head, his eyes and mouth. The driver moved quickly, turning the headlight on full, looking from side to side. Finally he said a word to the guide, and jerked his head back toward the women. The guide turned around in his seat, stretching his arm along the back of the upholstery.

"I must tell you," he said, softly and paternally, emphasizing nothing, "the comrade at the crossing warned us about a Fascist car somewhere on the streets that has just killed four policemen." He hesitated a moment. "The warning went out a little while ago. They may have shot it down by now."

Stronger than sleep, than love, than even fear, the horror returned to Olive's face. "Peter," she muttered to herself, and took Helen's hand, her eyes swimming with a violent nausea. It was true: she was at her most beautiful when she was most deeply moved, in acute fear, in horror, in despair. She muttered "Peter," but in a moment her life came back, and she was angry. "Those bitches!" she exclaimed, "he would have been here now if these bitches hadn't expected service. And we gave them service," she added loudly, mystifying the guide, "I'd like to get my hands on them for this."

"Murder?" asked Helen, smiling roundly. Hans! she thought.

"Why, yes," Olive answered. The car was going very fast now, blowing the horn One-Two-Three as the barricades on the side streets flickered by like hedges, careening around the Plaza de Cataluña, chasing up the *paseo* toward their street.

"You're safe, you and Hans," Olive said suddenly. "You decided quickly, and you really were clear all the way through." It was the first time she had shown any recognition. Helen did not speak, but let her go on, holding her hand, looking at the parting crowds of people, splitting before them in the window, behind them in the mirror above the driver. Memory and imagination, she thought, and returned to Olive's words. "Clear," she was saying, "I feel near it now, we will all end at different places after this. I know you want to stay here. But how can—"

The car swerved, skidding around a corner on two wheels, seeming for a moment to be headed directly into the lines on the curb waiting to cross the street.

"The woman!" Olive screamed. Just before the wheels the woman stood with the baby blanketed in her arms and asleep. The evening threw violet on her, whitening her blouse and casting her face in shadow. But they were close enough to see her eyes for one second as the car swung round, touching her skirt. They realized as they found her look that the doors were lettered for the government, that their fists were out and the guide was ready with a gun;

for in her look and in her posture of trust as she stood regarding the car was no feeling of harm, but presages of safety. Reckless! thought Helen for a moment, not knowing what she meant, or whom she accused. But the look of trust was stamped on them as they passed the woman with baby. The car crossed the avenue, swung into the Calle Boqueria, and pulled up before the black door of the Madrid.

"Anything we can do?" asked the guide, hurrying the suitcase and knapsacks into the darkness of the hallway.

"Only go back quickly," Olive's voice was begging. She leaned against the door a moment, her head next to the black knocker, the larger duplicate of the row in Moncada, the delicate large hand, the iron fruit; she watched the car vanish into the night, down the compressed street.

"HE'LL COME, HE'LL be here any minute now," Helen said, standing over the wide brass bed. Olive looked up, and moved her hand toward the window.

"Oh, God; he should have been here fifteen minutes ago." She threw her arms over her eyes. "Those bitches," she said, all rancor gone out of her voice, nothing but the tone of mourning left, "reading Karl Marx and risking other people's lives without a word." She sprang up suddenly and ran to the balcony. "Wasn't that a horn?" she asked eagerly, as children ask after a parade. But the triple beat retreated; she came in, and shut the windows. "I'm not going to look again," she promised, throwing herself on the bed, "I'm going to let him come up the stairs, and open the door, and then I'm going to see if I can be angry at him."

Helen laughed at her, "You're behaving like a mother with a lost child," she said, although of course it was real, she thought, the warning, the four policemen, the darkness in the streets, "and when the child comes in with his ice-cream cone, he'll get his thrashing."

Olive rolled over on her back, her head falling at the side of the bed, the tight curls off her face. "It would be nice to have some ice-cream," she said, smiling. "Lovely."

"Or even ice-water," Helen answered, sitting down. "Ice-water to drink, and swim in, and keep at the bedside."

"We're probably all like that," Olive said. "Let the English yell for tea . . ."

"Never mind," Helen went on (Peter, she thought, hurry), "we probably could get some cold wine."

"I'd be tight if it were wine," said Olive.

"I'd be tight if I looked at it."

"I've always hated to drink," Olive said suddenly, "I dread getting tight so much: it makes me feel as if I lost my center, myself. It's that; it gets me so angry."

"Do you have to?" Helen was surprised.

"Why yes, if you're drunk." They were explaining very naively now, like two little girls—"yes," she said, "you're all exposed, betrayed."

"How can you?" asked Helen, "you can't open yourself up that way, not as much as we have, living on the train."

Olive looked up at her. "Or that woman," she remembered, "the one with the infant, who was almost run over. I would have resented anybody who exposed me to a thing like that: I would have screamed in the street the way I did in the car. But she didn't, did she? She trusted them completely. I'd give anything to be like that woman," she said, "and I never felt like this before. And the baby, did you see? It slept through that entire shock, we took it like an earthquake." She threw her arm over her eyes again. "God, I wish Peter would come."

She sat up. "I'm going to get the bitches to take their baggage," she said positively, "and if he isn't here by the time they come for it . . ."

"I'll help you," said Helen. "That's a promise." She had an errand; the letter for Peapack; the postcard for the lady from South

America. They were in her pocket, and the postcard was crumpled and a little blurred already. "I've got to mail them somewhere," she said. "Peter will be here when we get back."

THE POTTED PALMS in the lobby concealed nothing: the wicker chairs ranged around, the chessboard, the big hotel register, were all obvious in the tall room. Dinner was being served, and nobody came until she had rung several times. The little manager could tell Helen nothing about the mails; all he knew was that it was impossible to walk to the lady's address.

"There's a mailbox at the next corner to the right," he directed. "Nobody knows when the mails will be collected again—when *anything* will be running smoothly—" he threw his hands up, and clapped them in mid-air—"but drop it in, drop it in, and see what happens."

The smell in the street was dinner, and the high windows were lit. But the stores were dark, the street was all shadowed, and the far blasts of horns sounded ominous and unreal. Helen turned into the lane that cut her street. Narrower still, it could not permit the passage of even one automobile; hardly four people could walk abreast here. It ended immediately, however, and the new street opened at a view of a small burned church, whose flames seemed to have been lit for an hour, and then killed; the facade was burned to its substructure, and only one sign was left, beneath the broken statue of some saint:

FRIEND OF ANIMALS

At the corner, the mailbox carried no mark of delayed or arrested services; the hours of delivery had been charted, and the bulletin remained; but, dropping her card and letter into the slot, Helen heard the soft taffeta sound. The box was almost full; there had been no postal system for days. She wondered what had become of the lady, Peapack, the rest of the train. There was nothing to think about them. What if they did reach Barcelona? What then?

Hans. Hans had reached Barcelona, she thought. It means always learning to accept a position deeper in a group, deeper in a society of one sort or another, she speculated, looking again at the ruined church-front: think—the compartment, the Catalan family, the Olympic people, the Americans, the train, the truck, Hotel Olympic.

Peter. He must be there!

She turned, hurrying up the narrowest lane. Light in the street caught her eye. Stopping to lean over the gutter, she saw what it was. Crushed, battered, still metallic, but distorted as if it had been violently jerked and kicked, a crumpled splendid helmet lay, crammed deep into a sewer, only the silver crest showing, the lines of chased metal, the suggestion of a plume, forced almost down the drain.

Gun-fire, across the city. More horns. Streets, haunted by horns.

He must be there by now.

She went into the room. Olive was standing by the window. "He hasn't come," she said dully.

"Did you take the book back to the bitches?" Helen asked, avoiding her look.

"Yes. I didn't have the heart to give them hell."

A car passed in the empty street, not stopping.

Steps on the stair. At the door. It flung open.

Olive turned to Peter, a fierce look of triumph on her. "What did you do, walk?" she asked.

"Sure," he said. "I guess I'm late."

"Didn't you know about the four policemen?" she went on, delicately, sadly.

"Yes. I was talking to some people. It's a nice walk in the evening. Did you hear?" he demanded, "they're all filled with rumors about the front—is it true that they've threatened to bomb Saragossa?"

CHAPTER FIFTEEN

¿Será bombardeada Zaragoza?
—El Diluvio *headline, July 22*

What is '*ot baby?*" asked the boy at the end of the table.

The American social worker who had come in that afternoon looked up as Helen came in.

"There!" they told him. "She'll explain: *enfant chaud, heisses Kind, niña caliente.*"

"Ah," she said, sitting down beside him in her place, "that's not fair, just because I'm late to dinner—what have they been saying to you?"

Peter looked over the table at her. "But, then, he's been telling us fine things, too," he said, smiling, and introducing them. "He's Belgian, and he recommends Antwerp—a beach, a workers' camp, thirty francs to the dollar, books for fifteen and twenty francs— sound investment, that country, for Americans."

Helen's throat contracted. They were talking about leaving! She stared at Peter and Olive, wondering if her fear showed in her eyes and mouth. The Belgian waited for her to answer. His face was brilliant white, narrow, keen as some highly civilized rodent's might appear. Blue softness marked the hollows of his cheeks, but the eager health in his eyes contradicted the color and the pallor.

She said gaily to them. "I think Antwerp has crowded Palma out."

"Tell me," he insisted, "what is '*ot baby*'? Nobody will help me with my English."

"Won't the English help you?"

"They won't help me," the Belgian answered, passing the olives, "and they won't be allowed to help you."

She did not know what he meant.

"They're meeting tomorrow with their consul, and they've said they'd like the Americans to sail with them. Wait and see the consul refuse."

Again: leaving! She passed it off. "They probably won't sail, from what they say," she answered. "Did you see the French off?"

He spoke with great passion, the brilliance whitened in his face. "I wouldn't go, I couldn't bear it. They let us down, they stopped the Games from taking place! Not that it was their fault"—he cut meat viciously—"they were misled, openly misled, betrayed over their own majority vote!"

"But the United Front—"

"Their Popular Front, that allows them to leave: when they had the most athletes—one thousand of them!—the most to contribute; when their government calls itself *Front Populaire*."

Helen tried to tell him about the afternoon, the songs, the leave-taking's giant birdflight.

He laughed. "They should have gone off to France shouting '*A Zaragoza!*' *That* would have been consistent."

"Why that?"

"Didn't you know—that's to be the slogan from now on. We had the whole thing explained to us this afternoon—one of the Spanish comrades from the radio bureau lectured to a few of the teams."

He went on eating, explaining rapidly.

"Madrid and Barcelona are both all right," he said. "The government was successful the first day, and Catalonia's strongly with the government—always has been, and for its own, the minute this takes hold; it's actually independent now, under Companys nominally, really under the Workers' War Committee. The two cities are the industrial centers, but that doesn't mean too much: the largest plants are foreign-owned, and most of the workers in Barcelona are women in the textile factories. It's feudal, feudal, all the way through, except for these centers; and the Fascists have other key positions: Saragossa, Valladolid, Seville. Their strength is in their money, their help in wealth and guns from Italy and probably Germany, and their mercenaries from Africa. But these are their weaknesses: the people anywhere, as they see them uncovered, are bound to turn more strongly to the *Frente Popular*. The thing to do now is to keep a complete line of communication from being set up by the Fascists. Did you see the mobilization station?"

Helen nodded.

"The column will send out its first people now, he told us. And the city is joining—women from the factories and the farm women, and the young boys, and the old men over military age, with the others. In the south, they must fight against a stream sent out of Africa—Morocco is the key, watch what happens there—and here, Catalonia is free now and must be free. The columns will rise from Madrid and cross from Barcelona, and there will be the rest of the war which has only begun. And it's a natural war. In the midst of all countries, here," he said passionately, "I see Europe break apart; Spain, from being a growth adhering to the Continent, like some vestigial organ, is the center again. And, if we feel swallowed up, as every foreigner I've talked to does, that is a short feeling. I think that will leave when we leave the country, and see that this is not a monster thing, that this is our lives catching up with us, the life of the world catching Spain and us."

"I didn't know war," he said, "I remember running through a field of upturned divots when I was three, and the bombs crashed like an enormous grown-up booming over my bed. I would tie myself over a gun to keep it from shooting. But this has reason,

this is the fight we face now, from German concentration camps—
the nameless Italian jails—the belfries here—the coalfires in Belgium—the single fight."

"I've seen the Borinage film Ivens made," she told him. But he
was finished, he was eating nimbly and fast. The others had stopped
talking and looked at him, the vehement white face, quick hands.

"You tell me Mae West stories," the Belgian had changed as they
watched him, "and I'll talk about the Borinage." He attacked his
dinner. "I have to improve my English."

The smell of burning had curled into the room and a thick trail
of smoke seeped past the shutters. The waiter ran cursing up the
black and white floor as dinner began to break up. There was an
obvious smell of burning horseflesh in the room by the time the
waiter could shut the window. "It's only refuse," he pleaded, blocking couples as they tried to leave.

"Let's go out. It's late."

"Too late for the party?"

"Hours, Helen. The Condal people said they'd begin at
dinnertime."

"—and the coal miners came out of their leaky crazy shacks,
carrying pictures of Karl Marx down the road."

"God," said Olive, "let's go out for a minute, and get past that
horse."

The stairs were black, and the ornate door swung slowly in.
The street was jagged black at night, steep with shadows. A gust of
"Mama Inez," scratched on a cheap phonograph, repeated inces-
santly, blew down at them from a tall window.

In the street corner, one streetlight lit a square poster newly
glued to a wall. Far down the way under the next light, the same
square was blanked out. Two of the American team stood under it,
puzzled.

"They've just put up a bulletin," he said. "Come help us
translate."

El Comité de las Milicias Antifascistas

A committee of antifascist troops of Catalonia has been organized and has ruled unanimously the following, compulsory for all citizens:

First—To establish revolutionary order, for the maintenance of which all the organizations included in the committee are pledged.

Second—For control and vigilance, the committee has numbered all vehicles necessary for the accomplishment of orders issued by the same. To this object, cars will be considered seditious and will suffer sanctions determined by the committee.

Fourth—Cars moving by night will be especially rigorous against those breaking revolutionary order.

Fifth—From one to five in the morning, circulation will continue limited to the following elements:
A) To all accredited members of any of the organizations which constitute the committee.
B) Persons who pass accompanied by any of those elements and who assure their moral responsibility.

"Not quite that," interpolated Peter, who was translating slowly, "it says '*su solvencia moral.*' Moral solvency!—There's a tag we could use." He went on:

C) Those who are justified in case of great necessity which obliges them to go out.

Sixth—With the object of recruiting elements for the antifascist militia, the organizations which constitute the committee have ordered corresponding centers for enlisting and training opened.
The conditions of enlistment will be detailed in an interior regulation.

Seventh—The committee hopes that, given the necessity of constituting revolutionary order to build an effective front against the Fascist nuclei, it will not be necessary to resort to disciplinary measure to effect obedience of the order.

El Comité:

E.R. de C.: Artemio Aqueadé, Jaime Miravitlles y J. Pons

Partidos "Acció Catalana" o Izquierda Republicana: Tomás Fábregas

"Unió de Rabassaires": José Torrens

Partidos Marxistas: José Miret Musté y José Rovira Canals

C.N.T.: José Acea, Buenaventura Durruti y J. García Oliver

F.A.I.: Aurelio Fernández y D.A. de Santillán

U.G.T.: José del Barrio, Salvador González y Antonio López

"It's martial law," said the blond American.

"It's all going ahead!" said Peter. "Now the committee should assume control of the Government."

"But do they want a soviet?" asked another American behind Helen. He turned to her. "The German's been looking for you. He had to go off with a couple of Hungarians, and wanted you to know."

Helen thanked him. She was shutting her mind to what he was doing; she knew his will was direct. She felt only his greatness, and the bulletin on the wall.

The young soldier leaned out of his corner window. "Allo!" he called. "They're putting 'bans' all over town—but I," he thumped his chest, "Antonio Carrano y Torres, am finished with the committee work, I shall see Saragossa by Sunday." He kissed his fingers, struck a pose, and quieted immediately. "No, but amigos," he continued, "all the antifascists in the street wish me to tell you they are glad you feel with us, they are happy to know the strangers also see their suffering and love the people's cause."

The American team was swarming from the hotel to hear him.

They crossed as he spoke, reaching up to take his hand, firing questions at him, moved by his fervor.

THE THREE WALKED away from the group. The others were still staring at the poster on the wall. From the Condal, where the English were having a party, the victrola was repeating "Mama Inzez," and one of the team took it up, whistling. Helen looked at the Condal, wondering if Hans were there. She saw the desolate walls. There was nothing in the street but one light over the bulletin, and a lamp high up, in a window. At the end, after the narrowness, the *passeig* looked lit and busy. Peter started down toward it.

"Come on," he said. "Just for a few minutes."

"Oh, God," said Olive. "That's what happened to the Frenchman."

"It's better than sitting still," said Peter. "Come on. Helen, you come, too—and here's the Belgian, Olive, try to think of some Mae West stories."

The *passeig* was crowded. Families sat on the benches, walked up and down the promenade in the center of the avenue. The city was quite still, there was no firing. Every few minutes the One-Two-Three of an automobile horn sounded like mallet-strokes. Rarely, an armed car passed, rattling over the holes where paving stones had been pried up for barricades. The people on the benches did not speak very much.

They turned up the *passeig*.

Passing the darkened Communist Party Headquarters, they stopped to salute the guard, and met four of the Hungarian team. The boys were stopping at the Palacio. They laughed when they said so. "But in splendor!" said the beautiful one. Toni crossed over to Helen. "How's it going?" he asked. "Where are you staying? What do the Americans intend to do?"

They stood for a few minutes, talking about the English-American meeting called for the morning. They found themselves in a little knot, grouped bulky on the sidewalk as the crowd streamed past. "Goodbye!" called the Hungarians. "*A Zaragoza!*"

Peter and Helen walked ahead of the others.

"Olive was right," he said. "But it's quiet now, it's safe. Look!" he said at the filled seats. "It's a workers' city. All we have to fear is stray bullets—the trigger-loose savages!" he mocked.

The Fascists.

A little farther on, a sign stood in a second-story window, advertising the Berlin games.

They stood under it for a moment, repelled. A girl laughed from a dark bench.

At the end of the *passeig*, fronting the Plaza de Cataluña, stood the splintered kiosk. CHILDREN! it said, and there was a wide gap . . . BE SURE TO JOIN THE CLUB SHIRLEY TEMPLE . . . over the wreckage and rags. The strip of print hung, fractured in the center, and the shutter over the counter had been extracted by shot.

All the kiosks were an ironic confusion of headlines, ads, wrecked woodwork.

"Let's find seats," said Peter.

They sat down near the plaza.

"General Strike!" he said, musing. "All the muscles and the shouting of the cartoons, missing, and the whole city so real and quiet. And if we fill the streets, with them, who's going to know us apart?—The strikes we've talked about! Remember the first day of the New York elevator strike? The prostitutes' strike in Mexico City?"

Helen nodded.

"Did you sit around with people and do slogans for that one?"

"And what was the best one?"

"I don't know," she answered, absent, not paying attention. A man was walking down the street, a shadow intersecting many shadows passing, gun over his shoulders, a large stained bandage on his arm.

"I remember ours," said Peter fondly. "It followed all the rules. It would have won a war."

"What was it?" Helen asked.

"Go Fuck Yourself."

They laughed. Her laugh was sharp, cut short.

The street seemed too quiet.

"If we could only hear some music," she said.

"Come hear our records when we get back," he answered. "We play Brahms, Sunday evenings—he would be right, now, or 'Fire Bird.' Or poetry," he added. "When we get back, I'll write a poem for you. And maybe you'll say one now," he ended, tentatively.

She smiled obscurely, and did not answer—a line of sound was coming down the *passeig*, drawing closer, a rush of *Vivas* following down. One of the big buses, filled with guns and waving men rolled down along the promenade and turned into the plaza. Olive and the Belgian, on the side nearer the sound, turned their heads. "People coming!" said Olive.

"It's part of the army, then!' exclaimed the Belgian. His thin face grew brilliant, the shadows under the skin were dissolved.

The battalion advanced down the promenade. From little metal seats under the trees, from black windows receding in the street, the cheering seethed, expanded into open shouting. People stood, clapped, called "¡Viva!" and "A Zaragoza!" They were all four on their feet. Helen heard her throat go, fantastically, "Viva . . ." and then lock.

They filed past, line by line their faces showed plain under some light, young, important, with their knotted throats and tense cheeks. They did not march in step, and their rope sandals made hardly any sound. Some carried soft red blankets over their shoulder, shrugging them up into position as they walked, many rested their hands on cartridge belts, one or two wore metal helmets, one or two were women. Many had red strips bound around their hair, and red brassards. They did not say anything. They lifted their fists in acknowledgment. The shouting rose to a roar of praise after them.

There were not more than two hundred in this group.

They were past in a moment.

She had to sit down, her knees had gone rotten. Her eyes burned dry. For a moment, she had a hundred lives, all marching by. She knew that she would not be able to recognize three of these faces if she ever saw them again.

Another bus full of soldiers clattered past.

"I hate it, it's hateful, it's death," said Olive.

They started back to the hotel. The *calle* was very dark, as narrow as the hall through which she had gone to bed when she was little, Helen thought. Her hip was beginning again, she could hardly walk, when they came to the group of Americans still standing in the street, she could not walk anymore. Johnson, the blond American, called to her.

"You go on up," she said. Peter and Olive went to the hotel, slowly, talking as if persuading themselves of something. The light caught Olive's cheek. She looked profoundly mulatto in the half-dark, in her sadness.

Johnson said, "It looks as though we might sail with the English. They've got a majority against going, but the consul says no."

"And our consul?"

"Says nothing—nothing—at—all. The English have asked us, and the English have the boats. We may have to go with them. The government's talking about evacuating all foreigners."

"But the meeting tomorrow," she protested.

"Yes—with the consuls," he said. "Things are moving fast. See him?" pointing among the group he had broken away from. "That's the C.I. man, and the whole United Front line may be changed, he says, depending on what happens in Spain in the next day or two."

"The notice—it's martial law now, isn't it?" she asked.

"Just about."

"That's workers' army, already—"

"Yes, and now would be the time to follow it up. If a soviet is to be built, now—" he moved aside for two women who came slowly up the *calle*. One had her arm around the shorter one, who wept. The Belgian came back.

"Her husband's gone to Saragossa," he said.

They looked after the pair. The street was narrow; they had retreated into darkness already. One note returned as the woman wept.

"Two of the Belgians volunteered today," said the Belgian. "They wouldn't take one—he's got a wife and child in Antwerp."

"And the other?" asked Helen fearfully, her drawn breath whistling against her teeth.

"He's going with the rest tomorrow," answered the boy, the Belgian.

A light went out. The thin slit of sky over the street was buzzing with stars. Everyone was impossibly sleepy. The Welshman came out of the Condal, singing in a low voice. The English party was almost over. Helen remembered the bed, and her room; sleep. She was fighting her hip's pain, pain of remembering.

She got down the street; as she turned for good night, she saw, lit shockingly by the lamp above them, a group of the English.

The twisted shadows made their faces wormy and grave-eaten.

Their throats were dark, like the knotted throats of that unprotected army.

They were deciphering the notice of martial law.

SHE LAY BETWEEN the sheets, running her hand over the turned-back top, running her fingers like spiders over the cold cloth. The luxury, the voluptuousness of being lapped in fine extravagant cloth, was very great. All luxury. The hot-water faucet with its flat shine. The chair at the foot of the bed with her clothes thrown over it. The opened suitcase, *Aaron's Rod*, fresh dresses. The wide *passeig* during General Strike, full of walking people, the smiles, the greeting fist. A black-and-white checkerboard of a dining room floor.

The luxury of this room, a black cave in the world of Spain.

The room was smaller than the connecting one at the Olympic, its ceiling lower, the wallpaper made it close in. Her big bed drew itself together, contracted tight, and hung suspended before the tall double shutter. A crack down the center showed a square black window a hand could touch, so close outside.

She ran her fingers back and forth, madly, along the sheet. Her hip was convulsed in pain, separately, while the rest of her body lay exhausted, thrown flat on the bed. Flaming cathedrals, smoky images. There was a crucifixion going on in her hip, and the long, writhing legs of Jesus stretched like a drawn nerve down her thigh. Moving.

The army must be out of the city by now, walking. Stumbling in the dark across the hills to the south. The dark, soul hills. *En una noche oscura . . .*

Or marching north, encountering mountains and other armies, the savage Pyrenees, the world in Spain, marching hallucinations flooding Europe, finding hostile polite troops in France, a friendly country, murder in Germany, the bony candid faces of British tithe-marchers, weapons everywhere, spreading wide, and then the planes, the new formal death, bombs, grenades, gas, reconnoiterings, skies, and then farther abroad, farther into the past, the anonymous men, the anonymous past . . .

She stretched suddenly in an agonized, stiff cat-stretch.

Mother, father, leader! she thought. The brave men, brave. The love, mature and Hans, recognized by strangers, muscles set; the dark tense army. Could we have gone like that, who come into wars as tourists, helpless, heavy with paraphernalia, delicate, asking for ice and hot water? The feted peeresses during the Russian Revolution, she thought.

Tourists in time of war.

No orders, no orders.

What could they do?

The scene in the committee-room at Moncada arrived before her, the bright hot room, the braided lines drawn down the secretary's cheeks, no foreign nationals, no foreign . . .

The stretch snapped, and her eyes opened frantic.

Image of oppression, a sea throwing up anonymous hearts, netted in veins, floundering, enmeshed.

Image of destruction. The shutter had moved with a wind. She had seen, cast at her eyes, a Fascist, a man with gold epaulets, breathing and hoarse, obscured behind the smoke of his fuming revolver. And another came, and more, each with a thousand workers in his pistol-smoke, Banquo's children against a shutter, fifty men, all hoarse with fear, all golden-shouldered.

She recognized this death: the spy's attack, the general's shot in the head: this was the worst. She sighed, and was fully awake again.

The leg was the past, and she was far away from it. It leapt now, cruelly, and settled to a steady throbbing, whose echo was pulsed in veins: the past, poetry, music, walking through thousands of streets, stone, a generation shrieking, stone, all the girls saying, we *will* be mastered, stone, plane's flight, flag's signal without war, where flags mean survival, the wheels of speed, books, gifts, war. With each throb, riding on throbs, she said the name of someone she loved, some place she could return to, trying to make herself believe the past, hush the insistent past.

The leg grew quiet.

Hans! she thought.

His fine, weird eyes deepened before her. The pure life! he had said. Mother, father, leader! How to have it? What to do now, how to make life in this, how to be part? His carved cheeks were certain as wood. Surely he had a plan, she was certain he had a plan, he would make a life happen. The soldier in all the pride and effort and naked poverty going to Saragossa, walking across range past range of impossibility, black and silver like the land, faces in midnight changing in a wind, conviction building them, darkness painting them out, passion reviving them, arson, phoenix.

Hans, remaining in Spain.

The word, she prayed obscurely, the word, some sign.

Sleep, but: first the word!

A memory broke through, splitting tempest, echoing oracular, vague and august and arbitrary, words of any meaning arriving with one meaning, a ship like a bird reaching, splitting the agony with bombs of sense:

LET EACH STAND IN HIS PLACE

CHAPTER SIXTEEN

Las Pompas Fúnebres

The crash of arsenals, chutes gasping for the air, fast bombers letting loose daytime destruction, death knocking on the ground, the knocking on the door. The knocking on the door.

Sleep crowding over, spilling black, knocks that march with brother faces through.

He was calling . . . HIS PLACE.

The Welshman.

He was saying, come down, come down. Time to start.

To start? Where?

Besieged by confusion again, days shattered, a whole life lived in a few days, shattering down into confusion again?

To start?

She pulled herself up through the end of the night.

The day was violent white through the slits, shutter light falling in slats on the floor. Her clothes fallen on the chair, voices at the near wall, voices at her door. The Welshman's voice, calling, "Come down, we're starting to march. We have to be in our places in ten minutes. We're marching with the army."

A Zaragoza!

Hans, at the Palacio.

She answered.

He would wait for her downstairs. Only hurry.

There was cold water, godsend, running between her fingers over her face and wrists, waking, morning. She was busy at the chair. Awake. To hurry. Before. Too late.

THEY WERE WAITING at the door, the heavy, carven door with its black African fruit was swinging back, the sharp street was struck white with morning, filled with people, the athletes, the city people, standing before the Madrid, before the jewelry store, the electrical appliance shop, all the hotels.

The young athletes stood about, one knot bound to the small Spanish soldier, back to the wall, in the friendly attitudes, against the wall, of a tram at the brick of the chapel-side. "There!" The picture was taken. The Dutch boy spooled the film further in his camera. "I'll get one of the pictures to you," he promised the soldier. The bayonet in the center of the group was bound with a red strip. Yes. But, knotted about it, ragged, was the strip of black.

A Spanish family was ripping a square of black cloth in front of the hotel.

Helen asked the Welshman.

"In memory," he said. "We're marching for the war dead, too."

She put her hand out to the family, with the Welshman's hand. He was binding his strip about his arm.

All the athletes wore the brassards now, black, bound tight about the arm.

She took the scrap. The week. In memory?

"Pin?" she asked the Welshman, smiling the thin, twisted smile down. He shook his head no. And then, with the twist, the smile, he unpinned from his lapel the Olympic pin and handed it to her.

"But do take it!" he insisted. "You should have one, anyway; here, I have one that fits the buttonhole. You take the pin."

The scrap of black pinned to the waist, carried for badge.

Peter and Olive came up, tied with black. He was carrying a

camera. "I've been taking pictures of the teams," he said. "The English are going today—oh, you don't know, do you—you slept late, didn't you?" He laughed. "Good for you," he said. "You missed all that mess of meetings."

"What mess?"

"Johnson went with the English to their consul this morning." He turned to the Welshman, who looked at him with the long unbelieving look he had before the gunboat. "The consul won't let us go with them," he said. "English boats for the English." The Welshman scowled in a painful quick grimace, and turned on his heel. He crossed the street to talk to the English captain.

"It's true," said Peter. "But Johnson's trying to find something else. The consul hasn't done a thing."

"But they didn't want to go!" Helen said.

"They're planning other Games," Peter went on. "Maybe, October. At the Olympic, they said . . ."

"I know . . ."

A whistle blew, at their heads.

The line was moving, up the street. The Americans blew the shrill sport-whistle to call their people together.

Johnson pulled the American flag out of his belt. It was small, after the banners: a Fourth-of-July flag with a gilt spearhead. Stationery stores, the front of tourist cars, the consulate over the wrecked square, the bullet hole channeled deep through the deep plate-glass of its bank-window door. He waved the flag over his head. "Americans!" he called. "Sweatshirts!"

They were slipping the blue jackets over their heads, lettered in white over the shoulder, PEOPLE'S OLYMPIAD.

The Spanish family finished the black cloth, and were running down the street to the avenue.

There was a motion ahead. The Dutch and the Belgians had already started. The English were falling into line.

"Four abreast," Johnson was calling. "We'll all go together. Here, Peter, Helen, Olive, everybody!" the social workers were here, the bitches came running, cured by sleep, glad of the action—they all crowded in behind the small team.

On either side of the street, families waved. The windows emptied, and the street ran along with them, waved, and calling, wearing the strips of black.

EL SERVICIO DE POMPAS FÚNEBRES
Citizens of Barcelona are advised that all matters pertaining to the funeral rites must be regulated through the offices installed in 82 Calle de Muntaner, telephone number, 80.020.

The line swung into the great avenue, broadening from cramped groups circled around their flags into the spaced formations of parade; they fell into the great crowds swamping the avenue, and, at first, were indistinguishable, part of the people. Little by little, as the line lengthened and the flags were raised, they became identified, and the waves of greeting fell on them like waves of heat, rolling over the blood.

The cheers were beginning to go up.

As they passed down, the crowds parted in the sunlight, drawing the children off the center, standing near the trees, stopping, waving. Fists went up.

The avenue was the same they had gone down last night: The sign of the Berlin games, the drug stores, the Church of Bethlehem, with its ruined front, its lean stone saints with the broken skulls darkened by fire in their hands, the signs "BEWARE OF FALLING RUINS." The dwarf hunchback passing rapidly before it, the tall man with his arm around the shoulders of the older woman (weeping violently, would not be comforted), the burned arches, rubble of plaster, twisted pillars, walls fallen to lay bare the skeleton of brick, cancelled altar. The people at the door, staring inside, wheeling to face the line of march.

They filed past, turning toward the church. A stream of fine smoke still flared up at one corner.

The flags were in order now. The leaders of each nationality put flags high in the air. Looking down the line, the countries began to be spaced off. Only, the French were not there.

Helen heard running behind her, and stopped, turning with a violent insistent motion backward. She must not be wrong.

He came up to her quickly, his face hardened. He had been looking up and down the line. It was because the flags went up that he could find her.

He said, "I knew you would understand about last night."

"Hans," she spoke quickly, walking fast to catch up with the march, "I shouldn't have gone away to the hotel. But it straightened us out. The American team talks about going, but there isn't any way for them to leave. I don't want to go."

"Will you stay?" He asked with great pressure behind the words; he smiled, the intensity was too much to carry. She wished again that something might be said on a less simple plane, that their words might not be all clichés and repetitions. But it was unnecessary and ruinous to hope for that, and it was only a flash; she saw down the great walk, down the stream of foreigners. No words could ever mark them down, the sun, the flags, the war. Here she was.

"Yes, I want to," she said.

He was looking up front, too, at the sweatshirts of the athletes. He fell out of step, and she looked questioningly at his face.

"I shouldn't be walking here, perhaps," he said tentatively. "The American team."

"None of us are in the team," Helen showed him the train people, the social workers, two other Americans who were attaching themselves, who had come out of the crowd to join the march. "But we could walk somewhere else, if you'd rather," she said, thinking, Shall I be cut off entirely, and, If we can be together through this thing . . . and, How romantic I am!

"So long as we are together," he answered, answering her, and stepped in line firmly. They were passing the Shirley Temple Club, still hanging torn and shattered, and entering the Plaza de Cataluña again.

Peter leaned over from the row ahead. "Do you know the line of march?" he asked.

"Around the plaza once, and then down the Rambla a block or so to wait for the army." Hans told him how the Palacio had heard the arrangements: the army was starting from mobilization head-quarters, swinging up toward the plaza, and around to fall in with the Olympic people.

Peter spoke to the two bitches, walking with him and Olive, and they changed places with Helen and Hans. The four of them made a line now.

The street opened out into the square. Cars raced down, the guns finding them, the salutes up. A brand-new open car squealed, tires on paving, as the brakes jammed on beside them. It was marked, in white lettering that staggered from over the rear fender across the doors: POPULAR FRONT. It escorted them through the open square.

Many pushed back, crowding to the sidewalks to watch them. Cheer after cheer arose, gathering sound, rising to a peak at the sight of the Americans, fist up to greet the city, arms lifted with the mourning bands trembling. The line swung around the park in the center, swerved in a ripple of mass to avoid the body of a horse, head extended, lying forward from the long neck on the curb.

"Oh, Jesus," Olive said, blankly. She was staring up.

Planes!

They followed her look. Not into the sky, but lower, at the upper-story windows of a corner building. At the window hung the long drooping American flag, extended on its pole.

The consulate.

Hanging from the window, crowding the window, the staff of the consulate, and at the front, answering to a cry of consul, the important face of the man fading into nothing, for, with the logic of a film, the action, the necessary move, his hand came up clenched. He held it there. The crowd shouted up to him. The team shook their flag joyously, madly. The American fists, strangely national, stamped with the eagle for the second, came up.

"Jesus," said Olive, singing out the words, "I never thought I'd live to see the day!"

Peter laughed. The Americans, red-faced, were smiling, amazed and open. "What I'd give for a picture of that!" he swore, smacking his fist down on his open palm.

"Go ahead, take it," Olive was pulling at his camera.

But at the window, they were turning, formally retreating now, as the line passed, as the black thin lines on the arms went into the Rambla.

LAS VÍCTIMAS DE LA TRAGEDIA
Partial list of identified
bodies and of those wounded
in the insurrection:
Grau Martinez, Juan Parisis, Celestino
Criado y Aguilar, Juan Pecus y Torelló,
Francisco Herrera y Santiago.
Antonio Agulló Santiago, Domingo Capuja,
Germinal Vidal, Ramón Jover Brufau,
Luciano Padua Jornet.

Pedro Ros Brugués, Juan Pragas Susagna,
Catalina Benedicto, Enrique Manzano
Carretero.
José Fernández, Diego Serrés Borrás,
Angel García, Benito Calvo, Francisco
Truñón, Jaime Teruel Puerto.
Florián Federico Pastor, José Villegas,
Juan Matas, Rafael Bellors, Abilio
Prado, Roque González, Enrique Fontbernat
y Verdaguer.
Captain Miguel Montesinos, Baltasar
Barrio, Modesto Moya, Pascual Asensio
Pradas, Vicente Picó Quiles, Antonio
Martínes González . . .

The Rambla was spick, the sun cleaned everything, the debris of
burned cars and broken wood was scarcely seen behind the trees,
the marching people; the white truce-flags hanging from the fine
apartment houses were gay, twinkling against the fretted iron of
balconies. Behind some of the flags the curious turned, watching
the parade; three girls leaned from a high window, there a couple
stood, the woman in the curve of the man's arm, standing against
the window-frame.

The black-streaked arms came up, always saluting.

A man with a mourning band remained immobile at the march's
edge, his eyes did not change, his arm stayed up, his head only nodded at the flags.

Two women ran behind the first line of watchers, following
someone in the march—and here, behind them, a woman with a
blond northern face fell in with the Norwegians.

They reached an intersection two blocks below the plaza.
Already the first ranks were breaking at a signal. The march broke,

split about its leaders, and gathered, circular, around the tall Welsh-man, hoisted to the shoulders of the Irish weight-thrower. The teams grouped, waiting for a word, a slogan, and the people follow-ing them and lining the inner walks crowded through. To one side of the Welshman the poster glared:

BÉNÉDICTINE
El Mejor
de los licores

behind him, the five-lamp streetlight stood, freak lily, and the striped awnings, the pale house, the twinkling trees about his head, the ABELLO sign he leaned on.

Gathered at his knee, the remnants of the faces first seen at the Olympic Hotel were recognizable among the Catalans and the Span-ish athletes pressed close: the purple lips of Toni, and the printer, the team manager in his straw hat; the beautiful Dutch-English boy with the darker, stockier others of the Dutch team; the Belgians, the man who had walked from Antwerp, lost in the Pyrenees, the thin scholastic face of the boy who had complained against the French; the Norwegians, latest arrived; the whole English team, long fair Derek, the captain, the Jewish sportgirl with her famished look; and the Americans, the Negro boxer, the blond head of Johnson, the dark partner, Johnny, the Negro girl; the German woman in the trench coat who had been in thirty years of revolution; the guide of the Olympic roof; a hero-seeming man with heavy light eyebrows who had stood in the hall of the Olympic as the foreigners came.

"Olympic athletes, friends of the *Olimpiada!*" the Welshman was saying. "The committee of the *Olimpiada* wishes to speak for us to the people of Barcelona."

The crowd pushed closer. A Catalan was repeating to them, to applause.

He was explaining that the Olympics would be held in October, that the athletes were here to demonstrate with the victorious army of free Catalonia . . .

       . . . Felisa Alonso, José Aragonés y
       Sardá, Juan Altisench y Prats,
       Rafael Aguilar y Padilia, Raul
       Anglada y Taavedra, Gerónimo
       Auret Sanvicente . . .

. . . that the French had left in the interests of the United Front, which now extended across the Pyrenees.

The clamor.

The waves of joy, black ribbons, signs, noise which overbore the ears with cheering.

And the Dutch boy up, to tell of hope, confidence in this war, wish from a neutral country for quick victory.

The English picture of a land at the point of wedge, the key of the arch, that would be swung to the side of Spain, because its people could swing it.

Gunboats, illusion, cheers.

The American, bringing greetings from the farthest off, wishes of trade union groups to a country now governed by those speaking for such groups. Victory. Peace. Solidarity.

And, here, the dark boy, pushing his hair back with a slow, meditative gesture, flinging the thrown-back hand up and out in an explosion of will, as if a ball could rise up to the sun, so thrown, crying for his country, among the bursts of love and backing, clusters of cheers,

listen, he cries,

for the Italian people,

who are with you and will show it at their first moment, their second of first speech again.

The crying applause, forever, tidal.

Sensation.

But far, now, far, the vibration, no sound, nothing in sight but the Italian boy pushing his hand back over his head and pitching it up to the sun,

but the vibration,

but the unheard clock,

the approach.

THEY WERE WAITING through the speech now.

The approach.

They fell back to the sides, under the sparkle of trees, the lamps, until the twinkling white caught their eyes. Truce.

The white traffic markings down the streets drew boundaries here. The march stayed well within, its officers calling the pace, songs, snatches of songs, beginning to rise, the march slowing, dissipating off into the two linings of the road as the column was broken into two long lines within which the army might pass.

The car, POPULAR FRONT, slowed alongside and came to a stop.

Its driver shouldered up in his seat, twisted around to watch for the approach.

An armored car, a truck with heavy metal plates nailed hurriedly in place, marked large C.N.T., rolled past, grinding its gears, filled with uniformed men.

> . . . Silverio Malo, Eloy Jiménez Martínez,
> Francisco Arromolo Garrido, Francisco
> González Arteche.
> Francisco Caparrós García, Alfonso Colón
> Queral, Juliana Vara Cerezuela, Blas
> Zannuy Centeno, Jaime Roselló Aznar,
> Agustín Tomás Navarro, José Cemalias,
> Diego Caparrós, Gregorio Estorche, Buena-

ventura Zofre Lozano y Juan Castellano.
El diputado del Parlamento de Cataluña
Amadeo Colldeforns y su padre . . .

Hans cried out, "Here they come!" he spoke swiftly, under his breath, to Helen, "I'll tell the other Germans that I'm here with them, and come right back."

THEY COULD NOT be seen, they could not yet be heard; it was the cry advancing with them, its front advancing as their front rank came up, that made them known: a great female animal cry, the victorious wail of spectators, the city acclaim of those on the edge and sympathetic, who still have throats to cheer, while those silent fighters pass between their lines.

And now the "Internationale" sprang up, strange, in foreign inflections, as the Norwegians began to sing, changing the wordfall, the sound, almost the song itself.

The Dutch, and the Hungarians; picked it up, unfamiliar, only the form carrying it through, the marching tune.

The French were missing.

But it reached the crowd of Belgians, the song came nearer, the great crying welcome to the army came, mixing, until the chorus became a crying greet:

"*C'est la lutte finale,*
"*Groupons-nous, et demain,*"

. . . El directivo de la C.N.T. Francisco
Ascaso, Eduardo Gorgot, José Biota,
Javier Noguera, Alejandro Prodonis y
Fuentes, Concepción Canet y Alcaráz.
Vicente Vázquez, Salvador Guerrero,
José González y Valencia, Enrique Arnau
y Erude, Julián Gil y González . . .

"L'Internationale . . ."

Here! The first line of set faces, brackets of arms set in perpetual fist, red bands about the head, straight stony foreheads dark.

"Sera le genre humain . . ."

In a high sung note, praising, crying, speeding an army of unarmed men, who walked rope-soled, blankets slung at the shoulder, their women with them, a few, among them, a few, running beside in the blaze, past the shining confiscated roadsters, the homemade armored cars, the lines of spectators, and the Olympic lines who backed them, singing the unique song, finally arriving to the double English version, the English and Americans singing, welcoming, as the army passed; an army, not in the pathetic small battalions of the night before, but rounded up, strong in numbers, unshakable, but barely clothed, barely helmeted, barely armed.

They passed for minutes, the lines of soldiers, passing to a new phase of war. The city was strong now in its own defense; in a day, everything would be running once more, the city would be held; but these were going to meet the outer front. Almost exhausted by the internal battle, with the strenuous look of purity on their faces, they must be renewed to the next front.

They must be renewed. They must be enough.

> . . . Francisco Sanchis y Fernández,
> Francisco López González, Salvador
> Vidal y Perrino, José Martí, Luis
> Pius, José Parera y Cabré, Alejo
> Sáez de Sanmiguel, Luis Botella y
> José M. Valenzuela.
> Francisco Albella Vázquez, Ginés
> Mula, Juan Fuster y Segú, Pedro
> González, Teresa Querol y Querol,
> Lorenzo Cabrizas y Mercader.
> Bonifacio González, Antonio Vicente

Marco, José A. Clemente, José Orriols.
A esta lista hay que añadir Eugenio
Preimau, José Vila y Peiró, Luis
Mitjavila, Guillermo Prat, José Pros,
José Mirato Fornés, José Fabrés, que
ingresaron ayer, por la tarde, a más
de nueve muertos ingresados también
al mismo tiempo, los cuales hasta
ahora no han podido ser identificados . . .

Now, they touched, the two streams, at different speeds, with different meanings, changing each other subtly, strengthening each other, and changing each other's speed, according to laws of hydraulics, streams of armies passing friends, leaving their cities, saluting each other.

A woman ran alongside the Americans. She was trying to reach her son. The line was moving again, falling in behind the army. Hans was back. Helen said to him, "Do they think we're going to Saragossa?"

The woman cut in, joining the line. "American?" she asked. "Are the Olimpiada people with the army?"

"Yes," said Hans across Helen.

"¡*Viva Olimpiada*!" answered the woman, with an abrupt nod of her head. "You see how they care how you sympathize with us."

"Do they think we're going to the Front?" Helen asked. The cheers, the welcomes, the acclaim the line was receiving seemed too much. They entered the Plaza de Cataluña again. The army should have all the cheering.

"Only a very few, perhaps," the woman answered. "They know you are with the Games."

"With Catalonia," said Hans.

"Bravo, you are good people," the woman said, dropping out of line. The plaza was opening before them.

The army was continuing, cutting an avenue of shouts and cries, vivid red and blue and black, and the few uniforms and helmets spotting the march with khaki and metal. They were going on very rapidly, their faces in the pure set, the vigor and effort very plain. This was where the Olympic line broke off. They slowed, swung flags, turning off, breaking parade formation; nobody proceeded, the Americans turned, the English and Norwegian, Belgian, Dutch, and the few Italians and Germans, all turning, watching the army go, marching through the shot stone, the streets of noise, the brilliant farewell, hurrying, with set, young faces to the Fascist line.

CHAPTER SEVENTEEN

MES HOMES!
MES ARMES!

As the army moved away from them, they broke ranks, standing in the street now as anomalous crowd, broken through by pedestrians. From the front, one of the Catalan speakers waved and shouted; they turned to hear; he waved them on with him to the next square. They followed in small groups, losing the line of nationality they had kept in the march, taking down the flags. The citizens who had been magnetized to the parade joined them, calling to friends in the street as they went along, so that the line grew, becoming half Barcelona, half Olympic.

Peter ran up to Helen and Hans. "I found it!" he said, out of breath. "They say we can go swimming off the end of the piers—" He had a little package of the suits under his arm. "That must be where those boys were swimming as the *Djeube* went out." He thrust his head up and looked over the crowd with a farsighted bird's look. "As soon as this is over," he said. "What's up?"

Hans watched him quietly. "One more meeting," he answered. He held Helen's hand very tightly, so that her knuckles pressed together in the fast grip. "The square's a few blocks off."

Peter turned and waved to Olive to come up. As he waved, a man standing on the curb noticed the gesture, and hurried over. It was Spanner. He looked from one to the other, the cheek-veins visibly purpling in his surprise and effort to straighten things out.

"Here," he said, " you don't have to be doing this, you don't have to be marching with a crowd like this, you're all right without it, you're Americans—"

"That's right," said Peter.

"Well," Spanner went on, his short legs pumping to keep up with them, "the city's not so bad by now, it'll all be cleaned up in a couple of days."

"Of course," Helen agreed, staying close to Hans, but hearing Peter and Spanner talking loudly beside her, "everybody's been saying the same thing."

"This can't last," Spanner said violently. "The reaction will set in any day now. The rebels will march in here and clean up, they'll put the city on its feet in no time. Why, the people here are religious, they won't have to wait for Mola's army—do you think they'll stand for these church-burnings? No sirree, they won't—"

Peter cut him short. "Do they look as if they wouldn't?" he asked, gripping Spanner's elbow and pulling him around to face the street.

"Oh, look!" Spanner said, contempt darkening his face, making the egg-blue eyes brighter and shallower. "They couldn't get any word out. But the post office is open now, and the cables—"

"See here, Spanner. If we thought the Fascists were coming in, we'd have got out of this city so damn fast, by foot, or any other way there was," Peter stopped him again. "We stayed because it was in the hands of people we trusted. And the same people are leading this march, and we're wearing this black"—he put out his arm like someone who asks to have his muscle felt—"for the same people. That's how it is."

"Well, then," said the newspaper man, pulling out a handkerchief to wipe his hands, "my mistake. But it seems to me—I thought you were just stringing along with these people for the time being . . ."

A new flood of people joined their line, and Spanner got cut off, wiping his hands, stepping back to stand on the curb; he made a few notes on a little pad, and was enclosed by the crowd and finally blotted out.

"If *that's* going into the *Paris Herald-Trib*," Olive remarked, "and if *that's* a sample of what the papers are saying . . . Look, Peter! He said the post office was open. Come on, we'd better send cables. Helen, you've got to."

The old connections were being set up.

"Yes," Helen answered, "I do. I'll hurry, Hans, I'll come to the square. I won't say anything about plans."

"No, don't," he looked down at her gravely, "they ought to give us all our orders today sometime."

"Don't you want to send a message, that you're safe?" Olive asked him.

He shook his head. "*Kann nicht*," he said.

THE POST OFFICE held long lines at all the windows. A representative from the Belgian team was cabling, and Toni was filling out a form for the Hungarians. He motioned them over to him. "I've had to cross out two," he told them, pointing with his pen at the form, "just don't say anything about the war. They seem to be nervous about spies."

They were sending the word *safe*. Olive looked down at the word, still in wet ink on the ruled line. "It's a very strange thing to say about us at this point," she said in a small voice. "The last things we've been feeling are courage, smugness, safety—what this sounds like."

Helen put her hand on Olive's shoulder, looking with her at the form. "Oh, it's simple enough. Whatever we said would be three-quarters untrue."

The clerk at the wicket counted words. He looked up at them, with the same detective look that the officers at the frontier had. "Straight English? No code?" he barked, and hammered the stamps down with military sharpness when they nodded. He urged them on with the sideway motion of his head.

Toni was waiting at the door, smiling into the sun.

"Hurry!" he said. "The meeting!"

THE LITTLE SQUARE shot out of the dark streets into full sunlight, watercolor bright, clasped around with the government buildings. The ornate, full-breasted statues, the scrollwork in stone, the pompous rows of windows—and, lined along a balcony, the officials, waving down at the Olympic members, who were lost in the city crowd that waved back with them.

The sun picked out every detail, heated the stones of the street, flamed through the wind, white. High up, on one of the rooftops, laundry flashed, whipped into flags like the white truceflags that recurred all through the residential sections. But this was a line of white, flapping, about the shoulders of the two soldiers in their blue uniforms, faced in red, with silver buttons. They leaned on their carbines, looking down at the crowd, backed by the pure blue and white of sky and laundry.

There should be churchbells ringing, bells, that is.

The line of government representatives, bowed and smiled, straightened, with the look of energy on their faces; as all those in authority had tapped, it seemed, the pure energy, either they had opened their reservoirs for this effort, or they were more tired than human beings can survive. The kids on thrones, Peter had said of the boy who relaxed against red velvet on the balcony of Communist headquarters. Here were the older statesmen, with the same look.

On the margin, the two American school teachers who had stayed at the Madrid were telling their story to Johnson; the adventure of being at Sitges, the resort, when the war broke out, of trying to get a cab in from the coast, and standing helpless until the first man with a gun came along to offer them reassurance and a place for the night; imagine, the first man we saw, armed to the teeth! they cried; the story of the boy on the shore who ran up the steps of the church as they were about to set fire to it, crying, "Don't do it, it brings tourists, and also, it is beautiful," and preventing the burning with his argument.

Deeper in the crowd, Toni talked to one of the volunteers. He would go to Saragossa later in the week. The organization was good, everything was moving ahead; all the trade union quarrels had been lost in this war, the Anarchists held, the P.O.U.M. was holding, the *Catalanistas* saw here a chance for their country and for the United Front together; if there was such complete organization now, it might be true, the rumor that Bela Kun had been down here during June; but he was reported in Argentina that month, in Hungary, in five different places. Preparations had been made, all over Spain; the government had been warned, and had been ready with arms; the two regiments that had revolted under Goded in Barcelona were fools to advance with the cry "Long live the Republic!" for those who answered their machine gun volley with football tactics, tackles, head-on charges, were shouting back the same slogan triumphantly, with rage.

Deeper in the crowd, Collins the Irishman helped back the bakery wagon against the curb for speakers to stand. Shoulder against it, he complained to the Welshman that, given broader shoulders, he might have been the weight-thrower he wanted to be; he gave the first speaker a hand up, and stood back among the English.

The straight lines of mourning black were dissipated now. Spotted among the Spaniards in the square, the Olympic people were hard to find, even by the armbands, for the opening was so completely filled that the crowd pressed tight; only the heads were seen, the arms below the shoulder were lost and invisible. The crowd became single minded, uniform, Catalans and foreigners welded finally. All the faces turned up to the balcony, the soldiers against the laundry, the fierce sky that rained light down on that coast, that city; they turned to look up to the speaker.

It was the committee-member who represented the Games, telling of the place of the Olimpiada in the fight, introducing representatives of all countries, to repeat here what had been said in the earlier meeting, and to tell the participants the government's position now.

Peter whispered to Olive in the crowd, "We were right, the Games have embarrassed the government all along. Foreigners, to create *situations*—what parasites we become!"

In the balcony, the metal-faced Communist appeared, leaning over, looking down with a recognizing glint at the heads of those he had brought in. The committee-member spoke of the glory of the war, and his words were blotted out. The Catalans shouted in a breathy cry of relief, the soldiers on the roof moved together, leaning on the bright guns. A painful line of sunlight ran down the metal of the guns and buttons. Quicksilver brilliance escaped over the square of faces, a noonday smile of light.

". . . all countries defending the Popular Front, the need we have now to keep it whole and fighting . . ."

A car blasted three times with its horn, trying to force through from a side street, but the group shifted for a moment at the corner, someone ran off to speak to the driver, and he backed down, taking another street. The entrance of every tributary was filling with people, who edged in, contracting the space around the speaker until the wagon he used for platform hardly showed, tided with listeners. Only a few heavily shadowed doorways stood free.

Helen found Hans in one of these, as Martín was announced. He climbed on top of the car, dominating the meeting immediately. She recognized him before the introduction; his square impressive head with the fierce blond eyebrows marked him. He had been in the doorway of the Olympic, he had spoken in the street for the

Olimpiada committee; but now he was introduced as the organizer
of the Games, the force that had set in action this week which had
become so different from what was planned, the leader of the committee, about to start for Saragossa. He would speak, in a few minu-
ets; but first, he wished to have a speaker for the French delegation
read the message from the French.

THE FRENCH DELEGATION TO THE PEOPLE'S
OLYMPICS, EVACUATED FROM BARCELONA AND
LANDED TODAY AT MARSEILLES . . .
>   the tranquil voyage, Mediterranean, the
>   tawny cliffs of the coast, cypress,
>   oranges, the sea, the smooth ship passing
>   all these scenes, promised for years,
>   from which they had been forced away
>   into familiar country, streets they
>   knew, more placid beaches

PLEDGE FRATERNITY AND SOLIDARITY IN
THE UNITED FRONT TO OUR SPANISH
BROTHERS . . .
>   the bird flight sailing forced
>   upon them, so that no beauty
>   found could ever pay for the
>   country from which they had
>   been sent home and the battle
>   which they had barely seen begun

WHO ARE NOW HEROICALLY FIGHTING THE
FIGHT WE SHALL ALL WIN TOGETHER

"Hans," she said, standing close to him in the recess of the doorway. The crowd almost reached them, sunny and receptive in the
square, pressing close to the speaker. She looked up into his face,

brown, darkened by the arch over them, and, turned on the speaker, the weird eyes. The loved mouth.

"I know what you are doing," she said in English, "bravery. Whatever has happened to change me is ended now, in this week, all added up. Whatever you do, I have come along—"

He looked down at her with an unchangeable mute look, still carrying something of the look he gave to the speaker, but darker, close.

"Oh, Hans," she said in his language. "I wish I spoke German."

Or English, either, she thought. The change, the proof in her, the moment of proof given her by the war, the academic sadness she knew before, reaching, inarticulate; all the life she was beginning to see belonged to him, discoverer, inventor.

He took her elbow with his arm that was deep in the shadow and held her against his side. He was strong, his will was clear, he knew quickly.

He spoke in French. "Helena, shall we play word-games?" His thought was always visible on him, small, a change like water change; he remembered the train. He went on. "The gifts of the revolution. Shall we say: if it had not been just so at Port Bou on a Sunday morning, if a certain train had not stopped at such a town—? The whole revolution. It gave us to each other, that doesn't end anywhere. We know what we have to do. Even when you go—" he turned his head painfully.

Her face came up, colored and blurred. All division, all the denial of the time was bearing down on her. She protested it.

The voice she spoke in was mad, she felt she cried out, but the words did not issue so very loud.

"Hans, shall I stay with you, shall I stay?" She was repeating and desperate now, wanting to be something else, in a different position, possible.

"We know what we have to do," he said evenly. He moved his head from side to side, with a menagerie-animal slinging motion.

"Helena," he repeated without looking at her, in a dull fever. "Helena."

The crowd shouted at something the speaker said. Martín was up again, on the car, his square face and heavy yellow eyebrows dominating the square.

"I *am* changed," Helen told him. "I want you to know. You began anew—you set in motion—it is as though I had gone through a whole other life," she said lamely. But she felt the truth of the words before she spoke them and they became timid and broken.

"Yes," he said. He was still suffering.

"I was almost born again, free from fear. The ride in, or the morning at the Olympic."

The crowd bore forward against the speaker on an immense cheer, drowning Hans's response. The boy standing on the roof of the car put up his hand for silence, and Martín went on, in Catalan. He was to repeat this speech in all the languages. The crowd quieted. Hans repeated the word.

"Earlier," he answered, and smiled for the first time that day. "I saw you on the station platform. It was there that I saw you, you know," he said, with love. She admitted all his feeling, she was ready for anything he would disclose, anything the crowd or the world disclosed, sensitized to their wish. Through Hans. Transformed. "There was a pregnant woman—and the Hungarian told you it was General Strike, and walked away. I saw your face change, and a look entered. It was a beautiful thing for me to watch."

She hardly heard his words, as the meaning struck her. She only saw his lips move, and felt the hot sunned space between herself and his body, and the hot truth of his biography. She saw quickly the children in the trees, the lady from South America who was mother to her in her half-day of adolescence, the friends, the leadership, the deep terrible truck ride, the whole progress of a life within her life. And then she saw what he was saying.

"And you!" she cried.

Now it was clear.

Life within life, the watery circle, the secret progress of a complete being in five days, childhood, love, and choice.

Now it was coming to this.

She could see what was coming.

She was riding to it, down its street, its track.

"I am German," he said.

Slowly and magnified, like automobile accidents in the hour-long moment before the fender smash.

"It was clear to me from the beginning."

All his life, moving so steadily, watercourse! she thought; only let me move, too, keep on pouring free. It had always been clear to him; he was continuing.

"Even before I came to Spain, I think it was clear. And the necessity."

The cheering of the crowd was growing tremendous. The speech was being finished for the first time, in its first language, going on, stopping for the cheers, swinging ahead like the truck, the fierce journey geared to halt at barricades, swinging through speeches and lifted fists.

They must go back to the demonstration.

He bent down and kissed her, tense; the rich sunlight, the rich shadow, the heady cheering, were lost, and she was absorbed again and dark, and knew she was about to change again, but without violence, through natural slow force.

"I love you," he said, and put his hand on her, again. "Red Front," flashing the memory. "I'll be back in a minute."

He was in the crowd, turning, moving so rapidly with his runner's acuteness, his entire body aware and turning, so fast that she could not see him as he passed through its depth. She went forward, to the first step at the doorway. Now she could see the crowd plainly. The long sea of faces was all one face, repeated always over the entire square and into the fingers of streets stretching away from it, one face always, set in vigor and effort.

After a moment it broke: she could see Olive and Peter standing about ten yards from her. She edged through the crowd to where they stood, listening.

"Now he will repeat in French," Peter whispered. Martín threw his head up. The short second introduction was over. He was beginning again.

"Comrades; Olympic athletes; spectators, friends of the Olympics, Catalans:

"You came to Barcelona to see the Games of the Popular Front . . . "

Olive swung to Peter with her whole body, frankly. "I want something," she said.

". . . You have been privileged to remain to see the glorious victory, the real victory, of that Front."

"I want a child. I want us to have a child," she said in a clear profound voice.

"Many of you come from countries which have begun this war, and you know that it is the war we all face, throughout the world. It is the war of our times. We know that now.

"Many of you come from countries suffering the same oppression we have suffered. Your countrymen will have another example of victory. The people of Spain have many gifts. This struggle is their gift to all countries.

The victory, thought Helen, in all countries. Planes, the bombs of war, the illustrious words, love, my love, my love. The coast, the voyage?

"You have come to this country as foreigners in the moment of our war, and you have felt the unreal constraint of acting as aliens when you are our brothers, when this war belongs to all of us. You have been placed in the position of provocation to the Fascists; they have fired on your demonstrations, they have killed your men.

The faces lifted in pride and knowledge. The crowd of nations sealed in, small, unified.

"You have felt the inaction of strangers, but you are not strangers to us.

The silence, the attention, the knowledge of all of them, now, finally, of each other, the hurrah in the enormous sunlight (soldiers, blazing white, the coast, the sea, the words at last, promise and condemnation) like the hurrah of big guns, and the speed like sleep, like victory, of the cheering in their ears.

"Now you are about to return to your own countries. The boats are ready: the English will leave on their own boat, the Belgians will take all others on a ship they have chartered. If you have felt inactivity, that is over now. Your work begins. It is your work now to go back, to tell your countries what you have seen in Spain."

ANNOTATIONS TO *SAVAGE COAST*

1 At some point Rukeyser edited the title of the novel to reflect the transnational nature of the text, calling it *Savage Coast* (*Costa Brava*).

11 Scheduled to take place July 19–26, 1936 in Barcelona, Spain, the *Olimpiada Popular*, or People's Olympiad, was an international event organized by the Second Spanish Republic, meant to be a protest and alternative to Hitler's Berlin games (scheduled for August) and one to which twenty-two countries were sending over two thousand athletes. Nine Americans were sent by the Committee of Fair Play in Sports. Two hundred athletes who had traveled to Spain for the games stayed or returned to volunteer in the International Brigades. More information on the People's Olympiad can be found in: Antony Beevor, *The Battle for Spain: The Spanish Civil War 1936–1939* (New York: Penguin Books, 2006); Peter N. Caroll, *The Odyssey of the Abraham Lincoln Brigade* (Stanford: Stanford University Press, 1994); the *New York Times* (February 22,1936); the *Daily Worker* (July 23, 1936), and in the ALBA Collection at the NYU Tamiment Library.

11 Robert Herring, the editor of *Life and Letters To-day*, asked Rukeyser to travel to Barcelona to report on the antifascist games; instead, they published her account of the war as "Barcelona, 1936" in the autumn of 1936. Her correspondences with Herring can be found in The Muriel Rukeyser Collection, Henry W. and Albert A. Berg Collection of English and American Literature, at the New York Public Library. You can read her essay in, *"Barcelona, 1936" & Selections from the Spanish Civil War Archive*, ed. Rowena Kennedy-Epstein, New York: Lost

and Found, The CUNY Poetics Document Initiative, Series II (March 2011).

15 C. Day Lewis, *The Magnetic Mountain* (1933).

16–17 "The Catalan women" on the train are debating contemporary politics; it is July 19, 1936 and the military revolt is already underway. The terms that Rukeyser is catching, "*anarquista, comunista, monàrquica*," etc., demonstrate the complexity of Spanish politics at the outbreak of war. Catalonia had and continues to have a long history of Anarchist resistance, and, as the novel depicts, the Anarchists were on the forefront of organizing in response to the coup, securing parts of Spain, including the industrial centers of Madrid and Barcelona, against the Fascists. The Second Spanish Republic, while Socialist-Democrat, was not particularly loved by many parts of the Left, for it had failed to make the kind of far reaching reforms necessary for a more equitable society. On the other hand, the people of Spain rallied in defense of their Republic against the church-, elite-, and fascist-backed coup, and in Catalonia particularly they did this with an eye toward revolutionary change—from the collectivization of the land and factories to women's liberation. One of the great issues on the left during the war was that the Communist Party proposed that the workers' revolution should wait until after the war was won in order to build a strong Popular Front against fascism, one that included the middle class and that framed the fight against Franco as one for the preservation of bourgeois democracy. The Anarchists believed that the revolution and winning the war were one and the same. Orwell, of course, wrote a famous critique of the Communist Party in Spain in *Homage to Catalonia* (1938).

19 "Hungarians from Paris": By the 1930s, Hungary, which had already instituted anti-Semitic laws in the post-war era, had become increasingly aligned with and dependent on the fascist powers. Many Jews and radicals moved to Paris. Robert Capa

(née Endre Ernő Friedmann), for example, perhaps the most famous photographer associated with the Spanish Civil War, was one of many Hungarian Jews working and living in Paris by the mid 30s.

20 "Revolt in Morocco": The military coup against the Second Spanish Republic began as a revolt in the Spanish garrisons in Morocco on July 17, 1936, and marked the beginning of the civil war. Spain's colonial history in North Africa, and its loss of empire worldwide, proved to be an important factor in the uprising. Not only was there a large and well-trained military class that wanted to maintain its political, economic, and social place in an era in which there was little opportunity for external military action, but, as Helen Graham describes in *The Spanish Civil War: A Very Short Introduction* (Oxford: Oxford University Press, 2005), because of this the war was fought like a colonial war turned inward against "insubordinate indigenous people." The military elite viewed themselves as having an "imperial duty" to maintain unity against the internal social and political changes in Spain. Not only did the military techniques practiced during the colonial war in North Africa play an important role, but the use of North African soldiers in Franco's army is an equally important and understudied part of this history.

27 "Scottsboro": Rukeyser had traveled to report on the second Scottsboro Nine trial in 1933 with the International Labor Defense (ILD). In 1931, nine black men were charged with raping two white women, and all but one were sentenced to death. The ILD worked on the case, and the Communist Party publicized it widely as indicative of racial and legal injustice under capitalism, engendering enormous attention from the international left, and forming important ties between the Communist Party and civil rights groups. During the trial, Rukeyser was jailed for fraternizing with African Americans and caught typhoid fever.

40 "General Strike": A work stoppage of all but the most necessary professions (pharmacists, doctors) was called on July 19 to defend the Spanish Republic against the fascist insurrection. A coalition of left-wing groups, anarcho-syndicalists, and communists, came together to form the Popular Front.

41 W.H. Auden, *The Orators* (1932).

43 Rukeyser spent most of her time with the Swiss and Hungarian Olympic Teams. The American, British, and French teams were already in Barcelona.

44 The six Americans on the train with Rukeyser were Ernest and Rose Tischter, David Friedman, Molly Sobel, Lillian Lefkowitz, and Mrs. Martha Keith "of Peapack, NJ" as described in the *New York Times* article "Start of Strife in Spain is Told by Eyewitness" (July 29, 1936).

48 Mur des Fédérés: "The Communards' Wall" in the Père Lachaise Cemetery, commemorates the execution of Parisians by the French army during the last days of the Paris Commune. Considered the first successful workers' revolution, the citizens controlled Paris from March 18 to May 28, 1871. Tens of thousands were massacred during the "bloody week," and a great many more imprisoned or executed after the revolution was suppressed by the government. For a good history, see Donny Gluckstein's *The Paris Commune: A Revolution in Democracy* (Chicago: Haymarket Books, 2011).

49 John Reed was the author of *Ten Days that Shook the World* (1919), a firsthand account of the 1917 revolution in Russia.

52 C.N.T., the Confederación Nacional del Trabajo (National Confederation of Labor), was formed in 1910. An anarcho-syndicalist union, during the civil war they joined with the F.A.I., the Federación Anarquista Ibérica (Anarchist Federation of Iberia), thus uniting as the C.N.T.-F.A.I. The U.G.T., the Unión General de Trabajadores (General Union of Workers) was a Marxist-Socialist union formed in 1888. At the outset of war they joined forces as the Popular Front, along with many other workers' parties. Both the C.N.T. and U.G.T. are still active unions.

55 Karl Marx and Friedrich Engels, *The Communist Manifesto* (1848).

61 General Goded was one of the many military leaders involved in the coup. When he surrendered, Lluís Companys, the president of Catalonia, forced him to make an announcement over the radio. He was executed that August. In his surrender speech he states, "Fortune has been against me and I am held prisoner. Therefore, in order to avoid more bloodshed, the soldiers loyal to me are free of all obligation."

Companys's speech that followed: "Citizens: Only a few words, for now is the time of action and not words. You have just heard General Goded, who led the insurrection and asks to avoid more bloodshed. The rebellion has been stifled. The insurrection is put down. It is necessary for everyone to continue following the orders of the Government of the Generalitat (The Autonomous Government of Catalonia), heeding its instructions. I do not want to end without fervently praising the forces who, with bravery and heroism, have been fighting for the Republican cause, supporting civil authority. Long live Catalonia! Long live the Republic!"

79 Sylvia Townsend Warner, *Summer Will Show* (1936).

79 Chapter five remained unfinished, and is quite fragmentary, almost more impressionistic than narrative. Rukeyser appended a note to the manuscript outlining what she intended to do:

> *(Note to the reader of this ms: The gaps in this chapter are conspicuous. They are the only gaps in the ms and they will be filled in a day or two, but that does not excuse them.*
>
> *One comes after p. 12 and is the story of the plans of the Hollywood executives to escape, their failure, and the transportation of a Spanish doctor to Barcelona in the car they had*

"commandeered." Then the mayor's committee representative arrives, thanks the train for its letter and collections, and warns them that they have one hour to provision themselves and then they are to lock themselves in the train, for the Fascists are expected. The grocery scene (unfinished) follows. It concludes with a fight between the two German children and the passage through the town of the gun-cars.

Next scene on the train, expecting the Fascists. Conversations between Helen and lady from S. Am., and Helen, Peapack and two Moncada boys. Helen goes for a walk with Peter, who has been looking for a place to swim, and stops for food at a peasant's house. She is left alone while he returns to the train. The house is fired on by snipers in the hills. She returns to the train. Bugle in town announces danger is past until further notice.)

92 In this scene, Helen and Peter are trying to grasp the situation and the experience on the train, while cautious not to romanticize or "dramatize it." Rukeyser crossed out a fantastic line, where Helen says: "It's very literary, that train," a phrase that encapsulates so much about the moment in which she was writing. The self-conscious awareness of the line speaks to how Rukeyser was positioning herself and this work in the context of her contemporaries. By keenly referencing the novelistic trope of travel as transformative, it also highlights a common theme in writing about the Spanish Civil War, one in which "going over" is reflected in the movement of the train, of crossing the border into Spain.

92 Rukeyser wrote a fragment that was never fully integrated into the chapter:

Helen looked over the water jug, as she drank, as its thick rim pressed against the bridge of her nose. The line of it set the little garden against the olive hill, cutting off the rest. The hill looked peaceful, cultivated. She finished drinking, and gave the jug to the woman.

"Peter!" she exclaimed, turned to the garden. "Vegetables!"

He sat the jug down at the wall, finished drinking in a moment, nodded to the nodding woman. "You have a fine appetite for water," he said to Helen. She felt again the hot fear in her stomach.

"Spain makes me thirsty," she answered, and smiled, looking at the hill.

"Scared?"

"Certainly." They stood over the row, in the little garden. The ripe peas were round in the pod, cleanly seen under the thin green cover, each full bubble casting a small shadow. Succulence and freshness, the pottery jug, the rows of peas, the little, quiet house.

The woman bobbed and laughed, at the praise of her garden. Behind her, a larger woman and an old man were sitting in the sun, on a bench against the house. They watched the foreigners. The old man pulled out a long rope lighter and touched off his cigarette.

"That's what I should bring back!" Helen said. "There's a man in Connecticut who's been wanting a lighter like that—" She repeated to the woman.

"That's easy, in Barcelona. You can get them anywhere. One peseta." Her face changed suddenly, and she laughed. "Not now," she said. "Wait. *Huelga General.*"

Peter suddenly snapped his fingers.

"Maybe she'll make lunch for us." he turned to her.

"Of course, anything, eggs, an omelette, perhaps?"

"Vegetables!" he said. "Could we have vegetables?" He grinned at Helen. "At this rate, I'll be a fresh-air fiend by tomorrow."

"Certainly vegetables." The woman turned and shouted at the other, larger one, in Catalan waiting for the answer.

"How many?" Peter counted them out: Olive, the bitches . . .

"And the Drews and the lady—" Helen added.

"All right, eight, then."

"But they've got a lot of provisions. They won't want to leave the train, anyway," Helen thought: And your provisions? Where had Peter been while they were buying food?

"Provisions! In the middle of the day! Well, say five then. Will you cook vegetables for at least five, please?" Peter was bargaining with the woman.

"Leave your young lady here," she was shrewd, she wrinkled her nose and eyes at Helen, she waved Peter on, "bring the rest back."

"You're hostage, Helen!"

Peter was running down the road.

93 Edwin Rolfe, "To My Contemporaries" (1933).

93 Chapter six opens with a passage from D.H. Lawrence's *Aaron's Rod* (1922). Including this text inside her own, such that her character is in communication with it, is significant. *Aaron's Rod*, like *Savage Coast*, is a travel narrative, one whose protagonist is also situated on the precipice between two eras. Rukeyser wrote in her journal about Lawrence during the period in which she was working on the novel, and his influence on her early work is clear, particularly his explicit renderings of sexuality and his discussion of a dynamics and metaphysics of poetry, and his *Studies in Classic American Literature*. Likewise, Rukeyser, like Lawrence, became a target of New Criticism, particularly by the critic R.P. Blackmur.

109 T.S. Eliot, *The Waste Land* (1922). The line to which she refers is in "Burial of the Dead," when Madame Sosostris reads the tarot cards: "Here is Belladonna, the Lady of the Rocks, the lady of situations."

111 Hart Crane, *For the Marriage of Faustus and Helen* (1923).

119 J.W. von Goethe, from *Wandrers Nachtlied* (*Wanderer's Nightsong*) (1870). The last two lines, which she recites, translate to "wait soon/you too shall rest."

120 André Malraux, *Le temps du mépris* (*Days of Wrath*) (1935).

140 Horace Gregory, "Abigail to Minerva" (1936).

141 "The little plaster saint": The Catholic church had long been aligned with the ruling class and worked in the interests of the monarchy. During the war it supported the fascists, legitimizing the coup d'etat.

158 Henry Adams, *A Dynamic Theory of History* (1904).

188 "*Notas Gráficas de la Sublevación Fascista*": Images of the Fascist Uprising.

202 "hero-faced woman": I suspect that Rukeyser might be describing Dr. Edith Bone, a Hungarian photojournalist who had become a British subject in the 1930s, and was in Spain with Felicia Browne, a painter who joined the people's militia in August. Browne was the first British subject to be killed at the front. Bone remained in Spain to support the Republic; eventually she returned to Hungary, where she was disappeared and imprisoned in 1949, accused of being a spy. Her book *Seven Years Solitary* (New York: Harcourt Brace, 1957) recounts her experience.

207 "*Il n'y a pas de Pyrenees*": There are no Pyrenees, a phrase made by French supporters of the Spanish Popular Front indicating that the "front" extended across the Pyrenees border (Martin Hurcombe. *France and the Spanish Civil War: Cultural Representations of the War Next Door: 1936–1945*. [Burlington, VT: Ashgate, 2011]). The hope that France would form a United Front with Spain, along with England, was short lived. By

August, France and England signed a nonintervention pact, along with Germany, Italy, and Russia, one that was supported by the United States. Nevertheless, Germany, Italy, and US corporations openly violated the agreement, and continued sending military aid to Franco's Nationalist Army. Mexico and Russia supported the Republican army, though minimally, in comparison.

219 Franz Mehring, *Karl Marx: The Story of His Life* (1935).

220 Hans refers to his political involvement with the militant *Rotfrontkämpferbund* (Red Front Fighters), part of the German Communist Party (KPD) during the Weimar republic. The party was suppressed by Hitler in 1933, and its leader Ernst Thälmann was imprisoned throughout the 30s, then shot at Buchenwald in 1944. German political exiles, like Hans, formed one of the first International Brigades in Spain, calling it the "Thälmann Brigade" in his honor, and saw the fight against fascism in Spain "as the German chance in or out of Germany."

232 Joris Ivens and Hanri Storick, *Misère au Borinage* (1933). A documentary film about a mining strike in Belgium.

257 *"MES HOMES! MES ARMES!"* was a slogan used on U.G.T. and P.S.U. propaganda posters during the war. The full poster reads: *MES HOMES, MES ARMES, MES MUNICIONS PER AL FRONT* (More Men, More Arms, More Ammunition for the Front).

266 Like Boch, between 1936 and 1939, around thirty-five thousand foreigners volunteered for the International Brigades.

WE CAME FOR GAMES*
A Memoir of the People's Olympics, Barcelona, 1936

W*e could see very little from the train. But what we could see was full of sunlight and mystery at the same time: the Vaterpolo team out there on the station platform doing exercises, and all the yellow flowering mimosa trees full of little boys trying to see into the windows of the compartments.*

There was the station, and the row of houses beyond. We showed no sign of starting. The engineer, somebody said, was sitting on the steps up front, eating bread and sausage.

I could hear a radio playing Bing Crosby songs, and then a wild yodeling broke in; it was the Swiss team in the car ahead.

An old Catalan woman said, "This train isn't going to move, not anymore."

I say "we," but I had been sent down from London by myself. It was the hot, beautiful summer of 1936, my first time out of America, with all the smiting days and nights of the month in England.

I was working for the people who had brought me over with them, and I had driven across to London from the landing in Liverpool on the first morning. Then the first tastes: many people who came to my friends' flat, people who afterward would be the Labour government, and the people I saw, poets and refugees and the League of Nations correspondent for the *Manchester Guardian*. A brilliant performance of *The Seagull*, and the Russian Ballet, and a

*Originally written for and published by *Esquire* magazine, October 1974.

tithe-marchers' day, all silent, with the signs reading WE WILL NOT BE DRUV. The feeling of Hitler in the sky, very highly regarded by many, the feeling of Mussolini. Adventures in meaning, too; curiosity about the cooperatives, for my friends were working on a book about co-ops in England and Scandinavia as well as in the U.S.; curiosity about Russia; all-absorbing delight and storm about people, for me, and my own wish not to be "druv," for I was driven.

When the editor of an English magazine said, "Will you go to Barcelona for me?" I put away a chance to go to Finland and Russia with my friends. The Olympic Games were to be held in Hitler's Berlin early in August, and there were going to be Games in Barcelona as a peaceful assertion and a protest. France had asked for more money for these Games than the sum allotted to the big Olympics, and the United States and many other countries were going to send teams. The wedding of the other editor of the magazine, a woman I had never met, came at that moment too—and my editor would have to go to the wedding. I told my editor I would go. He came to the station with me, and gave me a handy black and orange book, a *Guide to 25 Languages of Europe*.

Now that book was being passed among us on the train.

On the way south, there was a tantalizing hour in Paris, glimpses of avenues and buildings seen in movies and paintings and dreams, and kiosks with posters advertising gas masks for children. A change of trains, and the night, and the Spanish frontier at Port Bou, and then this train, going slowly, with a flash of the Mediterranean, and shoulders of olive hills, and a Catalan family in the wooden compartment with me. Slowly, and the olive, yellow-strapped uniform of the Civil Guard; the grins over English cigarettes and the Olympic teams, whom everybody had noticed at the frontier because one or two had some difficulty about the collective passports under which they traveled.

The train had gone more and more slowly, and then stopped here, Moncada. A small station after Gerona, a clearly unimportant town. The Spaniards begin to talk to the Hungarian athletes, partly in French, partly in a mixture of sign language and *25 Languages*. But the phrase-book language, "One o'clock exactly. Thank you very much," would not carry the questions about the Olympics, or politics. The Spaniards said, "The Army. Some on one side, some on the other. Not good to talk." These are not Spaniards; they are Catalans. Their own nation, their own language (not in the orange and black book), and they have been preparing for these Games, these *Jocs*, for a long time. People are hurrying to Barcelona from Paris, from Switzerland, from America, from all over France, from England, whose unions have sent a tennis team and some track people.

The train does not go. On the station platform, there are armed civilians patrolling, and now the small boys are climbing the little blossoming trees. Rumors begin to go through the train, and the Catalan family sitting with me begins to make a plan. The heavyset fine father talks to his mother, who agrees; he pats his young olive-colored son on the head. The boy is eleven; he looks at me with iodine-color eyes as his father invites me to come into the town with them. His father says, "It is General Strike."

At that moment two Americans come through the train. They have heard that an American woman is here. The lady from Pea-pack, New Jersey, had shared my compartment on the French train; she is up front, and is concerned about me. I decided for the train, and told the Catalan family I would find them later.

We went through the train, talking; really we were collectors of rumor. The engineer was in charge of us now, and the stationmaster spoke for the town. No, he could not say how long the strike would last. But the shooting had begun at the barracks in Barcelona that morning. It had something to do with the Games, they said; or something to do with the moment of the Games, at which several thousand foreigners were expected in the city. Some of the soldiers, at the appeal of the crowd before them, had refused to fire and had turned against their officers, to immense cheers. There was something about generals, a general flying in from the Islands.

The tourists, frightened and inconvenienced, murmur, make a kind of flutter and try to plan.

Who is on this train? Conspicuously, Catalan families on their way from town to town or back to Barcelona, and the two teams, the Hungarian water-polo team from Paris and the Swiss team. The Catalans leave the train, almost without exception, and find quarters in the town.

There is a German who has come to run in the Games, on his own, from France where he has been working as a cabinetmaker. Bavarian, with a broad strong face like a man in a Brueghel picture—or a Käthe Kollwitz—his cheekbones stand out. He smiles, a very dark brown flashing. He had been a *Rotfrontkämpfer* who left Germany soon after Hitler came to power.

In first class, there are Italian businessmen, and a German family with two children who are hitting each other; a very beautiful woman from South America; the French deputy, M. de Paiche, who has come officially to the Games, and his male secretary; two rather attractive English couples on their way to Mallorca on holiday, from a bank and from *The New Statesman*, and others in the two cars who are not at once identifiable. In the one Pullman, there are Hollywood people, a director and two cameramen.

A Spanish doctor emerges from the Pullman and tells us about the Hollywood men; he has offered to hire a car, and to go with them to the city. But they do not want that. They want to go back to the frontier.

The mayor of the town appears on the platform; very grave, wearing in his lapel a black ribbon of mourning. There have been deaths of men from this town today.

A tall man, distinguished face, thin, with fine movements, climbs down the steps of the train. We see him speaking for a while to the mayor, as the long evening closes down. The birds begin;

the boys whistle from the trees. Word comes back: the tall man is a professor of philosophy from the University of Madrid. He will act as go-between for the train.

FIRST OF ALL, household arrangements. The two English couples bring basins of water and the little cakes of soap they carry with them, for the use of the train.

"But we can wash on the train!" says the lady from Peapack. She has five white rawhide valises, I admired them in the compartment, one is a hatbox.

No, we can't wash on the train; that water was used up hours ago.

We sleep on the train. As we choose places—we have all moved to first class—the two teams are playing soccer outside. There is a rattle of guns from the olive grove on the hill. A dark figure moves to the steps where the professor of philosophy has stood. After about an hour, he comes out again; his face cannot be seen, but his shoulders are in grief.

The station is dark, except for three or four lights and the slight movement of mimosa flowers, shadow and yellow in a slight breeze coming down cool from the Pyrenees.

Night. Two families, the father wounded, walk in from Barcelona with news of a tremendous battle. The radio goes on at half-hour intervals: Beethoven's *Fifth*, government bulletins, tangos, *You're Driving Me Crazy*, sardanas, Catalan songs. As long as the radio goes, the government is in control. And now, over that booming, scratching sound, a tired voice. The general who had tried to take Catalonia. There are four of them: Goded, Mola, Sanjurjo, Franco. Sanjurjo has been killed; this is Goded. He sounds to me like the businessmen during the Crash, an endless tiredness in his defeated voice. He is telling his followers to lay down their arms. There has been enough bloodshed, he says.

We write a letter on the train—to the town—and take up a

collection for the wounded. We each give a little, the athletes do, too. No, not the German family, not the Italian businessmen, not the Cockney shoe salesman; not the six platinum blondes, the Rodney Hudson Young Ladies, who were supposed to open tonight in Barcelona. The passenger whose help counts most turns out to be a League of Nations observer from Switzerland. He revises our letter to the town, putting it in perfectly acceptable diplomatic language.

We take it into Moncada, to the next street over from the station, past the finer houses belonging to people who live in the capital and come there for weekends sometimes. In the next street, the Committee is in session at the mayor's office. The mayor accepts the money with a speech of thanks, and turns the letter over to the Committee—formed of members of the two unions, and the Anarchists. Catalonia is Anarchist country, the first I have ever seen. They say there has been fighting for a hundred years, but never like this.

One of us begins to speak in sympathy for the town, but the mayor puts his hand up, stopping him flat. "No," he says. "No foreign nationals can intrude in revolutionary situations."

The passengers' committee and the Committee shake hands, and we go back to the train.

The roosters crowed all night, after the radio shut down. At four-forty-five the train shook, and the branches of the trees. A spire of black smoke could be seen off to the side; the church had been bombed.

NOW WE BEGIN to hear the story. The dark figure who had come to the train last night had been the priest, come to ask the professor to hide him. For an hour, the professor had considered, and had finally given his answer: this was an international place, the church had been storing ammunition for the officers' revolt, and he could not. Years later, in America, I heard Spaniards debating this incident. The professor had become an ambassador by then;

but this incident had become one of the most well-known and a node of argument of the war, with the death of Lorca. The train had become famous for the story of the priest and the professor of philosophy.

Five officers had been shot that morning in Moncada, we heard, and before their deaths, one had said, "Do what you want with me. I've killed two or three hundred of your men already."

Gun cars begin to appear, with U.G.T. and C.N.T. painted on their sides—the initials of the united trade-union groups. The guns bristle, pointing at us as we walk in the town. The Committee has suspended the strike for an hour, to allow buying of food. Ernie and Rose, the American couple, face guns. He is a labor lawyer from New York, and he is comforting her. She is terrified of the guns this morning. I see her again at four in the afternoon, as the gun cars come through again. She is standing with her back to them, eating chocolate. The fear is absorbed very quickly.

The teams are doing exercises on the station platform. A member of the Committee comes to ask us not to come out of the train anymore. I am in third class when the word of the change of control in Moncada comes through. A Catalan woman has made a fire here, and is cooking soup. The Member of the Committee will speak for the town from now on, and Otto, the German, is speaking for the train.

The town has given the engineer permission to drive the train a hundred feet down the track, toward Barcelona. Damn fool passengers have been using the toilets; they must stop, and something must be done. The English couples have done all they can to get people to use the lavatories in the station but some few people are not listening, and PASSENGERS WILL PLEASE REFRAIN is not widely known. The town has two wells, and is giving us one of them. It also is giving us the use of the schoolhouse, the most modern building in Moncada. We can sleep on the tables. The two teams move to the schoolhouse at once; they have a playing field, too, even though they are warned not to go out for more than two hours, now. Officers and rebel men are escaping northward from Barcelona, and running battles are expected.

There is a sound of cannon from Barcelona.

One of the Englishmen comes back as the stores close, with a supply of gunnysacks to sleep on. "So cheap—really such a bargain," he commends them to us. "They're really clean."

The people on the train are becoming very jumpy. Now we all go to the schoolhouse, for trucks have been promised to take the two teams into Barcelona; but they do not come.

Otto and I begin to talk in the late afternoon, in a complex immediate closeness. He does not speak English, and my freshman German is very bad, clumsy, full of mistakes. I have never wanted language so much. We try, and laugh, and hand the orange and black book back and forth. We try the pale yellow section, English, Spanish, French, the Romance tongues; we can both speak French of a sort. Then the pale blue: German, Dutch, the Scandinavians, and English. Then the buff: Russian, Polish, Czech, Serbo-Croatian, Bulgarian, always English. And the green, that the Hungarians have been using (but Ernie speaks Hungarian, with the languages that most of us speak), with Finnish, Estonian, that group. And the orange, Greek, Turkish, Albanian, Arabic, Esperanto. English always. Never Catalan.

With our language of many colors, we make a beginning.

The French newspapers lie on the floor of the train aisle. A tiny paragraph can be read if you pick up the paper. It says that shooting broke out yesterday in Spanish Morocco. But you don't have to pick the paper up to see the big picture of the feature story. It is Nijinsky in his Swiss sanatorium, against the background of black cloth unrolled in the shape of a cross, dancing his black dance of the world.

Rattle of machine guns, in the town, all night.

The soldiers reappeared, as loyal troops. Civil Guard, for the government, patrolling the train, their yellow straps shining dark in the light from the platform.

In the morning a car came—not for the Hollywood men, who are shouting by now, but for the little Spanish doctor, who is needed in Barcelona. It goes off in that direction, the purple-faced director staring.

Now a curious panic begins on the train. Rumor has followed rumor, and now we hear that the looting has begun. "Rape," says one of the Rodney Hudson blondes, and the shoe salesman comforts her.

Down the street of houses belonging to absentee landlords, and facing the train, a methodical process, perfectly visible to the passengers. A group of young men—rather like the young men who went off in an open truck the first night to fight in Barcelona, no two firearms alike—go from door to door. Systematically, one opens the big heavy door with its black knocker in the shape of an iron hand dropped to sound on the door. If his key does not work, he forces the lock. Two young men go in, and after a moment, they can be seen with two or three religious prints and a hunting rifle and a pistol, perhaps. This goes on; the scene repeats. Suddenly, a boy of five or so ducks under the arm of the leader and disappears for a minute. Still running, he comes out with a heap of towels and cuts down the street. We all watch. "Spanish looting," says Ernie.

Halfway down the block, his mother catches him, walks in the sight of all to the young leader, returns the towels and makes her short speech.

Far off, among the olive trees on the hill, a man can be seen. He is running too. Shouts hurrah on the slopes. A plane flies far to one side, but one pulls one's head in. Everything is visible to the naked eyes, one feels.

At this moment the trucks arrive. There are two of them, open, with railings and stakes. They are for the teams and for anyone else who wants to try the ride. A car precedes them, a Communist

Party car. The Americans wonder about being saved by the Communist Party, each with his own feelings before that prospect. Two American school teachers, who have been reading pamphlets on *The Problems of the Spanish Revolution*. The two teams; Otto and I; Ernie and Rose; some of the others in the second truck. There is actually a united front now in Catalonia, Socialists, Communists, Anarchists, all backing the government.

The valises are set up around the sides of the truck for fortification. The Swiss team amazes the town with a burst of yodeling, part of our thanks. A machine-gun truck goes down the road; we are to follow in two minutes.

Sudden spasm of nerves and laughing. Ernie, in the voice of Groucho Marx—"Of course they know this means war!" A tiny boy in his shirt, holding his penis. Ernie—"Vive le sport!" And the truck starts off to Barcelona.

THE ROAD HAS fortifications, thrown-up bales of hay, later there are barricades of paving stones flying the red flag for unity. There are machine-gun nests, dead horses, dead mules, terrible spots that I cannot identify at several crossroads. A Ford sign on the way into the city.

As we reach Barcelona, the white flags are at all windows—towels, sheets, tablecloths hung over the windowsills for peace. Shooting is heard again and again—not cannons or machine guns (except once), but guns. My teeth feel the shots, and everything else, too; a nerve in my leg jumps. Ahead of us, a man falls, and our truck swerves and turns, taking a detour as some street-corner battle opens.

We are taking another road to the Hotel Olympic—immense building requisitioned for the athletes.

In the streets, there are no cars that are not armed and painted with initials or titles. VISCA (that's Viva) CATALUNYA.

Overturned cars, dead animals, coils and spires of smoke rising from burning churches. The coils of color climbing the architectural heart of the city, Gaudí's marvelous church, untouched by harm. The Chinese Quarter, money-set.

FROM THE ROOF of the hotel, the city is laid out before you, the wide avenues to the port, the Rambla, and there Columbus on a gilded ball and the water beyond. The heights over the city, Tibidabo, are very beautiful, the squares are illuminated, and the bullring, Monumental y Arena across the way, still a perfect place for snipers.

Look down, you can see the teams arriving still. Cars are overturned, here in the Plaza España, one of the two centers of the fighting. Guards stream into the building, and girls with rifles take their places in the cars.

In the dark, we set out for dinner at the stadium, with M. de Paiche (whose stomach has been badly upset by the diet of beans and soda) and his secretary. The windshield of the car we drive in is spangled by bullets, and there is blood on the cushion behind me. I sit upright; but the car goes up a winding road, and I can't help learning back.

Two thousand foreigners, thrown on the city as civil war began, are to be lodged and fed here.

The stadium is filled with athletes and stranded nationals. We eat beans; they are delicious. News goes around. We meet the English team, and at last the American team. Block parties have been held for months, and tryouts at Randall's Island—and here they are: Dr. Smith and George Gordon Battle in charge, and Al Chakin, boxing and wrestling; Irving Jenkins, boxing; Frank Payton, Eddie Kraus, Dorothy Tucker, Harry Engle, Myron Dickes, all track; Bernie Danchik, gymnast; Julian Raul, cycling; Charles Burley, William Chamberlain and Frank Adams Hanson.

In the meetings that night, the decisions are made to leave—the French, whose M. de Paiche says, "We have much to learn from

Spain"—and many others, to take the burden of thousands (some say twenty thousand) of foreigners off the government at this crucial and bloody moment. The French leave the next day on the *Chellé* and *Djeube*; we all see them off, waving from the dock. Even the gypsies, in red and pink, salute with clenched fists up. At the last moment, as on the deck the arms all rise together, the ship we watch appears to lift up on the sea.

The American and British athletes decide to stay, and ask us to come with them, to clear the Olympic building of as many people as possibly can go. The British are wonderful, brave, droll—they are feeling particularly humiliated, for they have had to lie down on the tennis courts while they were shot at—*lie down on the courts!* We go with them into the narrow streets, with barricades thrown breast high, paving torn up, the crowds in lyric late nighttime Catalan—to the Hotel Madrid in the Calle de Boqueria. Here, on the street, in the hotel and the two restaurants, the Condal and our own, we have the next days. We send our cables; the Telefònica, run by American business, is proud of a continued service.

At the American consulate, Drew Franklin tells us that Companys has asked him to supervise our leaving. There is no safe conduct, the consul tells us, don't try to go to the border by car. An art professor and a correspondent are there; the men should leave off their jackets, the women should not wear jewelry—"They will think you are proletarians." The hysterical reports have begun to register. Our three Hollywood men have reached the frontier, and have told reporters that they saw wild scenes of looting from the train, that they suffered deprivations and saw horrors.

Some of the athletes are talking of joining the fighting forces, which now include many members of the Assault Troops in their blue uniforms, the Civil Guard, and men and women who a week ago had been civilians.

We walk, going back always to the Madrid, talking with Otto, with the English athletes, smoking *Bisontes* (the Spanish relative of

Camels) and drinking wine. There was a moment outside a house in Moncada, when they taught me the double-spouted drinking; I learned laughing how to bite off the free-pouring drink. My practice drink was water, not wine, and they were shooting at the house—real practice conditions. We went in the house, and I learned. Now we drank from glasses, and from the pouring too; we came to our decisions in these days. It cleared and deepened between us; it was certain for Otto. He had found his chance to fight fascism, and a profound quiet, amounting to joy, was there; it was the German chance, in or out of Germany.

We talked with the athletes about what might happen. It was a matter of doing what we did *entire*, with our whole selves committed. What about King Edward, said the English. There was a rumor that something was happening so that his life was at last coherent, politically and erotically; it had something to do with the American woman, Mrs. Simpson, but there was a lot more besides.

Who would help the government and the people of Spain against the generals and the officers, the Fascist revolt backed by Germany and Italy? The checks and guns had been found in the Fascist strongholds. News of all this was published in the papers, which were coming out whole after the first days in which front-page stories were torn out, and sometimes hardly anything but the lists of the dead and wounded appeared. The death of the dancer La Argentina, whom I had loved to watch, was noted in a tiny paragraph.

But who would help? Not England, we thought. The English interests in cork, wine, many valuables, were visible. Her leaders liked Mussolini—"gentle," Churchill called him—and thought Hitler would improve. But the French were naturally and politically friendly. And America would surely be the friend of the Republic. "We can count on you," the poet Aribau had said.

The army begins to go. "A Zaragoza," is the word.

The city is under martial law. We are called to a meeting of the

Olympic people remaining, in a smaller square. The Norwegian speaks, briefly, and the Italian representative of his team. The Catalan speaks, in the language that is beginning to break open to us, glints like French, flashes like Spanish:

"This is what the Games stand for," not only to work against what is about to happen in Berlin, what is happening in Germany and through Hitler, but the true feelings of the Games, their finality: '*Amor i fraternitat entre els homes de tot el món i de totes les races.*'"

And Martín, the organizer of the Games, has the last word. He speaks to us as foreigners, as ourselves. He is speaking to me directly, at least that is how I hear his open words:

"The athletes came to attend the People's Olympiad, but have been privileged to stay to see the beautiful and great victory of the people in Catalonia and Spain.

"You have come for the Games, but you have remained for the greater Front, in battle and in triumph.

"Now you will leave, you will go to your own countries, but you will carry to them . . . the tense sunlit square, Martín about to start for Saragossa, the people in the streets, the train, the teams, the curious new loving friendship, the song of the *Jocs*:

No és per odi, no és per guerra
Que venim a lliutar de cada terra

". . . you will carry to your own countries, some of them still oppressed and under fascism and military terror, to the working people of the world, the story of what you see now in Spain."

Afterword

Now, a lifetime later, I think of all that followed. The British team had invited us to go out with them, but when the ship—*H.M.S. London*—arrived "from Gib," her officers would allow only British to board. So the Belgians, saying they were grateful for what the Americans had done to help them during World War I, took us on the *Ciudad de Ibiza*, taking almost twice the number she was supposed to carry.

The Catalan government told us we were welcome to stay, the men if they would fight, the women if we had experience in nursing or child care. I had none of that; work in a bookshop, in a theatre office, proofreading the Mu books, research (if that was what it was), and a first book of poems.

Otto, on the dock, looked deep into me. "You will do what you can in America," he said, "and I in Spain." He smiled, with his own happiness. He was not going to run in the Games. He had joined the militia, and he was going off to Saragossa. . . . We spoke of my coming back to Spain, but it was not very real. These days were all we could look at. "Gifts of the revolution," he said. He had been waiting to fight against fascism since Hitler came to power.

I waved to him from the deck. Ernie and Rose were there, the American team, the Belgians—the man who had walked over the Pyrenees—and the Hungarian team from France. The ship pulled away from the harbor, with Columbus standing on his black pillar.

All night toward France. We stayed on the dark crowded deck and talked. The Hungarian printer from Paris said to me, "And in all this—where is the place for poetry?"

"Ladis," I answered, "I know some of it now, but it will take me a lifetime to find it." We talked all night. With the morning light we saw the Cape of Agde, and then went into the harbor of Sète, to the canal, all at peace, and the houses with their red tile roofs and yellow deep cadmium awnings, and the swallows flying.

They took us in, and stamped our papers with police passes. There was dancing in the streets that night; I danced with Jo Gasco, who later left his shop and fought in Spain for six months of every year.

There were rumors that the People's Olympics might be held in October.

Sète produces vermouth and Valéry. It was at peace, a curious distant peace. I rented a little kayak and, after I paddled about two hundred yards out, let it drift and cried at last. I did not want to go on, but they came for me, and I paddled to the *plage*.

A week later, at the Berlin Olympics, Hitler refused to recognize the victory of Jesse Owens, the black American who won the hundred-meter race. The Berlin officials said the Negro had "a following wind" that helped him. He won three other events, however.

Everybody knows who won the war in Spain.

I COULD NOT get back; nobody would send me. You had to belong to a party or an organization or something, or have a press card. Nobody would give me a press card.

Otto's letters came, from training, from hillsides near Huesca, from Huesca, from near the Segre River. Then they stopped. I was able sometimes to hear about other people with the International Brigade—with the Lincoln Battalion—but nobody could send me word of Otto.

One freezing January evening, Ernst Toller came over to me in a restaurant and told me the news was very bad. The Republicans had been driven far north and the fighting seemed to be entering Barcelona.

The help that in Spain seemed sure to come from the United States to the Republic had never come. People here had a hard time sorting out the "teams"; Loyalists, in our American usage, were people against the Republic. And there were powerful, all-powerful, forces here on the side of Franco. Joseph Kennedy's argument to Roosevelt was one we would come to know—that Spain was the place to "stop communism."

I went home and sent a cable to Otto's Barcelona address, the permanent address, military headquarters, and slept a terrible sleep. The next day, the news of Barcelona's fall was on the radio.

Had the cable arrived? Had it fallen into the wrong hands? Had it killed Otto?

The stories of the Spanish walking in the rocks and snows of the Pyrenees were coming in. There was talk of a buffer zone to be created, and I thought: it will be a paradigm of all boundaries. Let me tell the story of the beginning and this first ending of the war, I had asked publishers. My publisher (by then there was another book of poems) said, "Of course, if you can get a press pass."

I called Henry Luce, for whom I had done a story with Margaret Bourke-White. "See Whit in the morning," said Luce. Now that was Whittaker Chambers. I had not even known there was a left wing until a story of Chambers', *Can You Hear Their Voices*, was done as a play my freshman year at college. I told him that, early the next morning, sitting at his desk at *Time*.

It was the last thing he wanted to hear. He was in a different incarnation by now, hating the Left, and living in an enormous hollow construct of his own.

He changed the subject. "What have you got for us on Spain?" he asked me.

I told him I wanted to get the story of the refugees and the buffer zone—the "end" of the war.

"But what can you give us?" he repeated. It was clear, slowly, that this was some game of his—a supposed deal in which I would have a story.

"I want to *get* the story, I want to write it," I said. It sounded foolish as I said it. He expected some spy stuff.

He exploded. "If you haven't got something for us—! I can send someone down from Paris." That ended it.

NEARER OUR OWN time. The Olympics in Mexico City, where the black athletes made their protest. In the meantime, the acts of this century, events which said in tragic clarity that our lives would not be shredded, not as athletes nor women nor as poets, not as travelers, tourists, refugees.

The high-rise apartment houses going up in Spain, the supermarkets, the tourist industry, the American naval bases.

NEARER. AT THE P.O.W. camp in Hanoi. The American prisoners want two kinds of news: word of the coming elections, and word of the Olympics just now held in Munich.

"Killed! Jewish athletes killed during the Games!" the prisoners say in horror. There are eight officers who have been brought down, safely, from their bombers.

"Eleven of them," answers Jane Hart, Senator Hart's wife. The prisoners respond to her coolness, her friendliness, her factuality. They are lean and tanned, wearing their Asian robes of dark red and purple.

"Athletes—shot!" they say. We tell them we will phone their families when we get back to the States.

THINGS THAT ENDURE to our own moment. Word finally came, through the Germans in Mexico, that Otto had been killed in the battle on the banks of the Segre River, at a machine-gun nest where six hundred out of nine hundred were killed that day. It is in the Franco histories. Their intelligence worked very well. They knew every gun position.

Not to let our lives be shredded, sports away from politics, poetry away from anything. Anything away from anything.

"Why do you care about Spain so much?" a friend asks me, a curious look in her green eyes, the question real on her fine face. She is watching the Derby on TV with passionate interest. During the time before starting, there are film clips of human runners. "It was so long ago," she said.

Going on now. Running, running, today.

ACKNOWLEDGMENTS

This project is indebted to the considerable help of a number of people. I'd like to thank William Rukeyser for his enthusiasm and permission to work on *Savage Coast*; Ammiel Alcalay for his tireless dedication to recovery projects, and for his invaluable intellectual guidance and friendship; and Jane Marcus for encouraging me to go into the archive in the first place, and especially for her mentorship, humor, and radical spirit of inquiry. Thanks to David Greetham and Richard Kaye for their insights, interest, and excitement; Jan Heller Levi for helping put the pieces together; Robin Vogelzang for her expertise and good eye. A special thanks to Aoibheann Sweeney, at the Center for the Humanities, CUNY, for consistently giving me a place to make this work visible; and to the participants in the Center for the Humanities 2011–12 Mellon Seminar, who workshopped part of the introduction. I'd also like to thank the participants in the Muriel Rukeyser celebration at the Century Club, the Modernist Studies Association seminar on Women's Documentary Forms, and the Modern Language Association Rukeyser Centenary Roundtable— in particular Anne Herzog, Elisabeth Däumer, Eric Keenaghan, and Stefania Heim—for affirming the importance of Rukeyser studies, and for their intellectual solidarity. The research for this project has spanned seven years, and much of it has been enabled by fellowships from the Graduate Center, CUNY, for which I'm very grateful. Thanks especially to Amy Scholder, Jeanann Pannasch, Elizabeth Koke, and Drew Stevens of the Feminist Press for their fantastic work on the book. To Cecily Parks, for her friendship through the student years, and now in work and motherhood; also to Miciah Hussey for his generosity and humor. To Theresa Epstein, Perry Kennedy, and Elizabeth Lapovsky Kennedy for their sustaining support, and to August, who's been an exciting beginning as I end this project. Most especially, thanks to Casey Hale, my best friend, for his dedication to our family and this book— "love's not a trick of light."

The Feminist Press is an independent, nonprofit literary publisher that promotes freedom of expression and social justice. Founded in 1970, we began as a crucial publishing component of second wave feminism, reprinting feminist classics by writers such as Zora Neale Hurston and Charlotte Perkins Gilman, and providing much-needed texts for the developing field of women's studies with books by Barbara Ehrenreich and Grace Paley. We publish feminist literature from around the world, by best-selling authors such as Shahrnush Parsipur, Ruth Kluger, and Ama Ata Aidoo; and North American writers of diverse race and class experience, such as Paule Marshall and Rahna Reizo Rizzuto. We have become the vanguard for books on contemporary feminist issues of equality and gender identity, with authors as various as Anita Hill, Justin Vivian Bond, and Ann Jones. We seek out innovative, often surprising books that tell a different story.

See our complete list of books at **feministpress.org**, and join the Friends of FP to receive all our books at a great discount.

THE FEMINIST PRESS
AT THE CITY UNIVERSITY OF NEW YORK
FEMINISTPRESS.ORG